The AMAZING WORLD OF GUMBALL™

RECIPE FOR DISASTER

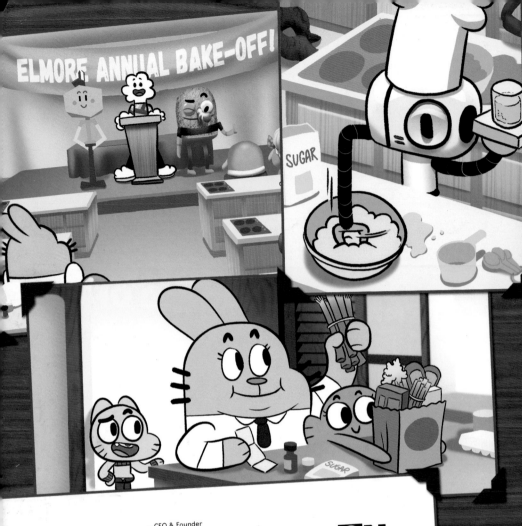

ROSS RICHIE ....CEO & Founder
MATT GAGNON ....Editor-in-Chief
FILIP SABLIK ....President of Publishing & Marketing
STEPHEN CHRISTY ....President of Development
LANCE KREITER....................VP of Licensing & Merchandising
PHIL BARBARO ....VP of Finance
BRYCE CARLSON ....Managing Editor
MEL CAYLO ....Marketing Manager
SCOTT NEWMAN ....Production Design Manager
KATE HENNING..Operations Manager
SIERRA HAHN...Senior Editor
DAFNA PLEBAN....................Editor, Talent Developent
SHANNON WATTERS..Editor
ERIC HARBURN...Editor
WHITNEY LEOPARD..Associate Editor
JASMINE AMIRI...Associate Editor
CHRIS ROSA...Associate Editor
ALEX GALER...Associate Editor
CAMERON CHITTOCK.......................................Assistant Editor
MATTHEW LEVINE..Assistant Editor
SOPHIE PHILIPS-ROBERTS ....Production Designer
KELSEY DIETERICH.....................................Production Designer
JILLIAN CRAB..Production Designer
MICHELLE ANKLEY.........................Production Design Assistant
GRACE PARK..Production Design Assistant
ELIZABETH LOUGHRIDGE ....Accounting Coordinator
STEPHANIE HOCUTT......................Social Media Coordinator
JOSÉ MEZA..Sales Assistant
JAMES ARRIOLA...Mailroom Assistant
HOLLY AITCHISON ....Operations Assistant
SAM KUSEK......................Direct Market Representative
AMBER PARKER...............................Administrative Assistant

kaboom!™ **CN** CARTOON NETWORK.

THE AMAZING WORLD OF GUMBALL: RECIPE FOR
DISASTER, May 2017. Published by KaBOOM!, a division
of Boom Entertainment, Inc. THE AMAZING WORLD OF
GUMBALL, CARTOON NETWORK, the logos, and all related
characters and elements are trademarks of and © Turner
Broadcasting System Europe Limited. Cartoon Network.
(S17) All rights reserved. KaBOOM!™ and the KaBOOM! logo
are trademarks of Boom Entertainment, Inc., registered
in various countries and categories. All characters,
events, and institutions depicted herein are fictional.
Any similarity between any of the names, characters,
persons, events, and/or institutions in this publication
to actual names, characters, and persons, whether living
or dead, events, and/or institutions is unintended and
purely coincidental. KaBOOM! does not read or accept
unsolicited submissions of ideas, stories, or artwork.

A catalog record of this book is available from OCLC and
from the BOOM! Studios website, www.boom-studios.com,
on the Librarians Page.

BOOM! Studios, 5670 Wilshire Boulevard, Suite 450, Los
Angeles, CA 90036-5679. Printed in China. First Printing.

ISBN: 978-1-60886-968-8, eISBN: 978-1-61398-639-4

The AMAZING WORLD OF GUMBALL™
RECIPE FOR DISASTER

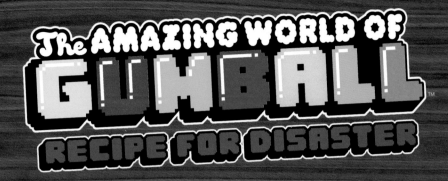

created by BEN BOCQUELET

script by MEGAN BRENNAN
art by KATY FARINA
colors by WHITNEY COGAR
letters by WARREN MONTGOMERY

"A PIE FOR A PIE"
script & art by KATE SHERRON

cover by KATY FARINA

designer JILLIAN CRAB
assistant editors MATTHEW LEVINE and MARY GUMPORT
editor SIERRA HAHN

with special thanks to MARISA MARIONAKIS, RICK BLANCO, JANET NO, CURTIS LELASH, CONRAD MONTGOMERY, MEGHAN BRADLEY and the wonderful folks at CARTOON NETWORK.

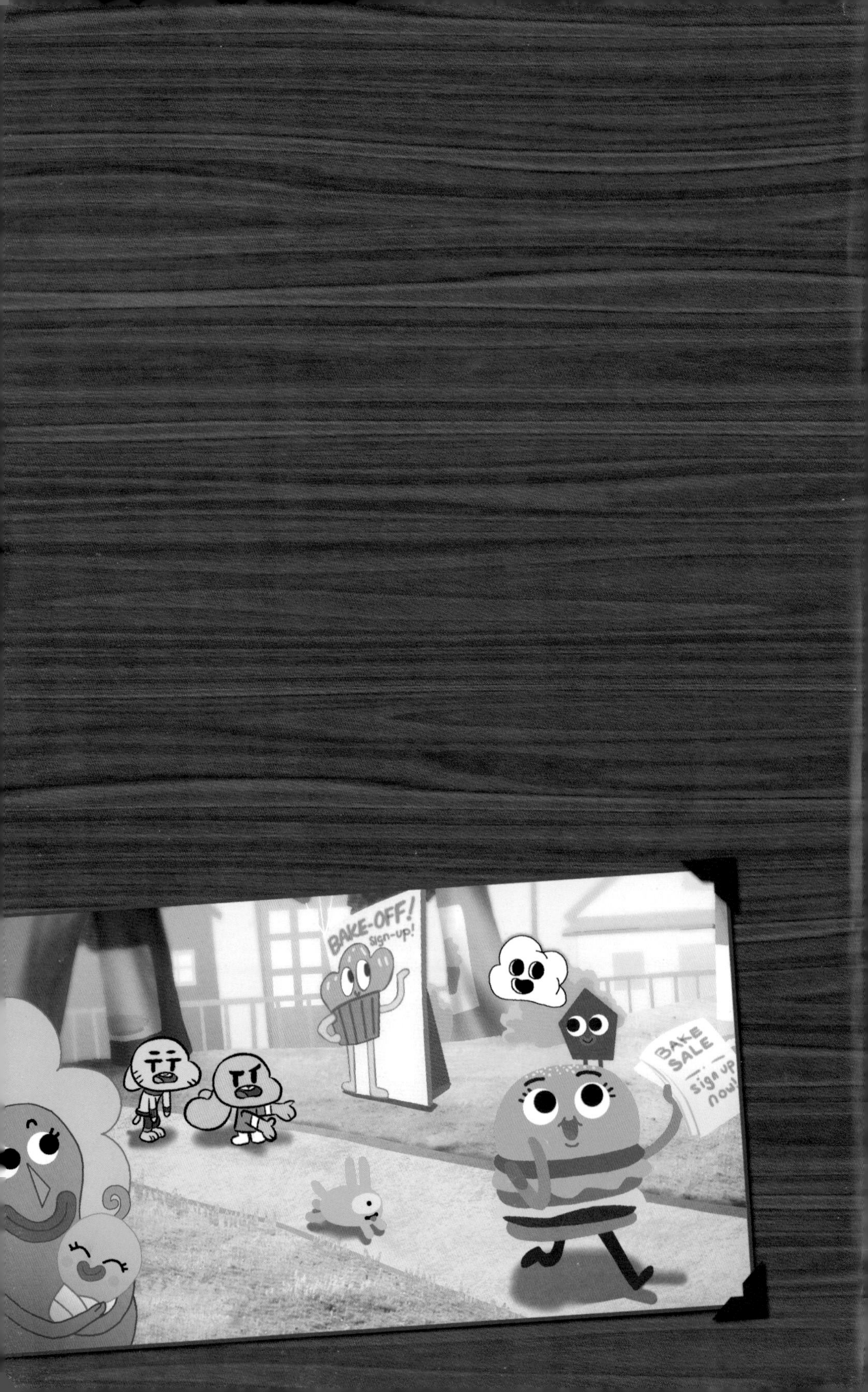
BAKE-OFF!
Sign-up!
BAKE SALE

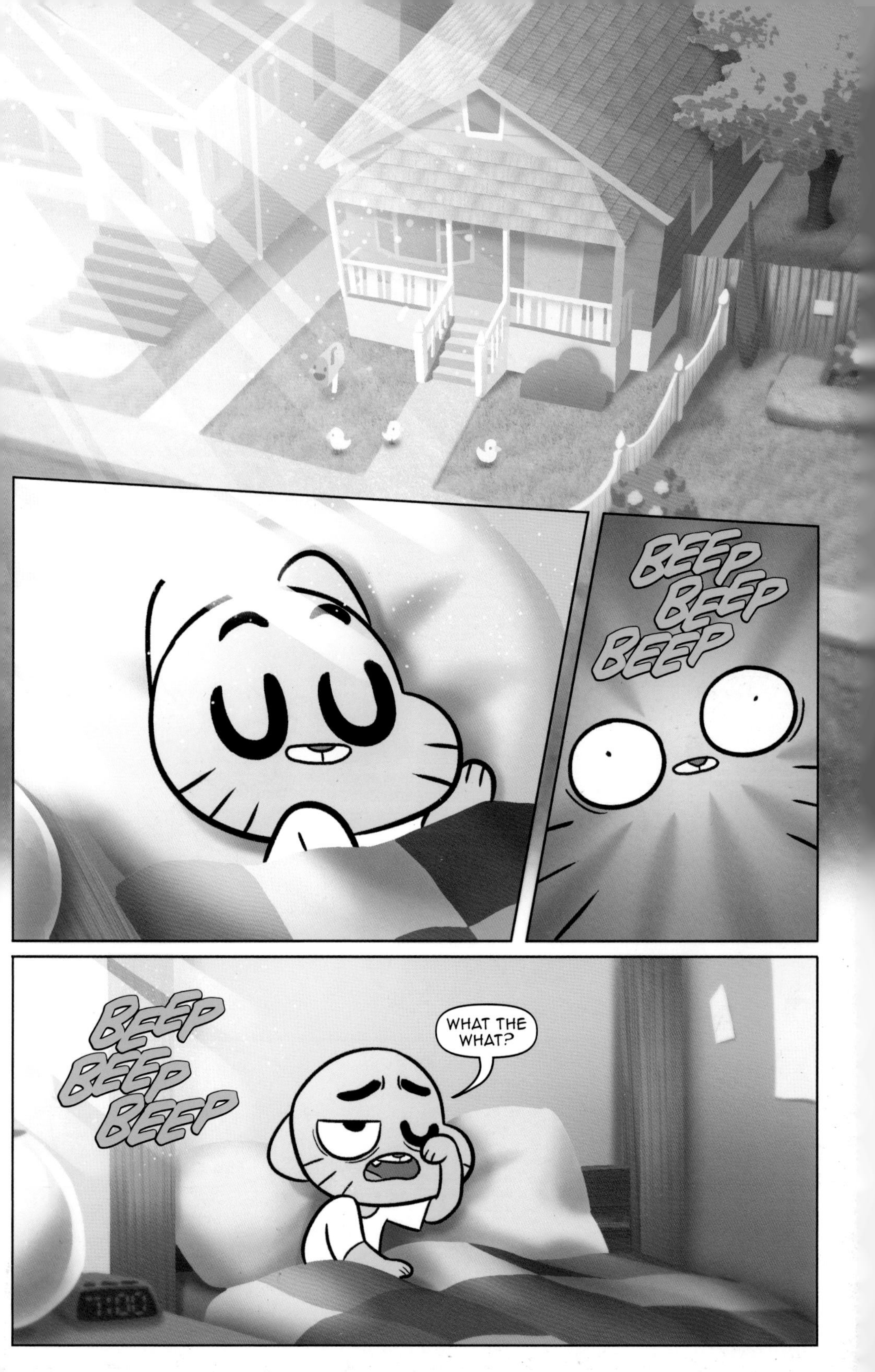
BEEP BEEP BEEP
BEEP BEEP BEEP
WHAT THE WHAT?

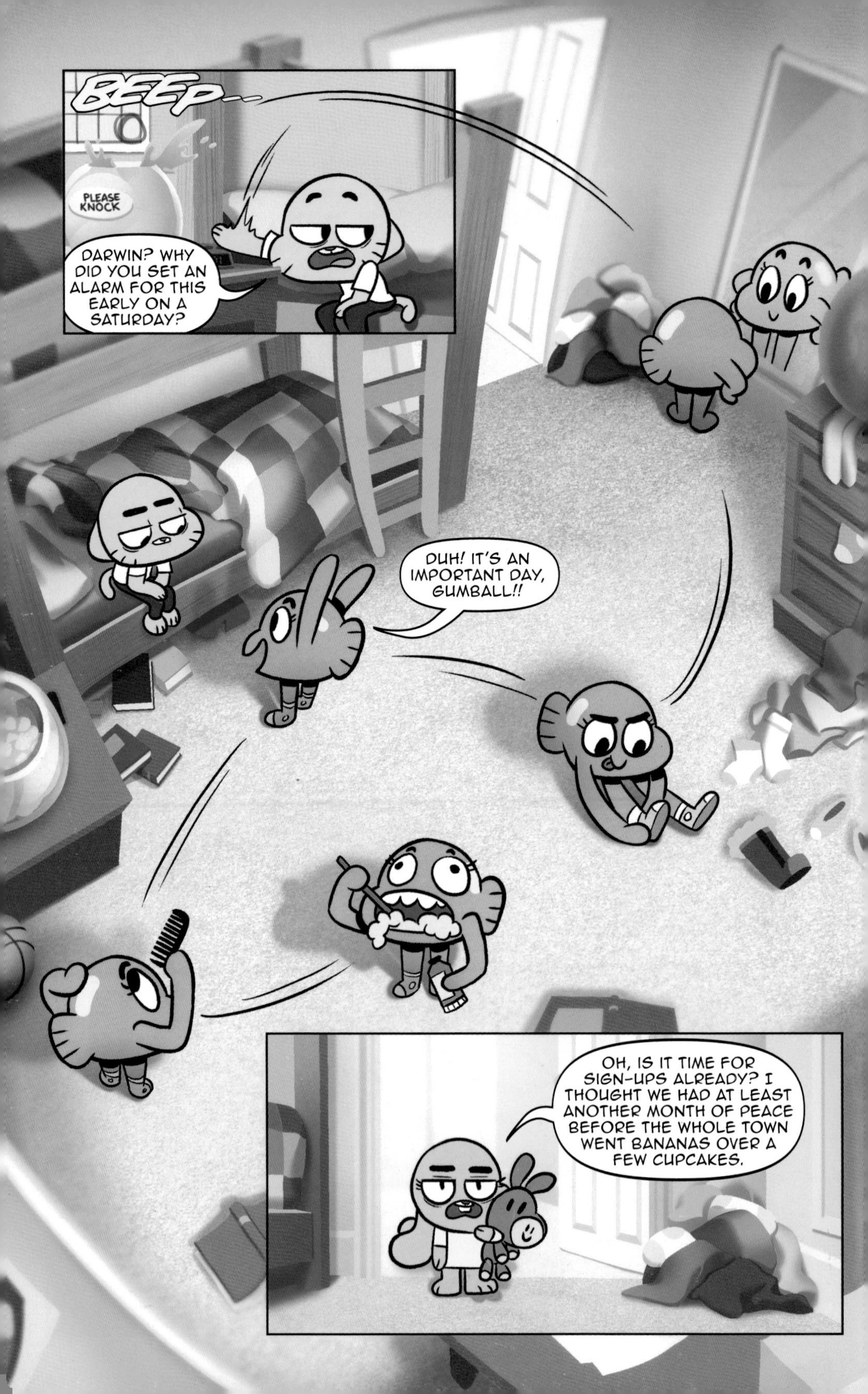
BEEP...
PLEASE KNOCK
DARWIN? WHY DID YOU SET AN ALARM FOR THIS EARLY ON A SATURDAY?
DUH! IT'S AN IMPORTANT DAY, GUMBALL!!
OH, IS IT TIME FOR SIGN-UPS ALREADY? I THOUGHT WE HAD AT LEAST ANOTHER MONTH OF PEACE BEFORE THE WHOLE TOWN WENT BANANAS OVER A FEW CUPCAKES.

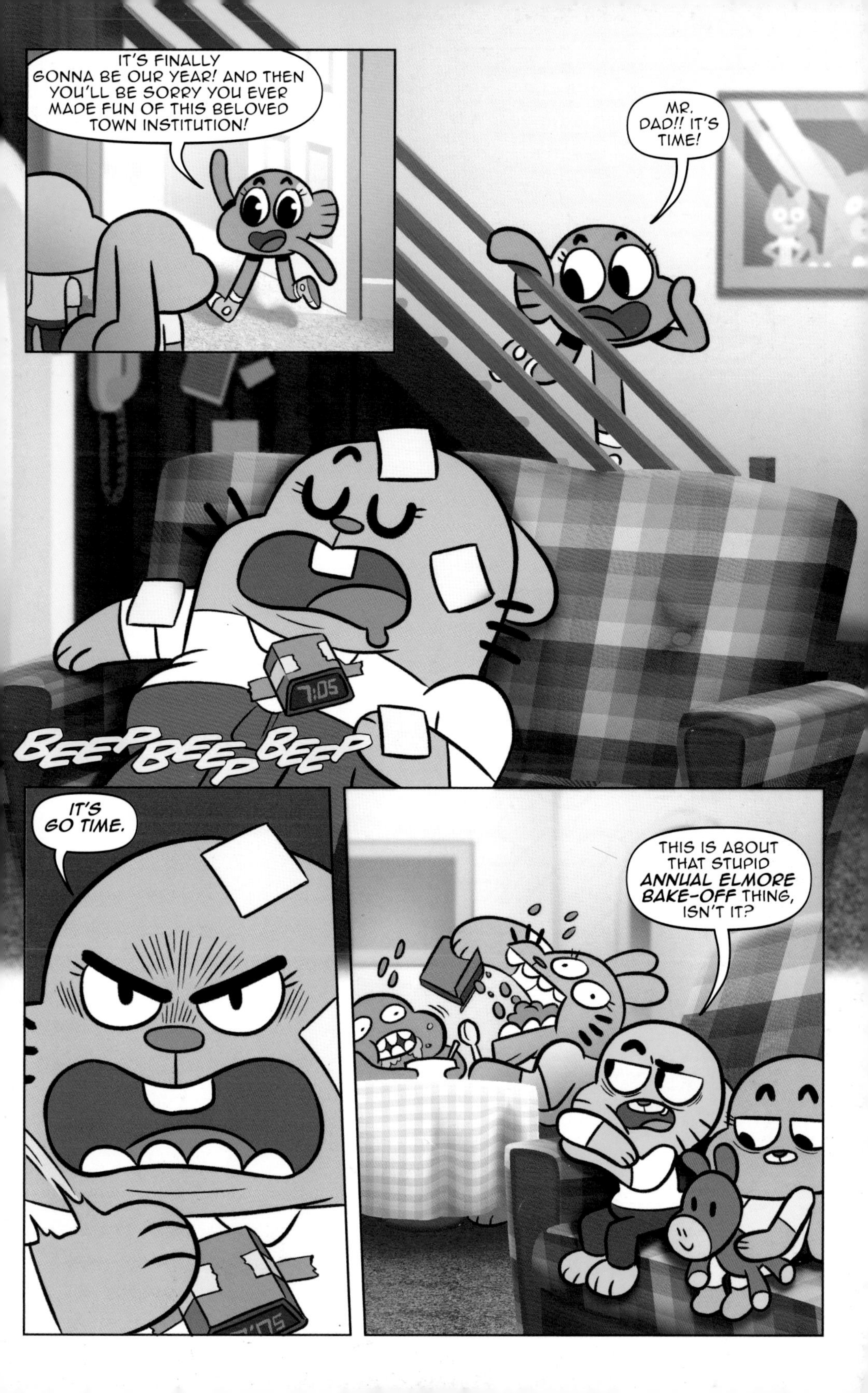
IT'S FINALLY GONNA BE OUR YEAR! AND THEN YOU'LL BE SORRY YOU EVER MADE FUN OF THIS BELOVED TOWN INSTITUTION!
MR. DAD!! IT'S TIME!
7:05
BEEP BEEP BEEP
IT'S GO TIME.
THIS IS ABOUT THAT STUPID ANNUAL ELMORE BAKE-OFF THING, ISN'T IT?

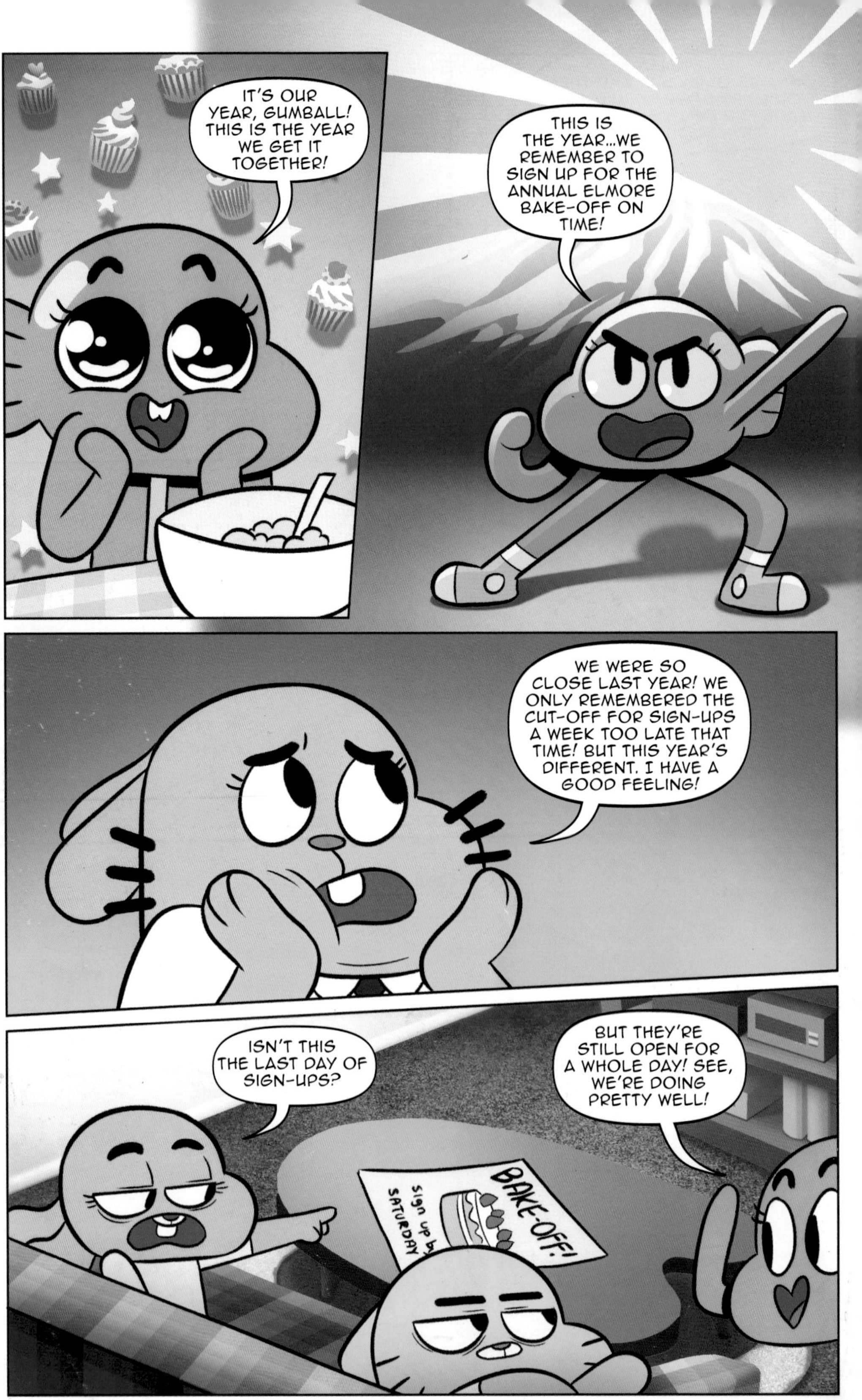
IT'S OUR YEAR, GUMBALL! THIS IS THE YEAR WE GET IT TOGETHER!
THIS IS THE YEAR...WE REMEMBER TO SIGN UP FOR THE ANNUAL ELMORE BAKE-OFF ON TIME!
WE WERE SO CLOSE LAST YEAR! WE ONLY REMEMBERED THE CUT-OFF FOR SIGN-UPS A WEEK TOO LATE THAT TIME! BUT THIS YEAR'S DIFFERENT. I HAVE A GOOD FEELING!
ISN'T THIS THE LAST DAY OF SIGN-UPS?
BUT THEY'RE STILL OPEN FOR A WHOLE DAY! SEE, WE'RE DOING PRETTY WELL!
BAKE-OFF!
sign up by SATURDAY

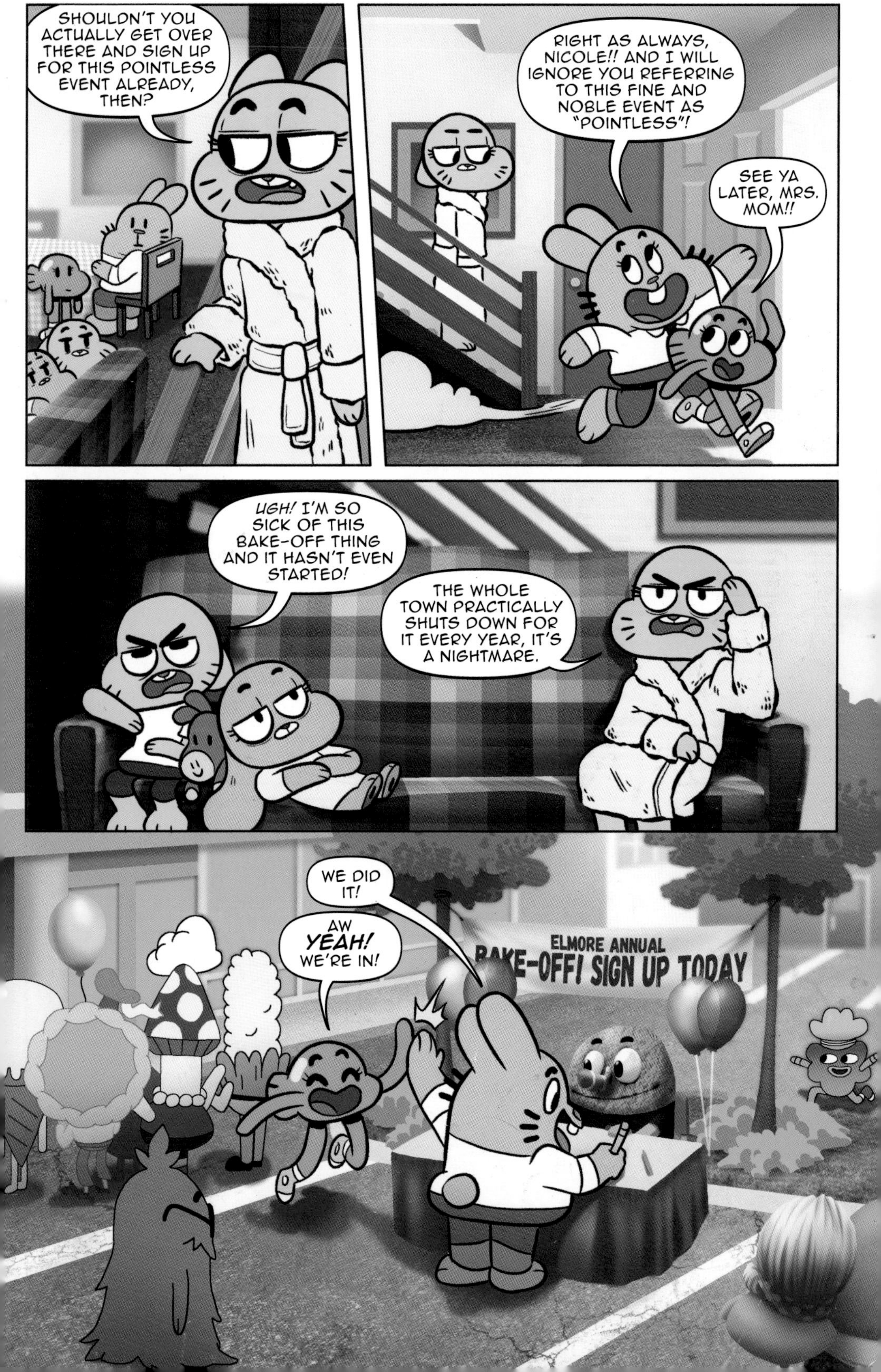
SHOULDN'T YOU ACTUALLY GET OVER THERE AND SIGN UP FOR THIS POINTLESS EVENT ALREADY, THEN?
RIGHT AS ALWAYS, NICOLE!! AND I WILL IGNORE YOU REFERRING TO THIS FINE AND NOBLE EVENT AS "POINTLESS"!
SEE YA LATER, MRS. MOM!!
UGH! I'M SO SICK OF THIS BAKE-OFF THING AND IT HASN'T EVEN STARTED!
THE WHOLE TOWN PRACTICALLY SHUTS DOWN FOR IT EVERY YEAR, IT'S A NIGHTMARE.
WE DID IT!
AW YEAH! WE'RE IN!
ELMORE ANNUAL
BAKE-OFF! SIGN UP TODAY

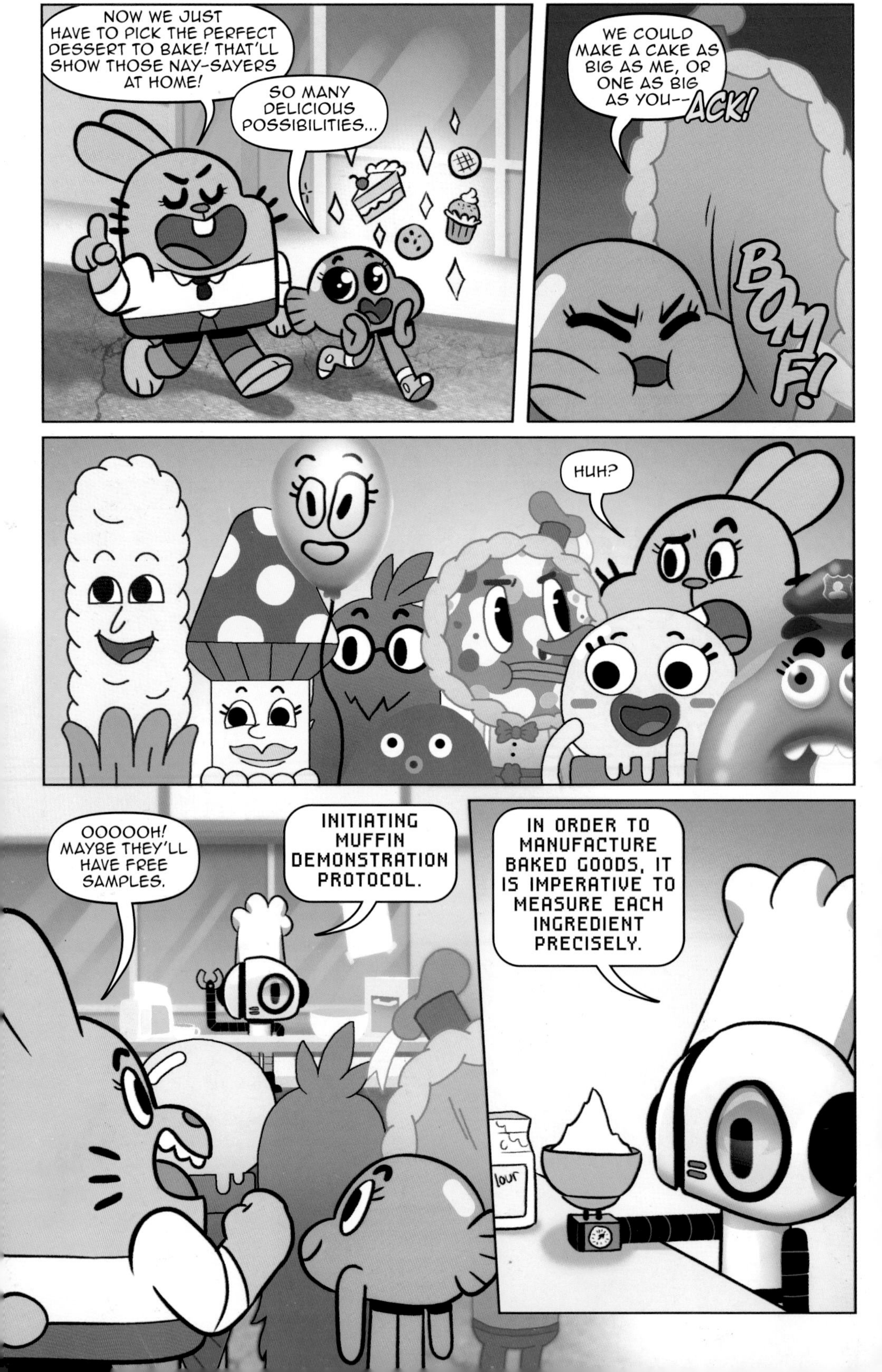
NOW WE JUST HAVE TO PICK THE PERFECT DESSERT TO BAKE! THAT'LL SHOW THOSE NAY-SAYERS AT HOME!
SO MANY DELICIOUS POSSIBILITIES...
WE COULD MAKE A CAKE AS BIG AS ME, OR ONE AS BIG AS YOU--ACK!
BOMF!
HUH?
OOOOOH! MAYBE THEY'LL HAVE FREE SAMPLES.
INITIATING MUFFIN DEMONSTRATION PROTOCOL.
IN ORDER TO MANUFACTURE BAKED GOODS, IT IS IMPERATIVE TO MEASURE EACH INGREDIENT PRECISELY.

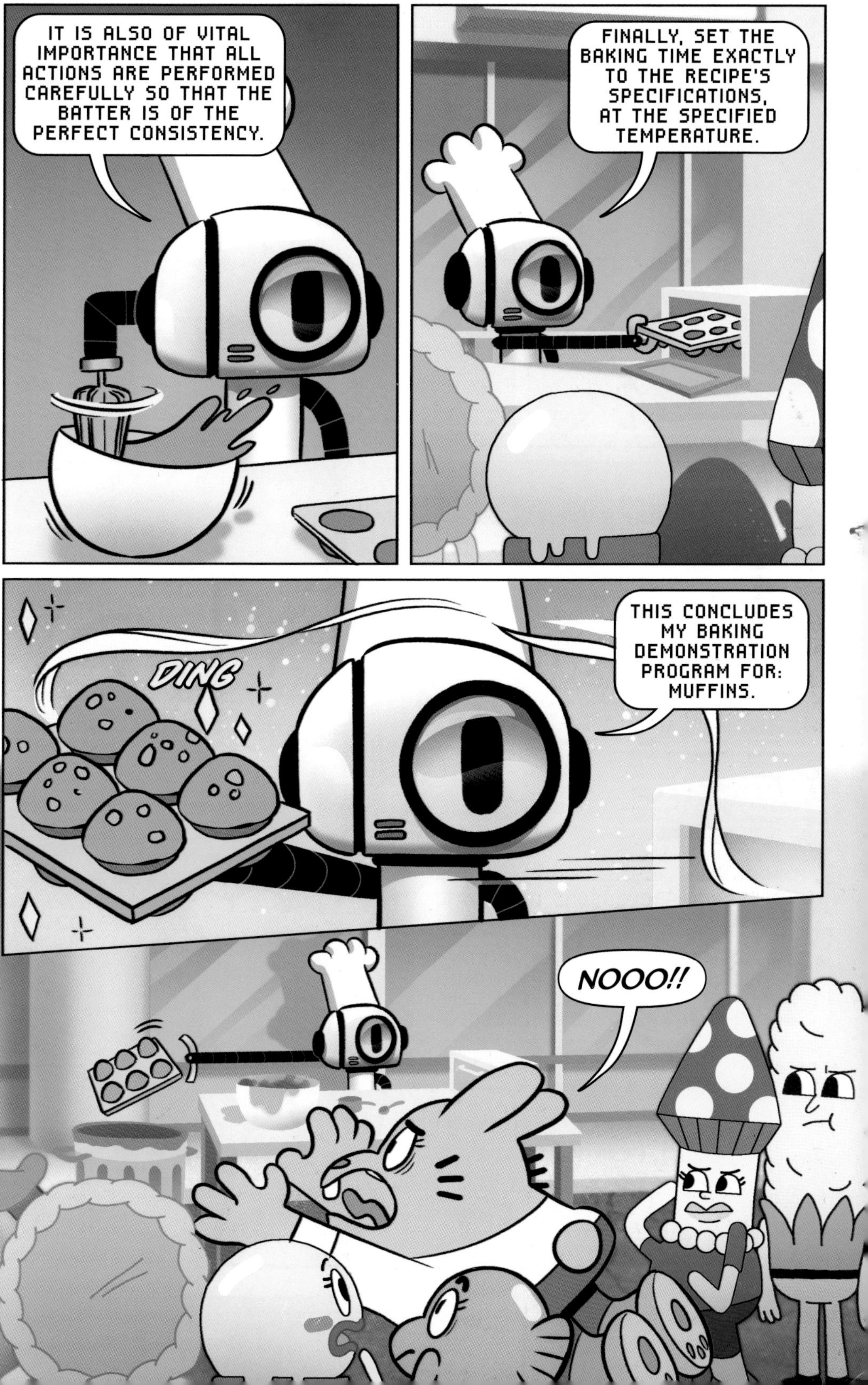
IT IS ALSO OF VITAL IMPORTANCE THAT ALL ACTIONS ARE PERFORMED CAREFULLY SO THAT THE BATTER IS OF THE PERFECT CONSISTENCY.
FINALLY, SET THE BAKING TIME EXACTLY TO THE RECIPE'S SPECIFICATIONS, AT THE SPECIFIED TEMPERATURE.
DING
THIS CONCLUDES MY BAKING DEMONSTRATION PROGRAM FOR: MUFFINS.
NOOO!!

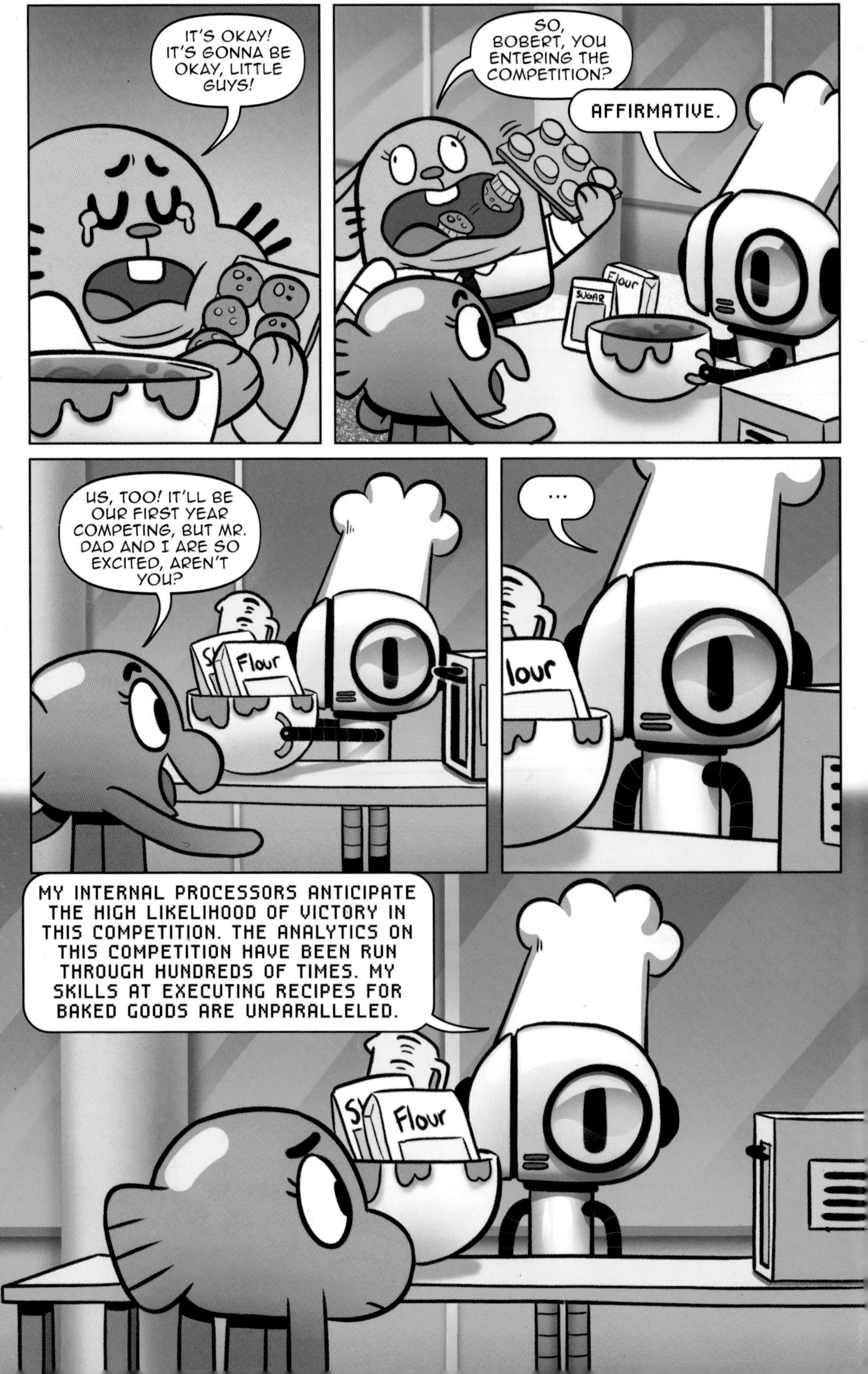
IT'S OKAY! IT'S GONNA BE OKAY, LITTLE GUYS!
SO, BOBERT, YOU ENTERING THE COMPETITION?
AFFIRMATIVE.
US, TOO! IT'LL BE OUR FIRST YEAR COMPETING, BUT MR. DAD AND I ARE SO EXCITED, AREN'T YOU?
...
MY INTERNAL PROCESSORS ANTICIPATE THE HIGH LIKELIHOOD OF VICTORY IN THIS COMPETITION. THE ANALYTICS ON THIS COMPETITION HAVE BEEN RUN THROUGH HUNDREDS OF TIMES. MY SKILLS AT EXECUTING RECIPES FOR BAKED GOODS ARE UNPARALLELED.

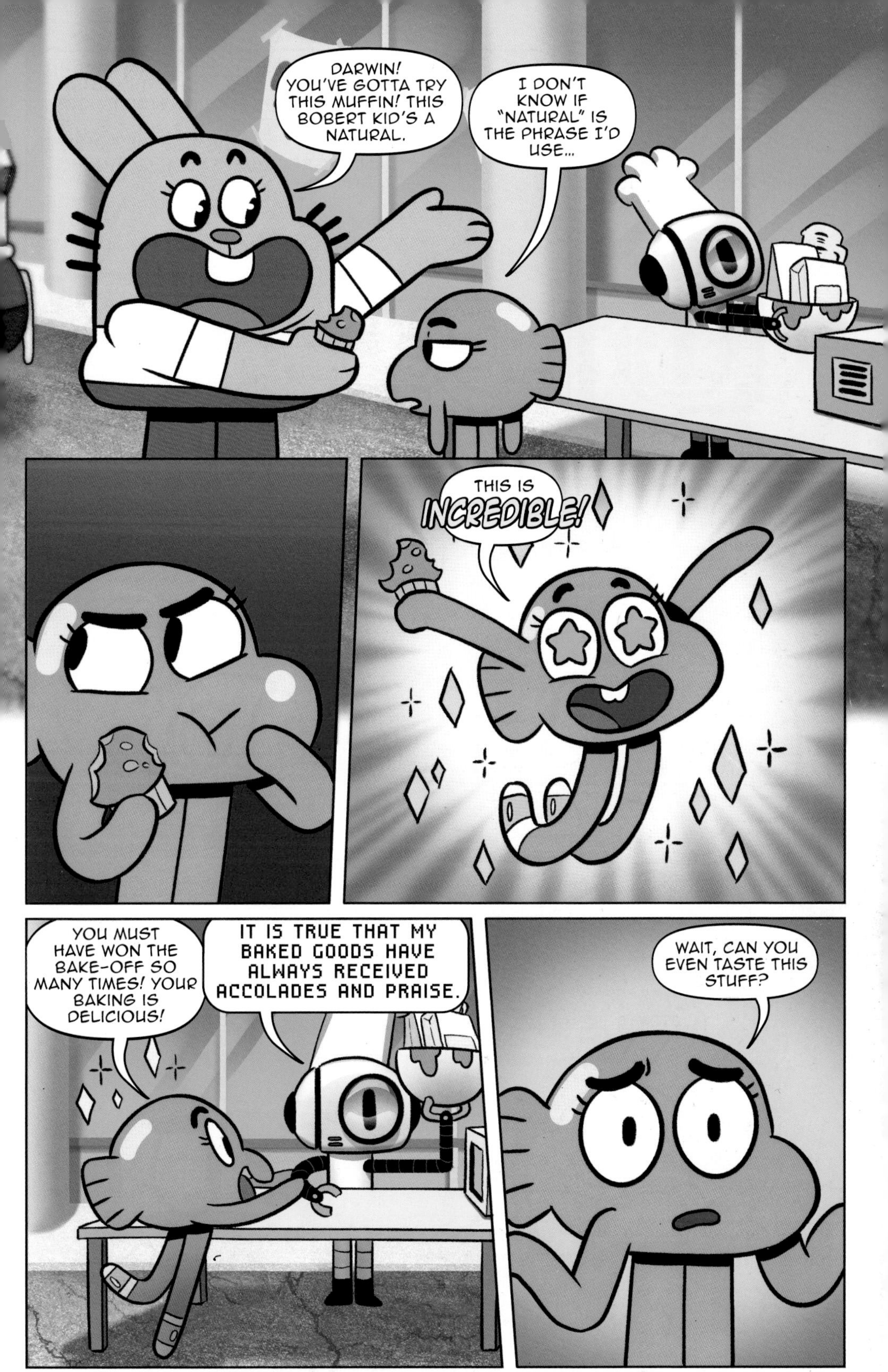
DARWIN! YOU'VE GOTTA TRY THIS MUFFIN! THIS BOBERT KID'S A NATURAL.
I DON'T KNOW IF "NATURAL" IS THE PHRASE I'D USE...
THIS IS INCREDIBLE!
YOU MUST HAVE WON THE BAKE-OFF SO MANY TIMES! YOUR BAKING IS DELICIOUS!
IT IS TRUE THAT MY BAKED GOODS HAVE ALWAYS RECEIVED ACCOLADES AND PRAISE.
WAIT, CAN YOU EVEN TASTE THIS STUFF?

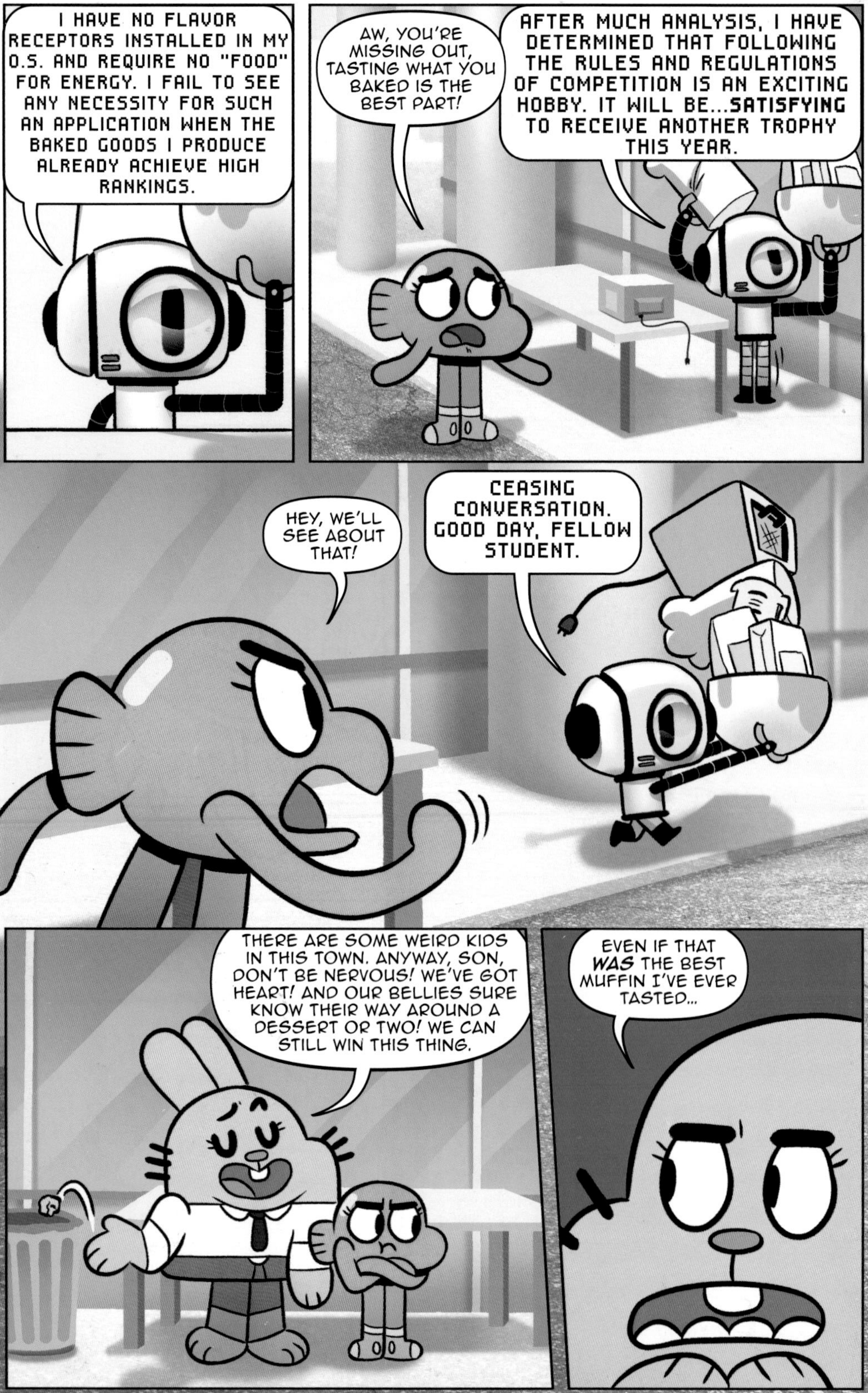
I HAVE NO FLAVOR RECEPTORS INSTALLED IN MY O.S. AND REQUIRE NO "FOOD" FOR ENERGY. I FAIL TO SEE ANY NECESSITY FOR SUCH AN APPLICATION WHEN THE BAKED GOODS I PRODUCE ALREADY ACHIEVE HIGH RANKINGS.
AW, YOU'RE MISSING OUT, TASTING WHAT YOU BAKED IS THE BEST PART!
AFTER MUCH ANALYSIS, I HAVE DETERMINED THAT FOLLOWING THE RULES AND REGULATIONS OF COMPETITION IS AN EXCITING HOBBY. IT WILL BE...SATISFYING TO RECEIVE ANOTHER TROPHY THIS YEAR.
HEY, WE'LL SEE ABOUT THAT!
CEASING CONVERSATION. GOOD DAY, FELLOW STUDENT.
THERE ARE SOME WEIRD KIDS IN THIS TOWN. ANYWAY, SON, DON'T BE NERVOUS! WE'VE GOT HEART! AND OUR BELLIES SURE KNOW THEIR WAY AROUND A DESSERT OR TWO! WE CAN STILL WIN THIS THING.
EVEN IF THAT WAS THE BEST MUFFIN I'VE EVER TASTED...

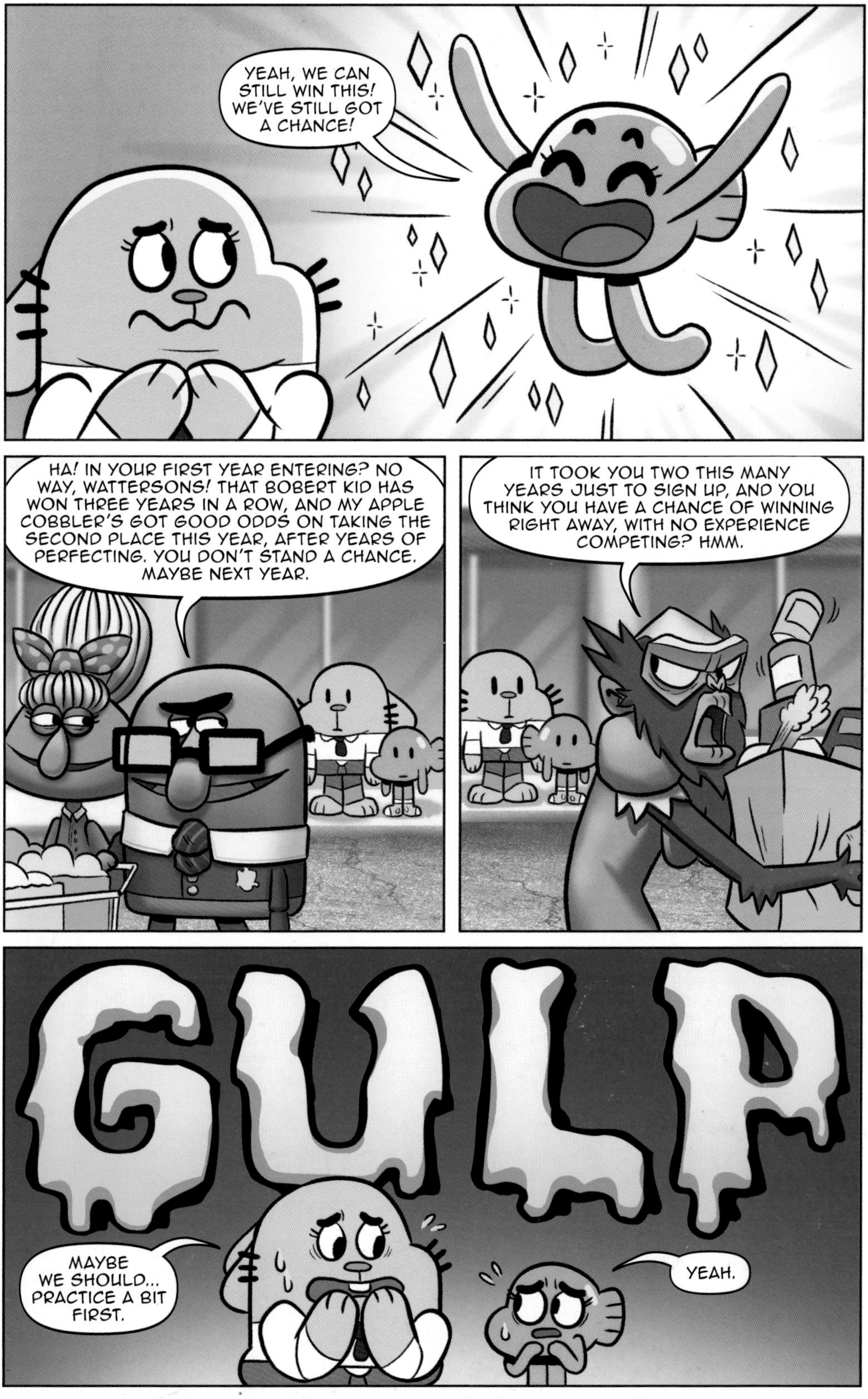
YEAH, WE CAN STILL WIN THIS! WE'VE STILL GOT A CHANCE!
HA! IN YOUR FIRST YEAR ENTERING? NO WAY, WATTERSONS! THAT BOBERT KID HAS WON THREE YEARS IN A ROW, AND MY APPLE COBBLER'S GOT GOOD ODDS ON TAKING THE SECOND PLACE THIS YEAR, AFTER YEARS OF PERFECTING. YOU DON'T STAND A CHANCE. MAYBE NEXT YEAR.
IT TOOK YOU TWO THIS MANY YEARS JUST TO SIGN UP, AND YOU THINK YOU HAVE A CHANCE OF WINNING RIGHT AWAY, WITH NO EXPERIENCE COMPETING? HMM.
GULP
MAYBE WE SHOULD... PRACTICE A BIT FIRST.
YEAH.

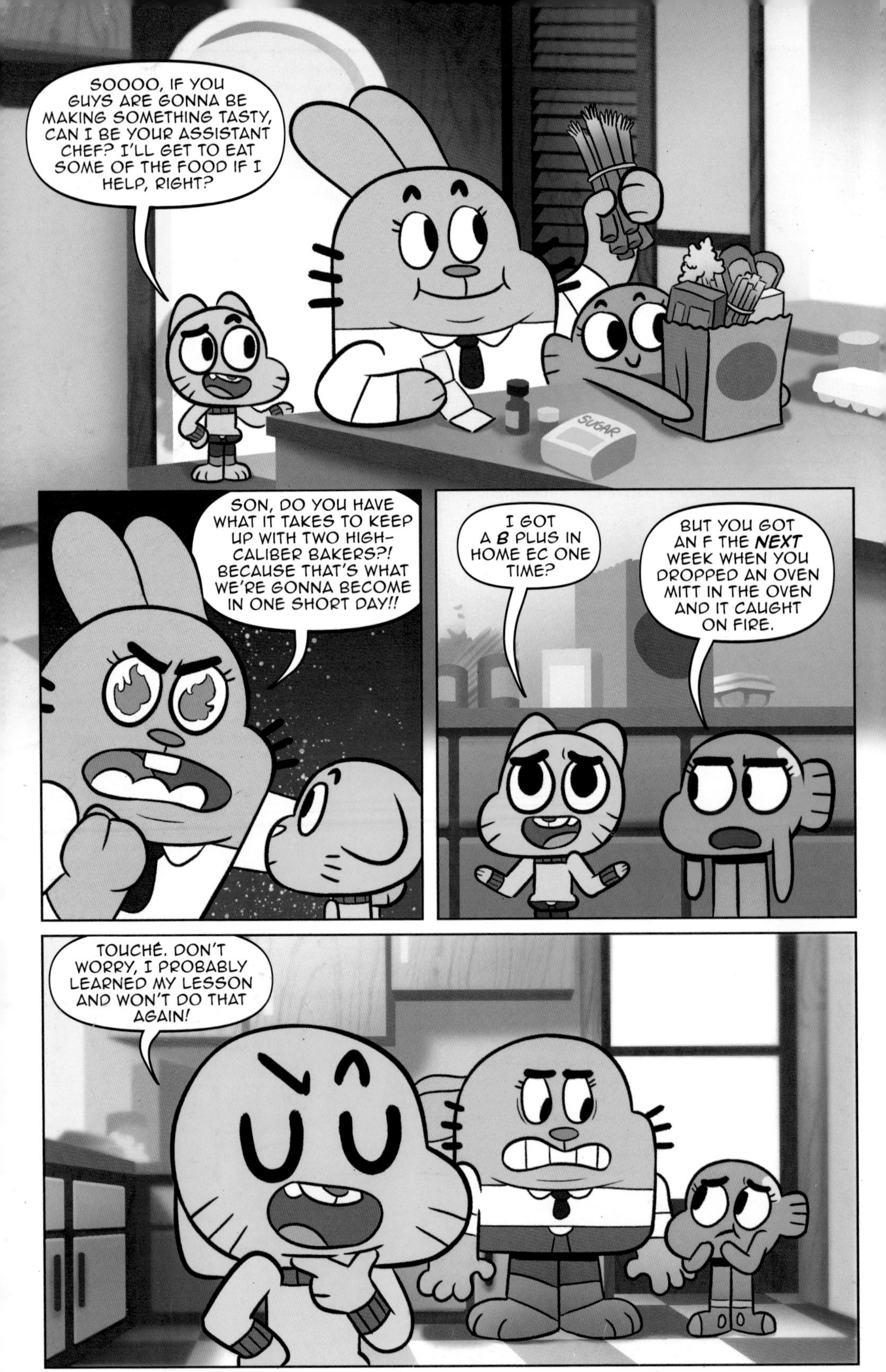
SOOOO, IF YOU GUYS ARE GONNA BE MAKING SOMETHING TASTY, CAN I BE YOUR ASSISTANT CHEF? I'LL GET TO EAT SOME OF THE FOOD IF I HELP, RIGHT?
SUGAR
SON, DO YOU HAVE WHAT IT TAKES TO KEEP UP WITH TWO HIGH-CALIBER BAKERS?! BECAUSE THAT'S WHAT WE'RE GONNA BECOME IN ONE SHORT DAY!!
I GOT A ***B*** PLUS IN HOME EC ONE TIME?
BUT YOU GOT AN F THE ***NEXT*** WEEK WHEN YOU DROPPED AN OVEN MITT IN THE OVEN AND IT CAUGHT ON FIRE.
TOUCHÉ. DON'T WORRY, I PROBABLY LEARNED MY LESSON AND WON'T DO THAT AGAIN!

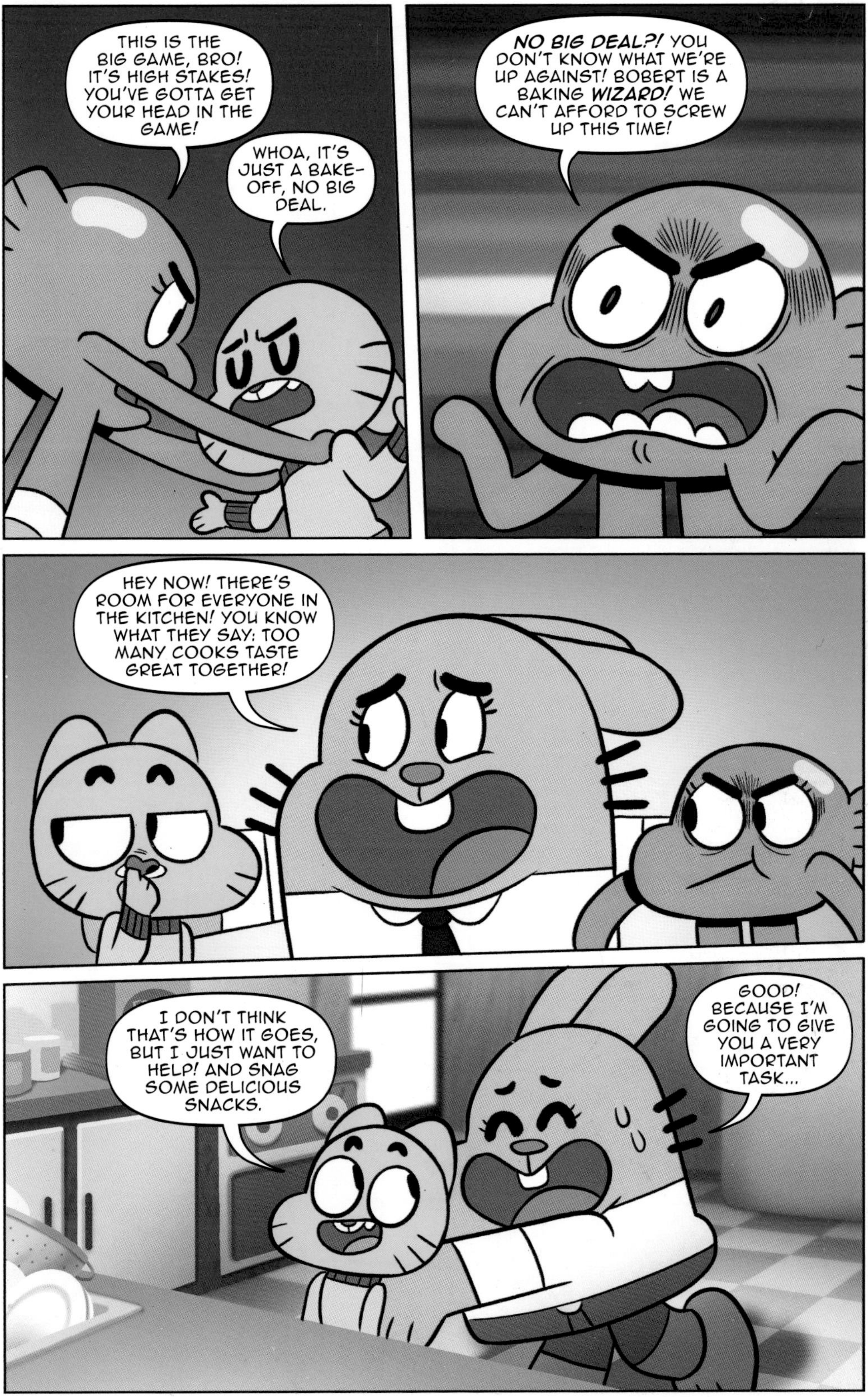
THIS IS THE BIG GAME, BRO! IT'S HIGH STAKES! YOU'VE GOTTA GET YOUR HEAD IN THE GAME!
WHOA, IT'S JUST A BAKE-OFF, NO BIG DEAL.
NO BIG DEAL?! YOU DON'T KNOW WHAT WE'RE UP AGAINST! BOBERT IS A BAKING WIZARD! WE CAN'T AFFORD TO SCREW UP THIS TIME!
HEY NOW! THERE'S ROOM FOR EVERYONE IN THE KITCHEN! YOU KNOW WHAT THEY SAY: TOO MANY COOKS TASTE GREAT TOGETHER!
I DON'T THINK THAT'S HOW IT GOES, BUT I JUST WANT TO HELP! AND SNAG SOME DELICIOUS SNACKS.
GOOD! BECAUSE I'M GOING TO GIVE YOU A VERY IMPORTANT TASK...

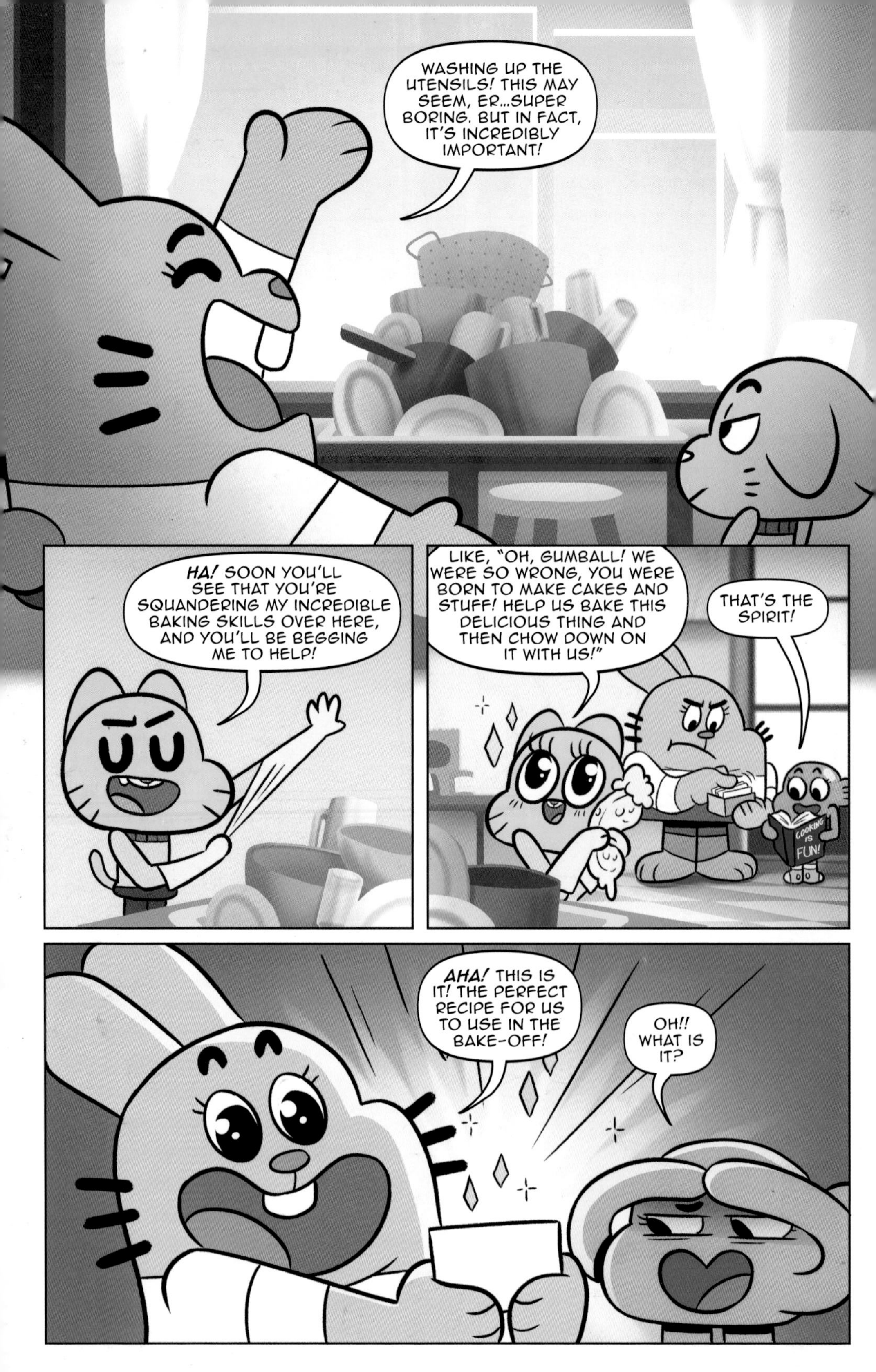
WASHING UP THE UTENSILS! THIS MAY SEEM, ER...SUPER BORING. BUT IN FACT, IT'S INCREDIBLY IMPORTANT!
HA! SOON YOU'LL SEE THAT YOU'RE SQUANDERING MY INCREDIBLE BAKING SKILLS OVER HERE, AND YOU'LL BE BEGGING ME TO HELP!
LIKE, "OH, GUMBALL! WE WERE SO WRONG, YOU WERE BORN TO MAKE CAKES AND STUFF! HELP US BAKE THIS DELICIOUS THING AND THEN CHOW DOWN ON IT WITH US!"
THAT'S THE SPIRIT!
COOKING IS FUN!
AHA! THIS IS IT! THE PERFECT RECIPE FOR US TO USE IN THE BAKE-OFF!
OH!! WHAT IS IT?

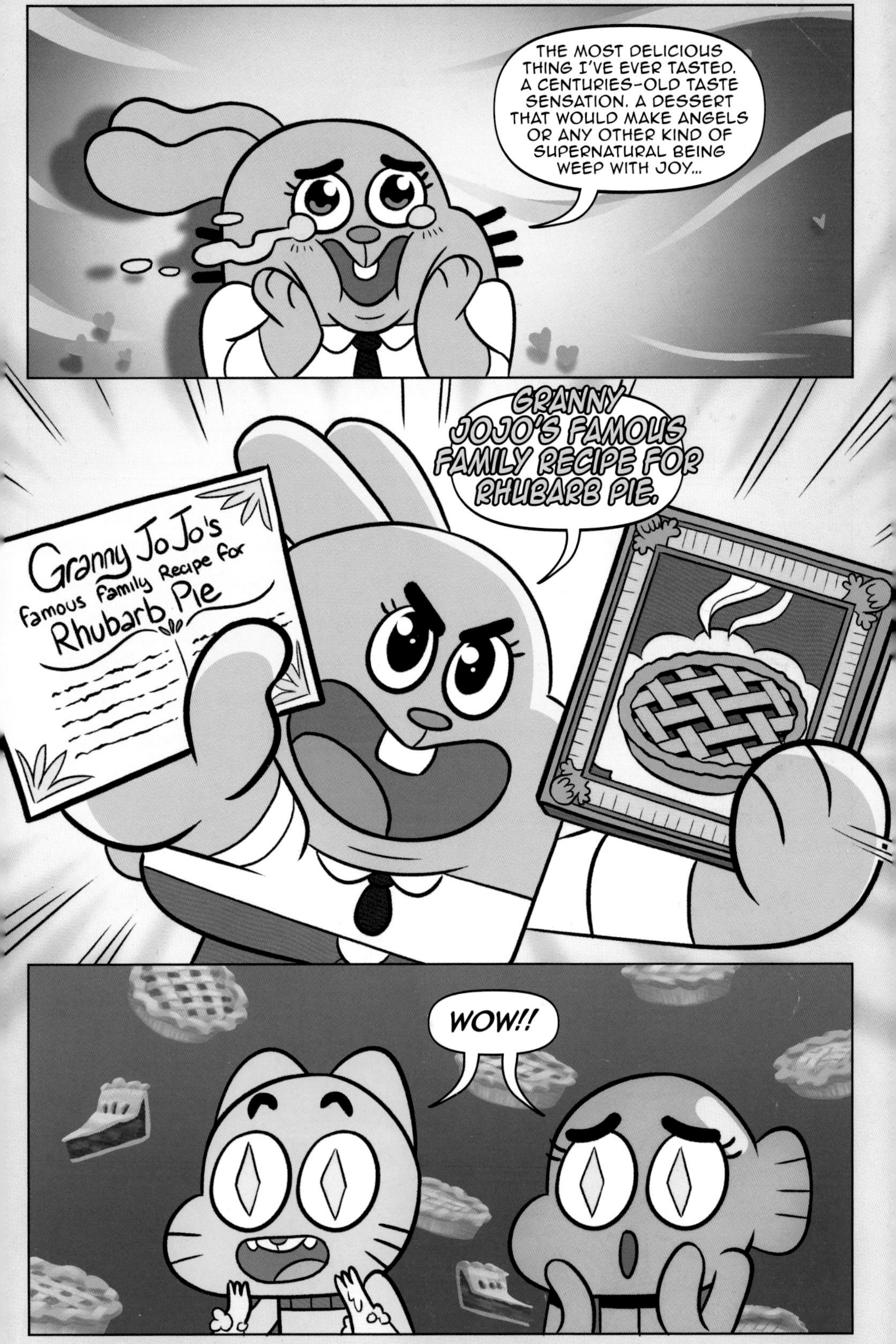
THE MOST DELICIOUS THING I'VE EVER TASTED. A CENTURIES-OLD TASTE SENSATION. A DESSERT THAT WOULD MAKE ANGELS OR ANY OTHER KIND OF SUPERNATURAL BEING WEEP WITH JOY...
GRANNY JOJO'S FAMOUS FAMILY RECIPE FOR RHUBARB PIE.
Granny JoJo's famous family Recipe for Rhubarb Pie
WOW!!

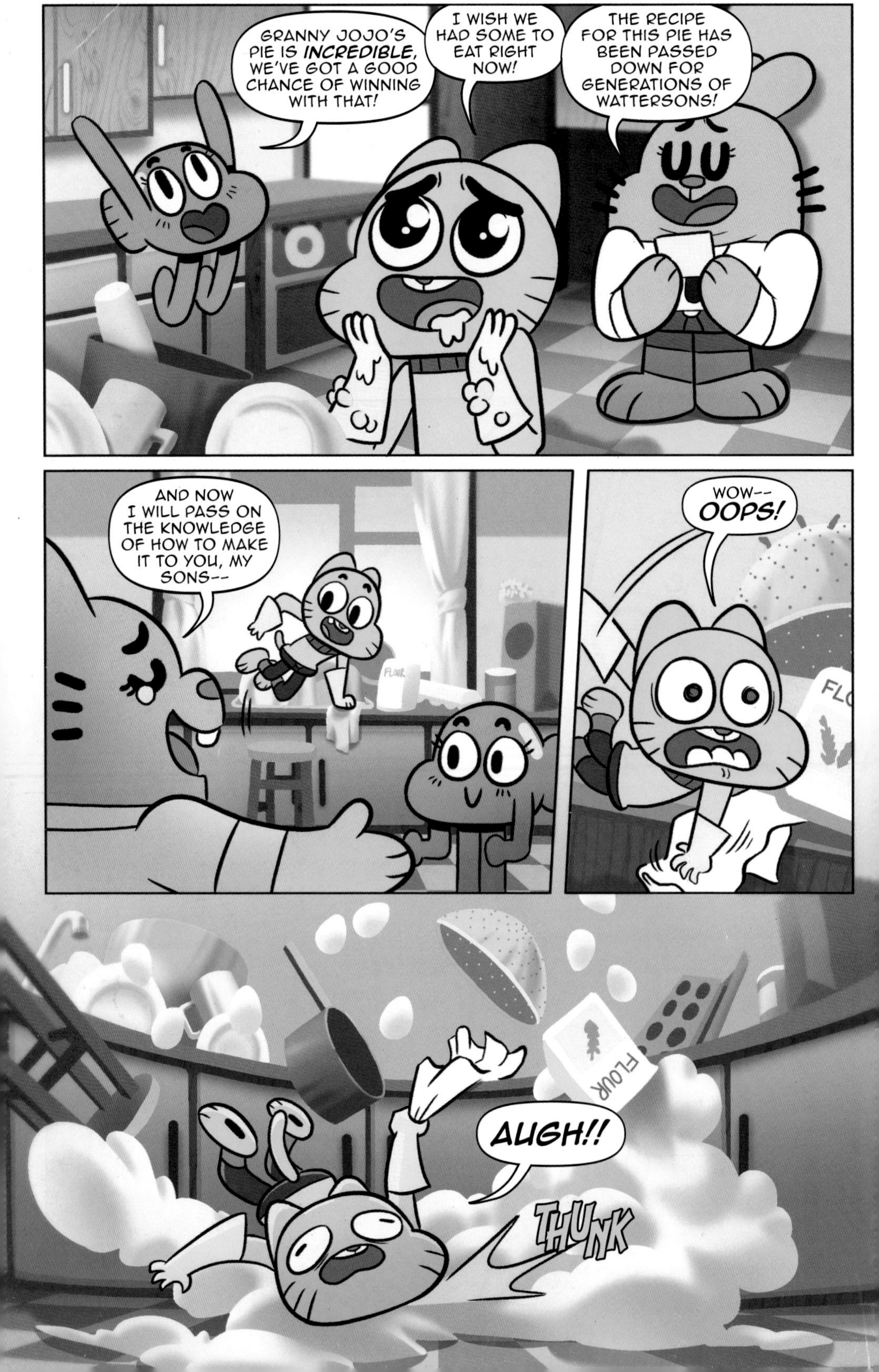
GRANNY JOJO'S PIE IS INCREDIBLE, WE'VE GOT A GOOD CHANCE OF WINNING WITH THAT!
I WISH WE HAD SOME TO EAT RIGHT NOW!
THE RECIPE FOR THIS PIE HAS BEEN PASSED DOWN FOR GENERATIONS OF WATTERSONS!
AND NOW I WILL PASS ON THE KNOWLEDGE OF HOW TO MAKE IT TO YOU, MY SONS--
FLOUR
WOW-- OOPS!
AUGH!!
FLOUR
THUNK

OH, DUDE. GROSS.

HEY, WHAT, THIS HUGE MESS HERE? THIS IS NOTHING.

GUMBALL, YOU'RE LIKE A KITCHEN JINX! WE DON'T HAVE TIME FOR THIS!

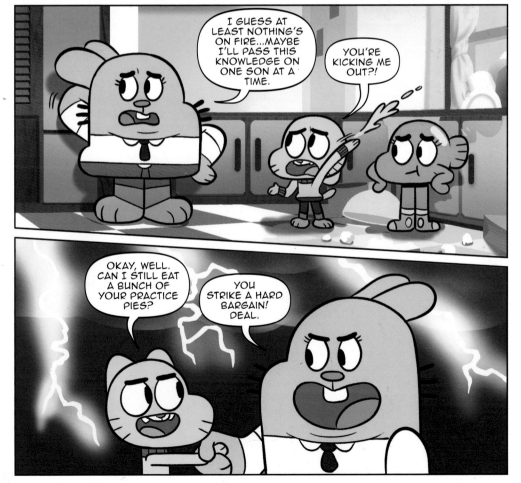

I GUESS AT LEAST NOTHING'S ON FIRE...MAYBE I'LL PASS THIS KNOWLEDGE ON ONE SON AT A TIME.

YOU'RE KICKING ME OUT?!

OKAY, WELL, CAN I STILL EAT A BUNCH OF YOUR PRACTICE PIES?

YOU STRIKE A HARD BARGAIN! DEAL.

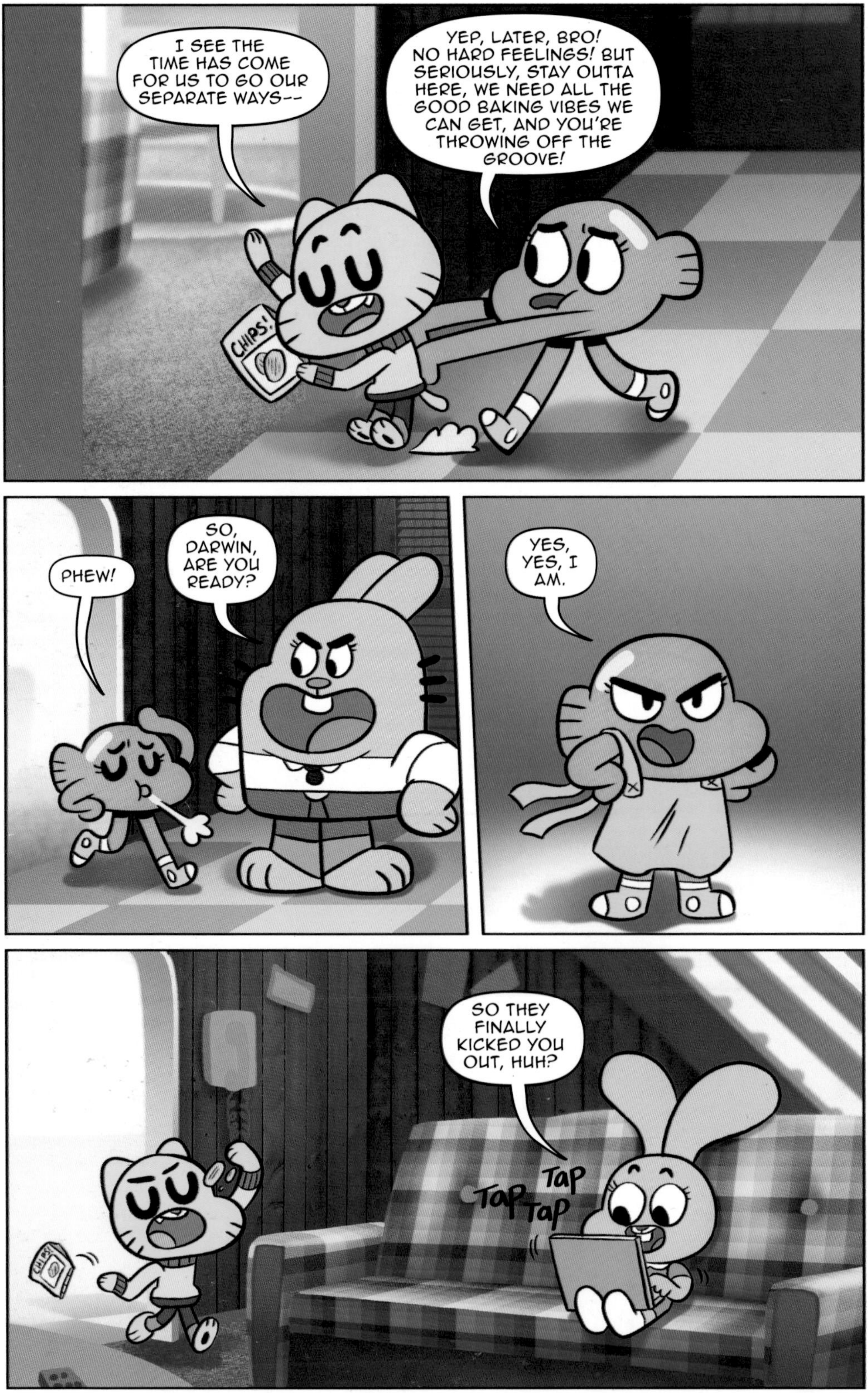
I SEE THE TIME HAS COME FOR US TO GO OUR SEPARATE WAYS--
YEP, LATER, BRO! NO HARD FEELINGS! BUT SERIOUSLY, STAY OUTTA HERE, WE NEED ALL THE GOOD BAKING VIBES WE CAN GET, AND YOU'RE THROWING OFF THE GROOVE!
CHIPS!
PHEW!
SO, DARWIN, ARE YOU READY?
YES, YES, I AM.
SO THEY FINALLY KICKED YOU OUT, HUH?
TAP TAP TAP

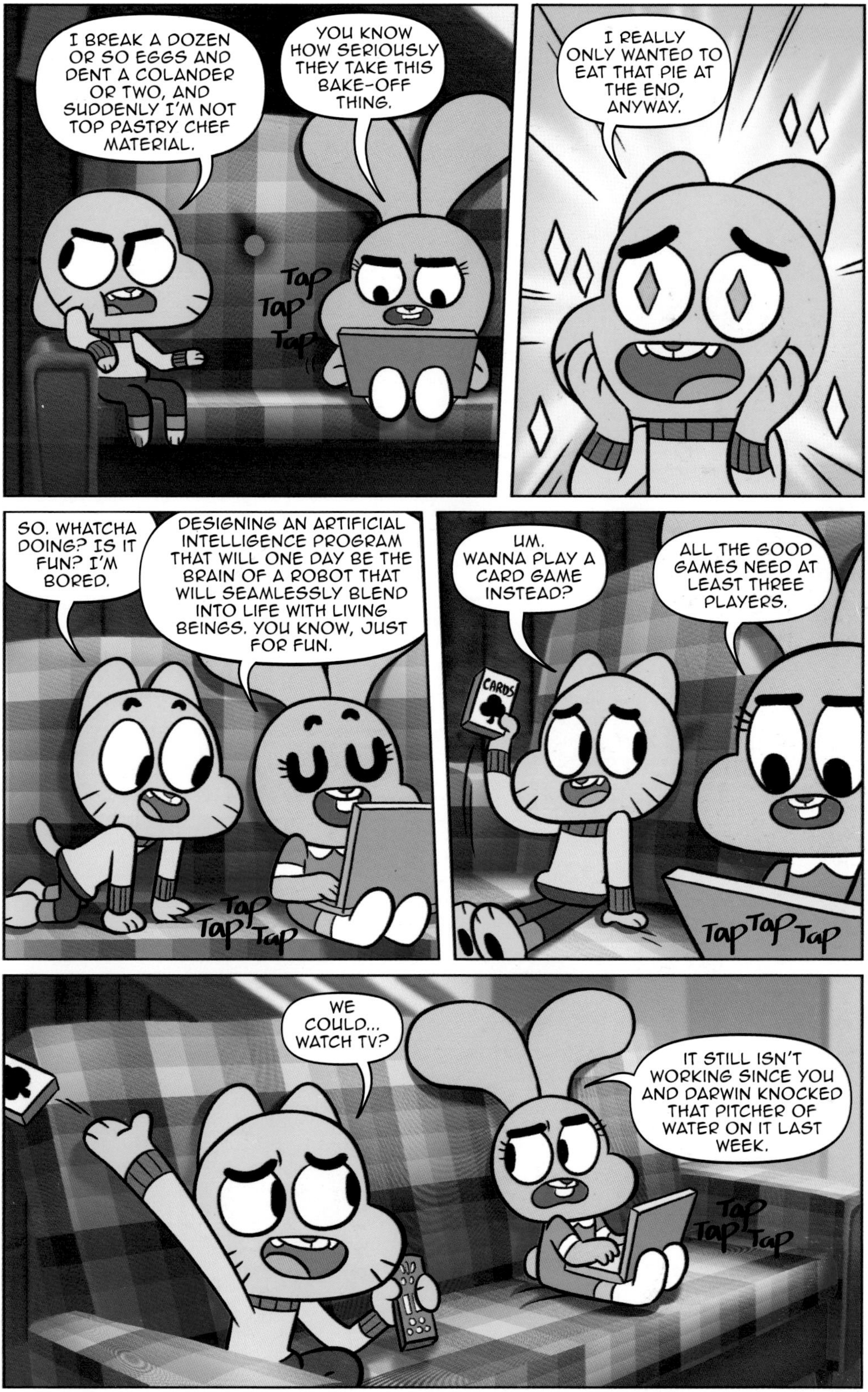

I BREAK A DOZEN OR SO EGGS AND DENT A COLANDER OR TWO, AND SUDDENLY I'M NOT TOP PASTRY CHEF MATERIAL.
YOU KNOW HOW SERIOUSLY THEY TAKE THIS BAKE-OFF THING.
Tap Tap Tap
I REALLY ONLY WANTED TO EAT THAT PIE AT THE END, ANYWAY.
SO. WHATCHA DOING? IS IT FUN? I'M BORED.
DESIGNING AN ARTIFICIAL INTELLIGENCE PROGRAM THAT WILL ONE DAY BE THE BRAIN OF A ROBOT THAT WILL SEAMLESSLY BLEND INTO LIFE WITH LIVING BEINGS. YOU KNOW, JUST FOR FUN.
Tap Tap Tap
UM. WANNA PLAY A CARD GAME INSTEAD?
CARDS
ALL THE GOOD GAMES NEED AT LEAST THREE PLAYERS.
Tap Tap Tap
WE COULD... WATCH TV?
IT STILL ISN'T WORKING SINCE YOU AND DARWIN KNOCKED THAT PITCHER OF WATER ON IT LAST WEEK.
Tap Tap Tap

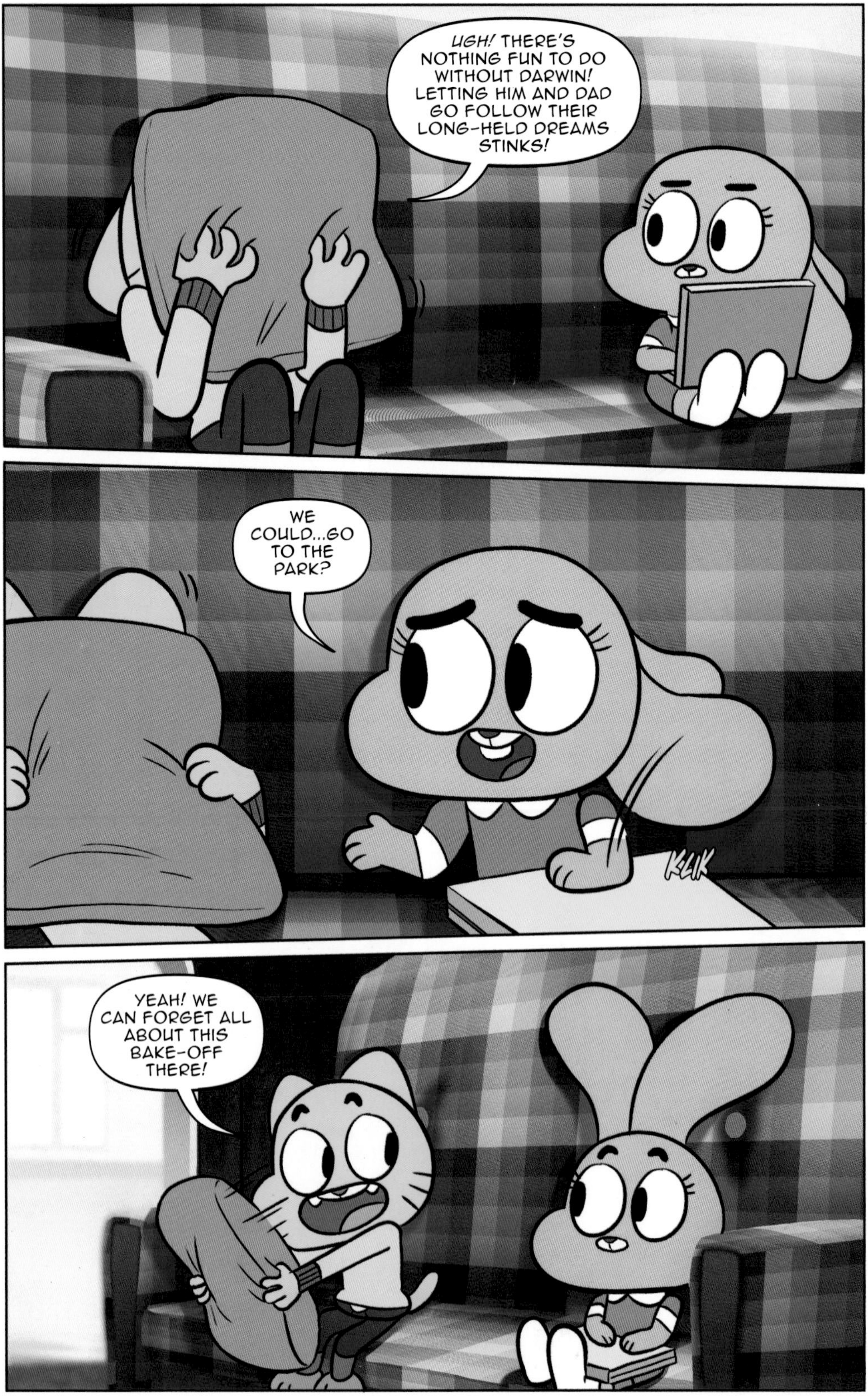
UGH! THERE'S NOTHING FUN TO DO WITHOUT DARWIN! LETTING HIM AND DAD GO FOLLOW THEIR LONG-HELD DREAMS STINKS!
WE COULD...GO TO THE PARK?
KLIK
YEAH! WE CAN FORGET ALL ABOUT THIS BAKE-OFF THERE!

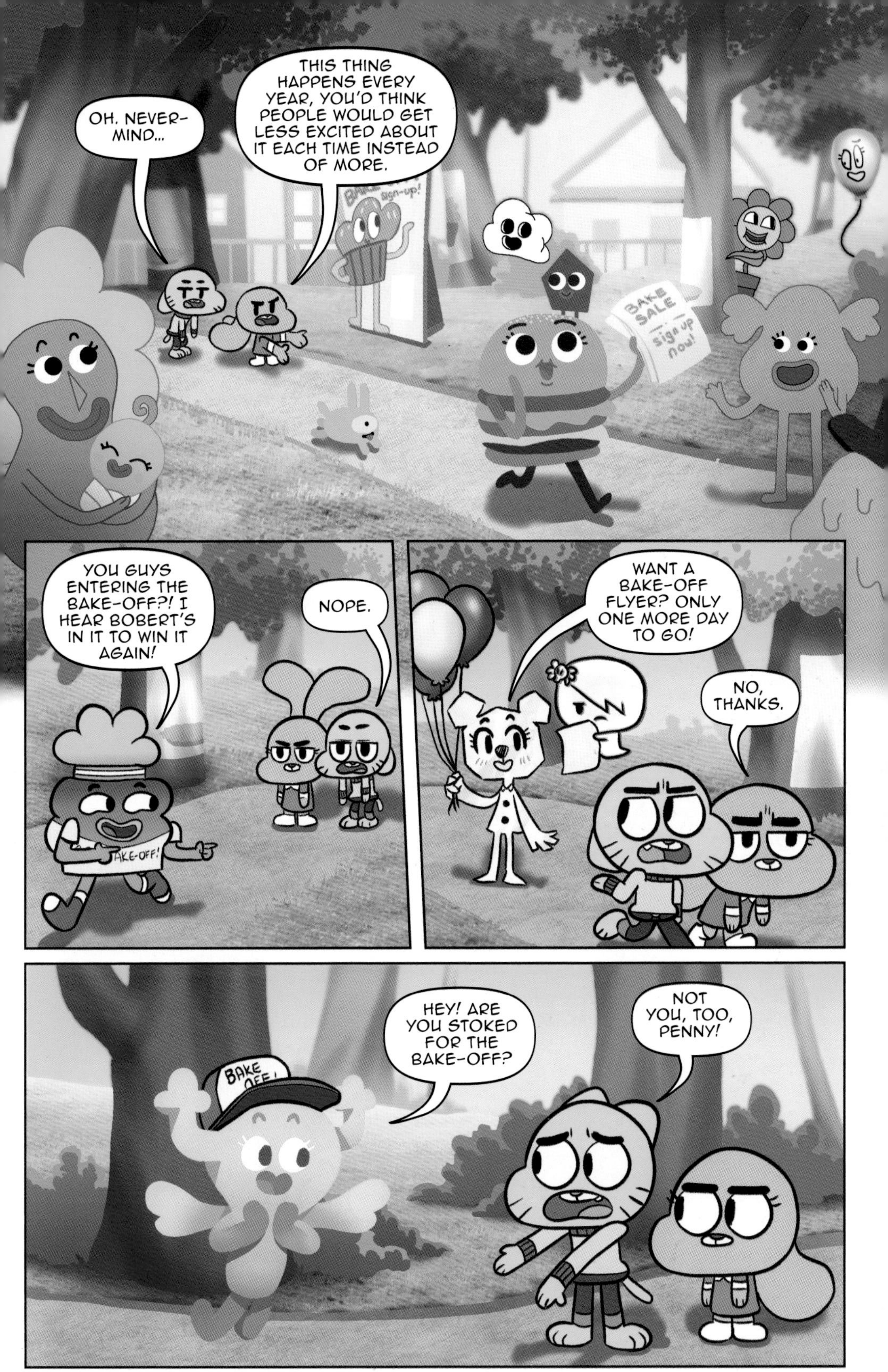
OH. NEVER-MIND...
THIS THING HAPPENS EVERY YEAR, YOU'D THINK PEOPLE WOULD GET LESS EXCITED ABOUT IT EACH TIME INSTEAD OF MORE.
Sign-up!
BAKE SALE sign up now!
YOU GUYS ENTERING THE BAKE-OFF?! I HEAR BOBERT'S IN IT TO WIN IT AGAIN!
NOPE.
AKE-OFF!
WANT A BAKE-OFF FLYER? ONLY ONE MORE DAY TO GO!
NO, THANKS.
HEY! ARE YOU STOKED FOR THE BAKE-OFF?
NOT YOU, TOO, PENNY!
BAKE

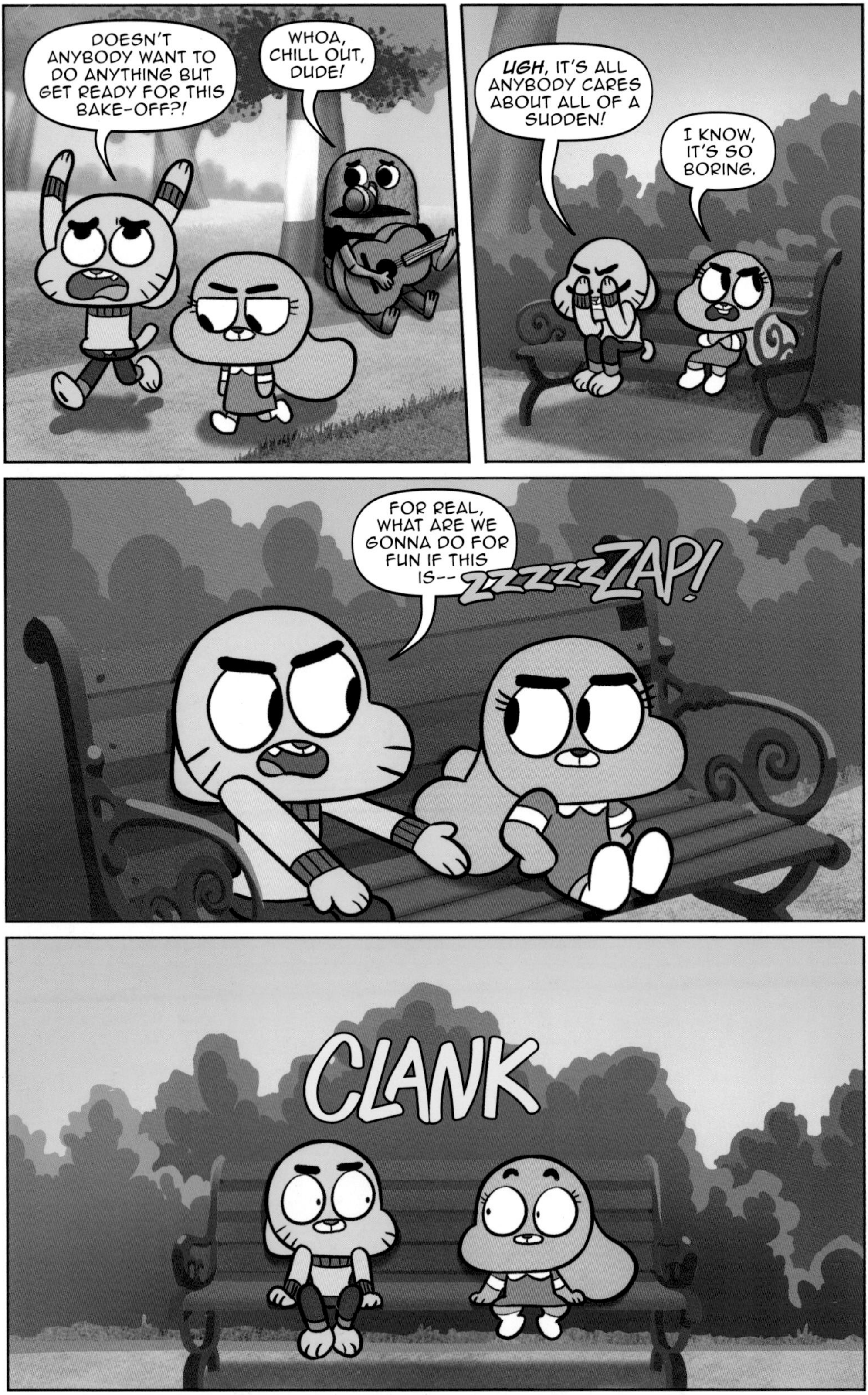

DOESN'T ANYBODY WANT TO DO ANYTHING BUT GET READY FOR THIS BAKE-OFF?!
WHOA, CHILL OUT, DUDE!
UGH, IT'S ALL ANYBODY CARES ABOUT ALL OF A SUDDEN!
I KNOW, IT'S SO BORING.
FOR REAL, WHAT ARE WE GONNA DO FOR FUN IF THIS IS--
ZZZZZZAP!
CLANK

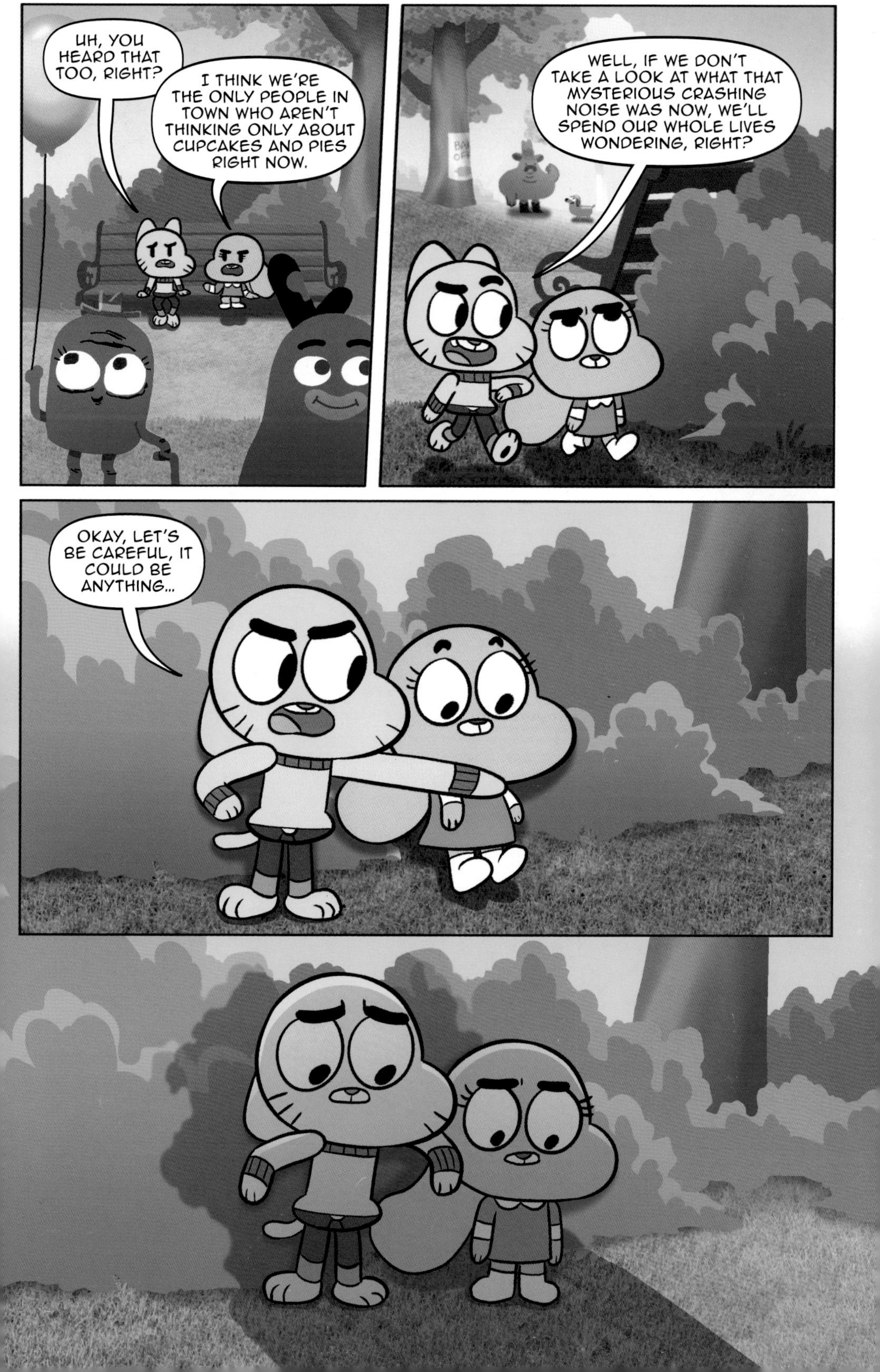
UH, YOU HEARD THAT TOO, RIGHT?
I THINK WE'RE THE ONLY PEOPLE IN TOWN WHO AREN'T THINKING ONLY ABOUT CUPCAKES AND PIES RIGHT NOW.
WELL, IF WE DON'T TAKE A LOOK AT WHAT THAT MYSTERIOUS CRASHING NOISE WAS NOW, WE'LL SPEND OUR WHOLE LIVES WONDERING, RIGHT?
OKAY, LET'S BE CAREFUL, IT COULD BE ANYTHING...

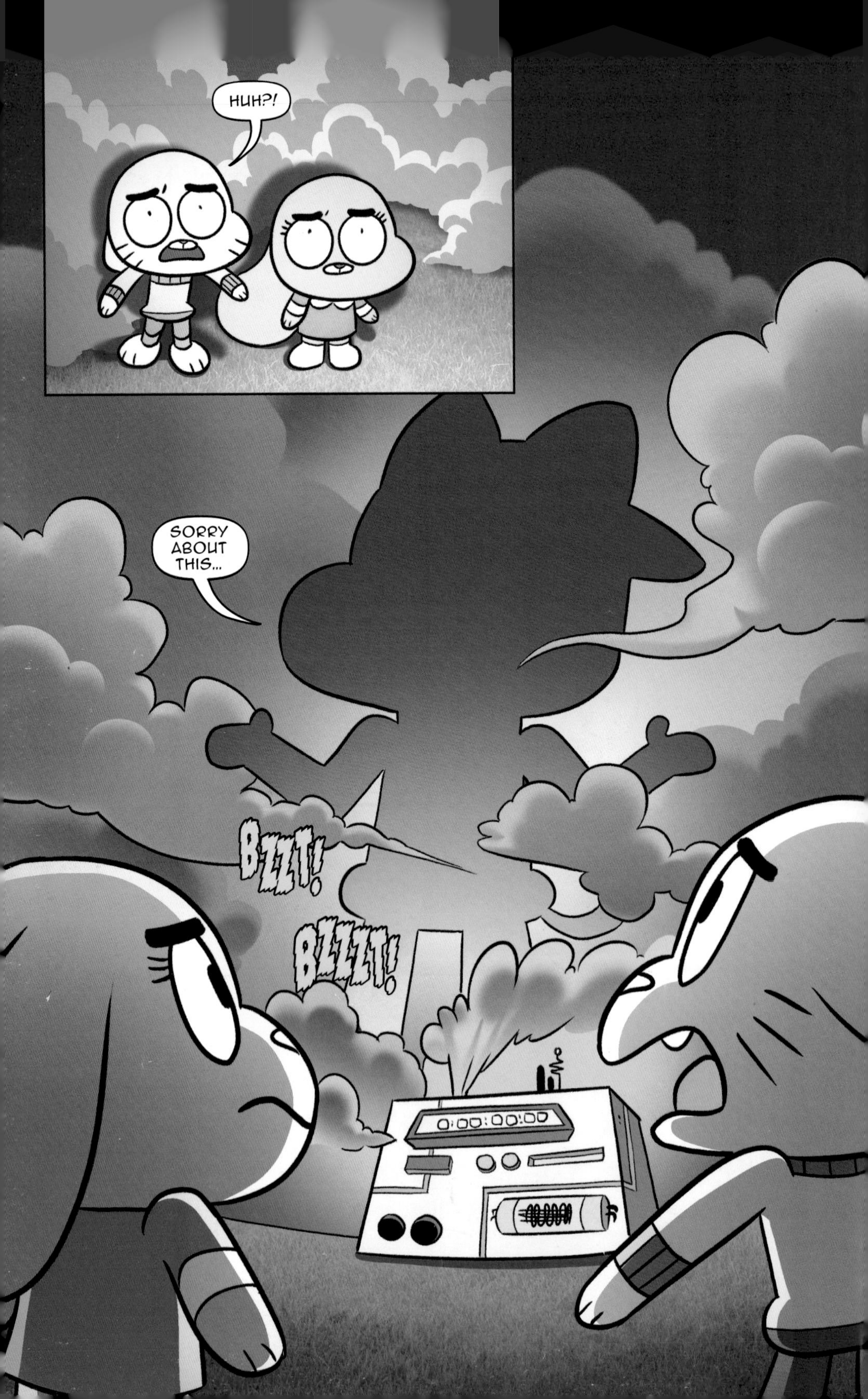
HUH?!
SORRY ABOUT THIS...
BZZT!
BZZZT!
0:00:00:00

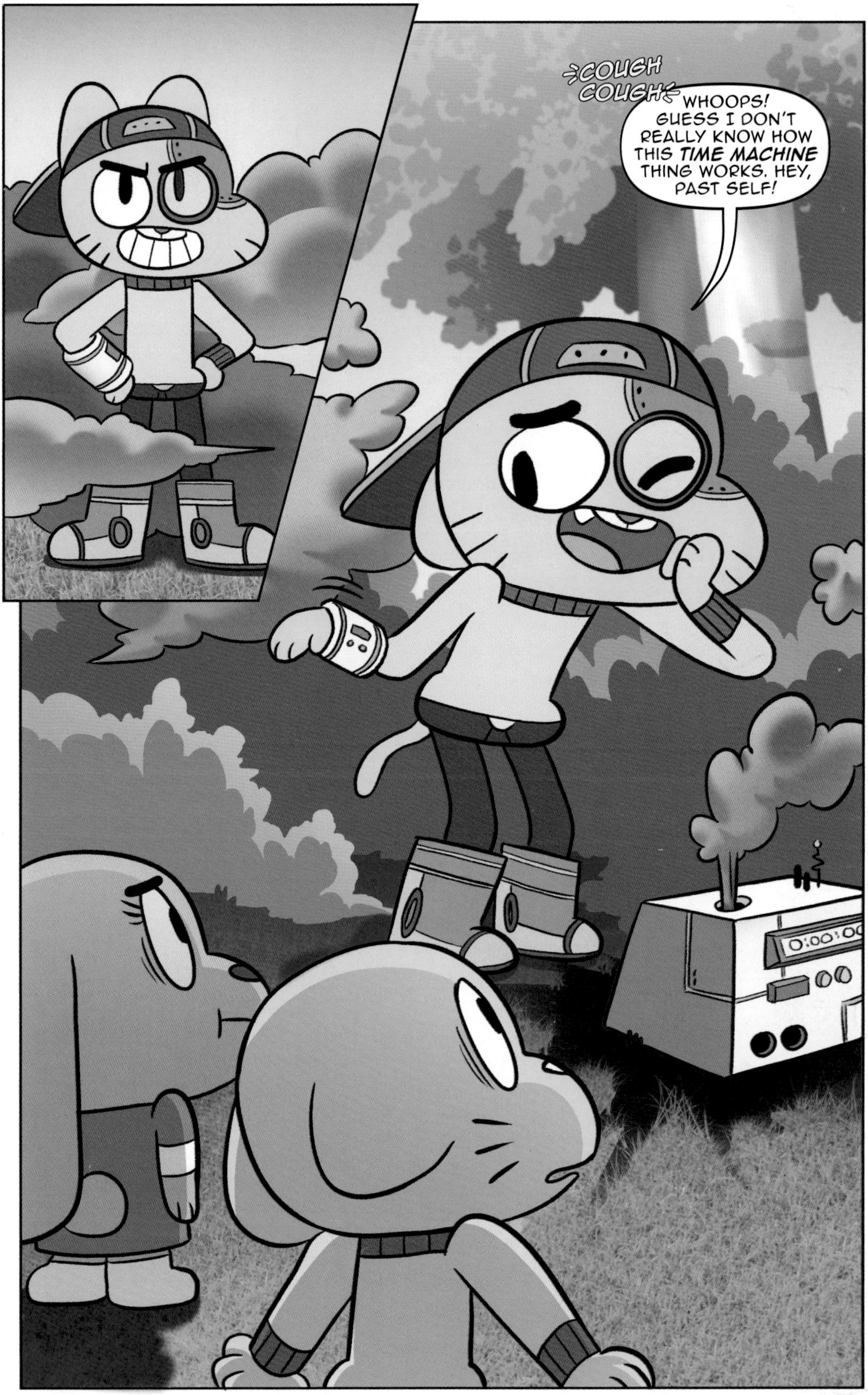

COUGH COUGH
WHOOPS! GUESS I DON'T REALLY KNOW HOW THIS *TIME MACHINE* THING WORKS. HEY, PAST SELF!

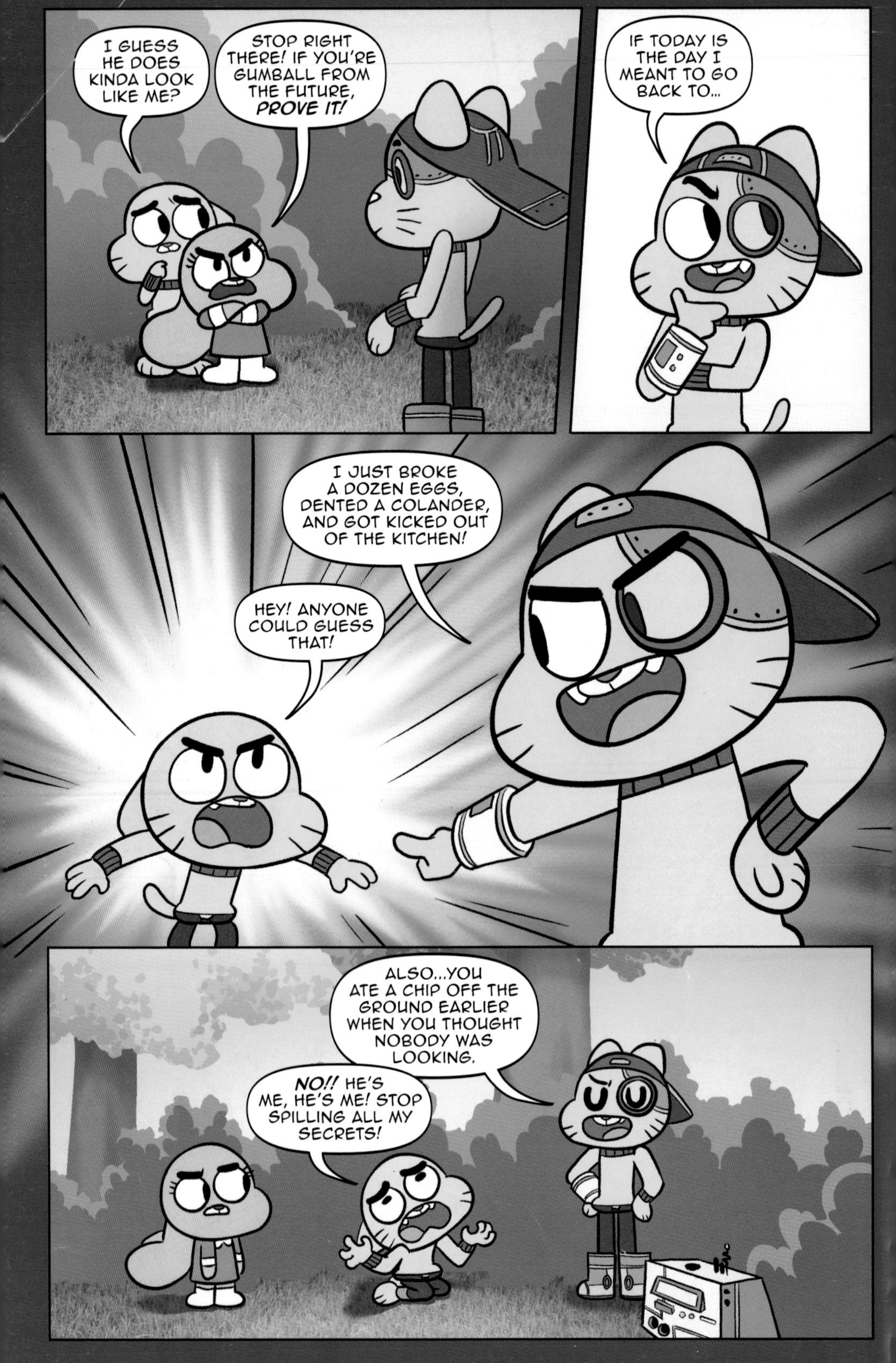
I GUESS HE DOES KINDA LOOK LIKE ME?
STOP RIGHT THERE! IF YOU'RE GUMBALL FROM THE FUTURE, *PROVE IT!*
IF TODAY IS THE DAY I MEANT TO GO BACK TO...
I JUST BROKE A DOZEN EGGS, DENTED A COLANDER, AND GOT KICKED OUT OF THE KITCHEN!
HEY! ANYONE COULD GUESS THAT!
ALSO...YOU ATE A CHIP OFF THE GROUND EARLIER WHEN YOU THOUGHT NOBODY WAS LOOKING.
NO!! HE'S ME, HE'S ME! STOP SPILLING ALL MY SECRETS!

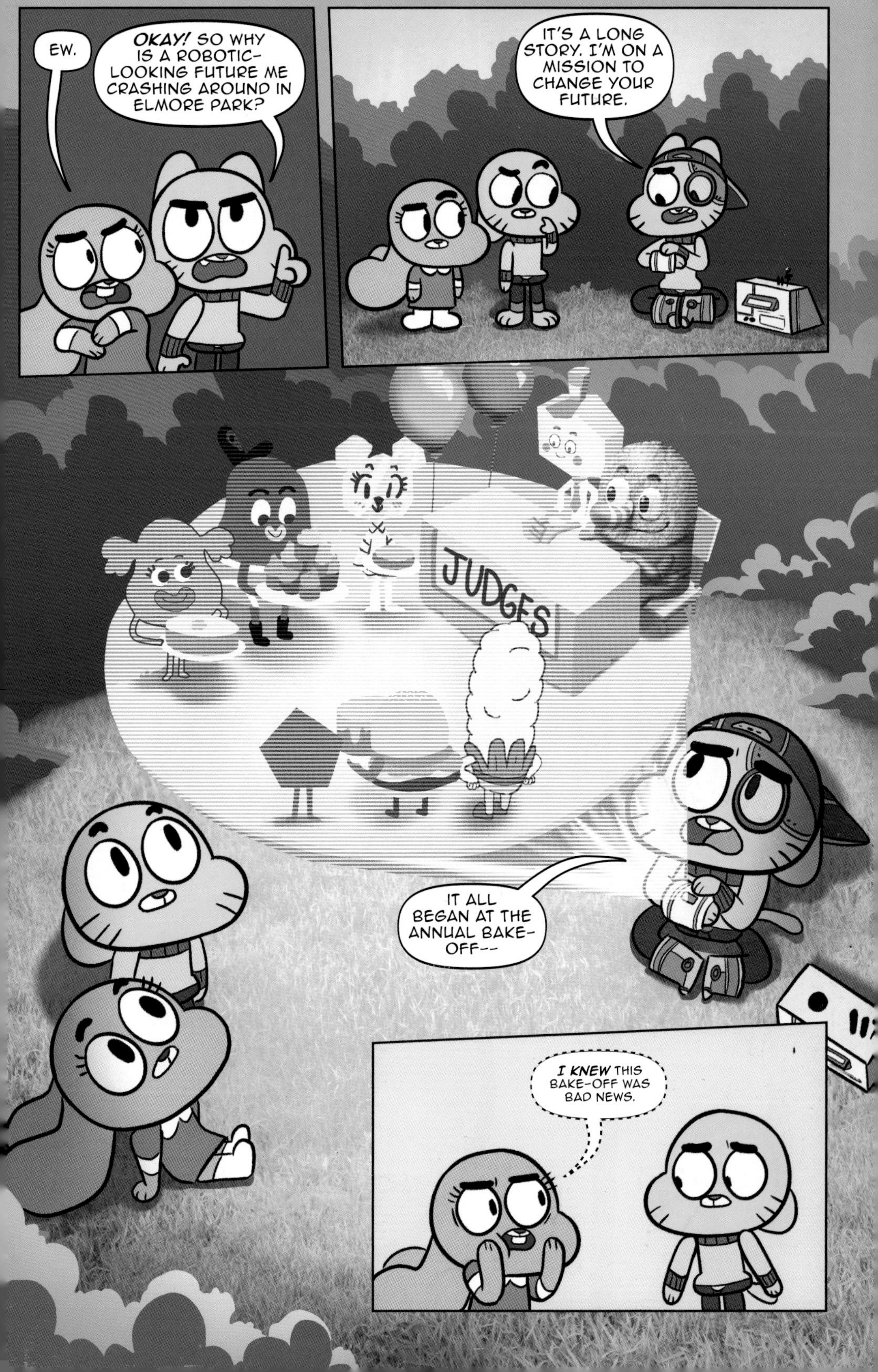
EW.
OKAY! SO WHY IS A ROBOTIC-LOOKING FUTURE ME CRASHING AROUND IN ELMORE PARK?
IT'S A LONG STORY. I'M ON A MISSION TO CHANGE YOUR FUTURE.
JUDGES
IT ALL BEGAN AT THE ANNUAL BAKE-OFF--
I KNEW THIS BAKE-OFF WAS BAD NEWS.

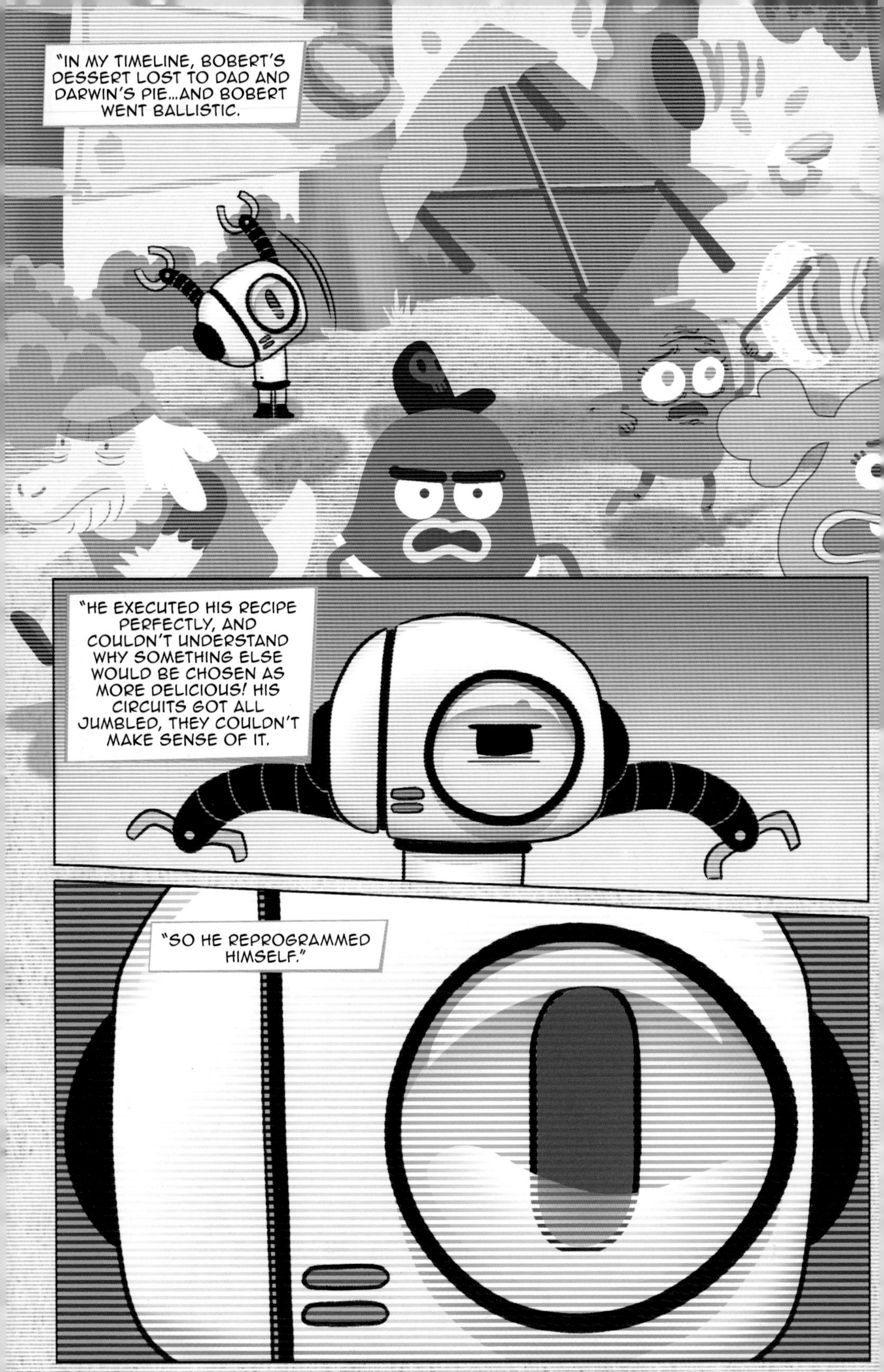
"IN MY TIMELINE, BOBERT'S DESSERT LOST TO DAD AND DARWIN'S PIE...AND BOBERT WENT BALLISTIC.
"HE EXECUTED HIS RECIPE PERFECTLY, AND COULDN'T UNDERSTAND WHY SOMETHING ELSE WOULD BE CHOSEN AS MORE DELICIOUS! HIS CIRCUITS GOT ALL JUMBLED, THEY COULDN'T MAKE SENSE OF IT.
"SO HE REPROGRAMMED HIMSELF."

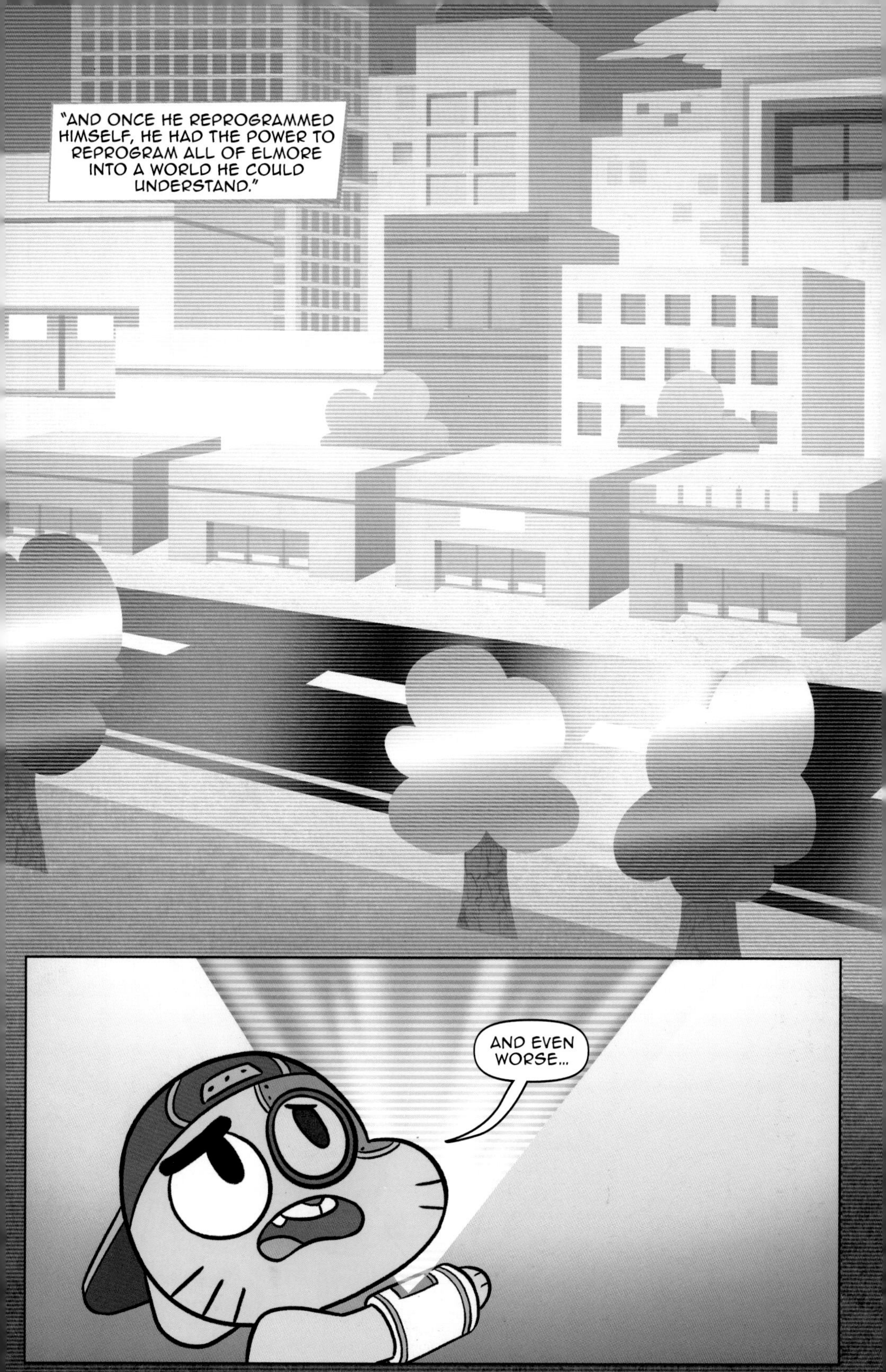
"AND ONCE HE REPROGRAMMED HIMSELF, HE HAD THE POWER TO REPROGRAM ALL OF ELMORE INTO A WORLD HE COULD UNDERSTAND."
AND EVEN WORSE...

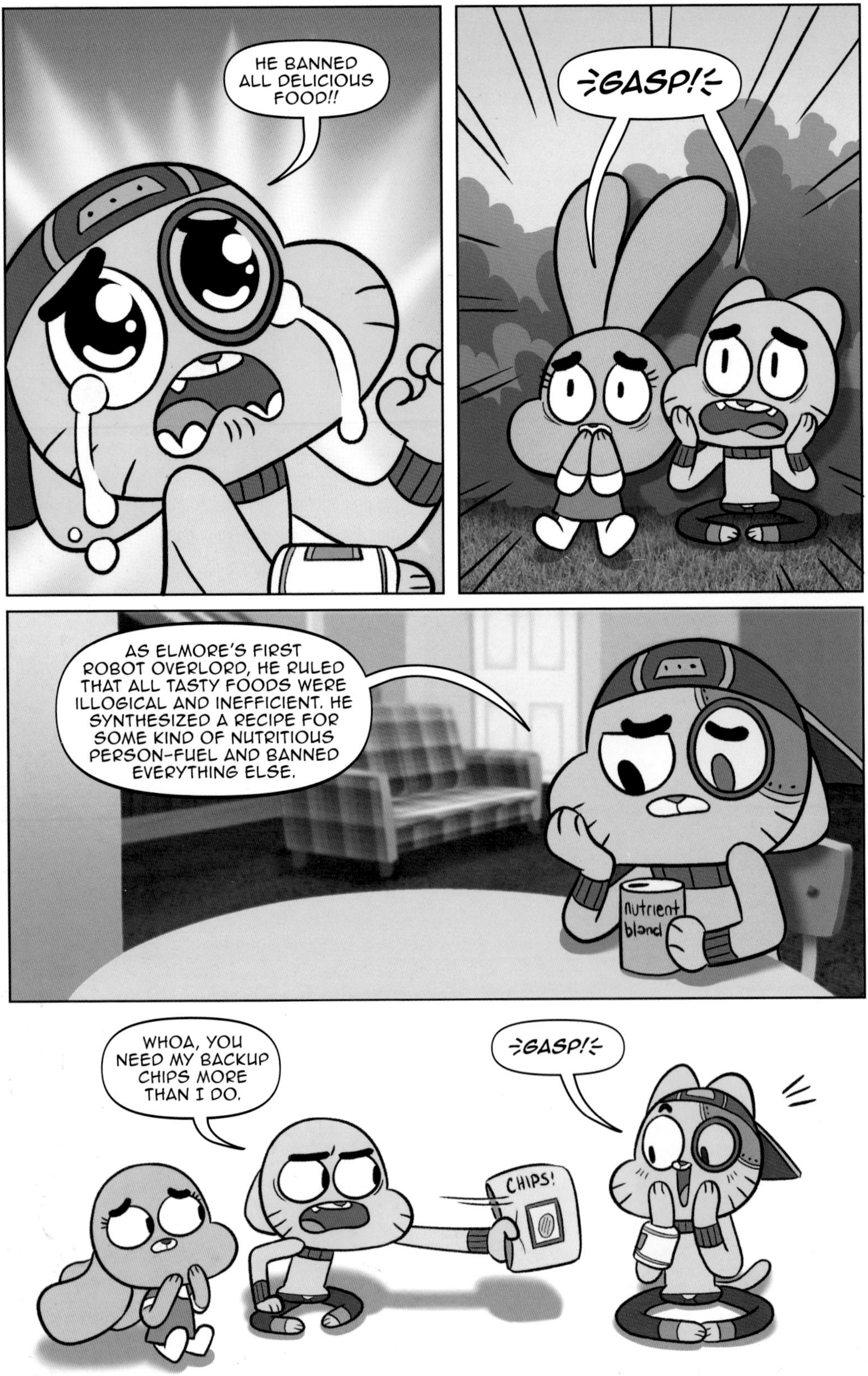
HE BANNED ALL DELICIOUS FOOD!!
GASP!
AS ELMORE'S FIRST ROBOT OVERLORD, HE RULED THAT ALL TASTY FOODS WERE ILLOGICAL AND INEFFICIENT. HE SYNTHESIZED A RECIPE FOR SOME KIND OF NUTRITIOUS PERSON-FUEL AND BANNED EVERYTHING ELSE.
nutrient blend
WHOA, YOU NEED MY BACKUP CHIPS MORE THAN I DO.
CHIPS!
GASP!

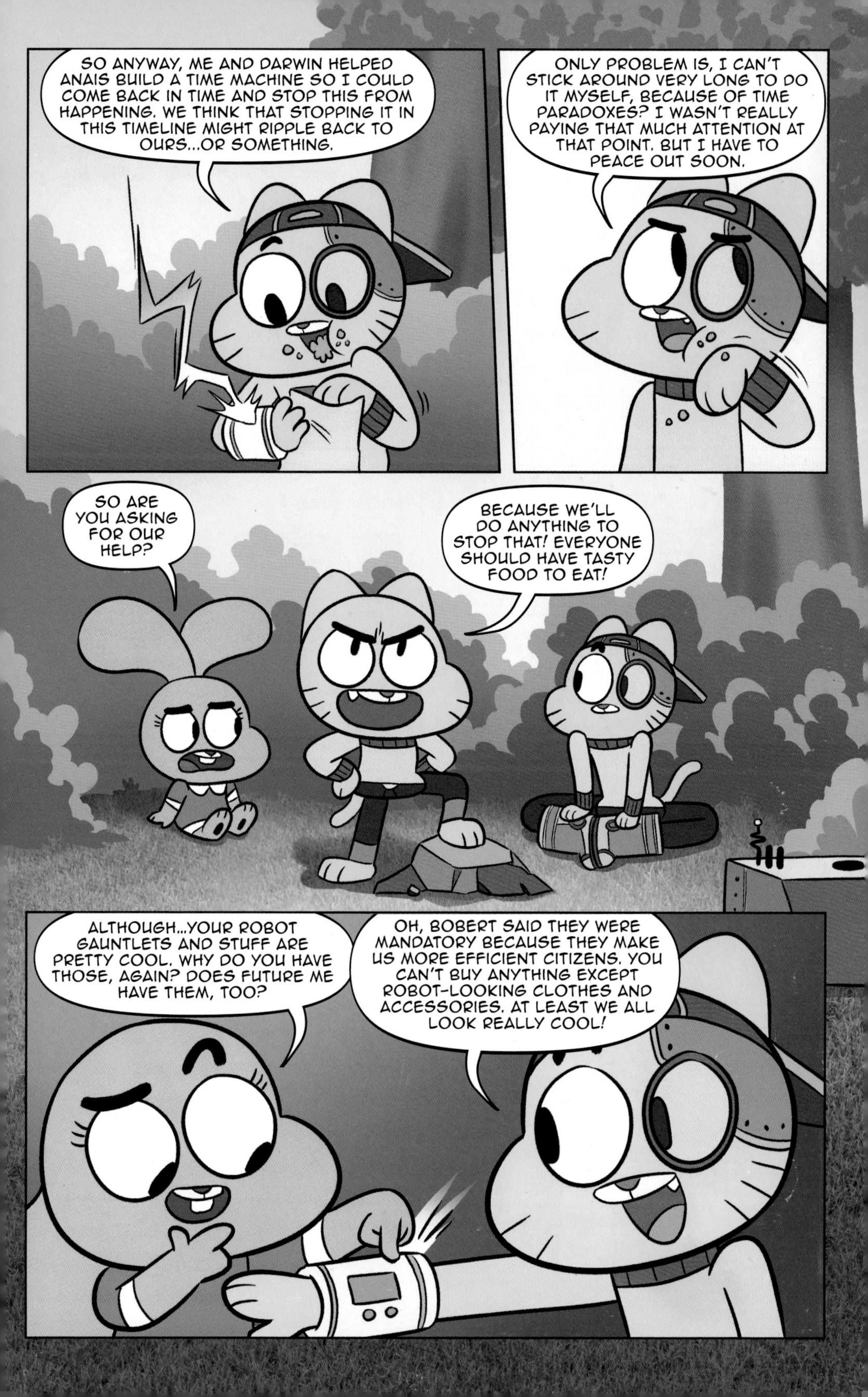
SO ANYWAY, ME AND DARWIN HELPED ANAIS BUILD A TIME MACHINE SO I COULD COME BACK IN TIME AND STOP THIS FROM HAPPENING. WE THINK THAT STOPPING IT IN THIS TIMELINE MIGHT RIPPLE BACK TO OURS...OR SOMETHING.
ONLY PROBLEM IS, I CAN'T STICK AROUND VERY LONG TO DO IT MYSELF, BECAUSE OF TIME PARADOXES? I WASN'T REALLY PAYING THAT MUCH ATTENTION AT THAT POINT. BUT I HAVE TO PEACE OUT SOON.
SO ARE YOU ASKING FOR OUR HELP?
BECAUSE WE'LL DO ANYTHING TO STOP THAT! EVERYONE SHOULD HAVE TASTY FOOD TO EAT!
ALTHOUGH...YOUR ROBOT GAUNTLETS AND STUFF ARE PRETTY COOL. WHY DO YOU HAVE THOSE, AGAIN? DOES FUTURE ME HAVE THEM, TOO?
OH, BOBERT SAID THEY WERE MANDATORY BECAUSE THEY MAKE US MORE EFFICIENT CITIZENS. YOU CAN'T BUY ANYTHING EXCEPT ROBOT-LOOKING CLOTHES AND ACCESSORIES. AT LEAST WE ALL LOOK REALLY COOL!

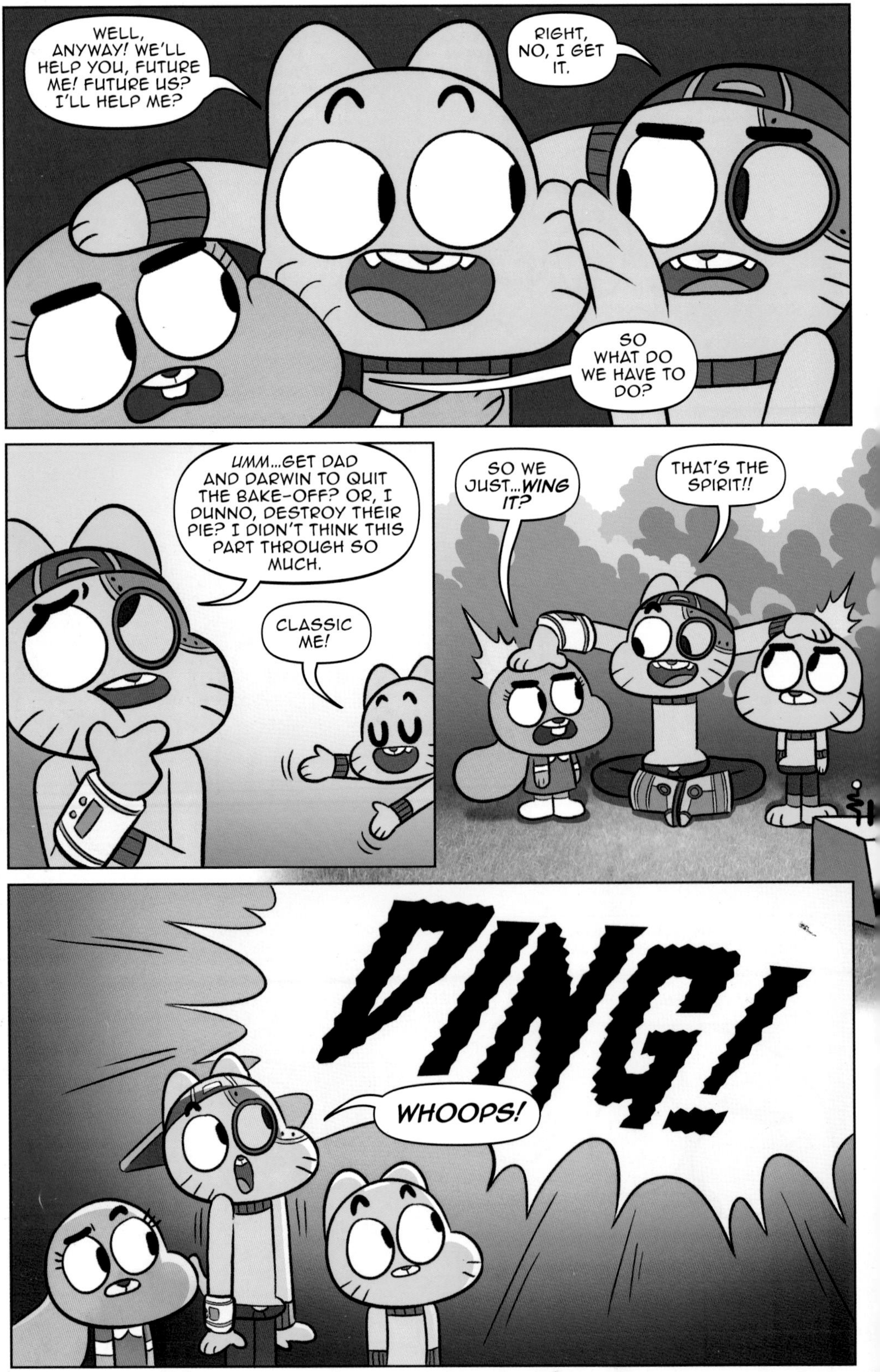
WELL, ANYWAY! WE'LL HELP YOU, FUTURE ME! FUTURE US? I'LL HELP ME?
RIGHT, NO, I GET IT.
SO WHAT DO WE HAVE TO DO?
UMM...GET DAD AND DARWIN TO QUIT THE BAKE-OFF? OR, I DUNNO, DESTROY THEIR PIE? I DIDN'T THINK THIS PART THROUGH SO MUCH.
CLASSIC ME!
SO WE JUST...WING IT?
THAT'S THE SPIRIT!!
DING!
WHOOPS!

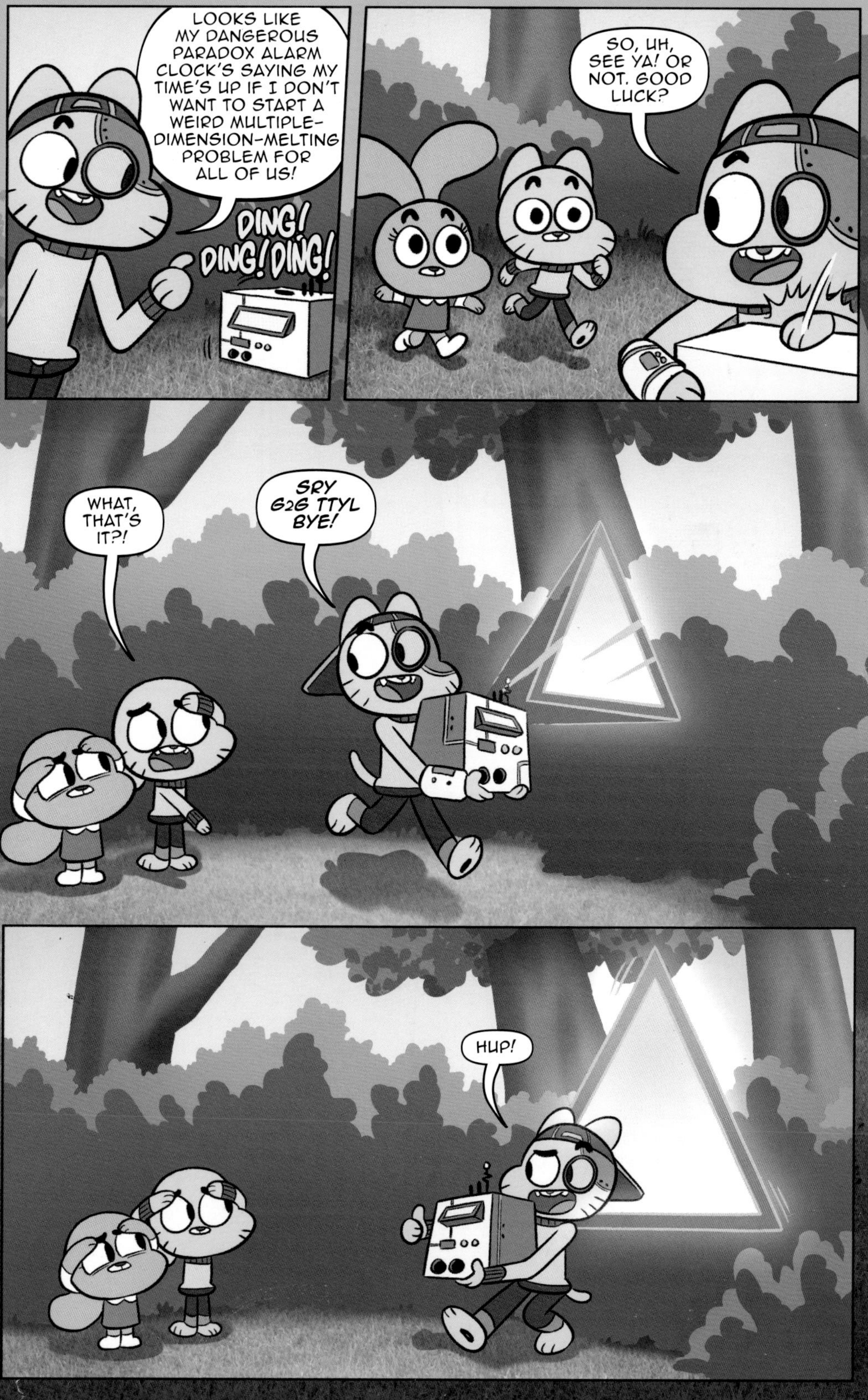
LOOKS LIKE MY DANGEROUS PARADOX ALARM CLOCK'S SAYING MY TIME'S UP IF I DON'T WANT TO START A WEIRD MULTIPLE-DIMENSION-MELTING PROBLEM FOR ALL OF US!
DING! DING! DING!
SO, UH, SEE YA! OR NOT. GOOD LUCK?
WHAT, THAT'S IT?!
SRY G2G TTYL BYE!
HUP!

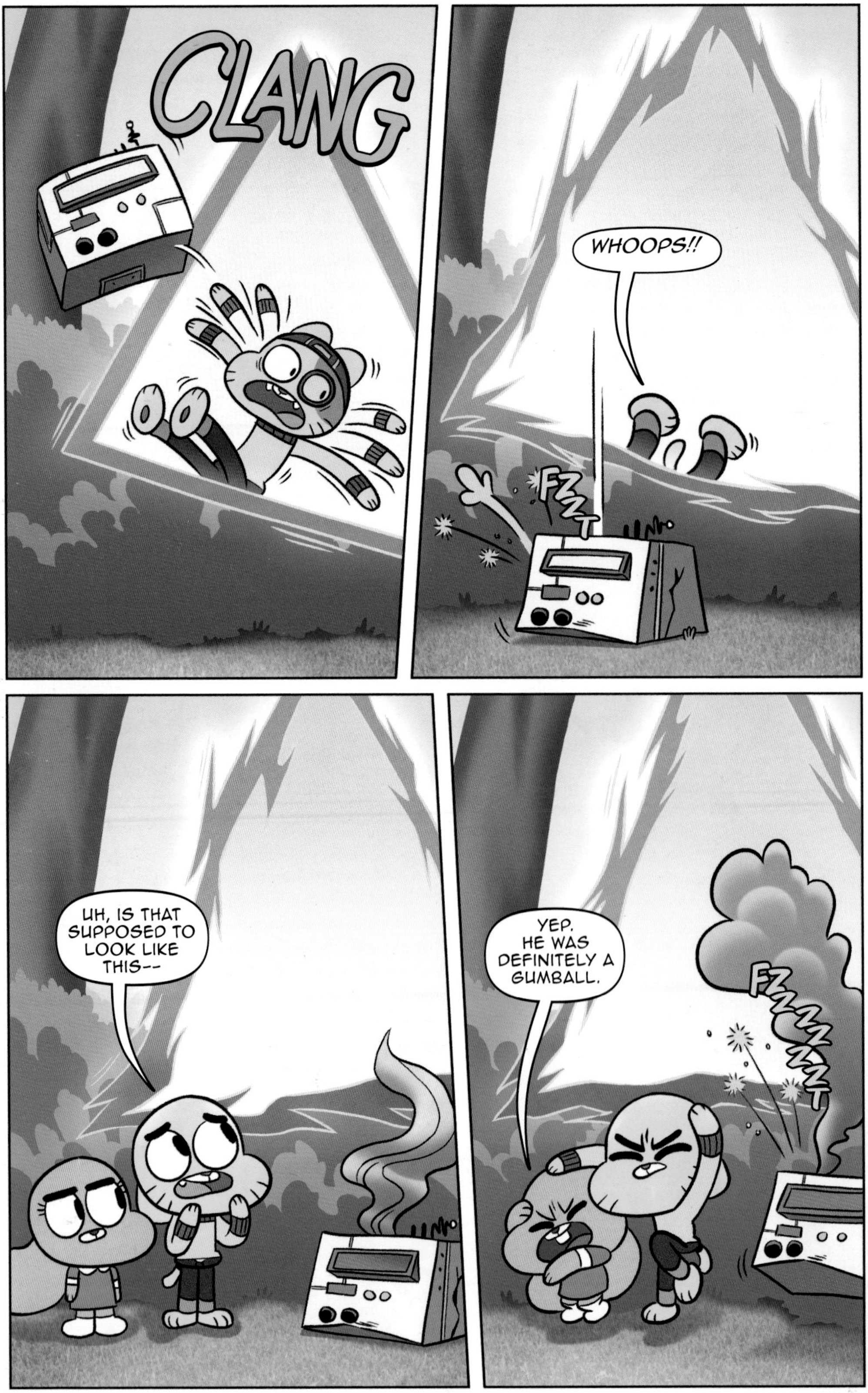

CLANG
WHOOPS!!
FZZT
UH, IS THAT SUPPOSED TO LOOK LIKE THIS--
YEP. HE WAS DEFINITELY A GUMBALL.
FZZZZZZT

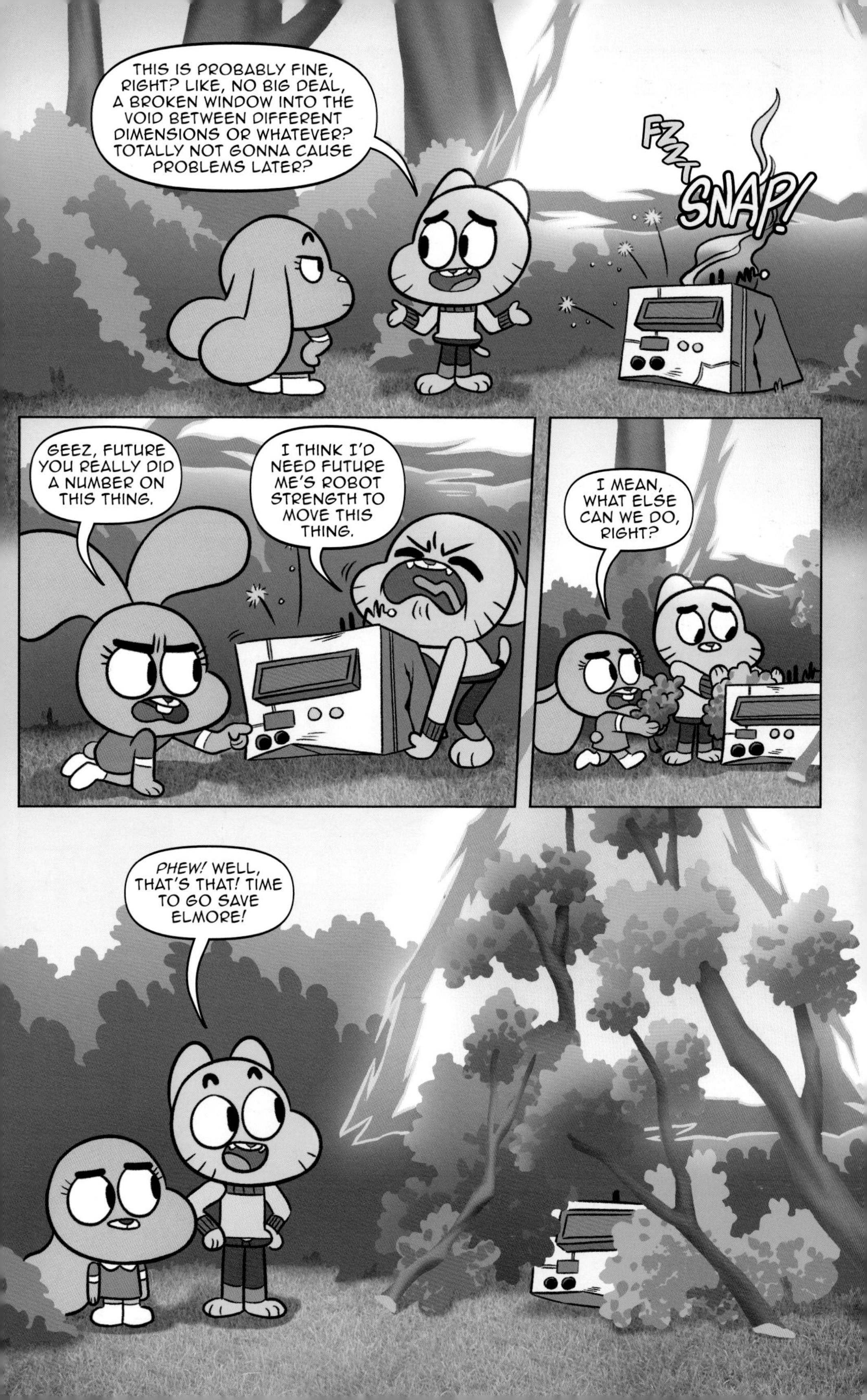
THIS IS PROBABLY FINE, RIGHT? LIKE, NO BIG DEAL, A BROKEN WINDOW INTO THE VOID BETWEEN DIFFERENT DIMENSIONS OR WHATEVER? TOTALLY NOT GONNA CAUSE PROBLEMS LATER?
FZZZT
SNAP!
GEEZ, FUTURE YOU REALLY DID A NUMBER ON THIS THING.
I THINK I'D NEED FUTURE ME'S ROBOT STRENGTH TO MOVE THIS THING.
I MEAN, WHAT ELSE CAN WE DO, RIGHT?
PHEW! WELL, THAT'S THAT! TIME TO GO SAVE ELMORE!

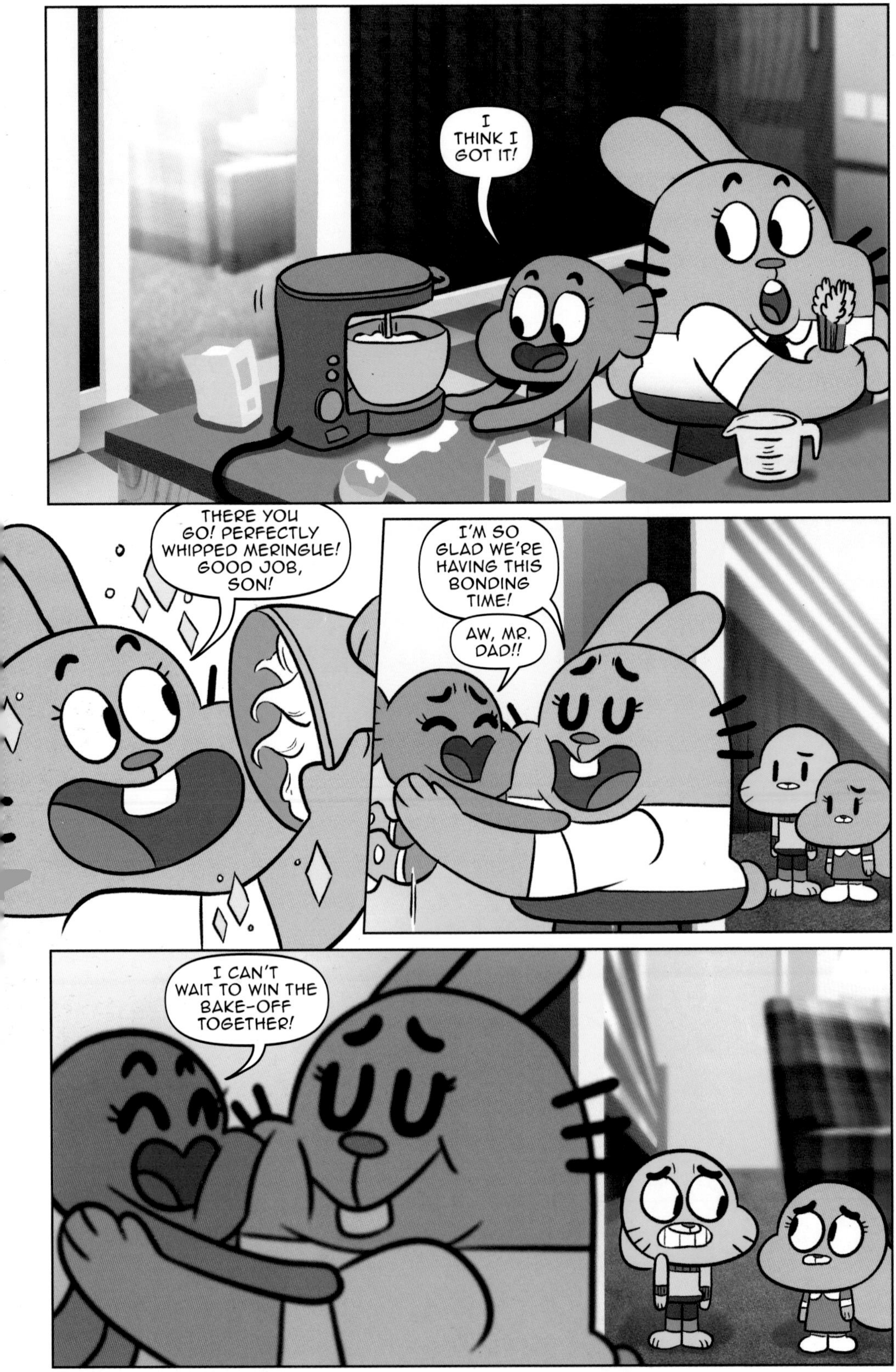
I THINK I GOT IT!
THERE YOU GO! PERFECTLY WHIPPED MERINGUE! GOOD JOB, SON!
I'M SO GLAD WE'RE HAVING THIS BONDING TIME!
AW, MR. DAD!!
I CAN'T WAIT TO WIN THE BAKE-OFF TOGETHER!

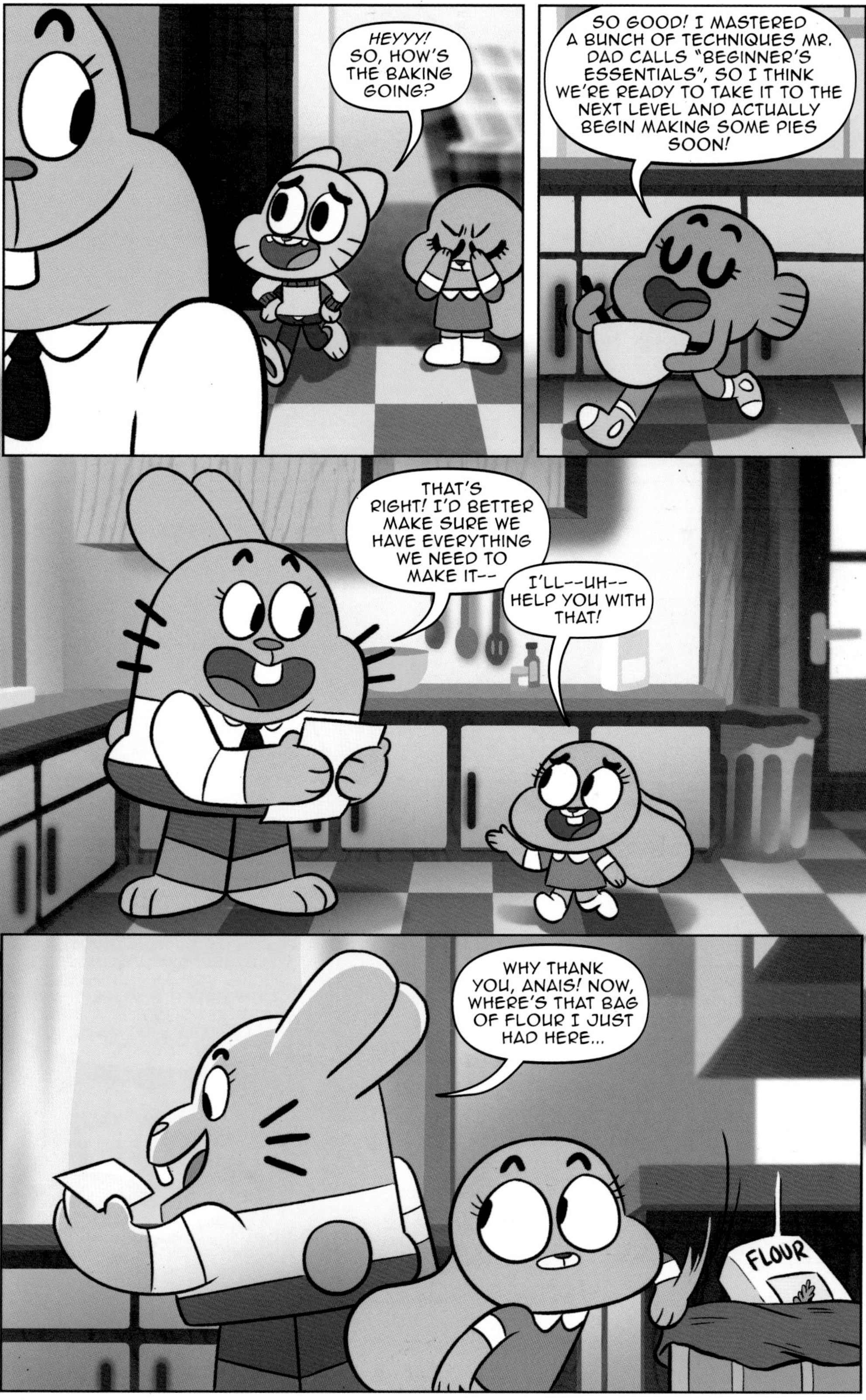
HEYYY! SO, HOW'S THE BAKING GOING?
SO GOOD! I MASTERED A BUNCH OF TECHNIQUES MR. DAD CALLS "BEGINNER'S ESSENTIALS", SO I THINK WE'RE READY TO TAKE IT TO THE NEXT LEVEL AND ACTUALLY BEGIN MAKING SOME PIES SOON!
THAT'S RIGHT! I'D BETTER MAKE SURE WE HAVE EVERYTHING WE NEED TO MAKE IT--
I'LL--UH--HELP YOU WITH THAT!
WHY THANK YOU, ANAIS! NOW, WHERE'S THAT BAG OF FLOUR I JUST HAD HERE...
FLOUR

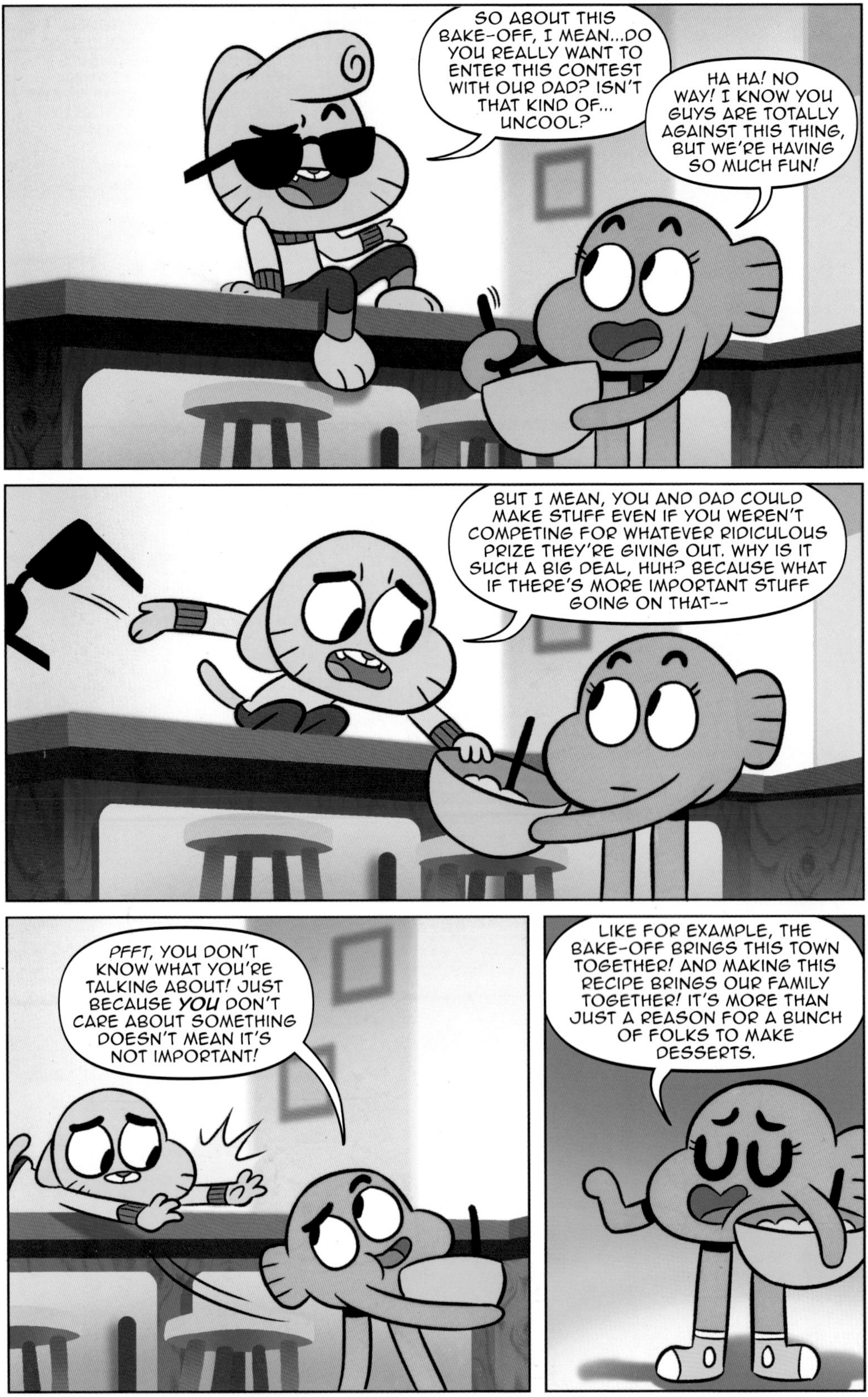
SO ABOUT THIS BAKE-OFF, I MEAN...DO YOU REALLY WANT TO ENTER THIS CONTEST WITH OUR DAD? ISN'T THAT KIND OF... UNCOOL?
HA HA! NO WAY! I KNOW YOU GUYS ARE TOTALLY AGAINST THIS THING, BUT WE'RE HAVING SO MUCH FUN!
BUT I MEAN, YOU AND DAD COULD MAKE STUFF EVEN IF YOU WEREN'T COMPETING FOR WHATEVER RIDICULOUS PRIZE THEY'RE GIVING OUT. WHY IS IT SUCH A BIG DEAL, HUH? BECAUSE WHAT IF THERE'S MORE IMPORTANT STUFF GOING ON THAT--
PFFT, YOU DON'T KNOW WHAT YOU'RE TALKING ABOUT! JUST BECAUSE YOU DON'T CARE ABOUT SOMETHING DOESN'T MEAN IT'S NOT IMPORTANT!
LIKE FOR EXAMPLE, THE BAKE-OFF BRINGS THIS TOWN TOGETHER! AND MAKING THIS RECIPE BRINGS OUR FAMILY TOGETHER! IT'S MORE THAN JUST A REASON FOR A BUNCH OF FOLKS TO MAKE DESSERTS.

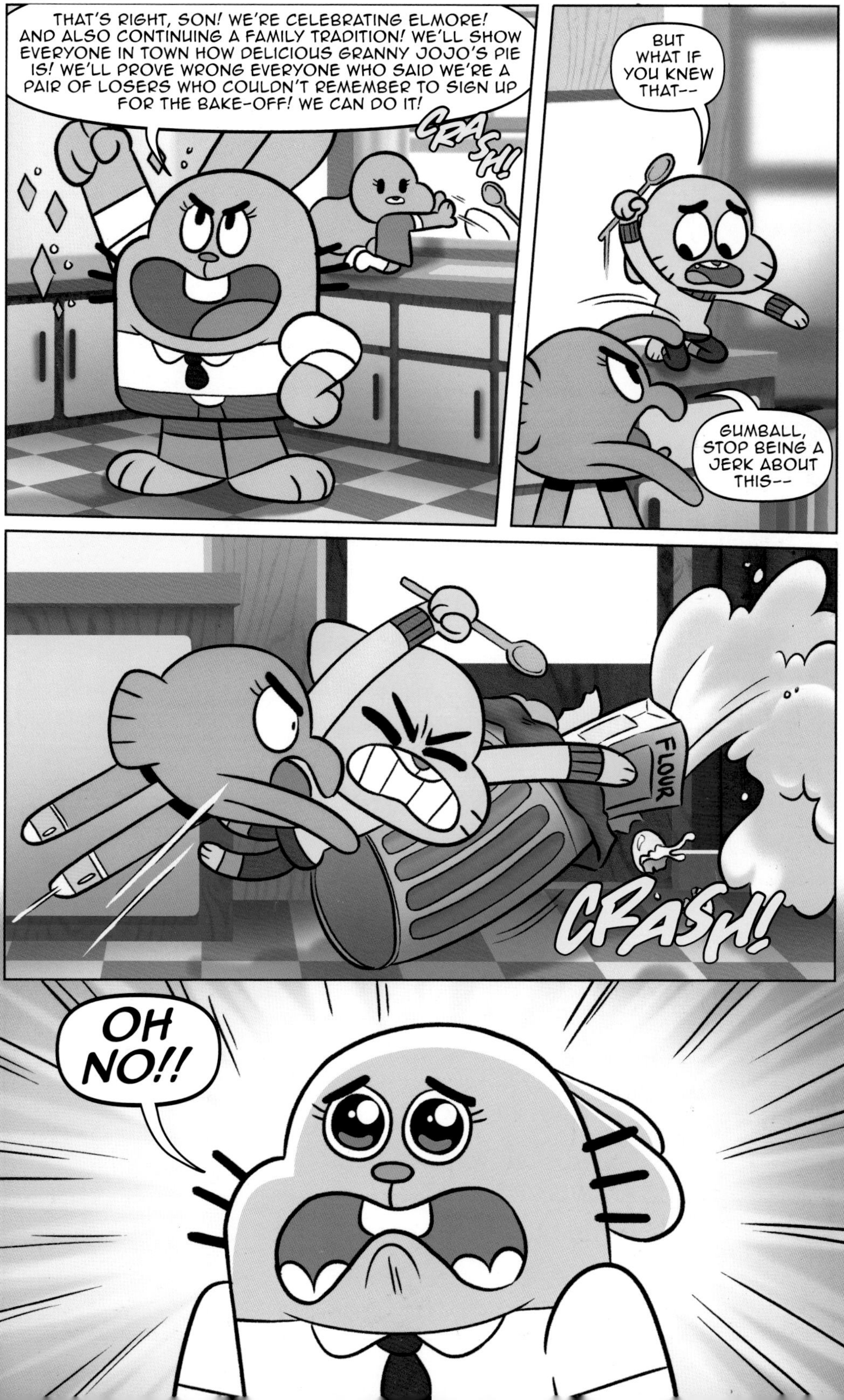
THAT'S RIGHT, SON! WE'RE CELEBRATING ELMORE! AND ALSO CONTINUING A FAMILY TRADITION! WE'LL SHOW EVERYONE IN TOWN HOW DELICIOUS GRANNY JOJO'S PIE IS! WE'LL PROVE WRONG EVERYONE WHO SAID WE'RE A PAIR OF LOSERS WHO COULDN'T REMEMBER TO SIGN UP FOR THE BAKE-OFF! WE CAN DO IT!
CRASH!
BUT WHAT IF YOU KNEW THAT--
GUMBALL, STOP BEING A JERK ABOUT THIS--
FLOUR
CRASH!
OH NO!!

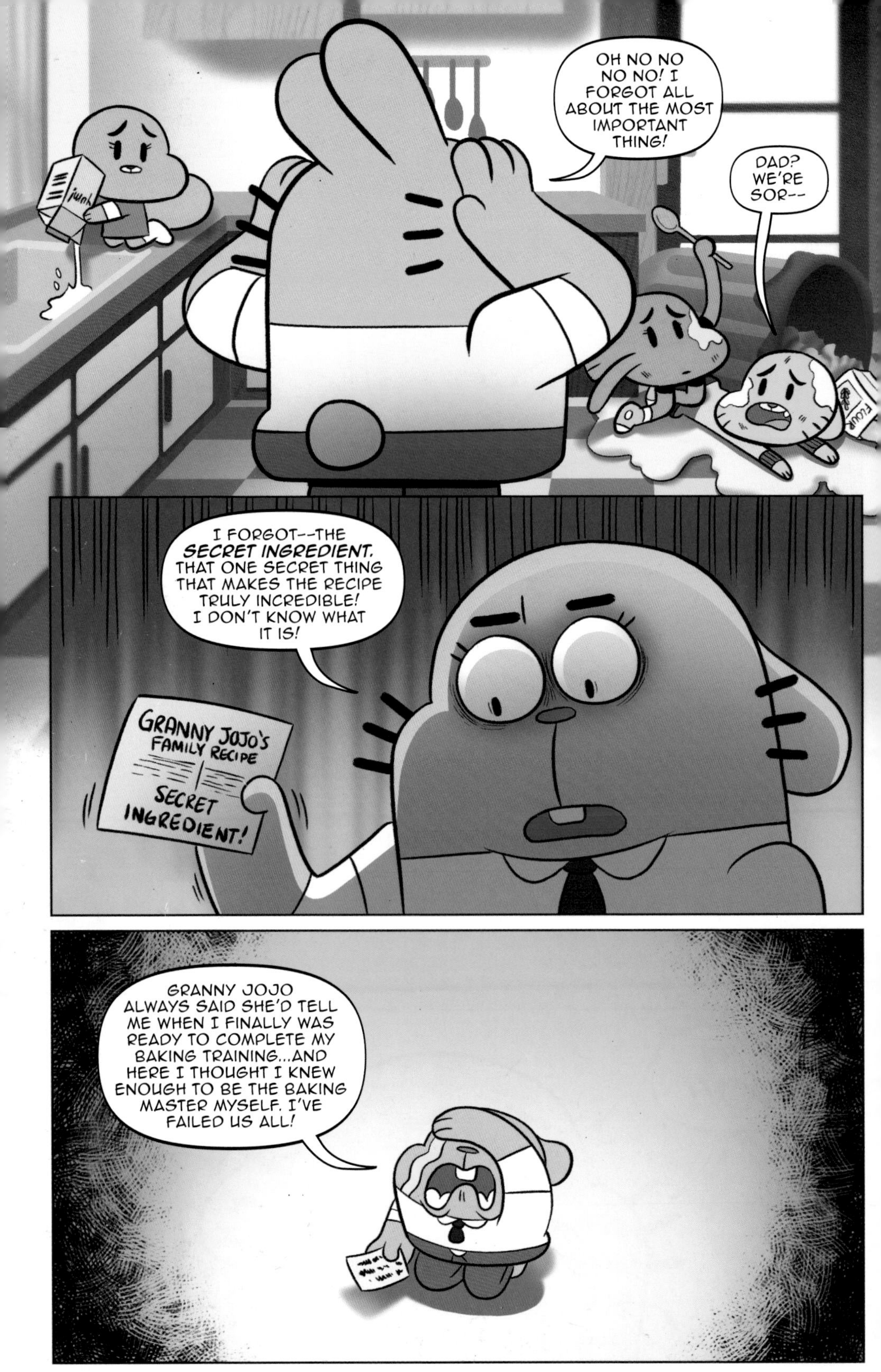
junk
OH NO NO NO NO! I FORGOT ALL ABOUT THE MOST IMPORTANT THING!
DAD? WE'RE SOR--
FLOUR
I FORGOT--THE SECRET INGREDIENT. THAT ONE SECRET THING THAT MAKES THE RECIPE TRULY INCREDIBLE! I DON'T KNOW WHAT IT IS!
GRANNY JOJO'S FAMILY RECIPE
SECRET INGREDIENT!
GRANNY JOJO ALWAYS SAID SHE'D TELL ME WHEN I FINALLY WAS READY TO COMPLETE MY BAKING TRAINING...AND HERE I THOUGHT I KNEW ENOUGH TO BE THE BAKING MASTER MYSELF. I'VE FAILED US ALL!

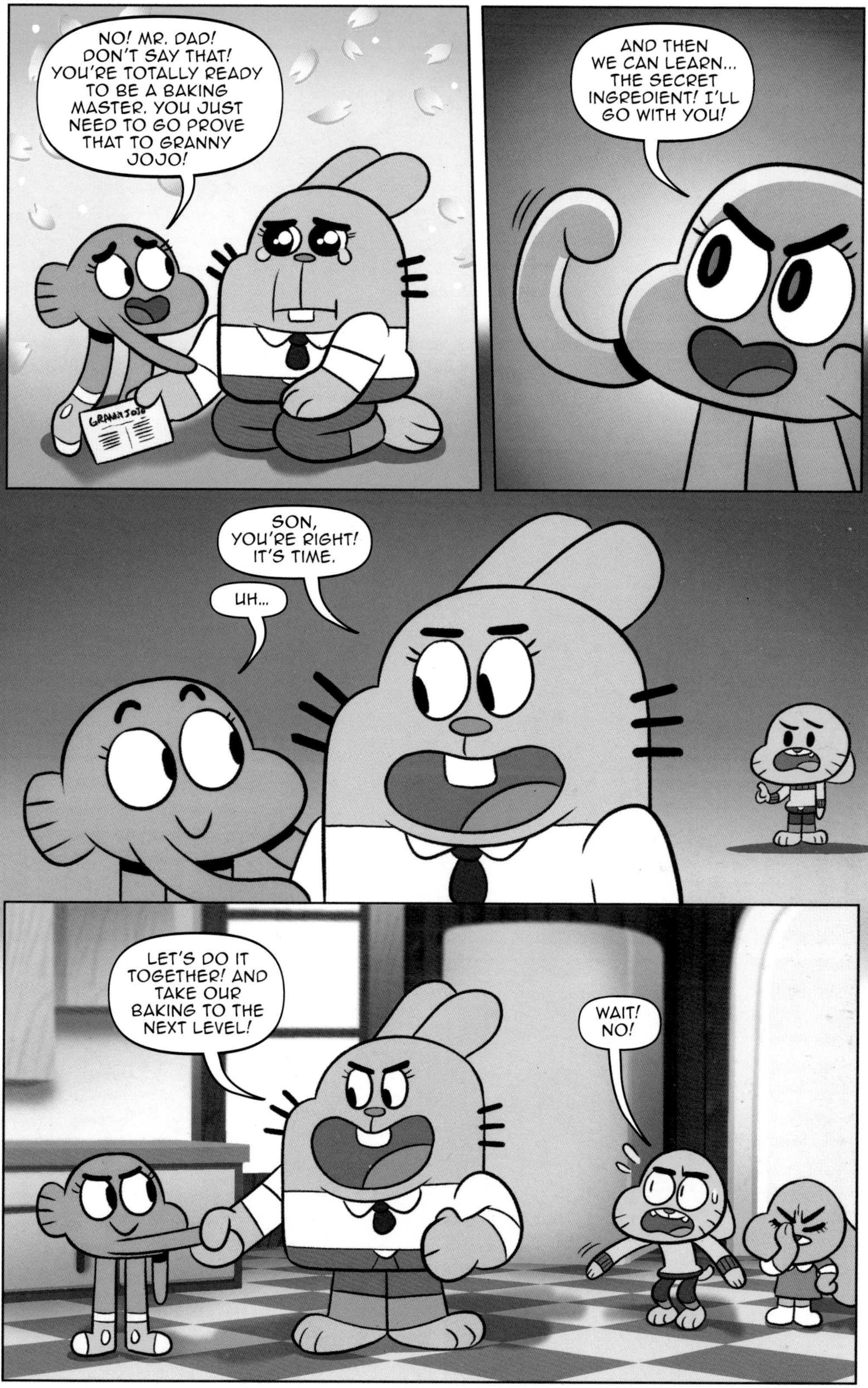
NO! MR. DAD! DON'T SAY THAT! YOU'RE TOTALLY READY TO BE A BAKING MASTER. YOU JUST NEED TO GO PROVE THAT TO GRANNY JOJO!
GRANNY JOJO
AND THEN WE CAN LEARN... THE SECRET INGREDIENT! I'LL GO WITH YOU!
SON, YOU'RE RIGHT! IT'S TIME.
UH...
LET'S DO IT TOGETHER! AND TAKE OUR BAKING TO THE NEXT LEVEL!
WAIT! NO!

HEY! YOU'VE GOTTA LISTEN TO ME, IT'S IMPORTANT--

I'VE GOT A MEETING WITH DESTINY, SON! WHATEVER IT IS CAN WAIT! NEXT TIME YOU SEE YOUR POPS, HE'LL BE A NEW MAN!

WHAT JUST *HAPPENED?*

FWUMP!

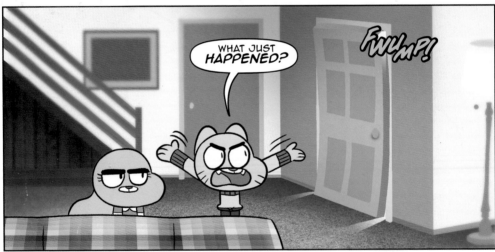

LOOKS LIKE IT'S BACK TO THE DRAWING BOARD.

I GOT RID OF AS MANY INGREDIENTS AS I COULD, BUT THEY COULD ALWAYS STOP BY THE STORE AGAIN.

MAYBE GRANNY JOJO WON'T EVEN TELL THEM THE MISSING INGREDIENT. AND EITHER WAY, NOW WE HAVE A FEW HOURS TO DO... *SOMETHING.*

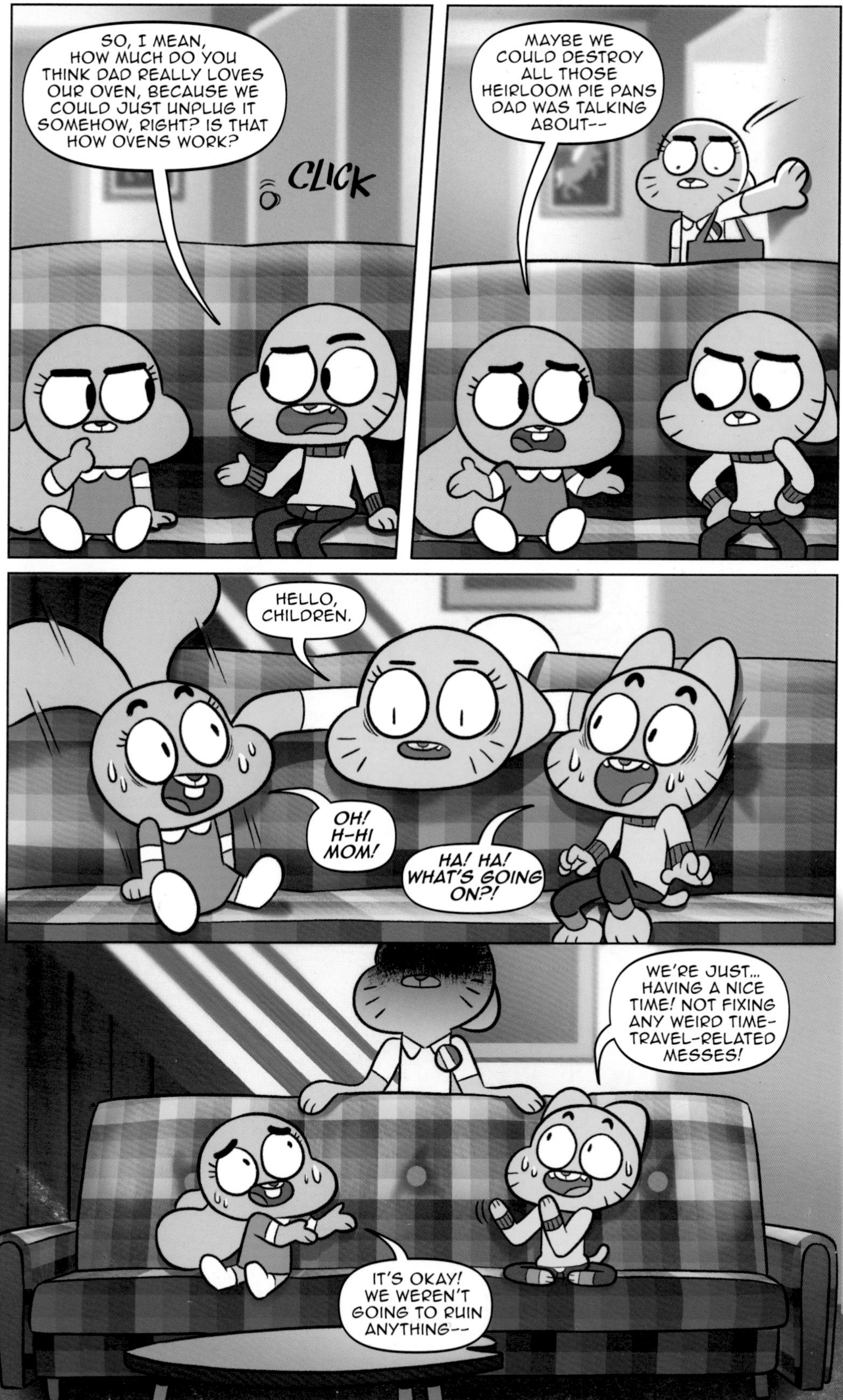
SO, I MEAN, HOW MUCH DO YOU THINK DAD REALLY LOVES OUR OVEN, BECAUSE WE COULD JUST UNPLUG IT SOMEHOW, RIGHT? IS THAT HOW OVENS WORK?
CLICK
MAYBE WE COULD DESTROY ALL THOSE HEIRLOOM PIE PANS DAD WAS TALKING ABOUT--
HELLO, CHILDREN.
OH! H-HI MOM!
HA! HA! WHAT'S GOING ON?!
WE'RE JUST... HAVING A NICE TIME! NOT FIXING ANY WEIRD TIME-TRAVEL-RELATED MESSES!
IT'S OKAY! WE WEREN'T GOING TO RUIN ANYTHING--

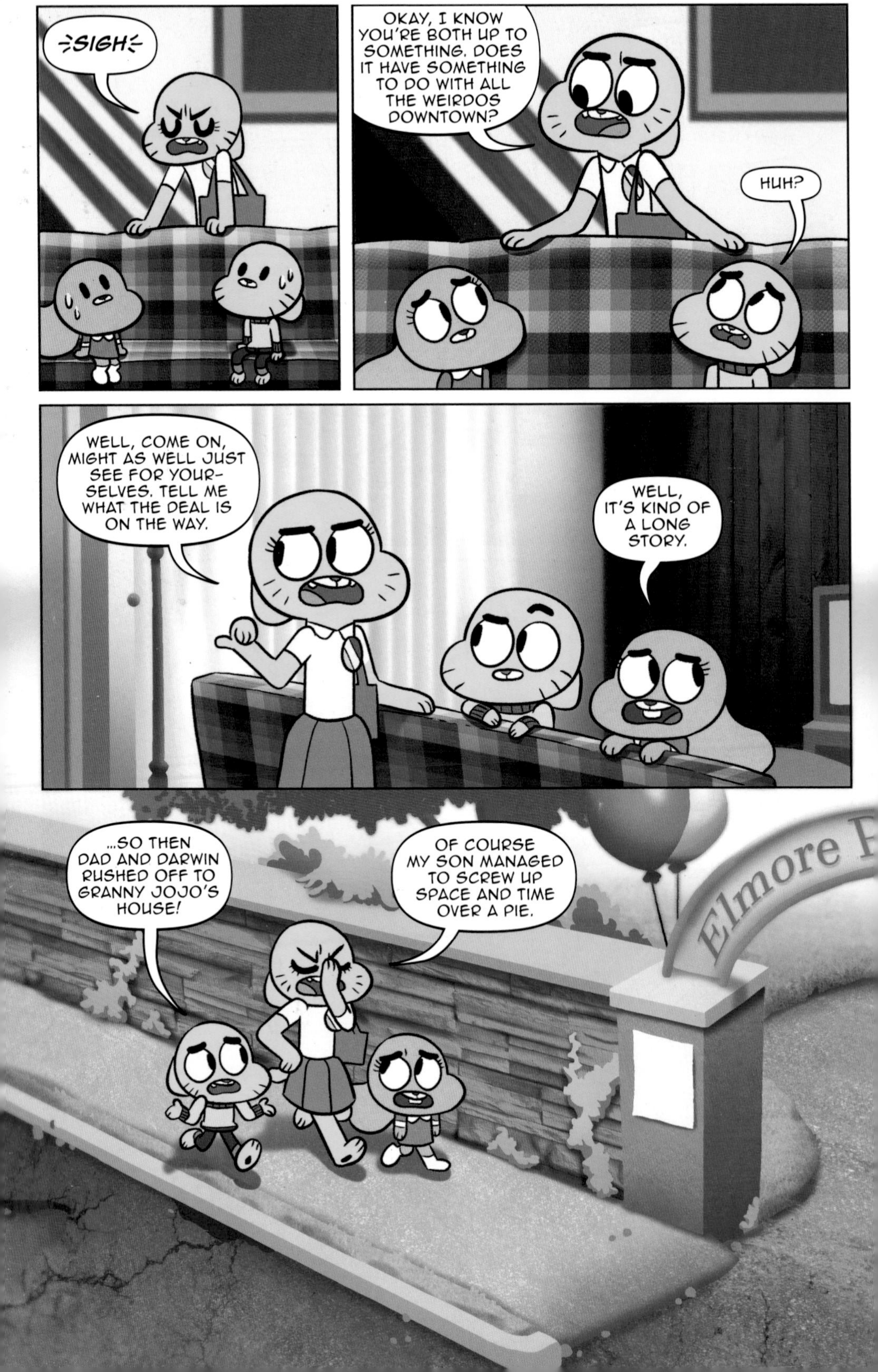
SIGH
OKAY, I KNOW YOU'RE BOTH UP TO SOMETHING. DOES IT HAVE SOMETHING TO DO WITH ALL THE WEIRDOS DOWNTOWN?
HUH?
WELL, COME ON, MIGHT AS WELL JUST SEE FOR YOURSELVES. TELL ME WHAT THE DEAL IS ON THE WAY.
WELL, IT'S KIND OF A LONG STORY.
...SO THEN DAD AND DARWIN RUSHED OFF TO GRANNY JOJO'S HOUSE!
OF COURSE MY SON MANAGED TO SCREW UP SPACE AND TIME OVER A PIE.

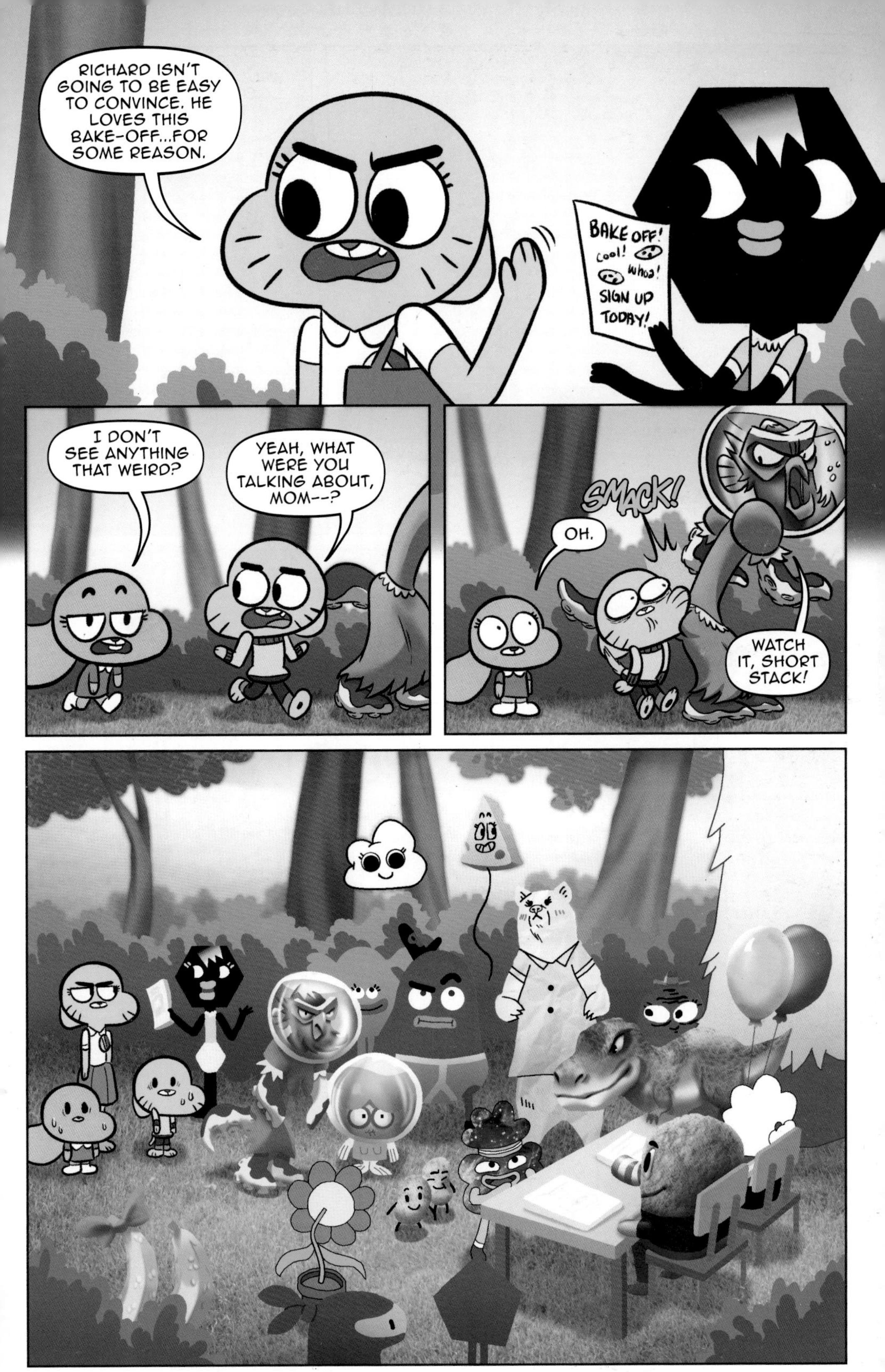

RICHARD ISN'T GOING TO BE EASY TO CONVINCE. HE LOVES THIS BAKE-OFF...FOR SOME REASON.
BAKE OFF! cool! whoa! SIGN UP TODAY!
I DON'T SEE ANYTHING THAT WEIRD?
YEAH, WHAT WERE YOU TALKING ABOUT, MOM--?
SMACK!
OH.
WATCH IT, SHORT STACK!

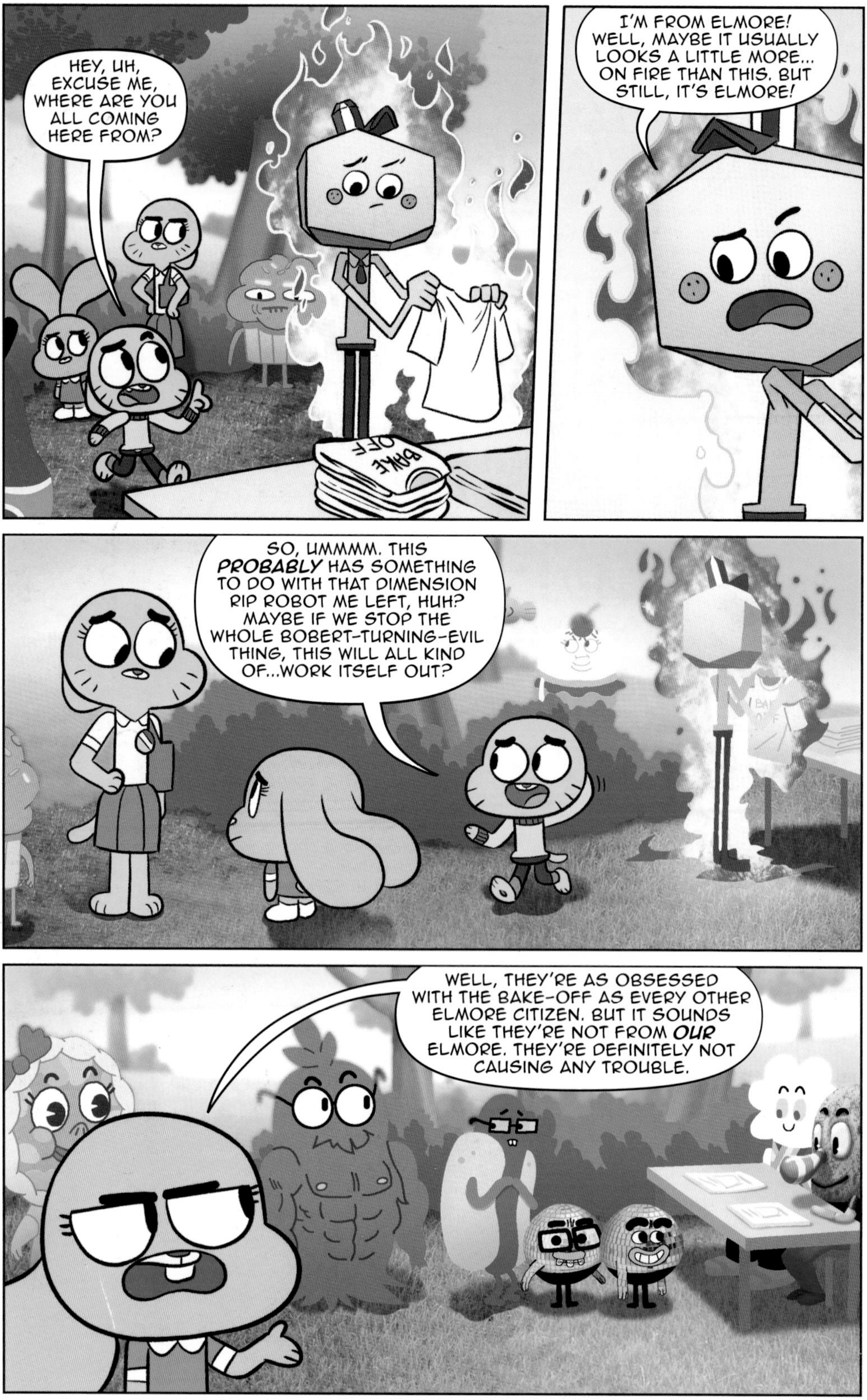
HEY, UH, EXCUSE ME, WHERE ARE YOU ALL COMING HERE FROM?
BAKE OFF
I'M FROM ELMORE! WELL, MAYBE IT USUALLY LOOKS A LITTLE MORE... ON FIRE THAN THIS. BUT STILL, IT'S ELMORE!
SO, UMMMM. THIS *PROBABLY* HAS SOMETHING TO DO WITH THAT DIMENSION RIP ROBOT ME LEFT, HUH? MAYBE IF WE STOP THE WHOLE BOBERT-TURNING-EVIL THING, THIS WILL ALL KIND OF...WORK ITSELF OUT?
WELL, THEY'RE AS OBSESSED WITH THE BAKE-OFF AS EVERY OTHER ELMORE CITIZEN. BUT IT SOUNDS LIKE THEY'RE NOT FROM *OUR* ELMORE. THEY'RE DEFINITELY NOT CAUSING ANY TROUBLE.

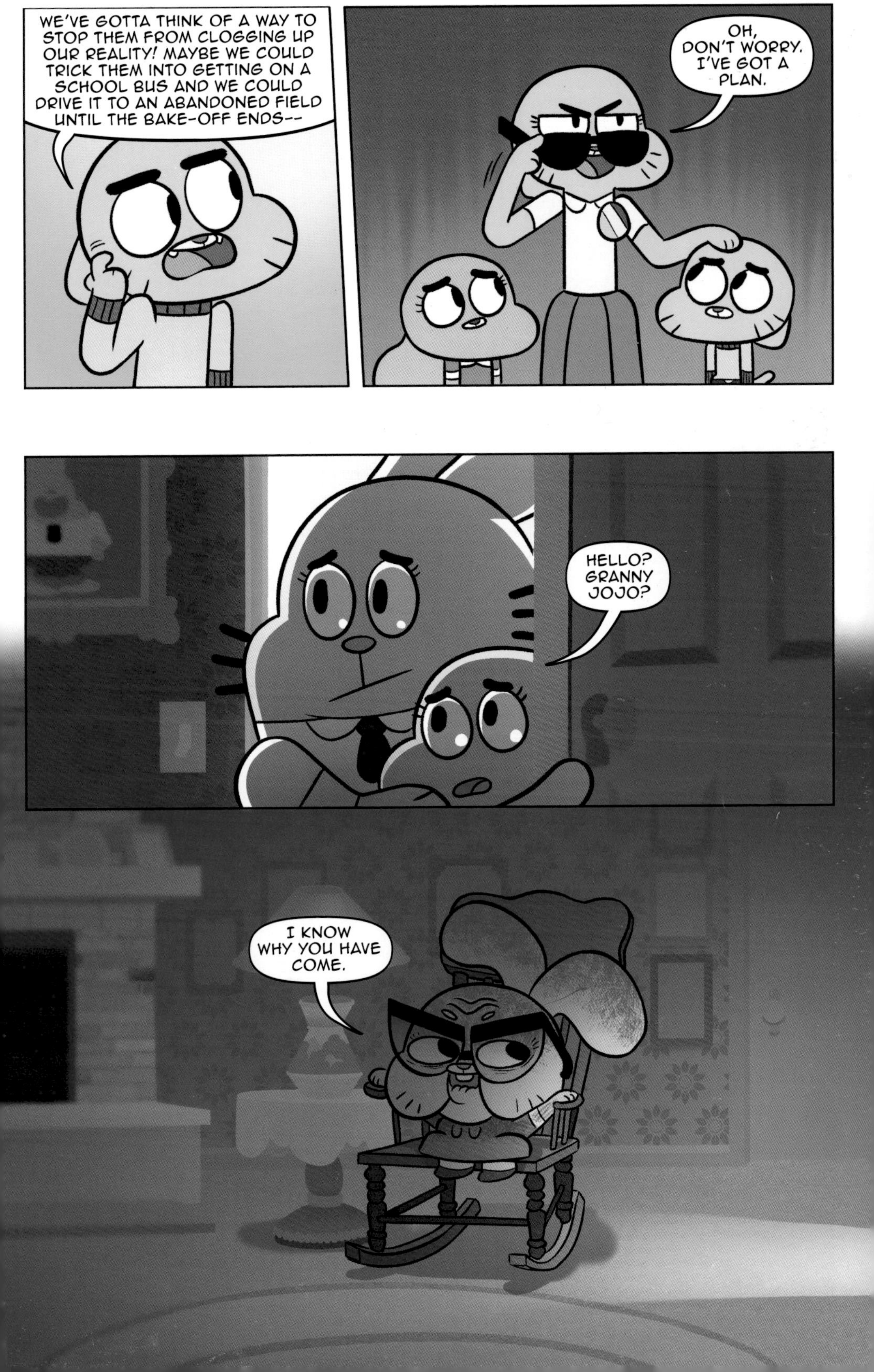
WE'VE GOTTA THINK OF A WAY TO STOP THEM FROM CLOGGING UP OUR REALITY! MAYBE WE COULD TRICK THEM INTO GETTING ON A SCHOOL BUS AND WE COULD DRIVE IT TO AN ABANDONED FIELD UNTIL THE BAKE-OFF ENDS--
OH, DON'T WORRY. I'VE GOT A PLAN.
HELLO? GRANNY JOJO?
I KNOW WHY YOU HAVE COME.

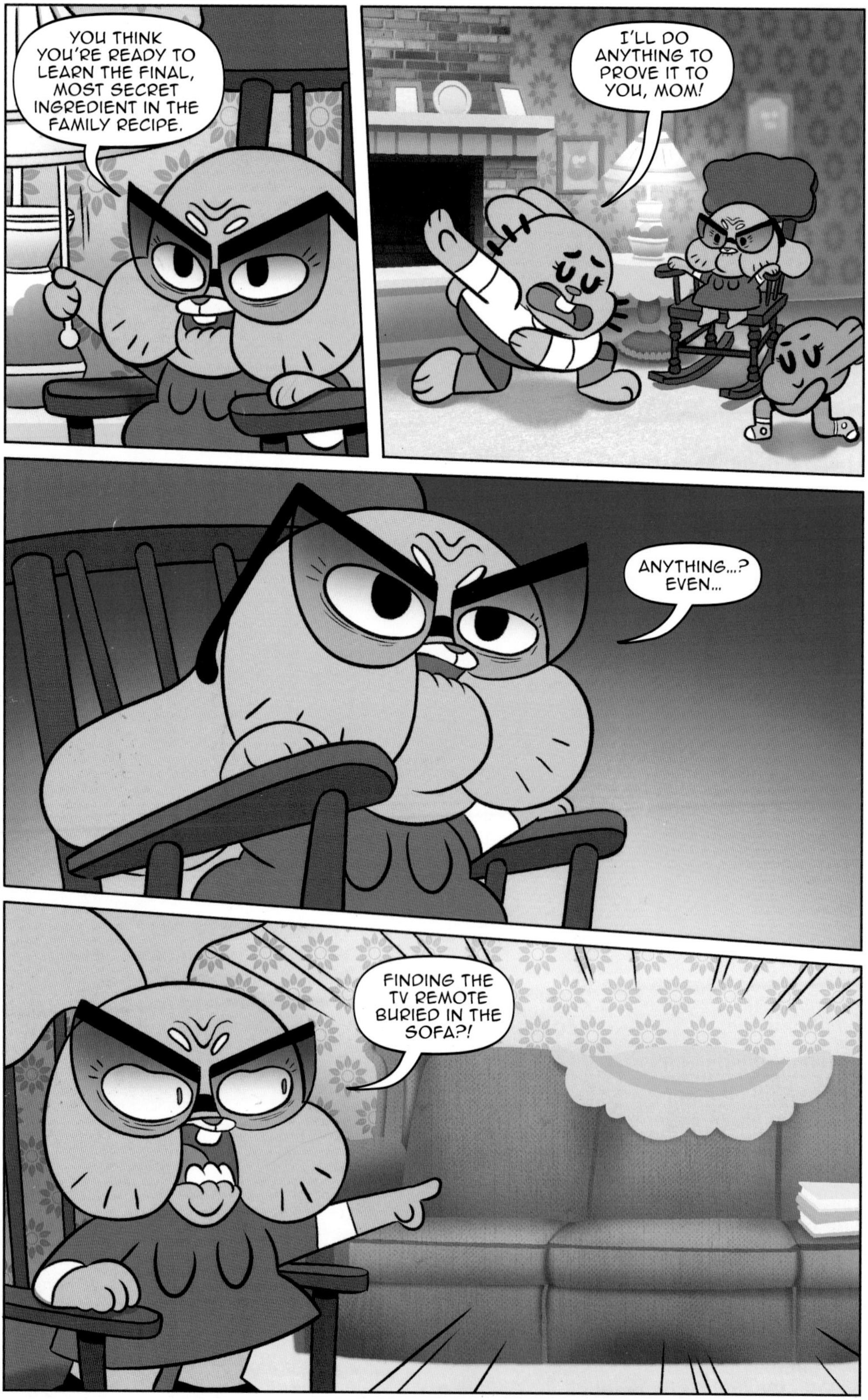
YOU THINK YOU'RE READY TO LEARN THE FINAL, MOST SECRET INGREDIENT IN THE FAMILY RECIPE.
I'LL DO ANYTHING TO PROVE IT TO YOU, MOM!
ANYTHING...? EVEN...
FINDING THE TV REMOTE BURIED IN THE SOFA?!

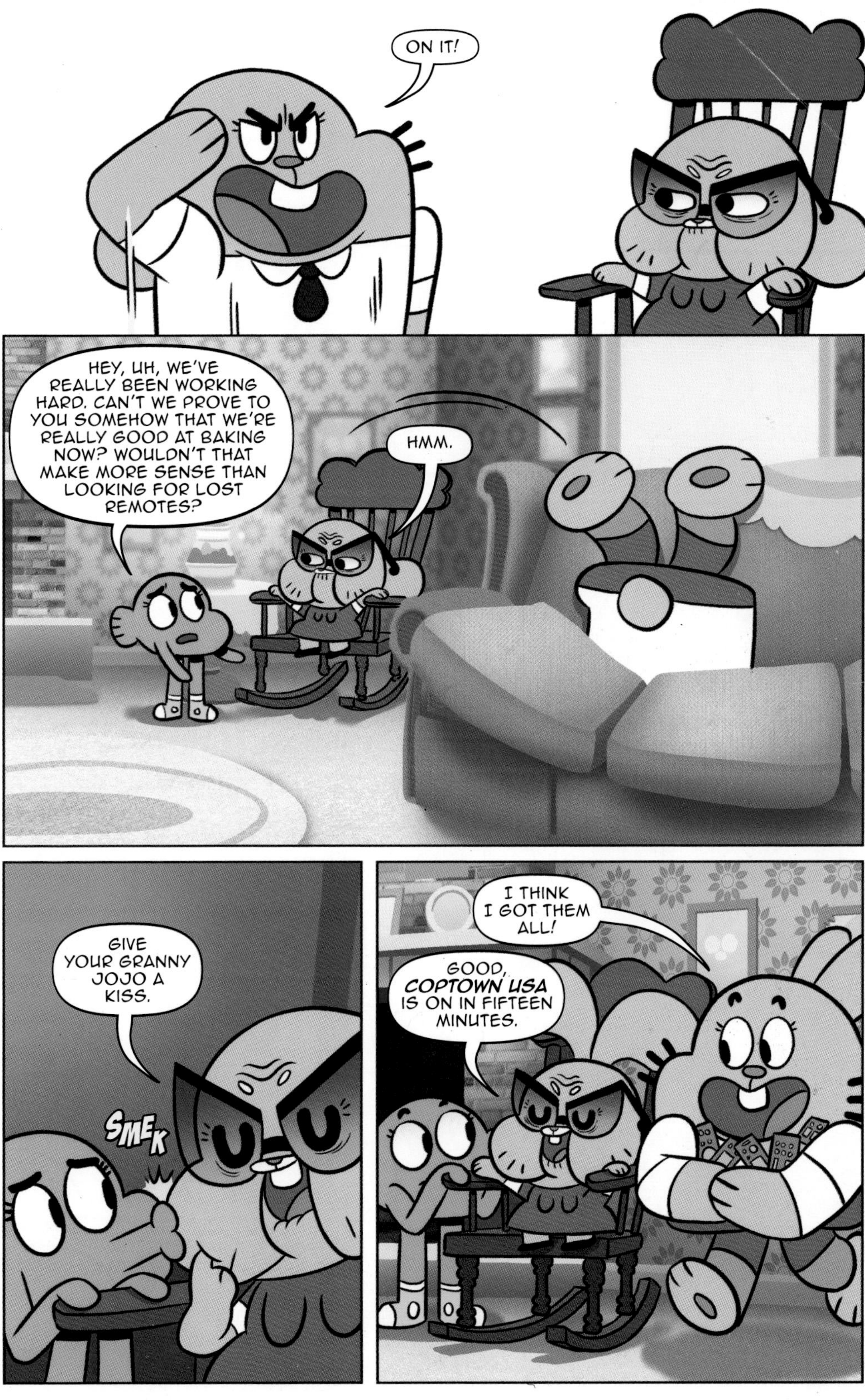
ON IT!
HEY, UH, WE'VE REALLY BEEN WORKING HARD. CAN'T WE PROVE TO YOU SOMEHOW THAT WE'RE REALLY GOOD AT BAKING NOW? WOULDN'T THAT MAKE MORE SENSE THAN LOOKING FOR LOST REMOTES?
HMM.
GIVE YOUR GRANNY JOJO A KISS.
SMEK
I THINK I GOT THEM ALL!
GOOD, *COPTOWN USA* IS ON IN FIFTEEN MINUTES.

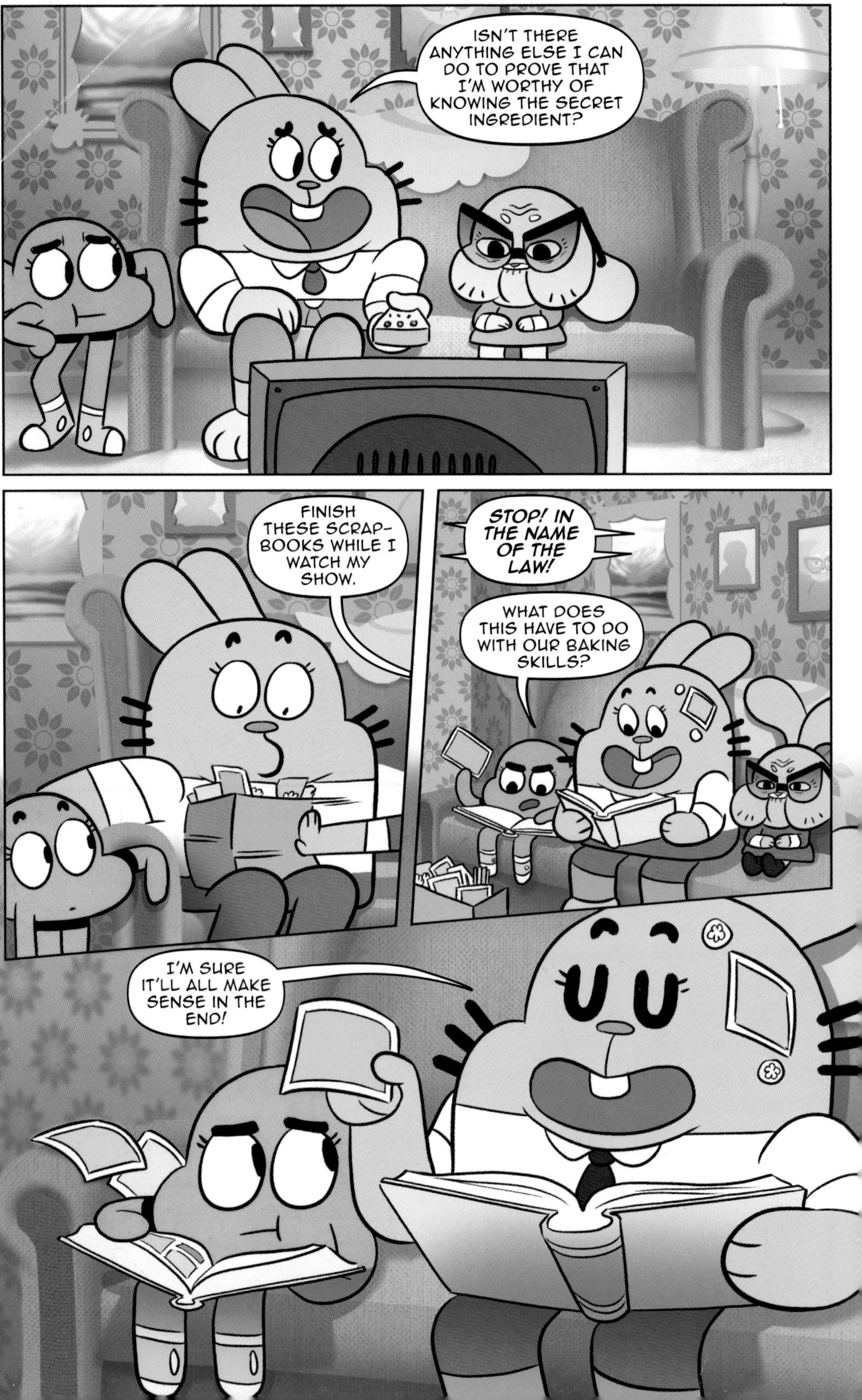
ISN'T THERE ANYTHING ELSE I CAN DO TO PROVE THAT I'M WORTHY OF KNOWING THE SECRET INGREDIENT?
FINISH THESE SCRAP-BOOKS WHILE I WATCH MY SHOW.
STOP! IN THE NAME OF THE LAW!
WHAT DOES THIS HAVE TO DO WITH OUR BAKING SKILLS?
I'M SURE IT'LL ALL MAKE SENSE IN THE END!

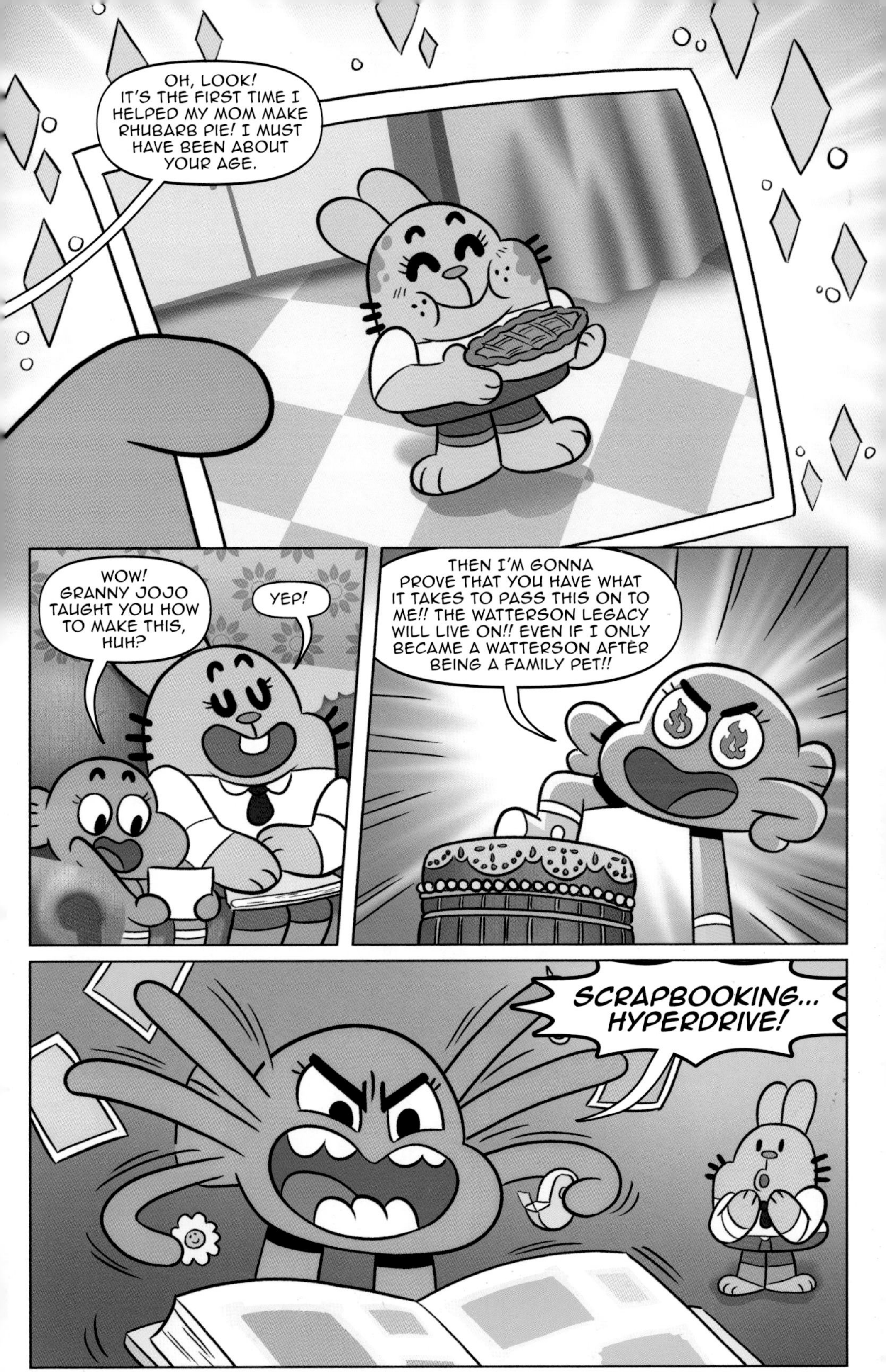
OH, LOOK! IT'S THE FIRST TIME I HELPED MY MOM MAKE RHUBARB PIE! I MUST HAVE BEEN ABOUT YOUR AGE.
WOW! GRANNY JOJO TAUGHT YOU HOW TO MAKE THIS, HUH?
YEP!
THEN I'M GONNA PROVE THAT YOU HAVE WHAT IT TAKES TO PASS THIS ON TO ME!! THE WATTERSON LEGACY WILL LIVE ON!! EVEN IF I ONLY BECAME A WATTERSON AFTER BEING A FAMILY PET!!
SCRAPBOOKING... HYPERDRIVE!

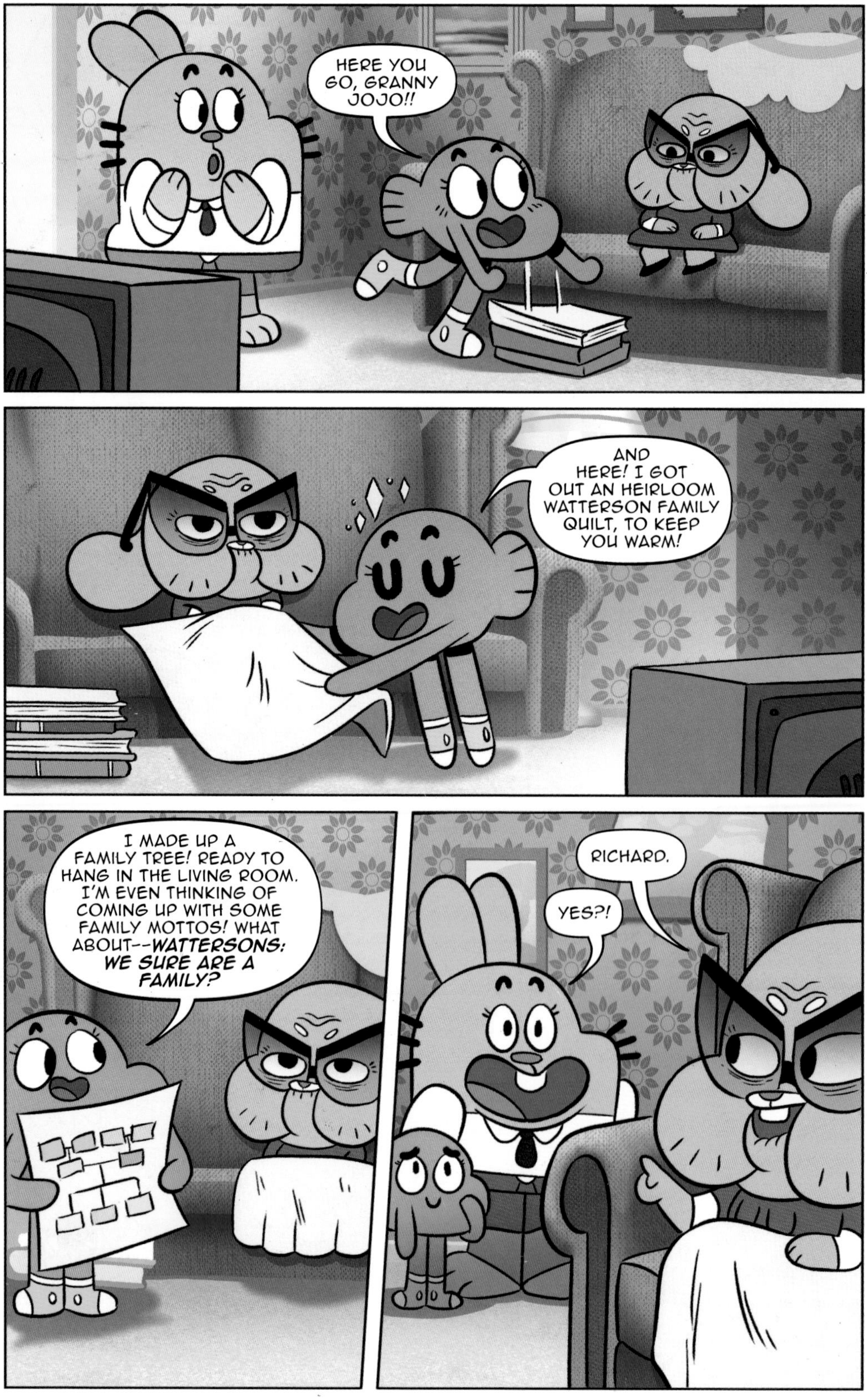
HERE YOU GO, GRANNY JOJO!!
AND HERE! I GOT OUT AN HEIRLOOM WATTERSON FAMILY QUILT, TO KEEP YOU WARM!
I MADE UP A FAMILY TREE! READY TO HANG IN THE LIVING ROOM. I'M EVEN THINKING OF COMING UP WITH SOME FAMILY MOTTOS! WHAT ABOUT--*WATTERSONS: WE SURE ARE A FAMILY?*
RICHARD.
YES?!

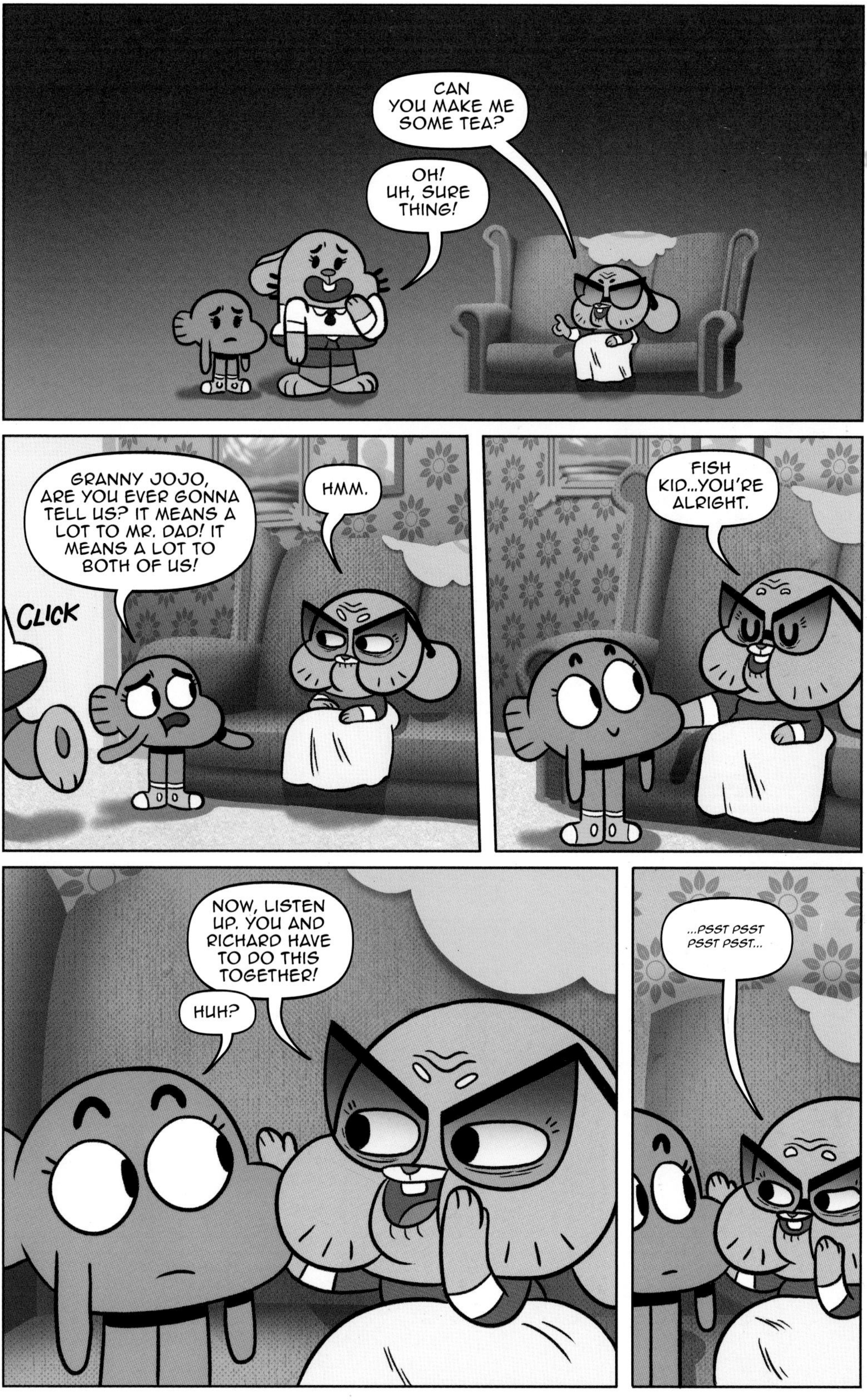
CAN YOU MAKE ME SOME TEA?
OH! UH, SURE THING!
GRANNY JOJO, ARE YOU EVER GONNA TELL US? IT MEANS A LOT TO MR. DAD! IT MEANS A LOT TO BOTH OF US!
HMM.
CLICK
FISH KID...YOU'RE ALRIGHT.
NOW, LISTEN UP. YOU AND RICHARD HAVE TO DO THIS TOGETHER!
HUH?
...PSST PSST PSST PSST...

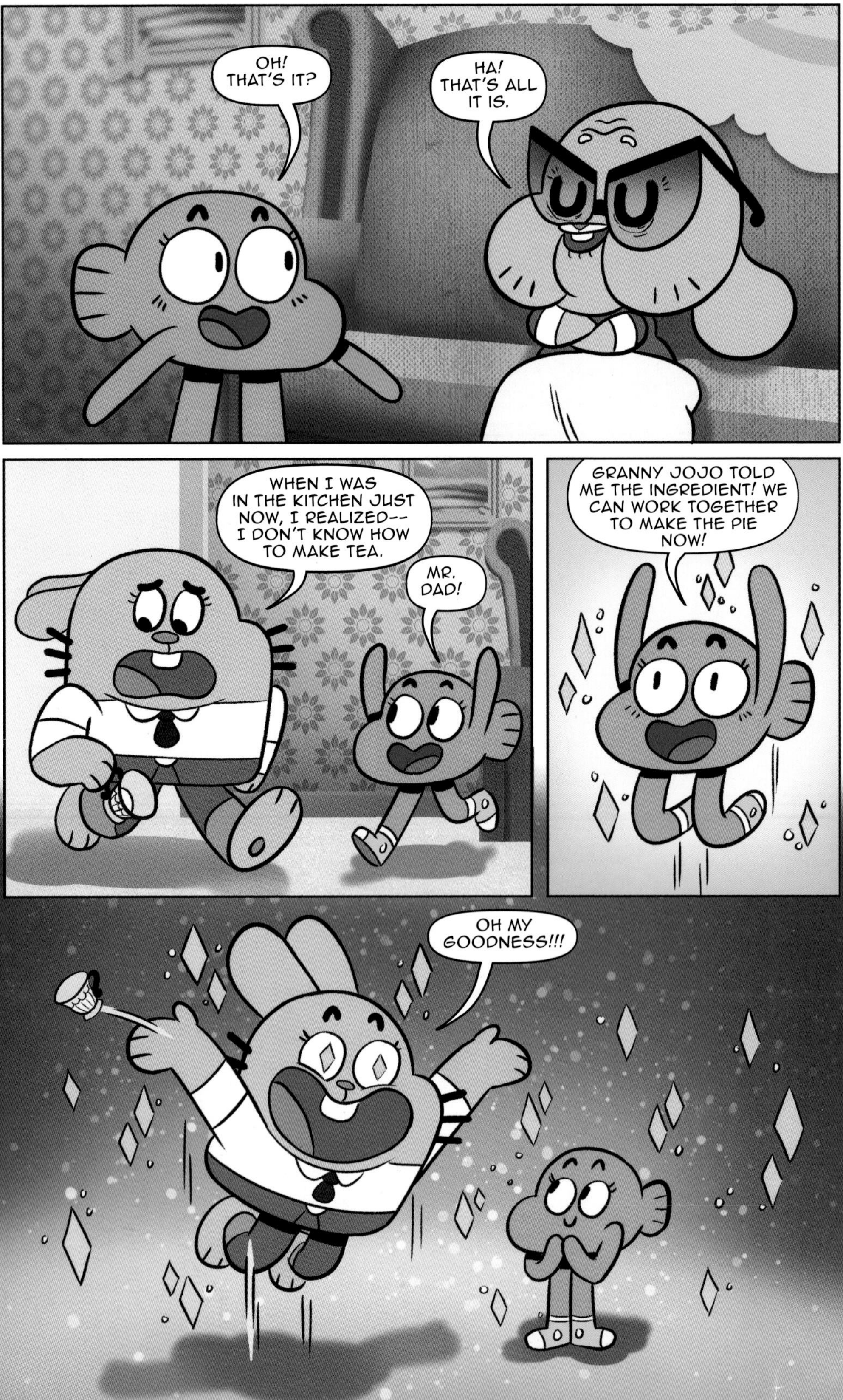
OH! THAT'S IT?
HA! THAT'S ALL IT IS.
WHEN I WAS IN THE KITCHEN JUST NOW, I REALIZED-- I DON'T KNOW HOW TO MAKE TEA.
MR. DAD!
GRANNY JOJO TOLD ME THE INGREDIENT! WE CAN WORK TOGETHER TO MAKE THE PIE NOW!
OH MY GOODNESS!!!

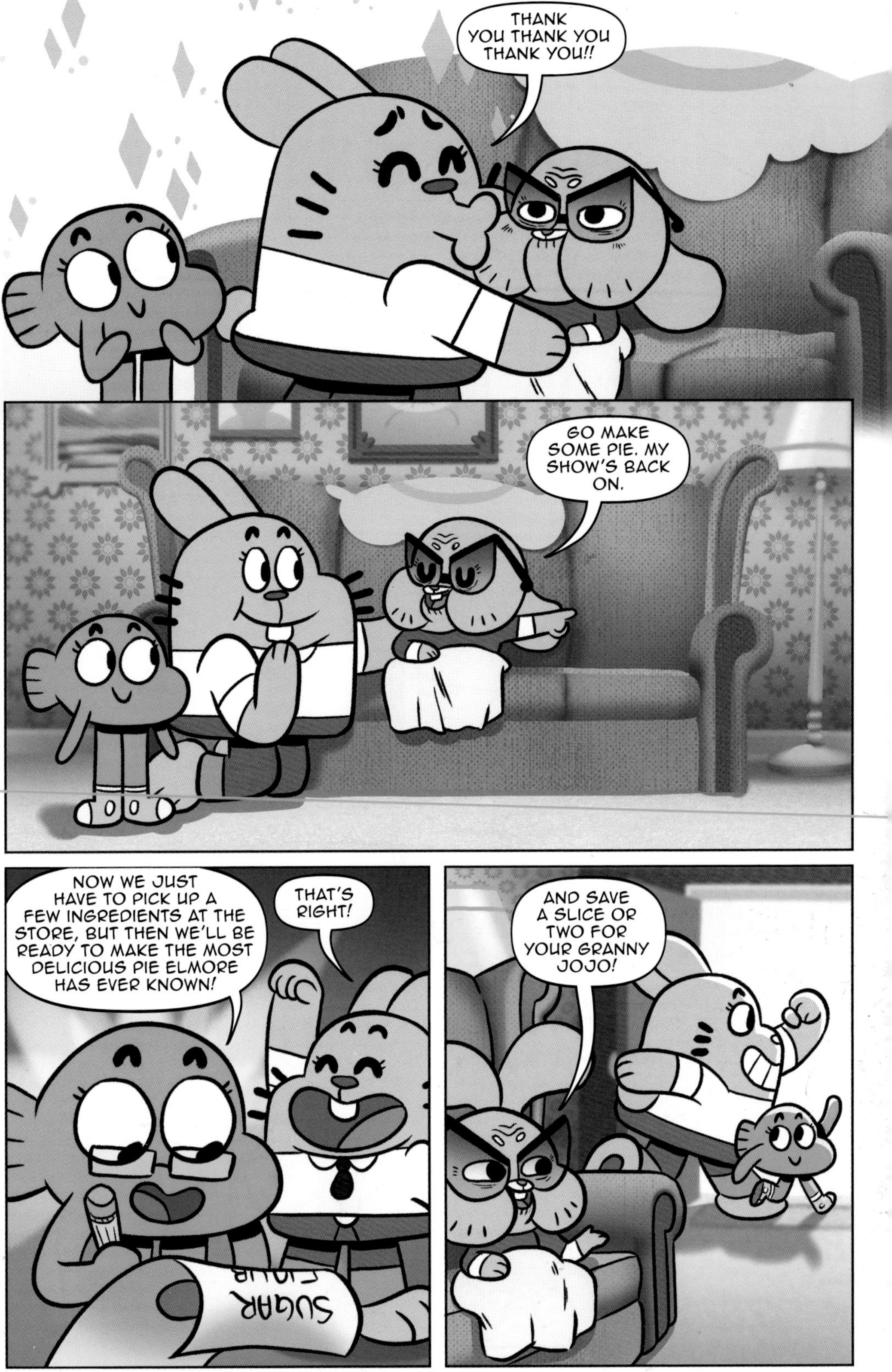
THANK YOU THANK YOU THANK YOU!!
GO MAKE SOME PIE. MY SHOW'S BACK ON.
NOW WE JUST HAVE TO PICK UP A FEW INGREDIENTS AT THE STORE, BUT THEN WE'LL BE READY TO MAKE THE MOST DELICIOUS PIE ELMORE HAS EVER KNOWN!
THAT'S RIGHT!
SUGAR
AND SAVE A SLICE OR TWO FOR YOUR GRANNY JOJO!

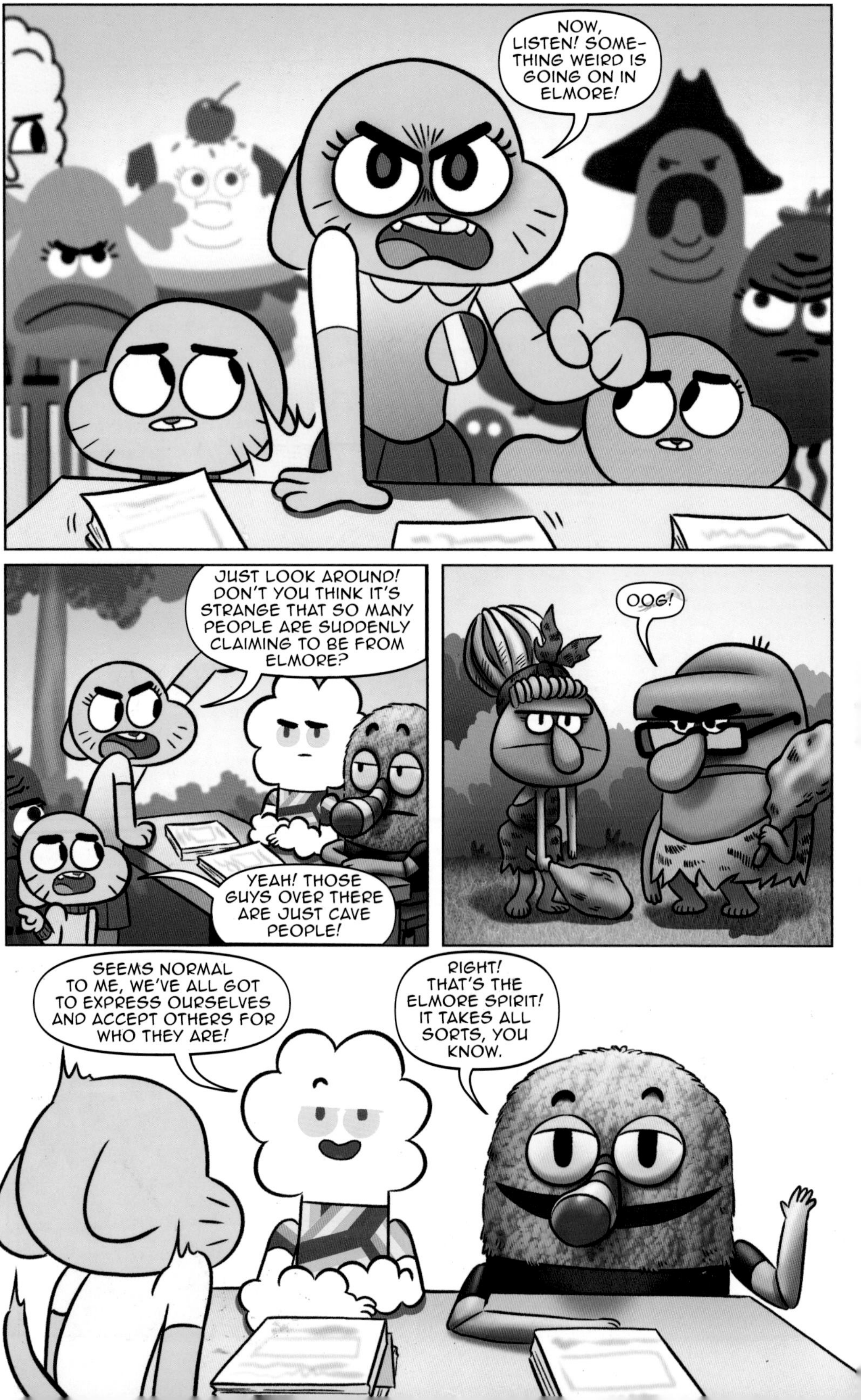
NOW, LISTEN! SOMETHING WEIRD IS GOING ON IN ELMORE!
JUST LOOK AROUND! DON'T YOU THINK IT'S STRANGE THAT SO MANY PEOPLE ARE SUDDENLY CLAIMING TO BE FROM ELMORE?
YEAH! THOSE GUYS OVER THERE ARE JUST CAVE PEOPLE!
OOG!
SEEMS NORMAL TO ME, WE'VE ALL GOT TO EXPRESS OURSELVES AND ACCEPT OTHERS FOR WHO THEY ARE!
RIGHT! THAT'S THE ELMORE SPIRIT! IT TAKES ALL SORTS, YOU KNOW.

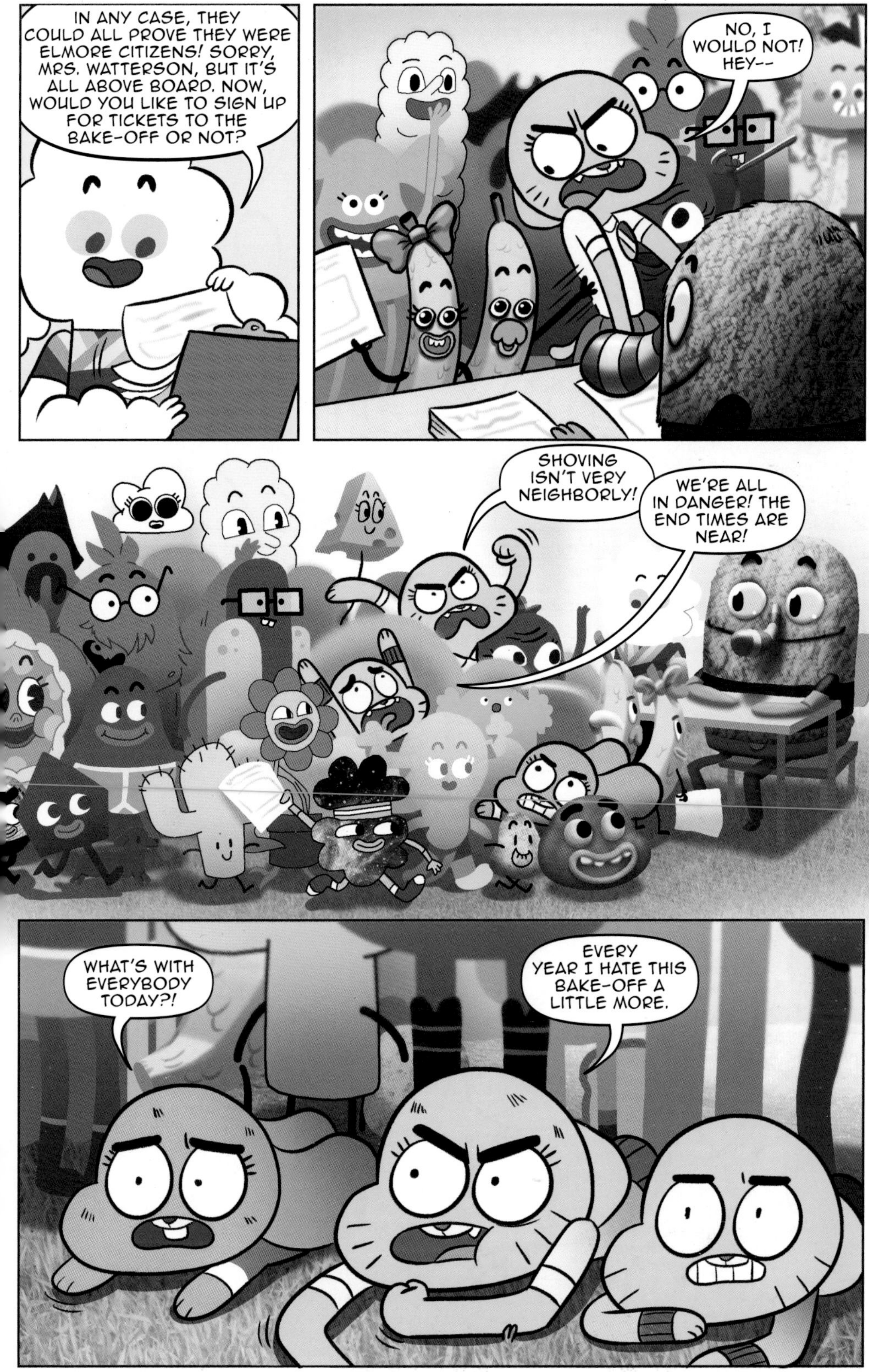
IN ANY CASE, THEY COULD ALL PROVE THEY WERE ELMORE CITIZENS! SORRY, MRS. WATTERSON, BUT IT'S ALL ABOVE BOARD. NOW, WOULD YOU LIKE TO SIGN UP FOR TICKETS TO THE BAKE-OFF OR NOT?
NO, I WOULD NOT! HEY--
SHOVING ISN'T VERY NEIGHBORLY!
WE'RE ALL IN DANGER! THE END TIMES ARE NEAR!
WHAT'S WITH EVERYBODY TODAY?!
EVERY YEAR I HATE THIS BAKE-OFF A LITTLE MORE.

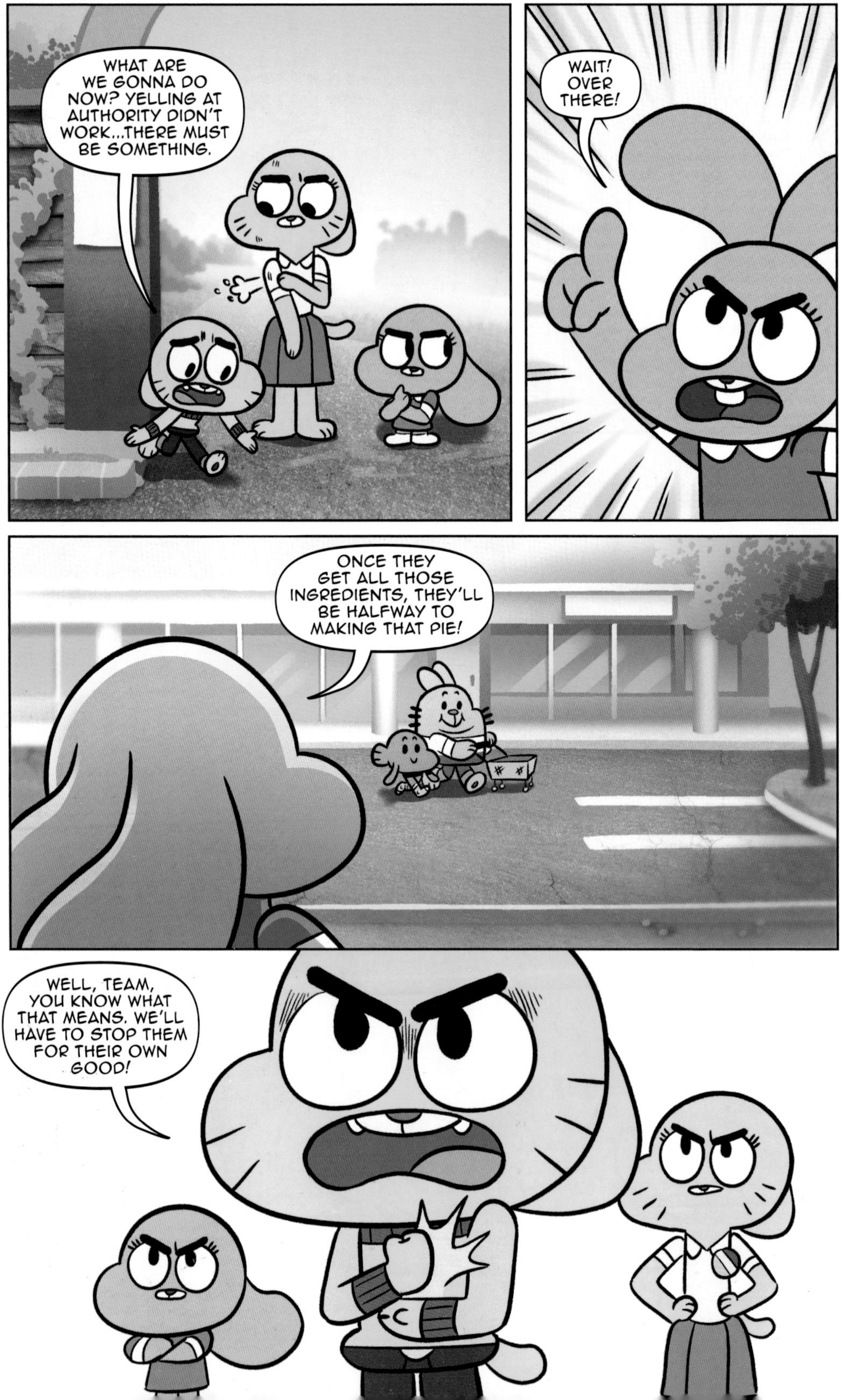
WHAT ARE WE GONNA DO NOW? YELLING AT AUTHORITY DIDN'T WORK...THERE MUST BE SOMETHING.
WAIT! OVER THERE!
ONCE THEY GET ALL THOSE INGREDIENTS, THEY'LL BE HALFWAY TO MAKING THAT PIE!
WELL, TEAM, YOU KNOW WHAT THAT MEANS. WE'LL HAVE TO STOP THEM FOR THEIR OWN GOOD!

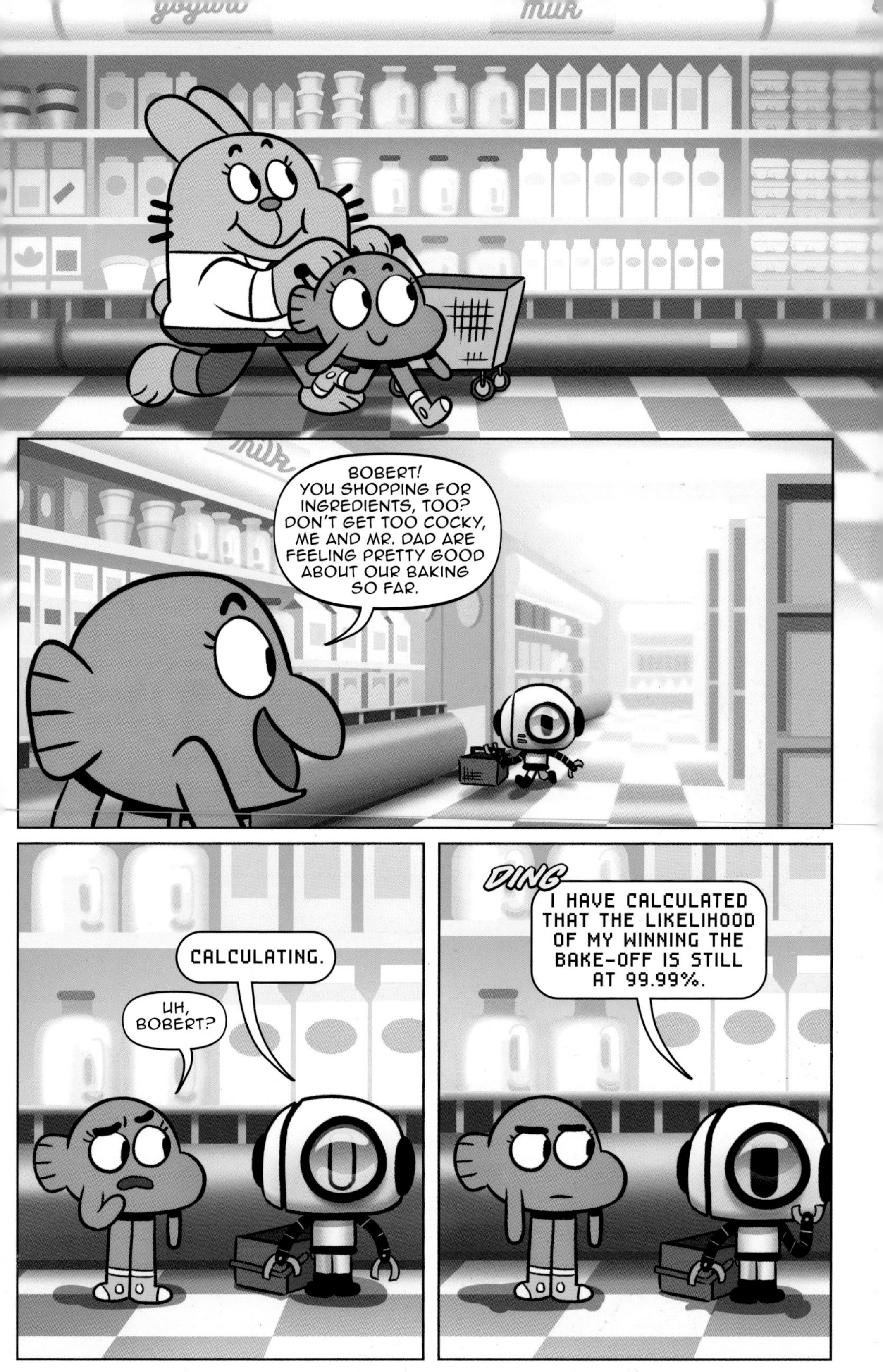
yogurt
milk
BOBERT! YOU SHOPPING FOR INGREDIENTS, TOO? DON'T GET TOO COCKY, ME AND MR. DAD ARE FEELING PRETTY GOOD ABOUT OUR BAKING SO FAR.
CALCULATING.
UH, BOBERT?
DING
I HAVE CALCULATED THAT THE LIKELIHOOD OF MY WINNING THE BAKE-OFF IS STILL AT 99.99%.

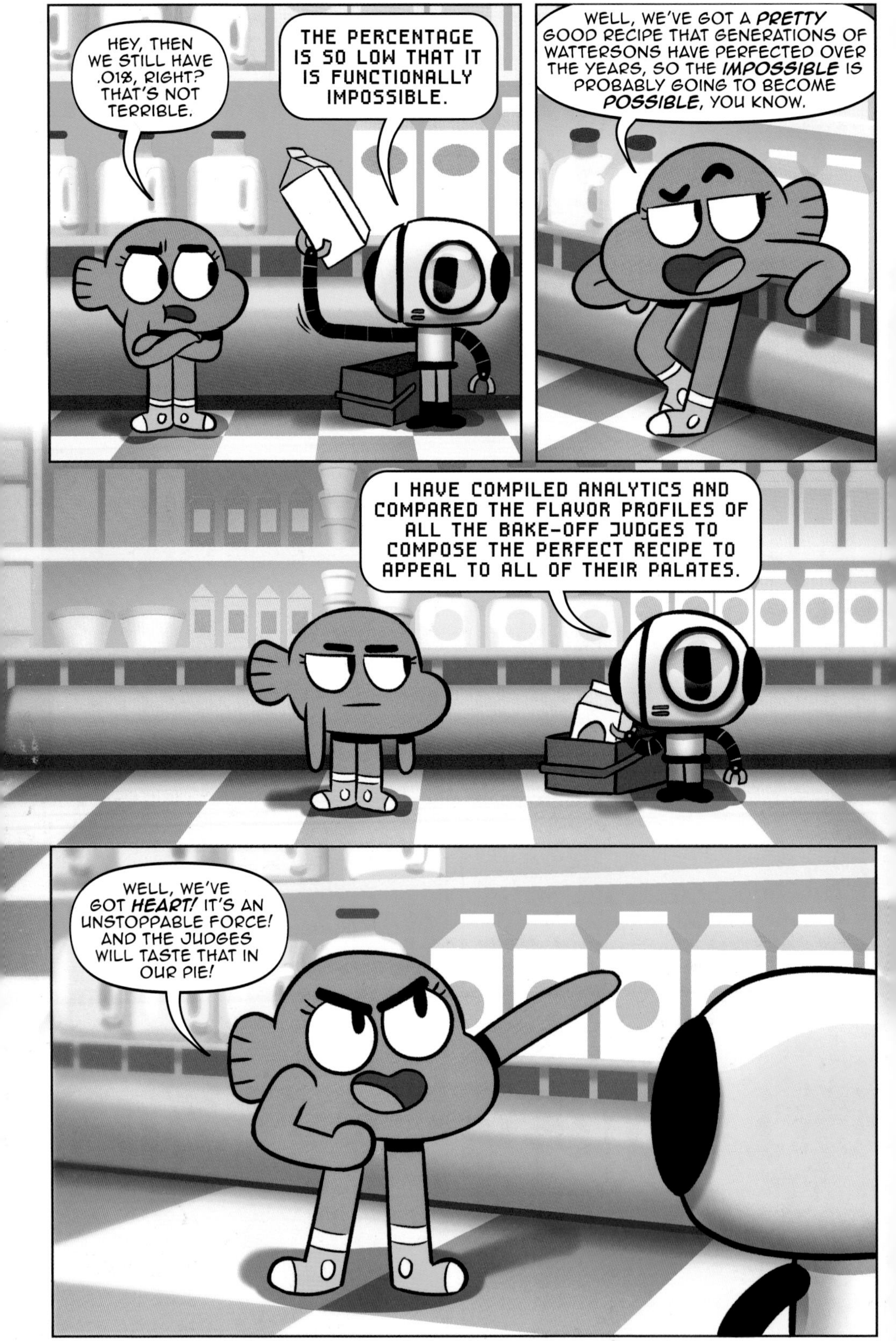
HEY, THEN WE STILL HAVE .01%, RIGHT? THAT'S NOT TERRIBLE.
THE PERCENTAGE IS SO LOW THAT IT IS FUNCTIONALLY IMPOSSIBLE.
WELL, WE'VE GOT A PRETTY GOOD RECIPE THAT GENERATIONS OF WATTERSONS HAVE PERFECTED OVER THE YEARS, SO THE IMPOSSIBLE IS PROBABLY GOING TO BECOME POSSIBLE, YOU KNOW.
I HAVE COMPILED ANALYTICS AND COMPARED THE FLAVOR PROFILES OF ALL THE BAKE-OFF JUDGES TO COMPOSE THE PERFECT RECIPE TO APPEAL TO ALL OF THEIR PALATES.
WELL, WE'VE GOT HEART! IT'S AN UNSTOPPABLE FORCE! AND THE JUDGES WILL TASTE THAT IN OUR PIE!

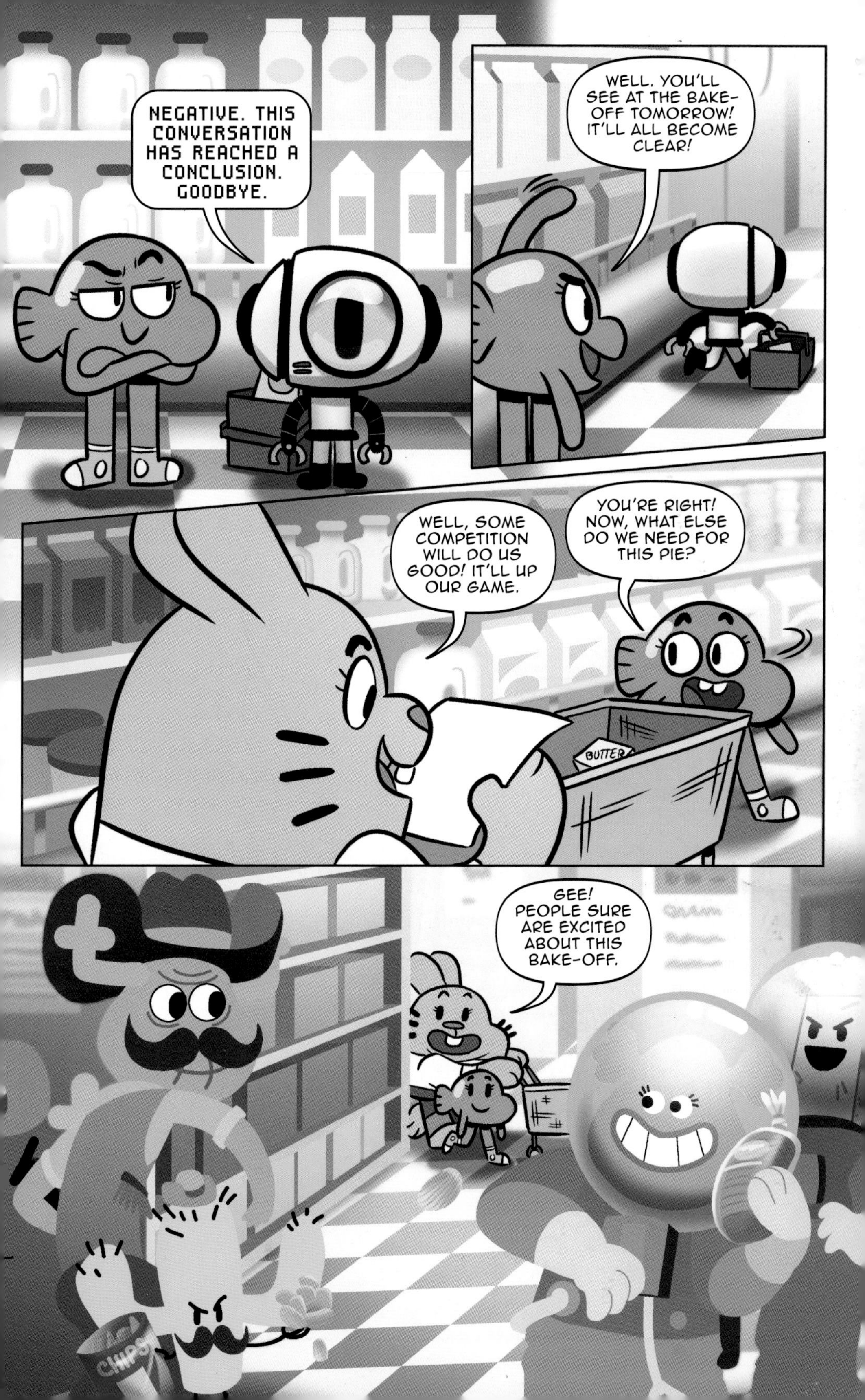
NEGATIVE. THIS CONVERSATION HAS REACHED A CONCLUSION. GOODBYE.
WELL. YOU'LL SEE AT THE BAKE-OFF TOMORROW! IT'LL ALL BECOME CLEAR!
WELL, SOME COMPETITION WILL DO US GOOD! IT'LL UP OUR GAME.
YOU'RE RIGHT! NOW, WHAT ELSE DO WE NEED FOR THIS PIE?
BUTTER
GEE! PEOPLE SURE ARE EXCITED ABOUT THIS BAKE-OFF.
CHIPS

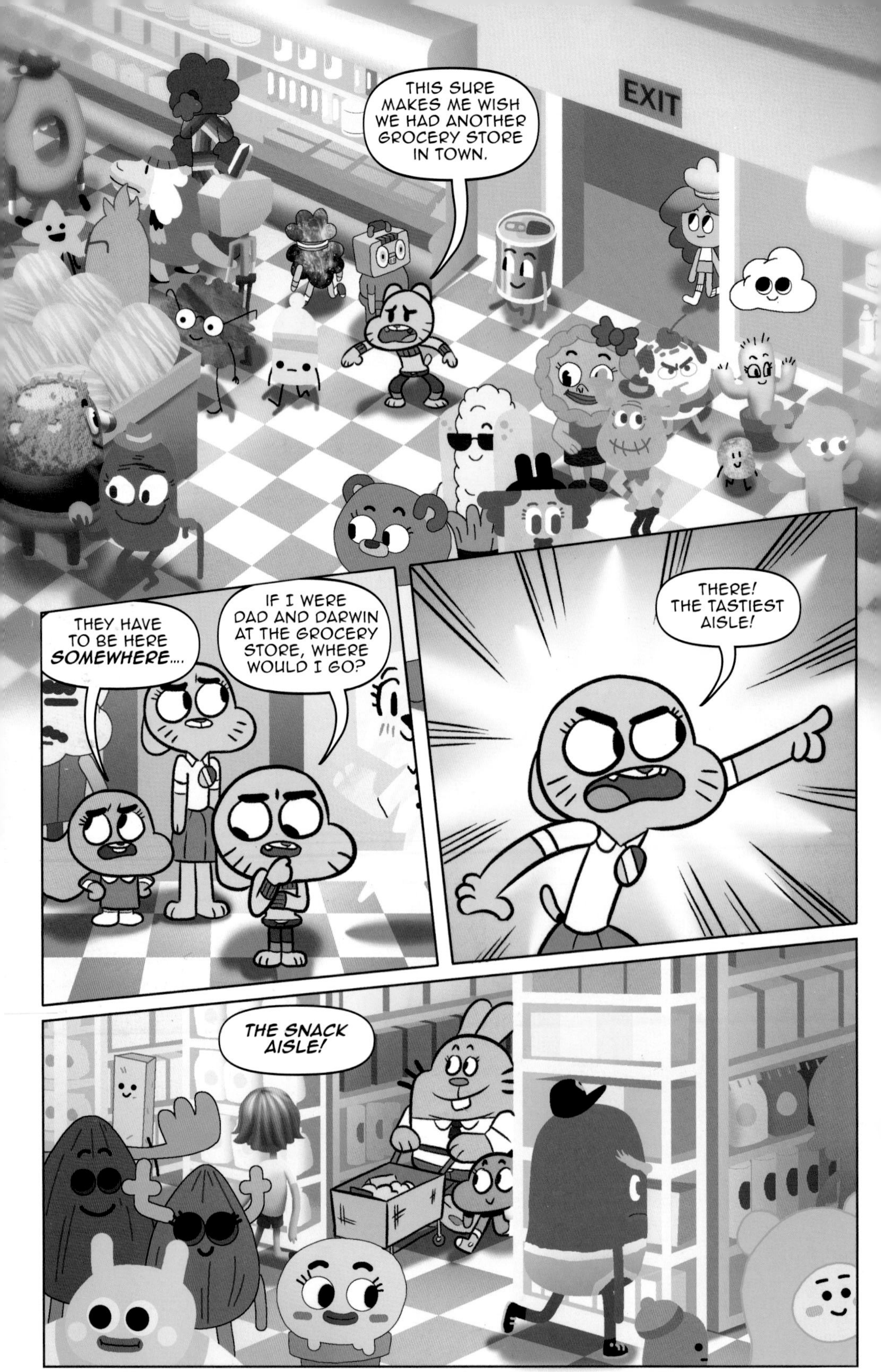
EXIT
THIS SURE MAKES ME WISH WE HAD ANOTHER GROCERY STORE IN TOWN.
THEY HAVE TO BE HERE *SOMEWHERE*....
IF I WERE DAD AND DARWIN AT THE GROCERY STORE, WHERE WOULD I GO?
THERE! THE TASTIEST AISLE!
THE SNACK AISLE!

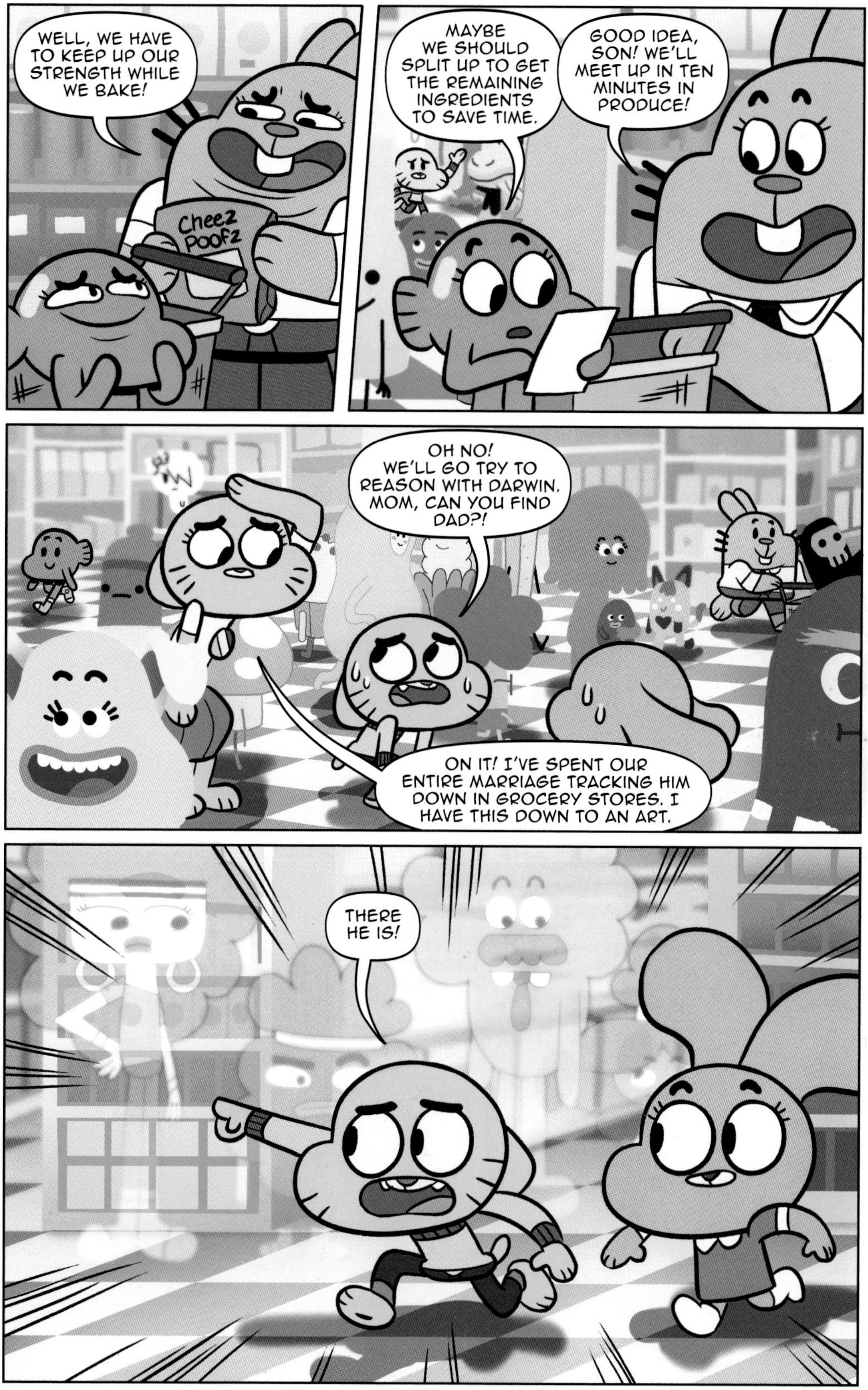
WELL, WE HAVE TO KEEP UP OUR STRENGTH WHILE WE BAKE!
Cheez Poofz
MAYBE WE SHOULD SPLIT UP TO GET THE REMAINING INGREDIENTS TO SAVE TIME.
GOOD IDEA, SON! WE'LL MEET UP IN TEN MINUTES IN PRODUCE!
OH NO! WE'LL GO TRY TO REASON WITH DARWIN. MOM, CAN YOU FIND DAD?!
ON IT! I'VE SPENT OUR ENTIRE MARRIAGE TRACKING HIM DOWN IN GROCERY STORES. I HAVE THIS DOWN TO AN ART.
THERE HE IS!

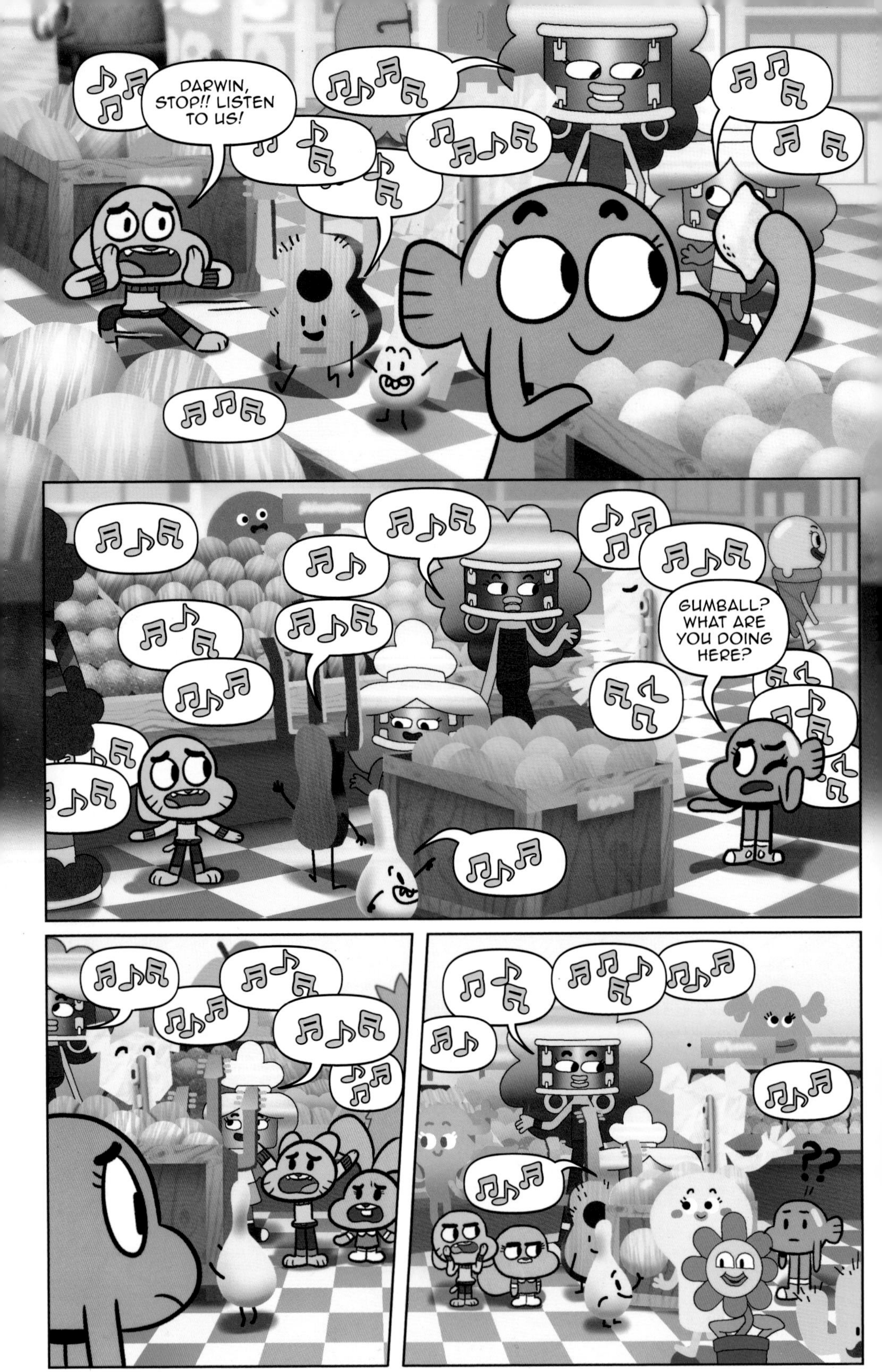
DARWIN, STOP!! LISTEN TO US!
GUMBALL? WHAT ARE YOU DOING HERE?
??

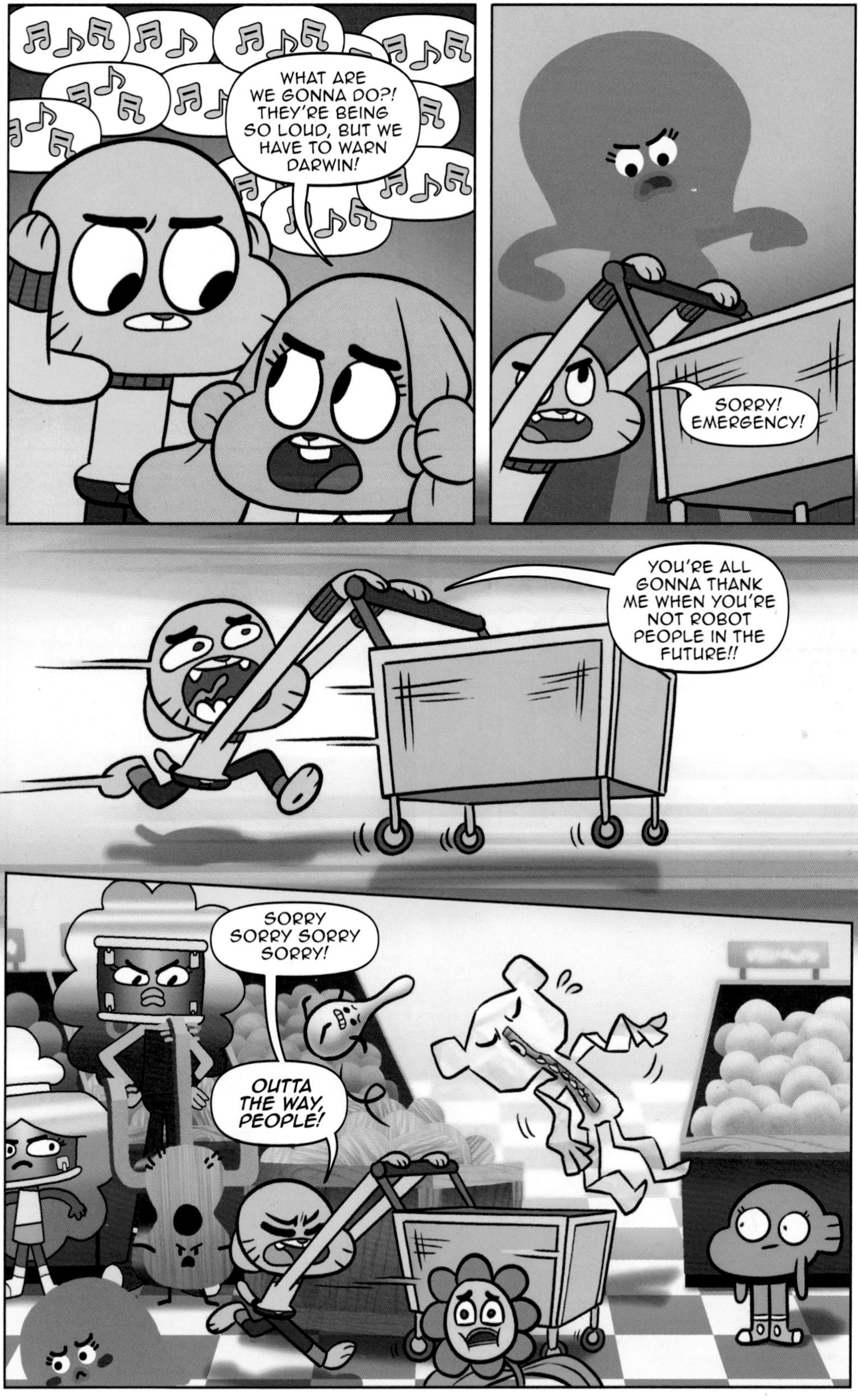
WHAT ARE WE GONNA DO?! THEY'RE BEING SO LOUD, BUT WE HAVE TO WARN DARWIN!
SORRY! EMERGENCY!
YOU'RE ALL GONNA THANK ME WHEN YOU'RE NOT ROBOT PEOPLE IN THE FUTURE!!
SORRY SORRY SORRY SORRY!
OUTTA THE WAY, PEOPLE!

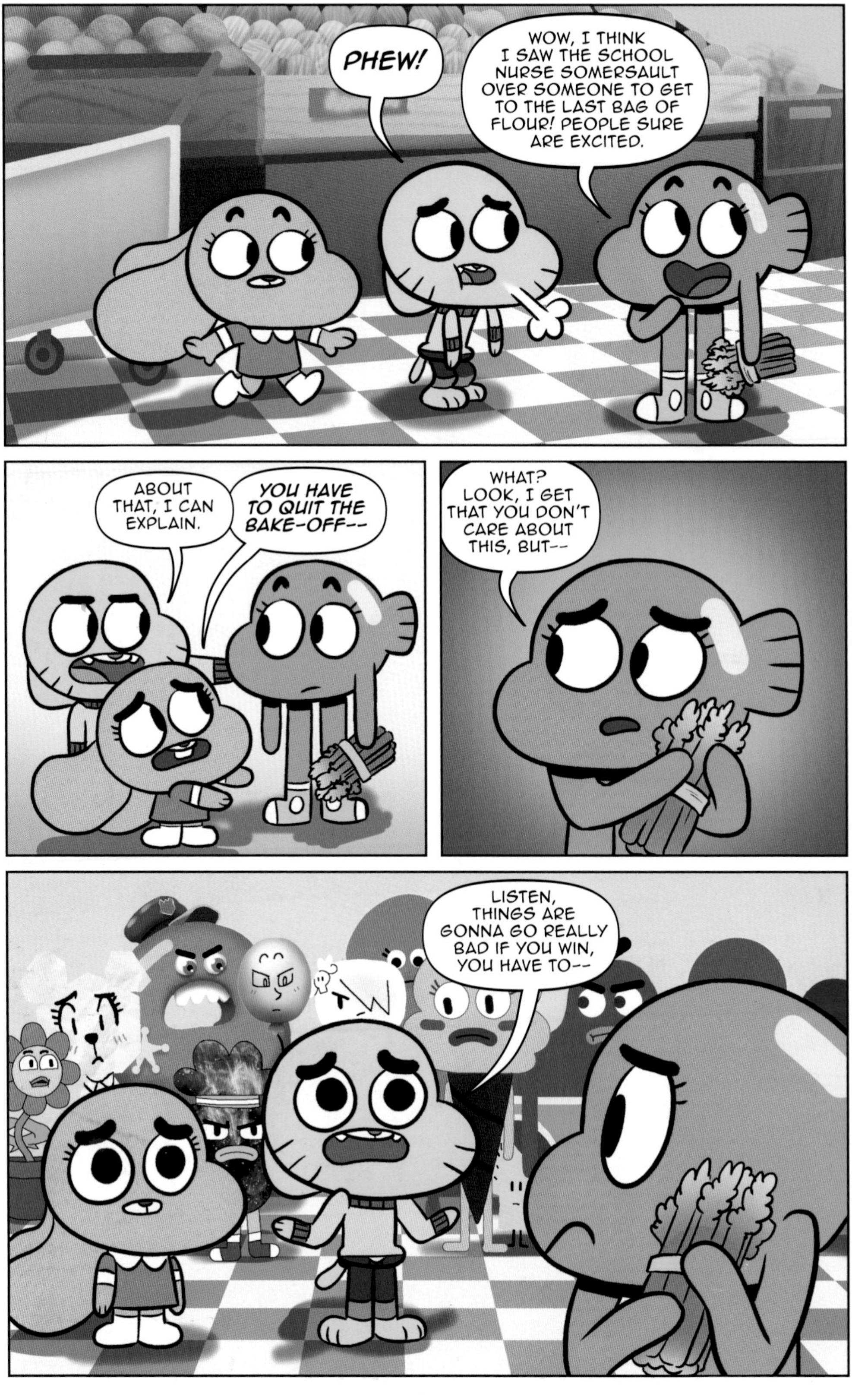
PHEW!
WOW, I THINK I SAW THE SCHOOL NURSE SOMERSAULT OVER SOMEONE TO GET TO THE LAST BAG OF FLOUR! PEOPLE SURE ARE EXCITED.
ABOUT THAT, I CAN EXPLAIN.
YOU HAVE TO QUIT THE BAKE-OFF--
WHAT? LOOK, I GET THAT YOU DON'T CARE ABOUT THIS, BUT--
LISTEN, THINGS ARE GONNA GO REALLY BAD IF YOU WIN, YOU HAVE TO--

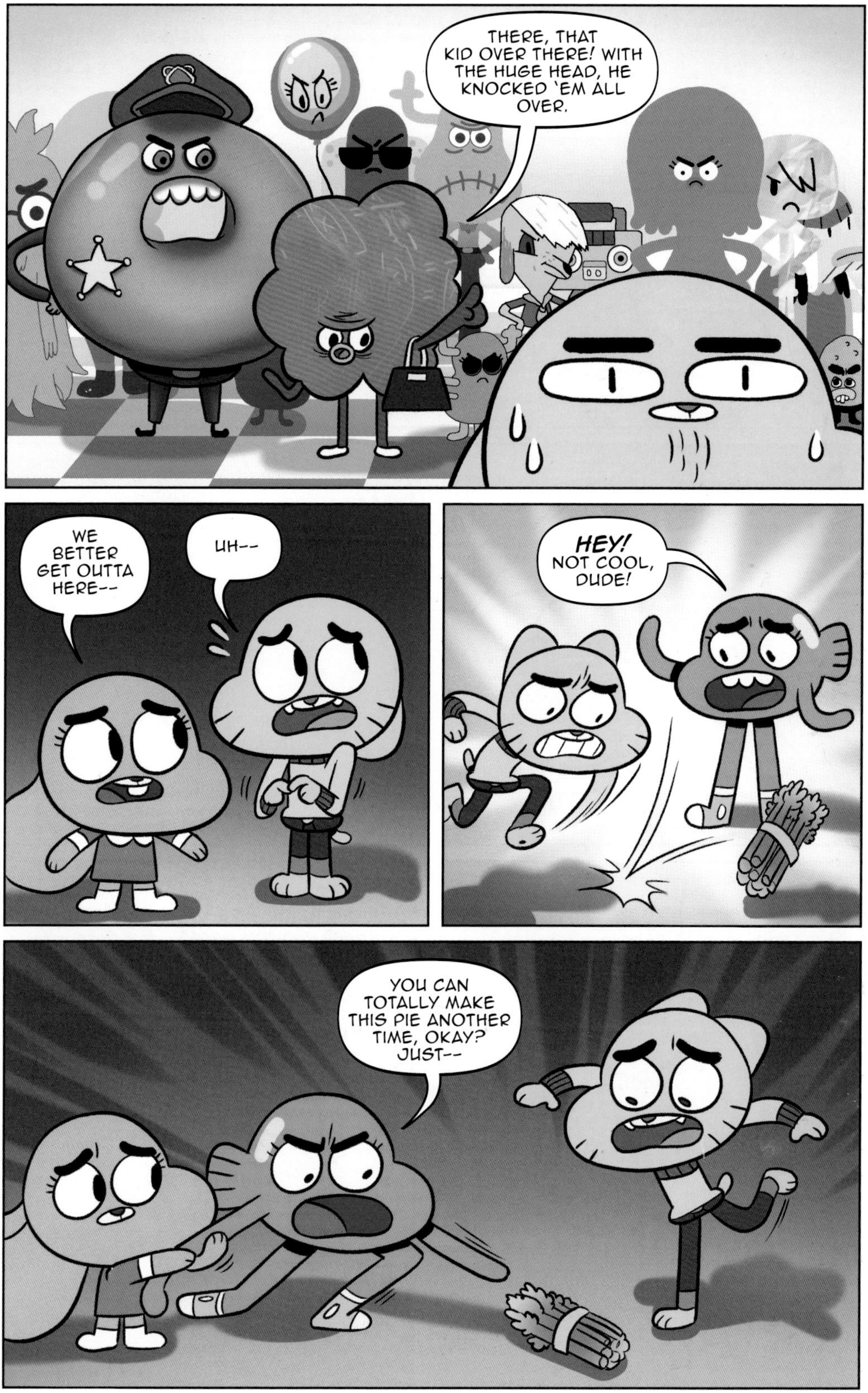
THERE, THAT KID OVER THERE! WITH THE HUGE HEAD, HE KNOCKED 'EM ALL OVER.
WE BETTER GET OUTTA HERE--
UH--
HEY! NOT COOL, DUDE!
YOU CAN TOTALLY MAKE THIS PIE ANOTHER TIME, OKAY? JUST--

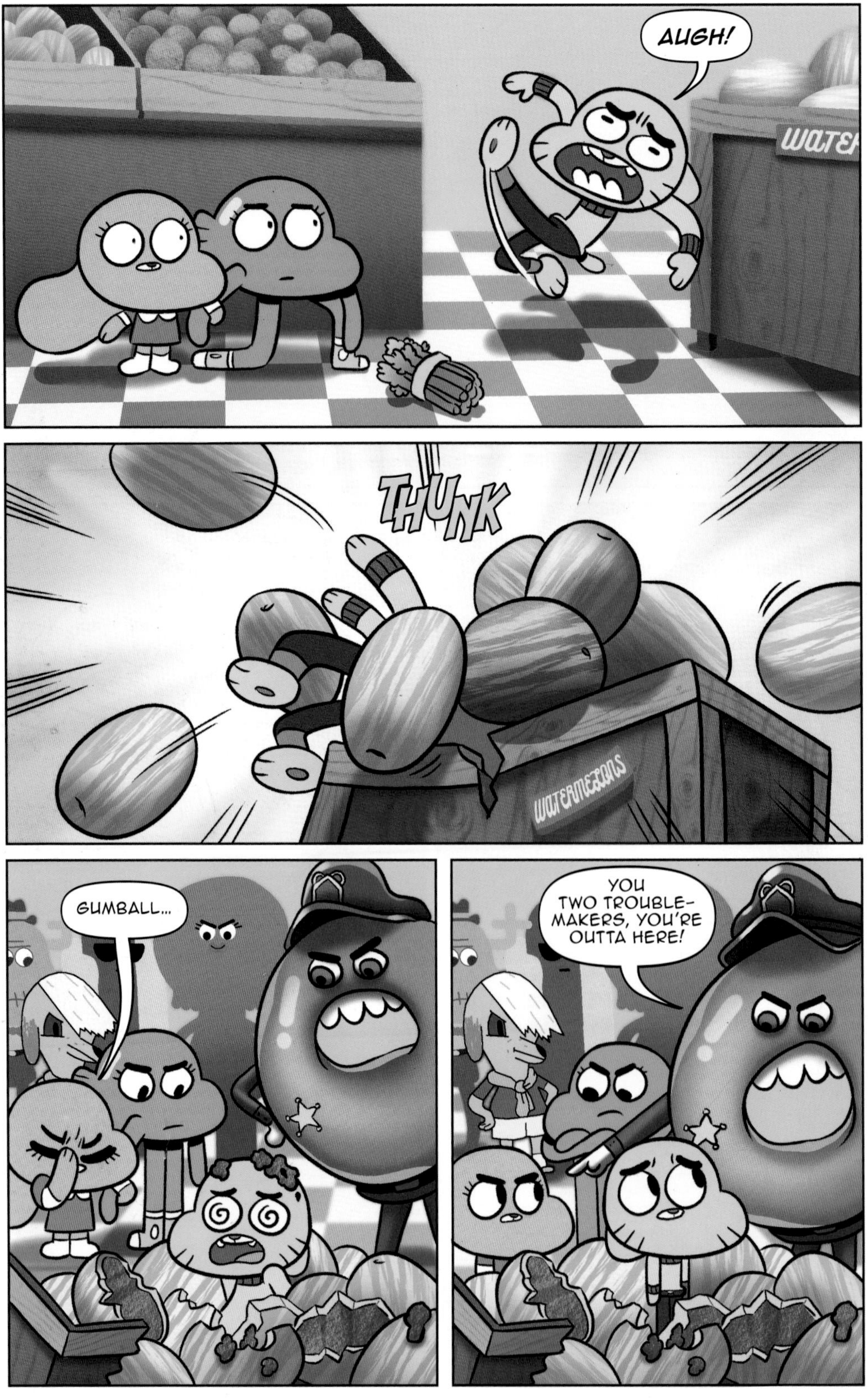
AUGH!
THUNK
WATERMELONS
GUMBALL...
YOU TWO TROUBLE-MAKERS, YOU'RE OUTTA HERE!

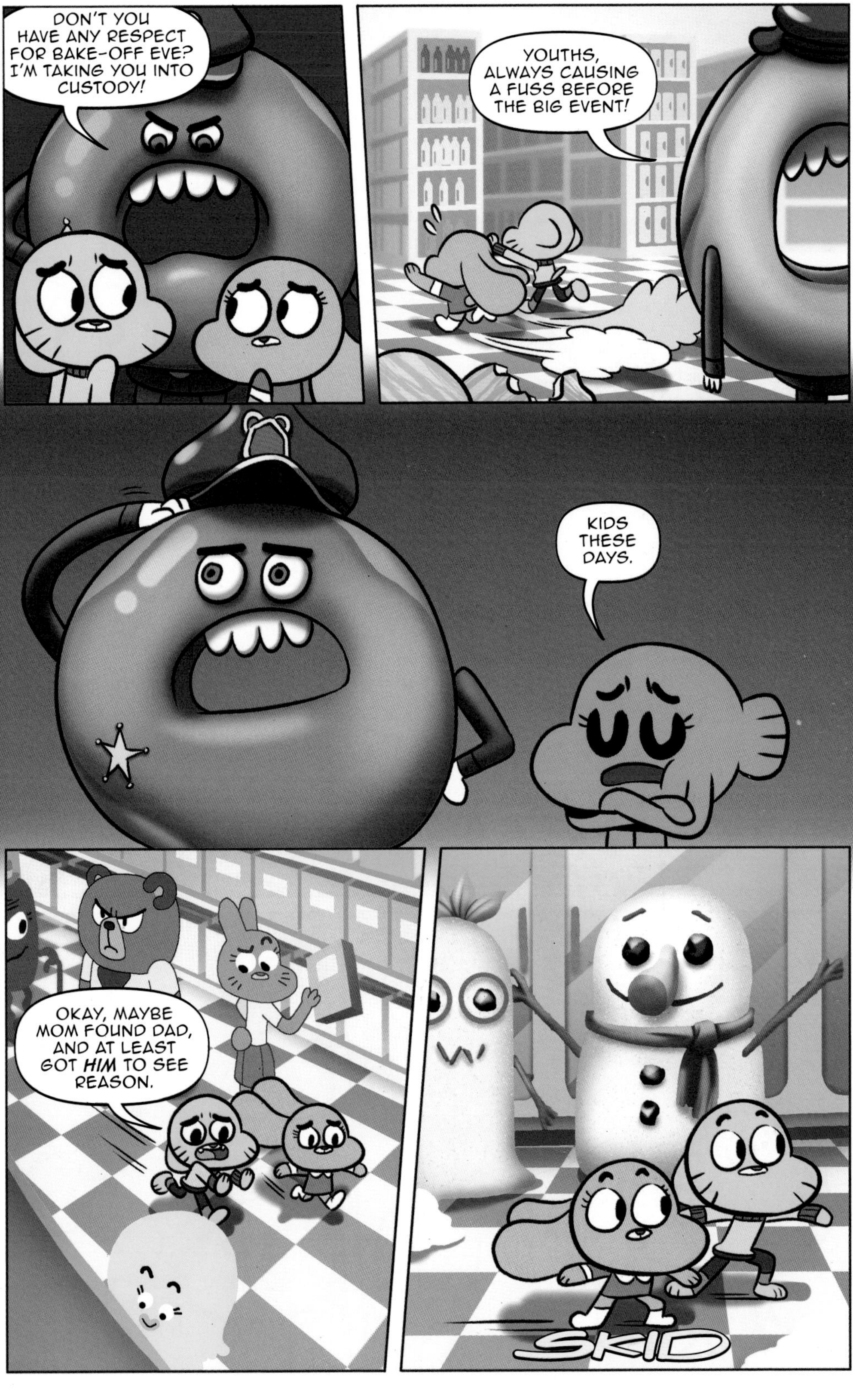
DON'T YOU HAVE ANY RESPECT FOR BAKE-OFF EVE? I'M TAKING YOU INTO CUSTODY!
YOUTHS, ALWAYS CAUSING A FUSS BEFORE THE BIG EVENT!
KIDS THESE DAYS.
OKAY, MAYBE MOM FOUND DAD, AND AT LEAST GOT *HIM* TO SEE REASON.
SKID

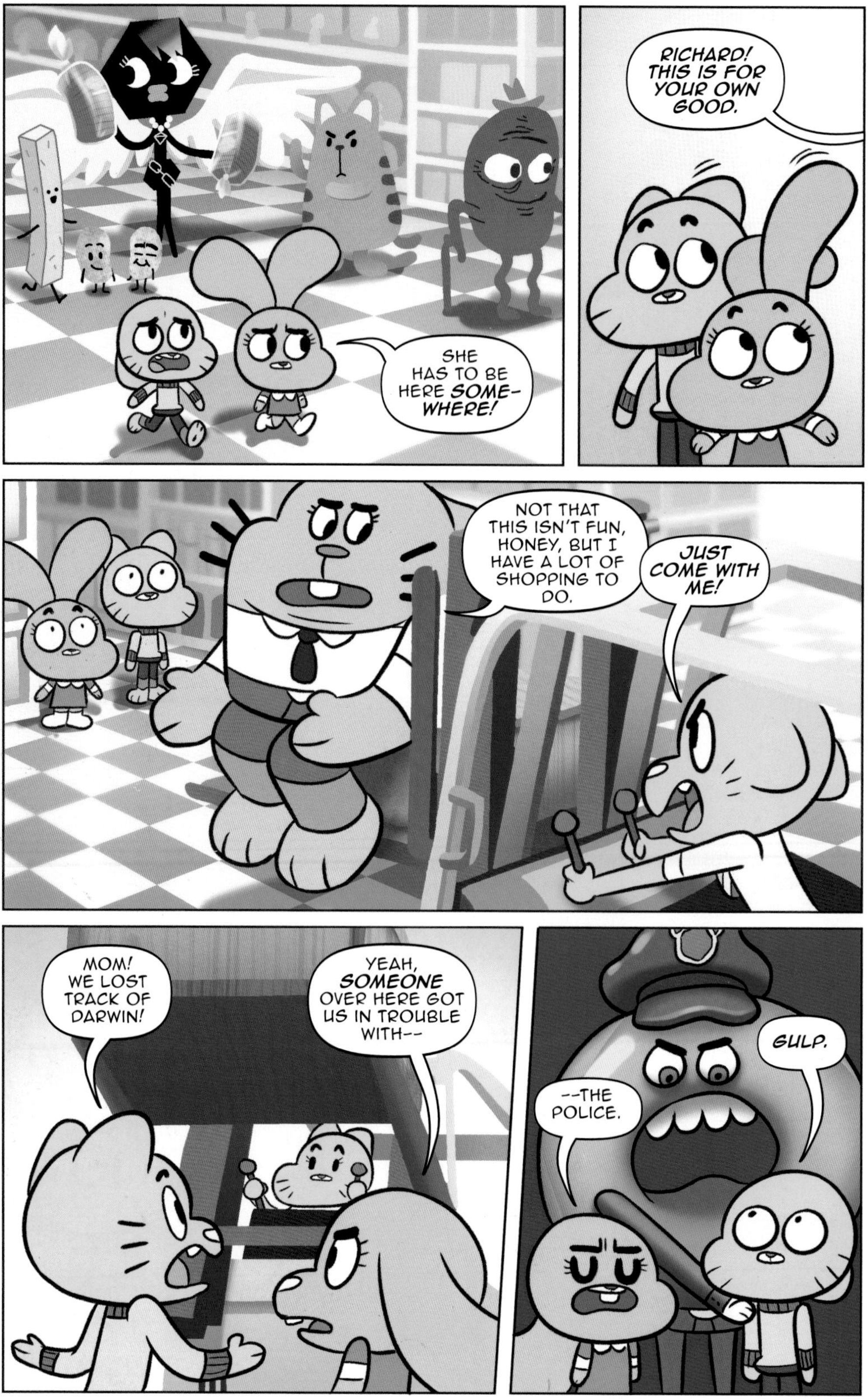
SHE HAS TO BE HERE SOME-WHERE!
RICHARD! THIS IS FOR YOUR OWN GOOD.
NOT THAT THIS ISN'T FUN, HONEY, BUT I HAVE A LOT OF SHOPPING TO DO.
JUST COME WITH ME!
MOM! WE LOST TRACK OF DARWIN!
YEAH, SOMEONE OVER HERE GOT US IN TROUBLE WITH--
--THE POLICE.
GULP.

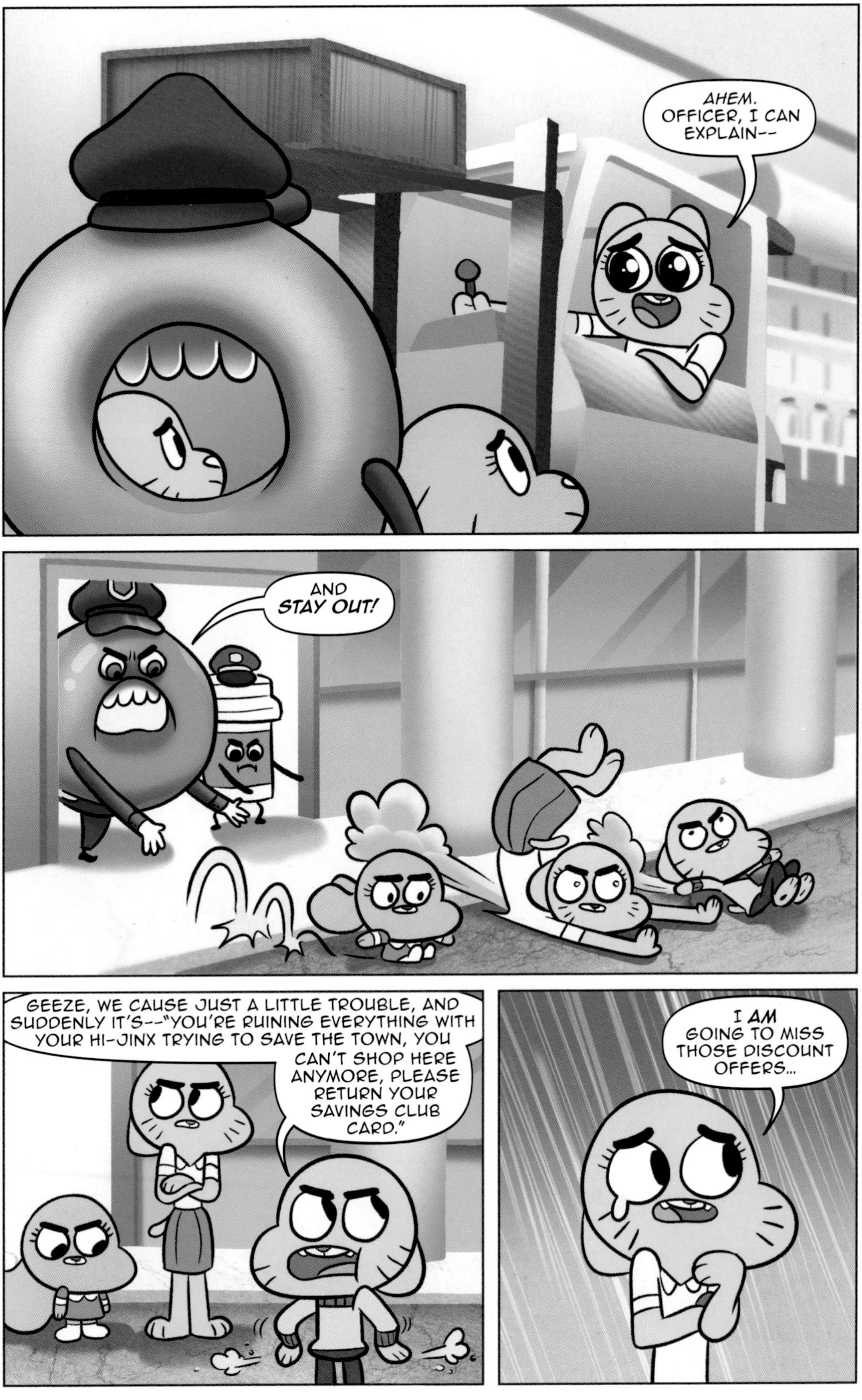
AHEM. OFFICER, I CAN EXPLAIN--
AND STAY OUT!
GEEZE, WE CAUSE JUST A LITTLE TROUBLE, AND SUDDENLY IT'S--"YOU'RE RUINING EVERYTHING WITH YOUR HI-JINX TRYING TO SAVE THE TOWN, YOU CAN'T SHOP HERE ANYMORE, PLEASE RETURN YOUR SAVINGS CLUB CARD."
I AM GOING TO MISS THOSE DISCOUNT OFFERS...

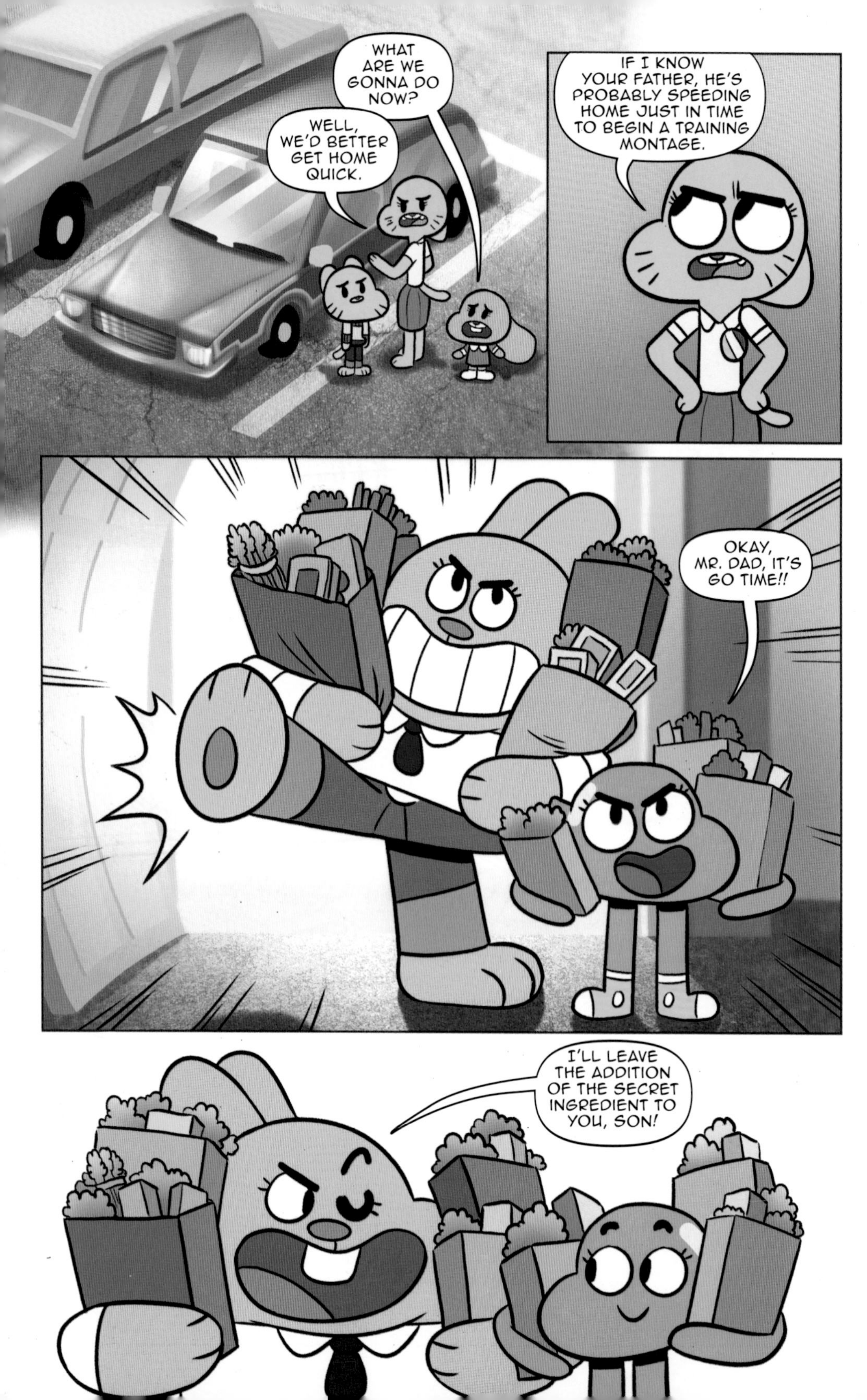

WHAT ARE WE GONNA DO NOW?
WELL, WE'D BETTER GET HOME QUICK.
IF I KNOW YOUR FATHER, HE'S PROBABLY SPEEDING HOME JUST IN TIME TO BEGIN A TRAINING MONTAGE.
OKAY, MR. DAD, IT'S GO TIME!!
I'LL LEAVE THE ADDITION OF THE SECRET INGREDIENT TO YOU, SON!

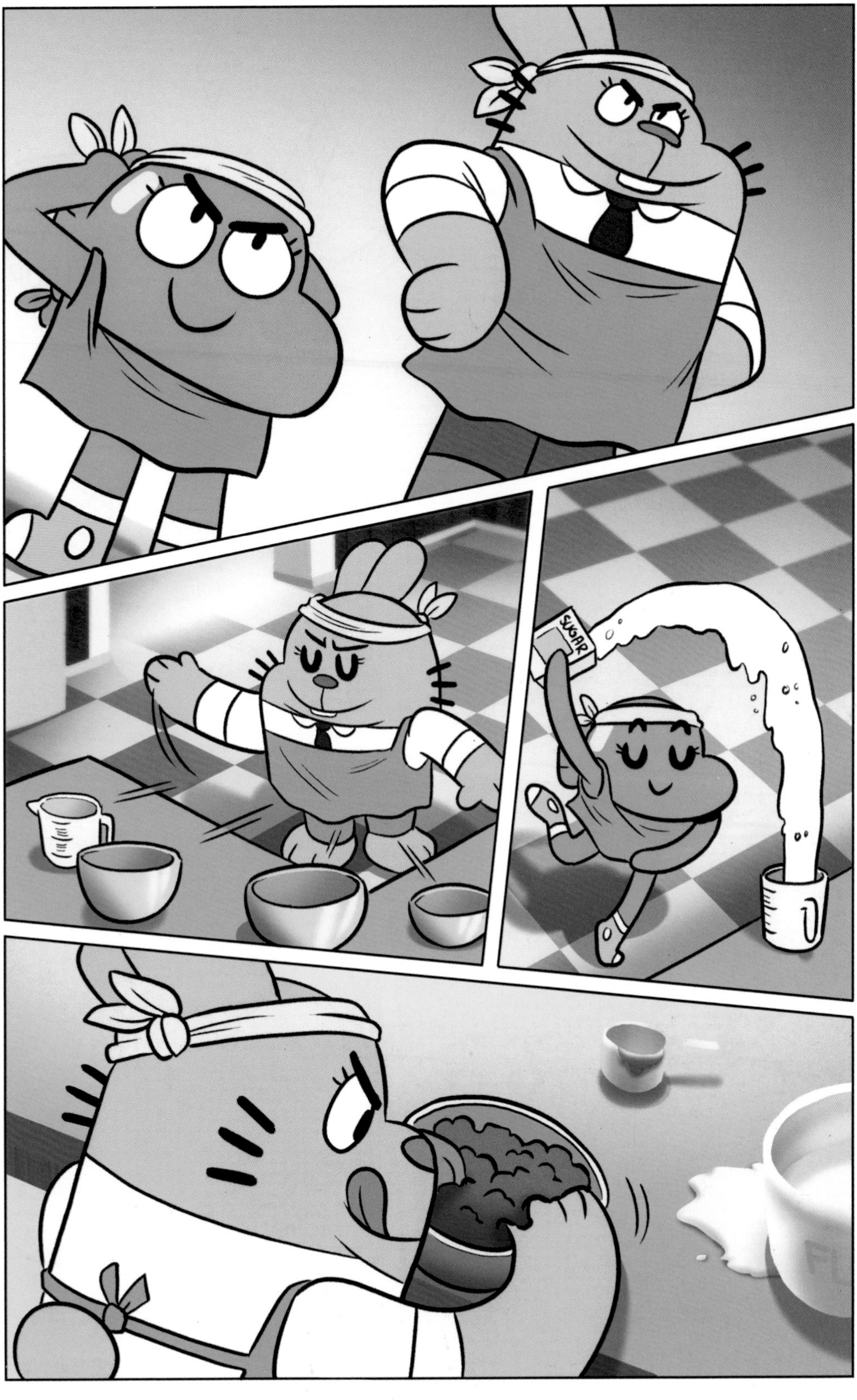
SUGAR

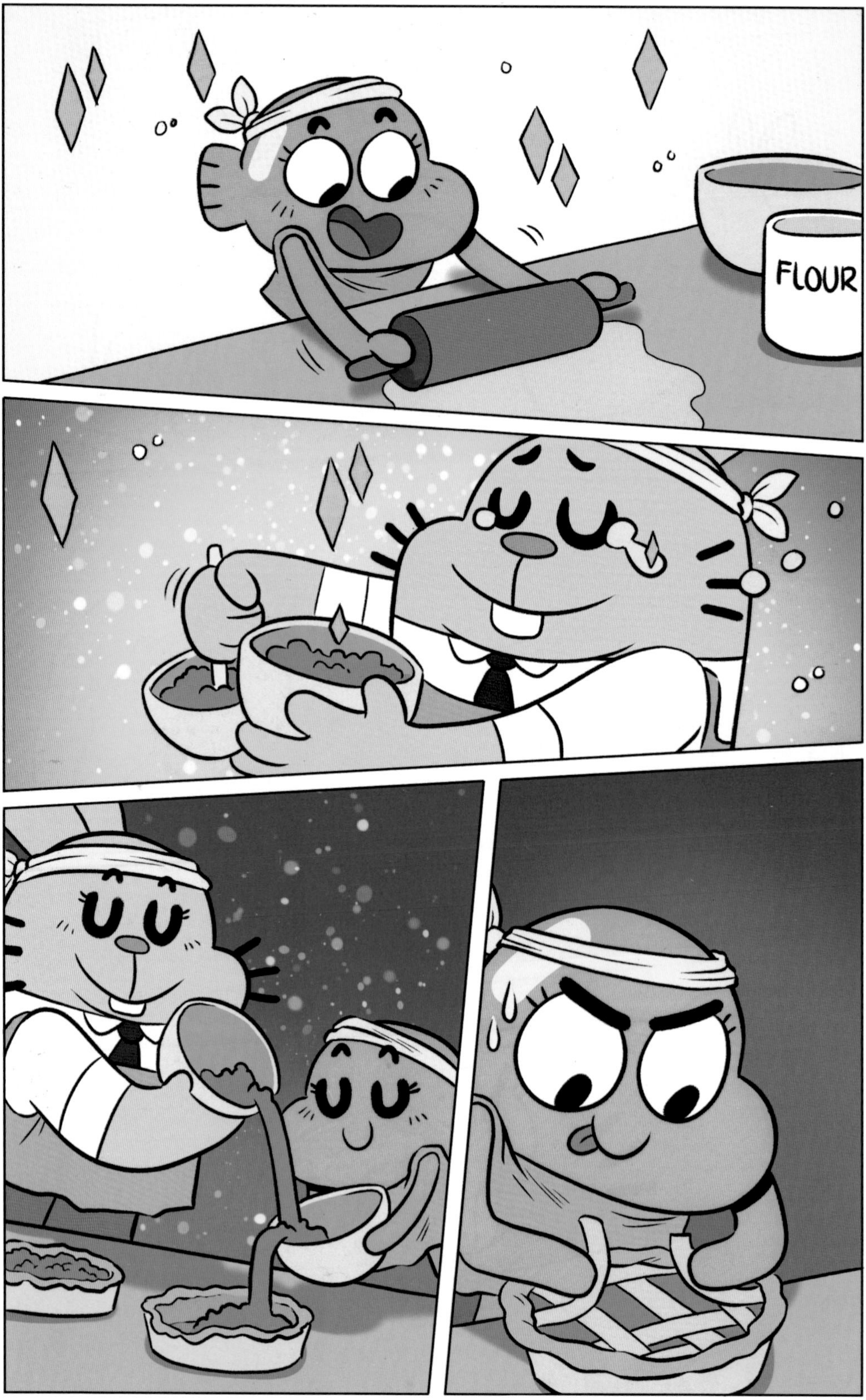
FLOUR

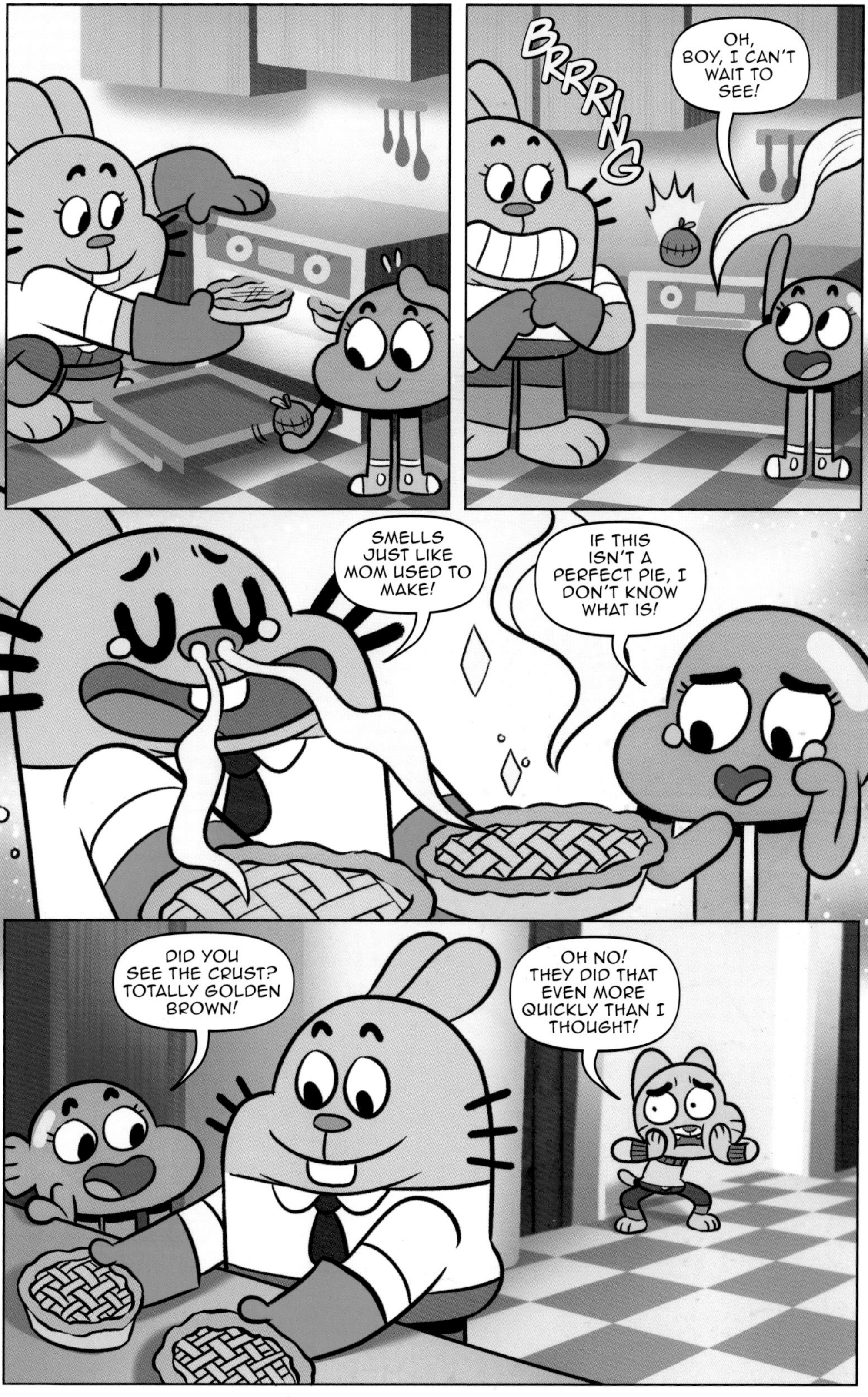
BRRRING
OH, BOY, I CAN'T WAIT TO SEE!
SMELLS JUST LIKE MOM USED TO MAKE!
IF THIS ISN'T A PERFECT PIE, I DON'T KNOW WHAT IS!
DID YOU SEE THE CRUST? TOTALLY GOLDEN BROWN!
OH NO! THEY DID THAT EVEN MORE QUICKLY THAN I THOUGHT!

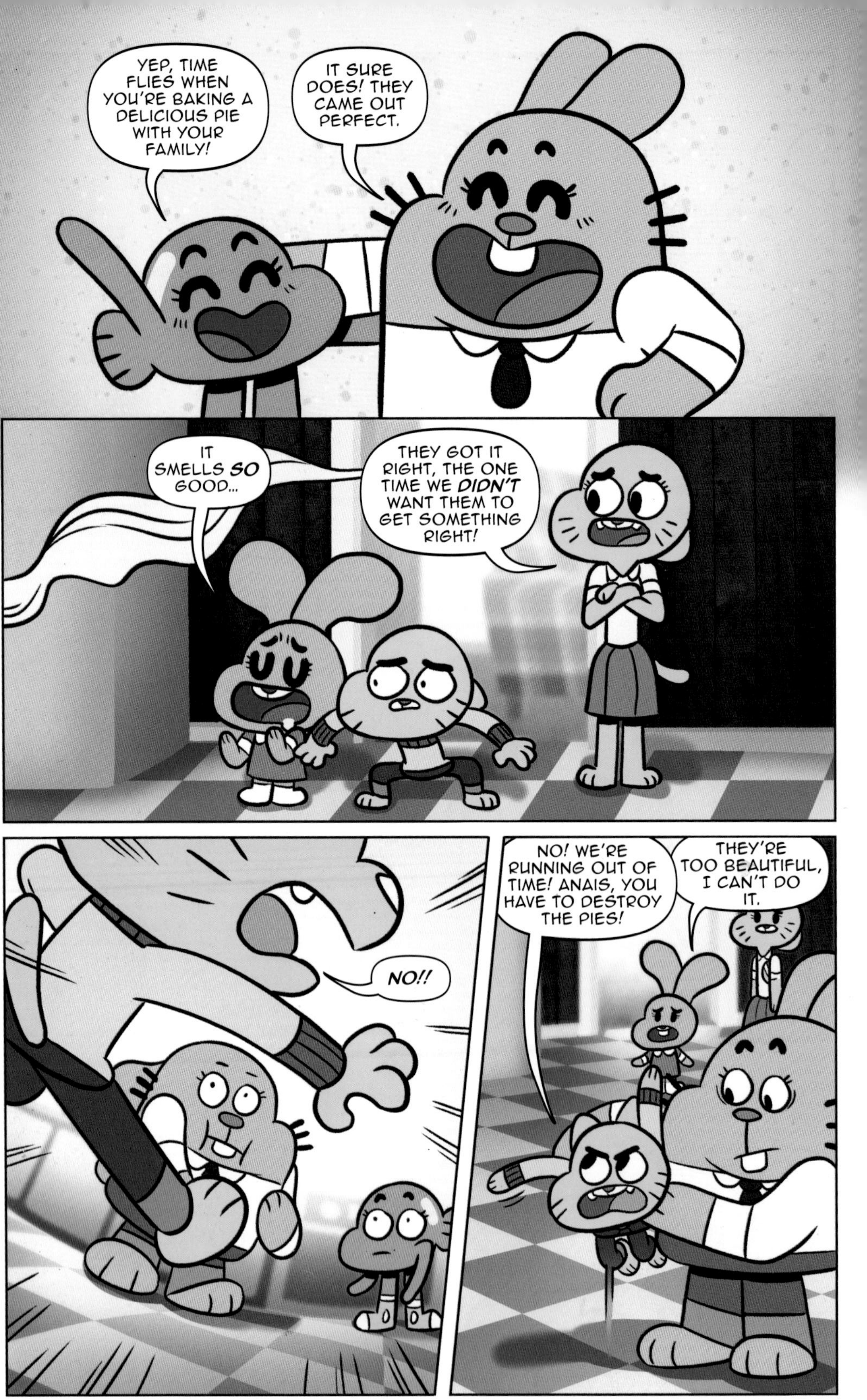
YEP, TIME FLIES WHEN YOU'RE BAKING A DELICIOUS PIE WITH YOUR FAMILY!
IT SURE DOES! THEY CAME OUT PERFECT.
IT SMELLS **SO** GOOD...
THEY GOT IT RIGHT, THE ONE TIME WE ***DIDN'T*** WANT THEM TO GET SOMETHING RIGHT!
NO!!
NO! WE'RE RUNNING OUT OF TIME! ANAIS, YOU HAVE TO DESTROY THE PIES!
THEY'RE TOO BEAUTIFUL, I CAN'T DO IT.

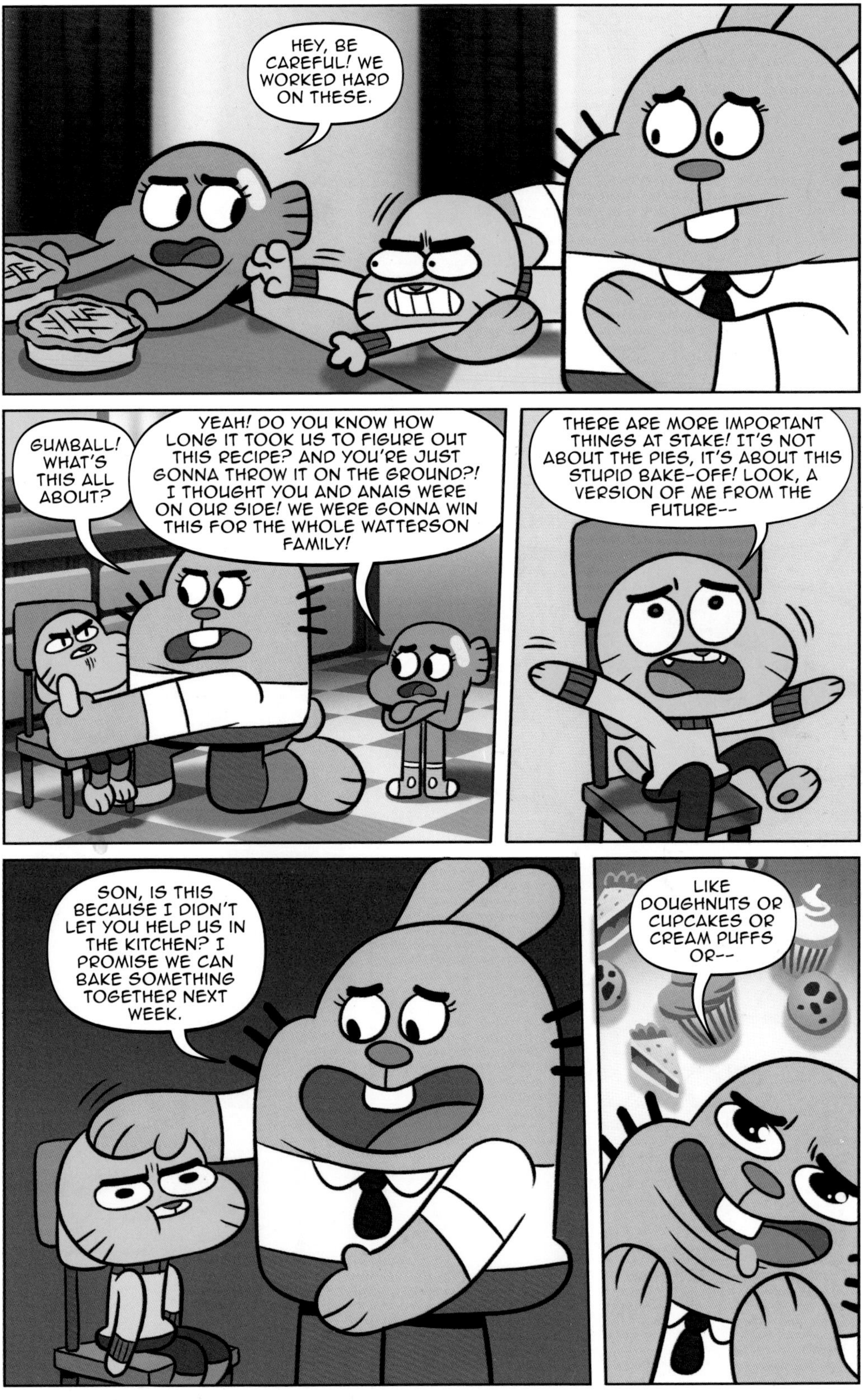
HEY, BE CAREFUL! WE WORKED HARD ON THESE.
GUMBALL! WHAT'S THIS ALL ABOUT?
YEAH! DO YOU KNOW HOW LONG IT TOOK US TO FIGURE OUT THIS RECIPE? AND YOU'RE JUST GONNA THROW IT ON THE GROUND?! I THOUGHT YOU AND ANAIS WERE ON OUR SIDE! WE WERE GONNA WIN THIS FOR THE WHOLE WATTERSON FAMILY!
THERE ARE MORE IMPORTANT THINGS AT STAKE! IT'S NOT ABOUT THE PIES, IT'S ABOUT THIS STUPID BAKE-OFF! LOOK, A VERSION OF ME FROM THE FUTURE--
SON, IS THIS BECAUSE I DIDN'T LET YOU HELP US IN THE KITCHEN? I PROMISE WE CAN BAKE SOMETHING TOGETHER NEXT WEEK.
LIKE DOUGHNUTS OR CUPCAKES OR CREAM PUFFS OR--

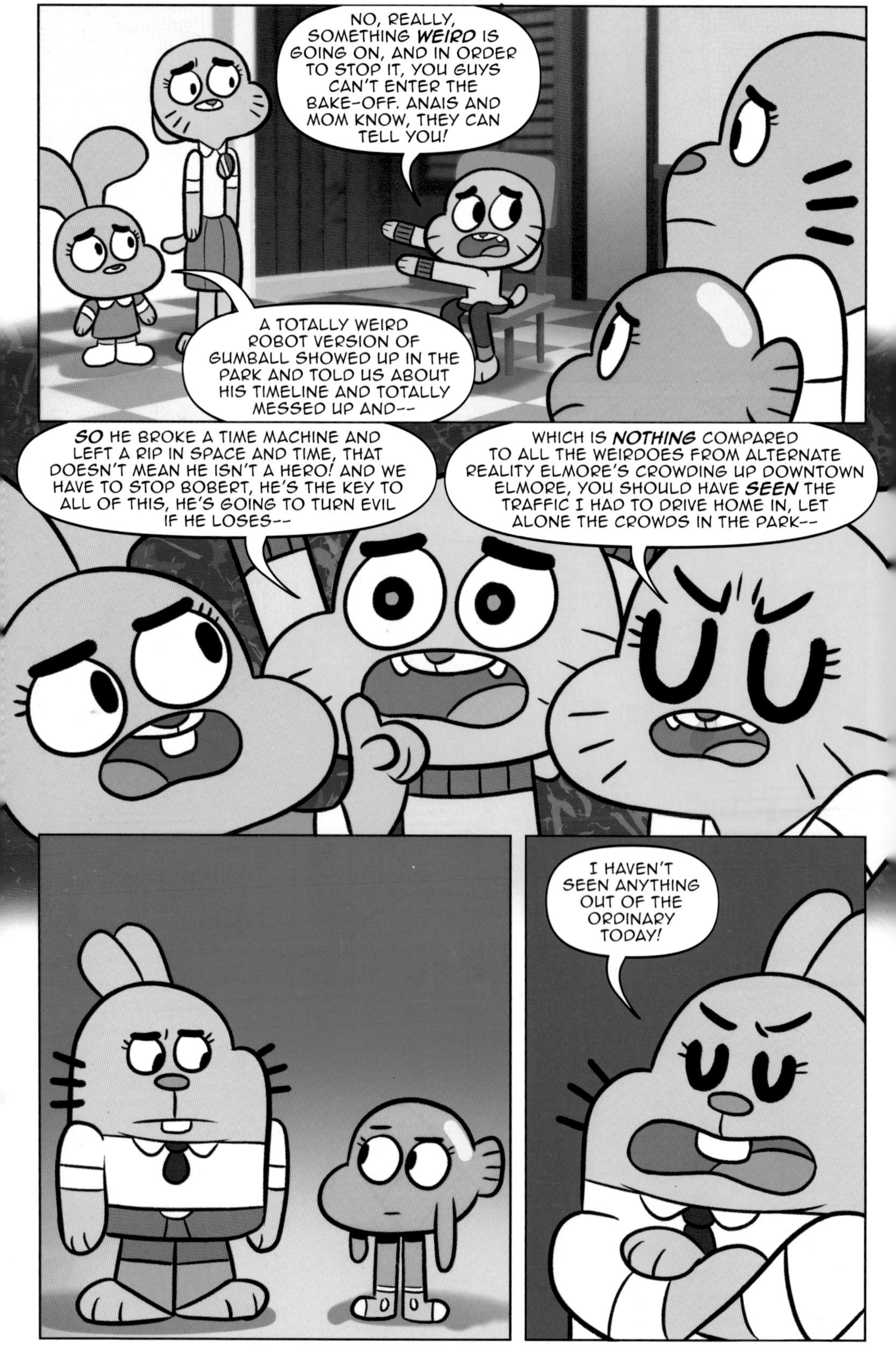
NO, REALLY, SOMETHING WEIRD IS GOING ON, AND IN ORDER TO STOP IT, YOU GUYS CAN'T ENTER THE BAKE-OFF. ANAIS AND MOM KNOW, THEY CAN TELL YOU!
A TOTALLY WEIRD ROBOT VERSION OF GUMBALL SHOWED UP IN THE PARK AND TOLD US ABOUT HIS TIMELINE AND TOTALLY MESSED UP AND--
SO HE BROKE A TIME MACHINE AND LEFT A RIP IN SPACE AND TIME, THAT DOESN'T MEAN HE ISN'T A HERO! AND WE HAVE TO STOP BOBERT, HE'S THE KEY TO ALL OF THIS, HE'S GOING TO TURN EVIL IF HE LOSES--
WHICH IS NOTHING COMPARED TO ALL THE WEIRDOES FROM ALTERNATE REALITY ELMORE'S CROWDING UP DOWNTOWN ELMORE, YOU SHOULD HAVE SEEN THE TRAFFIC I HAD TO DRIVE HOME IN, LET ALONE THE CROWDS IN THE PARK--
I HAVEN'T SEEN ANYTHING OUT OF THE ORDINARY TODAY!

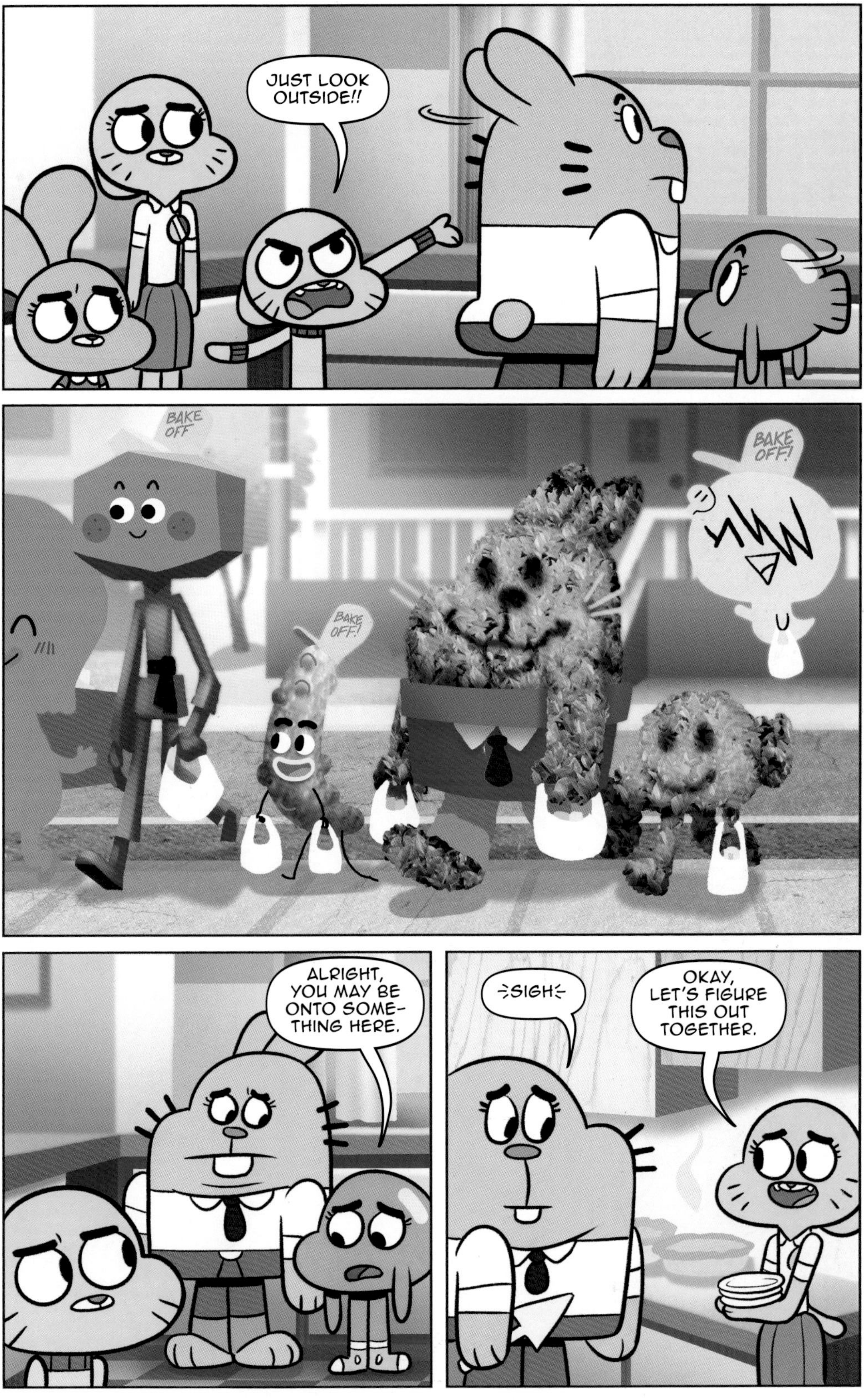
JUST LOOK OUTSIDE!!
BAKE OFF
BAKE OFF!
BAKE OFF!
ALRIGHT, YOU MAY BE ONTO SOME-THING HERE.
-SIGH-
OKAY, LET'S FIGURE THIS OUT TOGETHER.

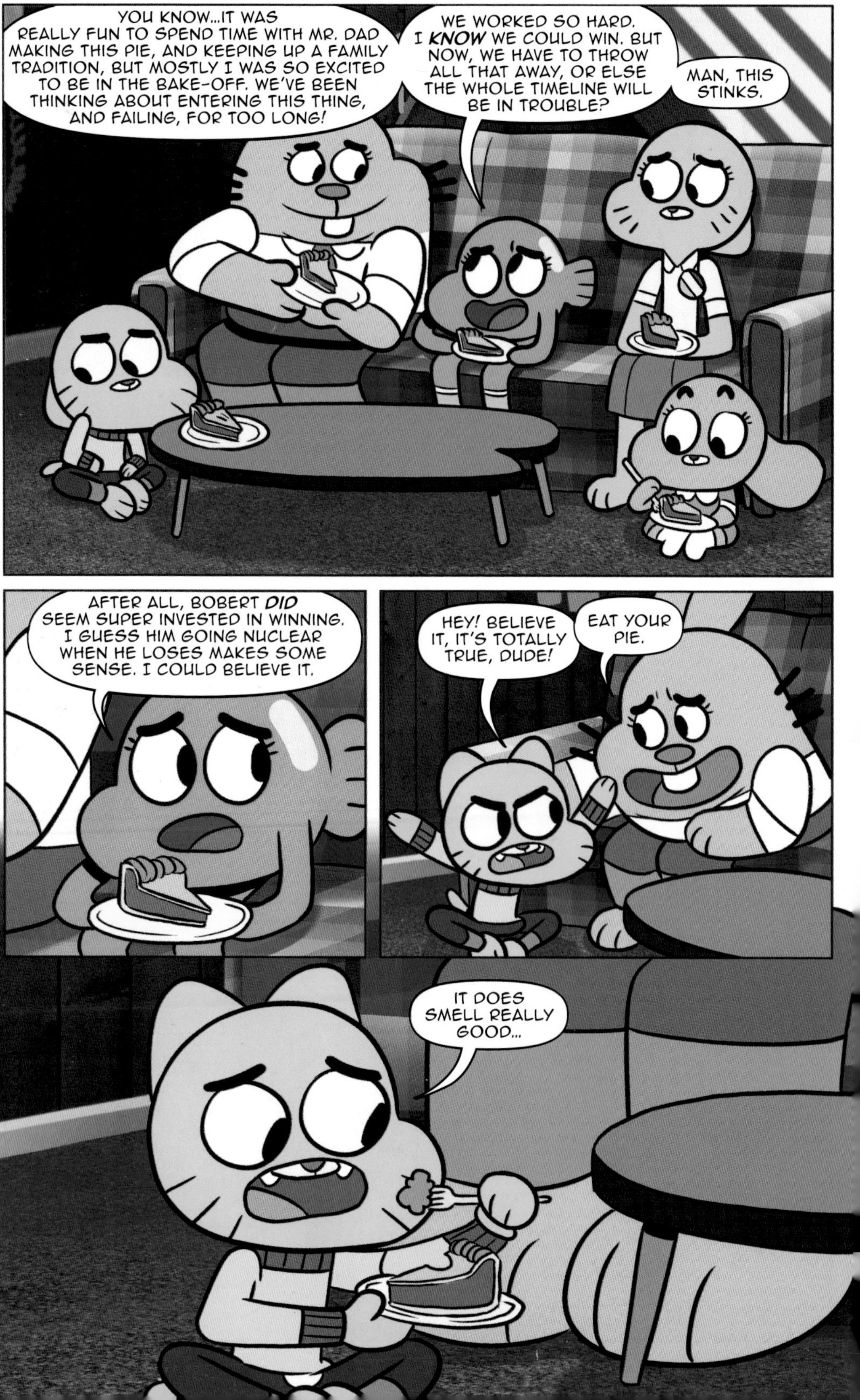
YOU KNOW...IT WAS REALLY FUN TO SPEND TIME WITH MR. DAD MAKING THIS PIE, AND KEEPING UP A FAMILY TRADITION, BUT MOSTLY I WAS SO EXCITED TO BE IN THE BAKE-OFF. WE'VE BEEN THINKING ABOUT ENTERING THIS THING, AND FAILING, FOR TOO LONG!
WE WORKED SO HARD. I *KNOW* WE COULD WIN. BUT NOW, WE HAVE TO THROW ALL THAT AWAY, OR ELSE THE WHOLE TIMELINE WILL BE IN TROUBLE?
MAN, THIS STINKS.
AFTER ALL, BOBERT *DID* SEEM SUPER INVESTED IN WINNING. I GUESS HIM GOING NUCLEAR WHEN HE LOSES MAKES SOME SENSE. I COULD BELIEVE IT.
HEY! BELIEVE IT, IT'S TOTALLY TRUE, DUDE!
EAT YOUR PIE.
IT DOES SMELL REALLY GOOD...

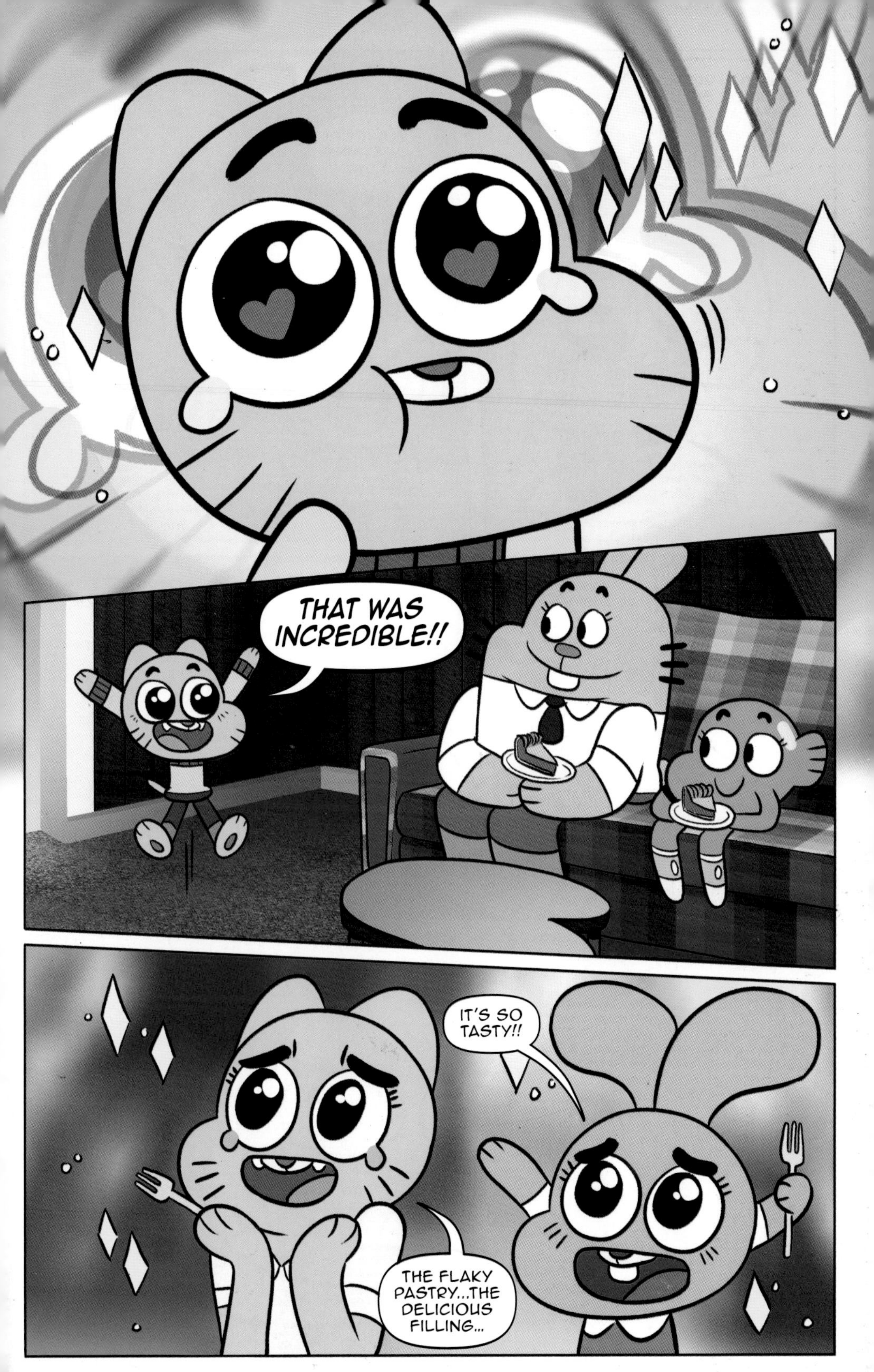
THAT WAS INCREDIBLE!!
IT'S SO TASTY!!
THE FLAKY PASTRY...THE DELICIOUS FILLING...

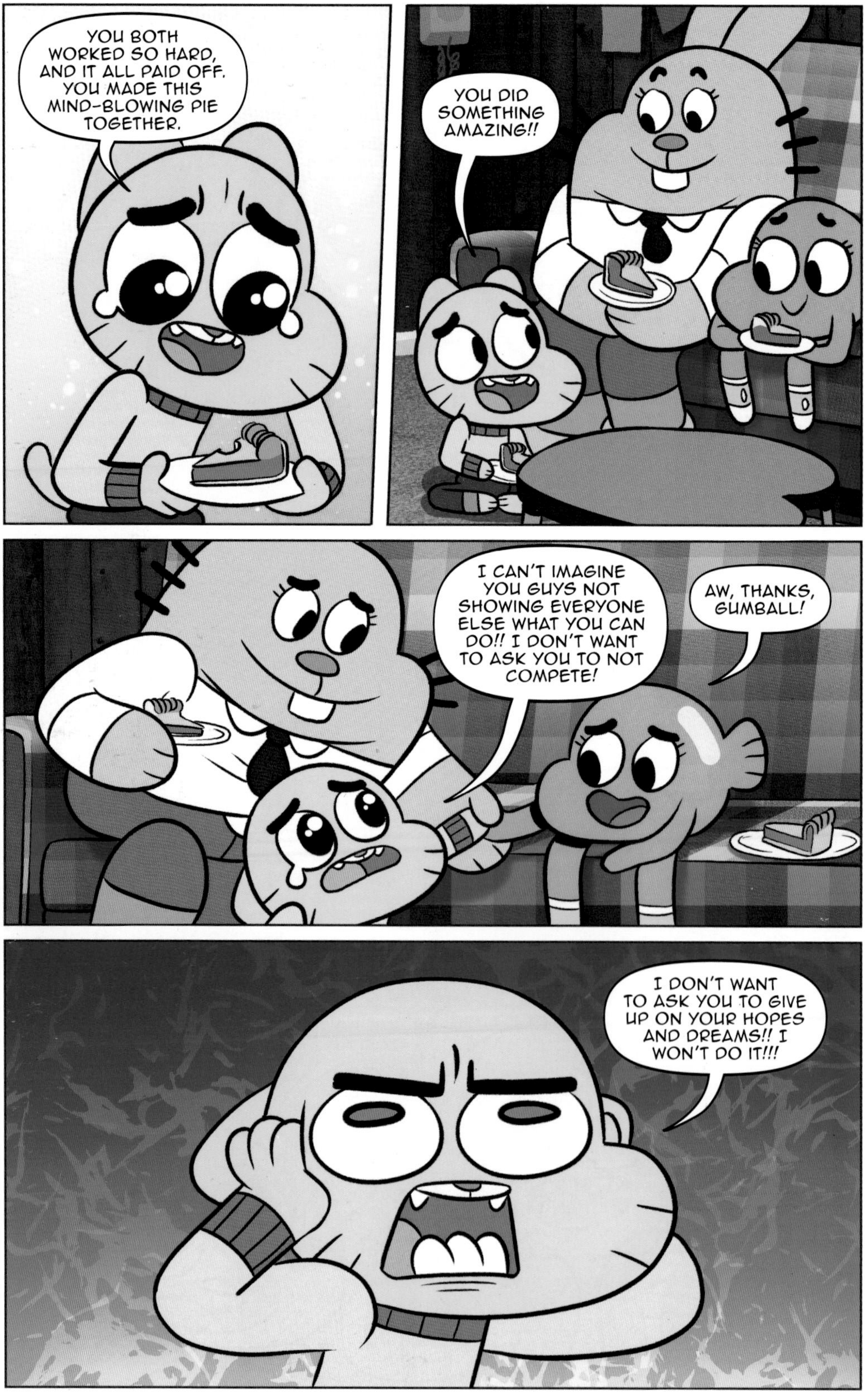
YOU BOTH WORKED SO HARD, AND IT ALL PAID OFF. YOU MADE THIS MIND-BLOWING PIE TOGETHER.
YOU DID SOMETHING AMAZING!!
I CAN'T IMAGINE YOU GUYS NOT SHOWING EVERYONE ELSE WHAT YOU CAN DO!! I DON'T WANT TO ASK YOU TO NOT COMPETE!
AW, THANKS, GUMBALL!
I DON'T WANT TO ASK YOU TO GIVE UP ON YOUR HOPES AND DREAMS!! I WON'T DO IT!!!

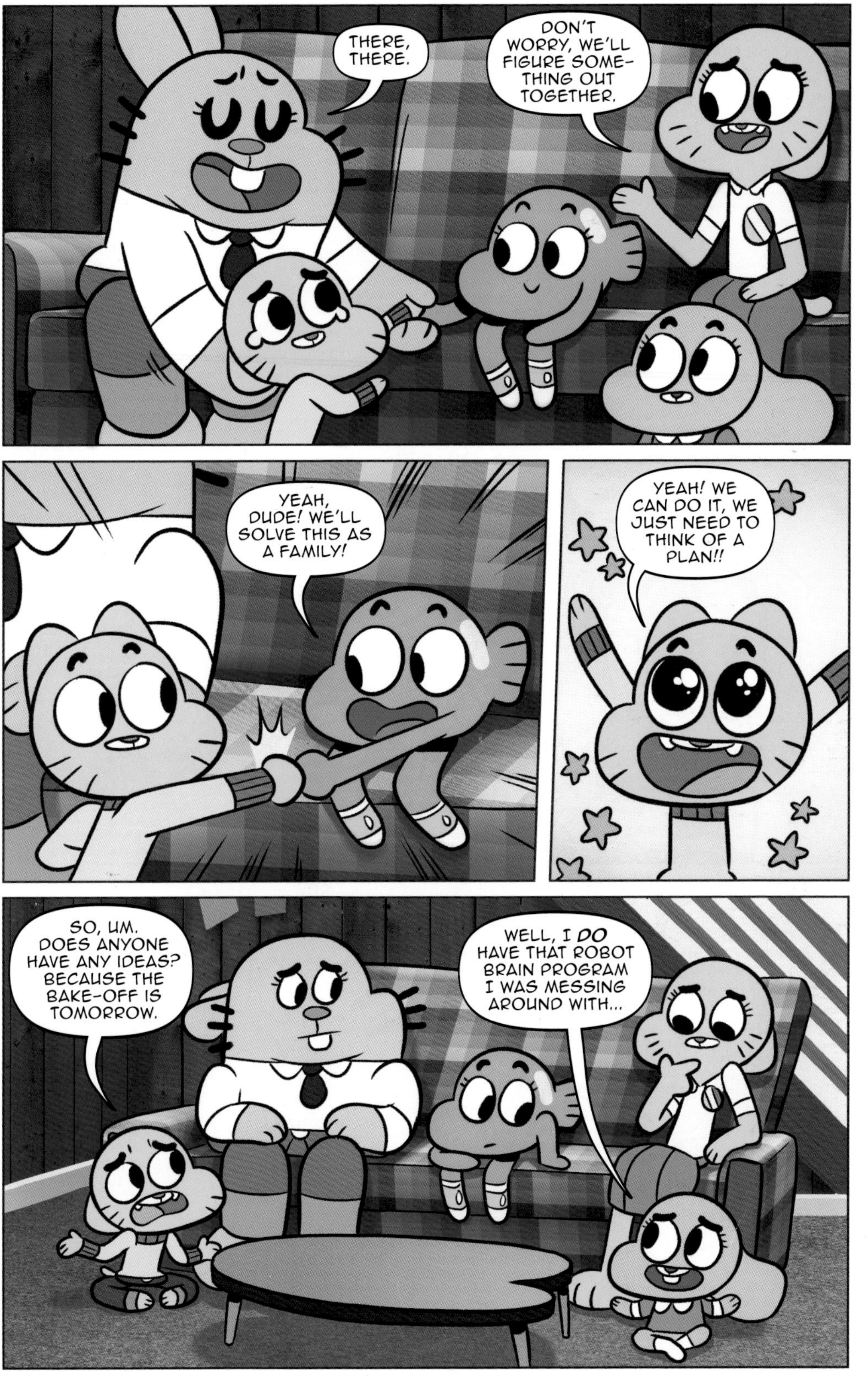
THERE, THERE.
DON'T WORRY, WE'LL FIGURE SOME-THING OUT TOGETHER.
YEAH, DUDE! WE'LL SOLVE THIS AS A FAMILY!
YEAH! WE CAN DO IT, WE JUST NEED TO THINK OF A PLAN!!
SO, UM. DOES ANYONE HAVE ANY IDEAS? BECAUSE THE BAKE-OFF IS TOMORROW.
WELL, I DO HAVE THAT ROBOT BRAIN PROGRAM I WAS MESSING AROUND WITH...

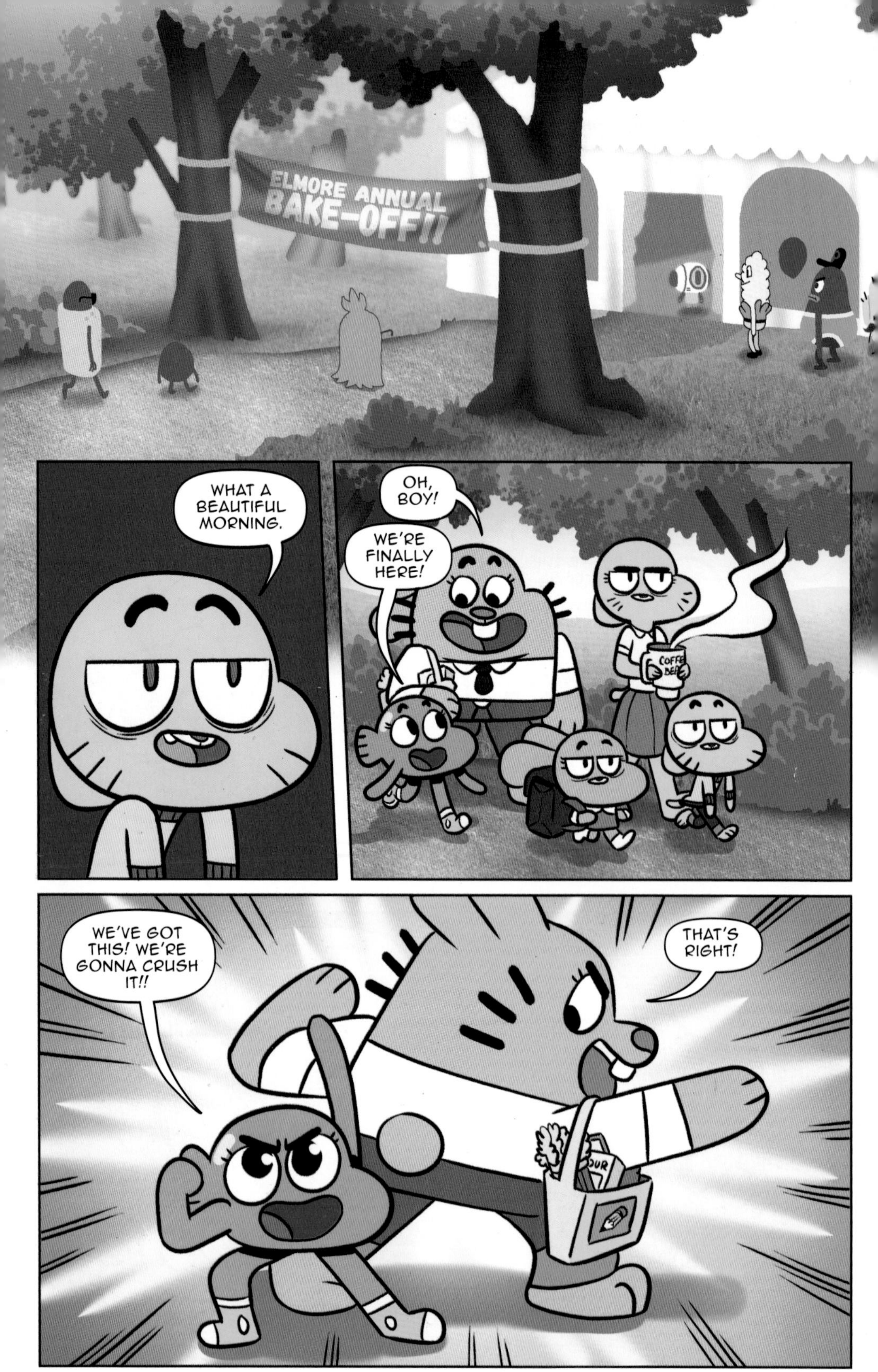
ELMORE ANNUAL BAKE-OFF!!
WHAT A BEAUTIFUL MORNING.
OH, BOY!
WE'RE FINALLY HERE!
COFFEE BEA
WE'VE GOT THIS! WE'RE GONNA CRUSH IT!!
THAT'S RIGHT!

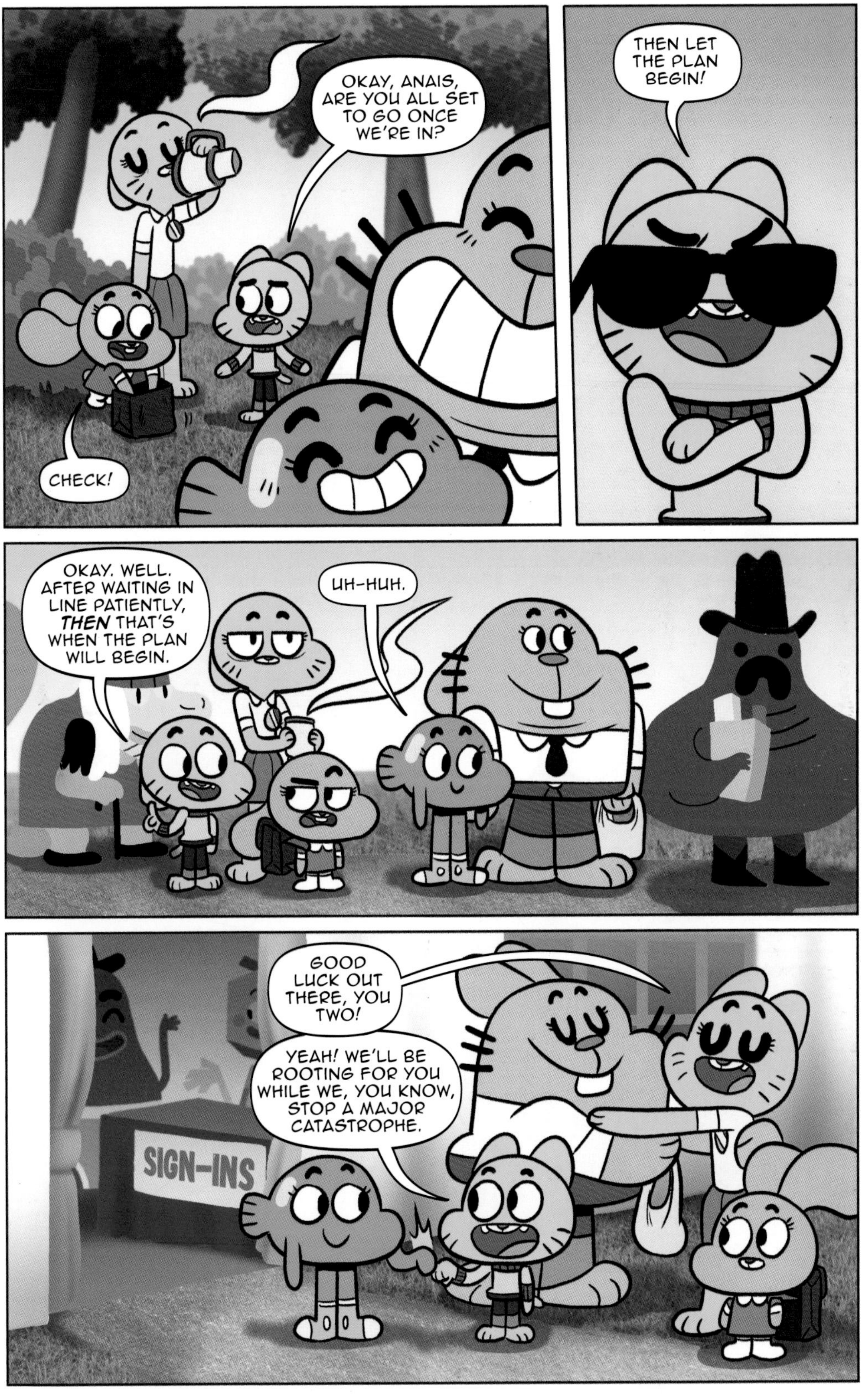
OKAY, ANAIS, ARE YOU ALL SET TO GO ONCE WE'RE IN?
CHECK!
THEN LET THE PLAN BEGIN!
OKAY. WELL. AFTER WAITING IN LINE PATIENTLY, *THEN* THAT'S WHEN THE PLAN WILL BEGIN.
UH-HUH.
GOOD LUCK OUT THERE, YOU TWO!
YEAH! WE'LL BE ROOTING FOR YOU WHILE WE, YOU KNOW, STOP A MAJOR CATASTROPHE.
SIGN-INS

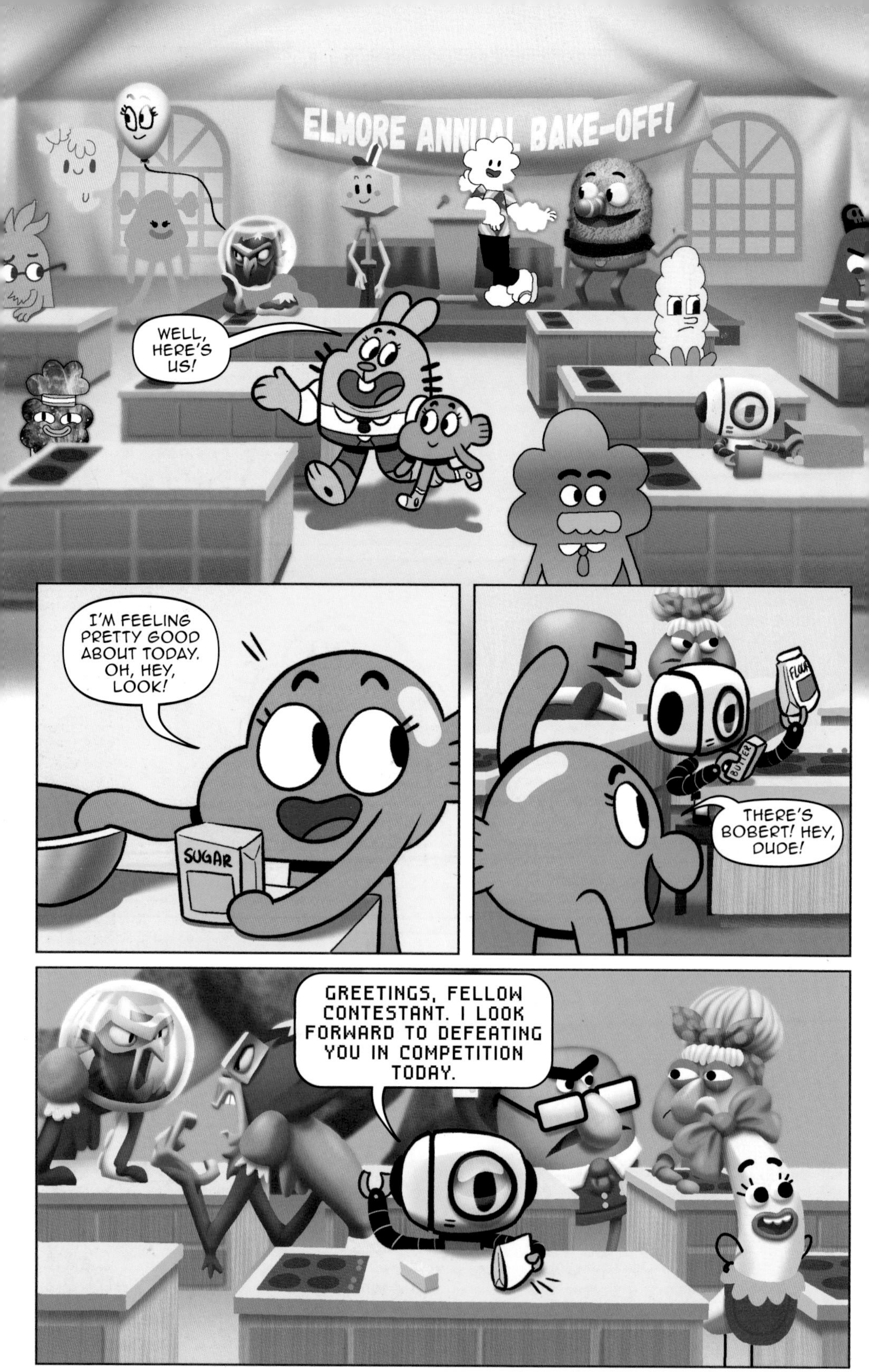

ELMORE ANNUAL BAKE-OFF!
WELL, HERE'S US!
I'M FEELING PRETTY GOOD ABOUT TODAY. OH, HEY, LOOK!
SUGAR
FLOUR
BUTTER
THERE'S BOBERT! HEY, DUDE!
GREETINGS, FELLOW CONTESTANT. I LOOK FORWARD TO DEFEATING YOU IN COMPETITION TODAY.

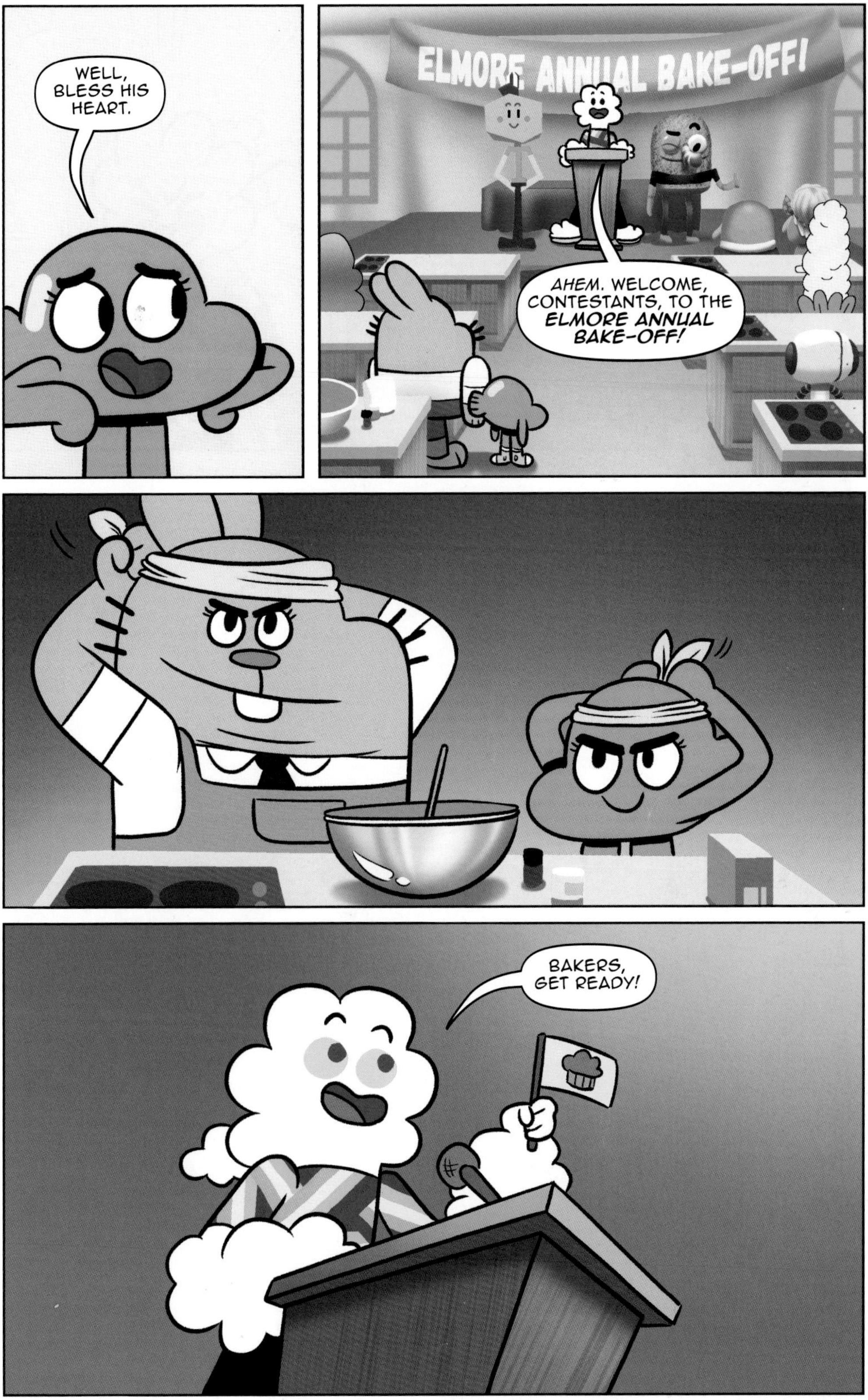
WELL, BLESS HIS HEART.
ELMORE ANNUAL BAKE-OFF!
AHEM. WELCOME, CONTESTANTS, TO THE ELMORE ANNUAL BAKE-OFF!
BAKERS, GET READY!

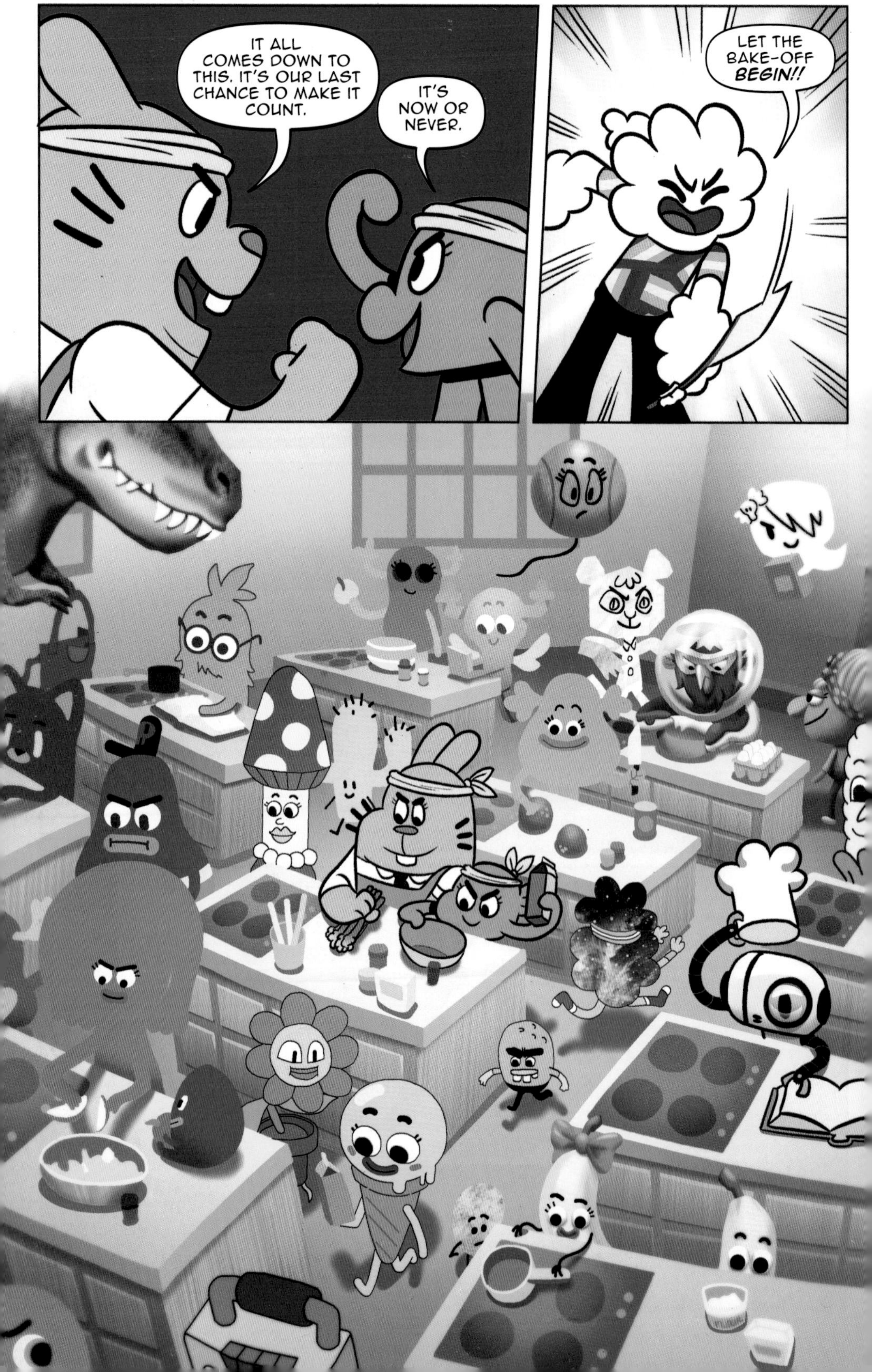
IT ALL COMES DOWN TO THIS. IT'S OUR LAST CHANCE TO MAKE IT COUNT.
IT'S NOW OR NEVER.
LET THE BAKE-OFF BEGIN!!

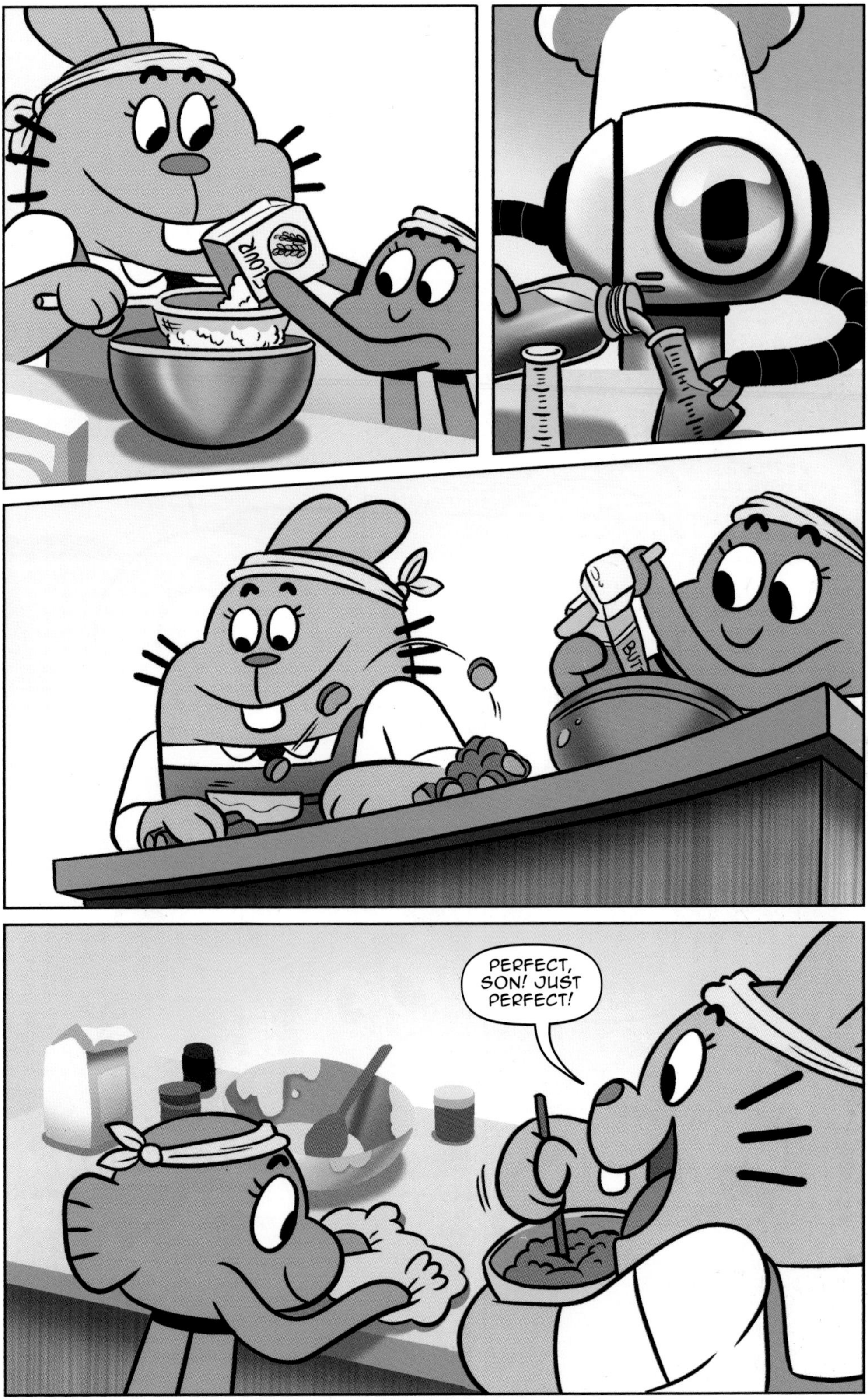
FLOUR
PERFECT, SON! JUST PERFECT!

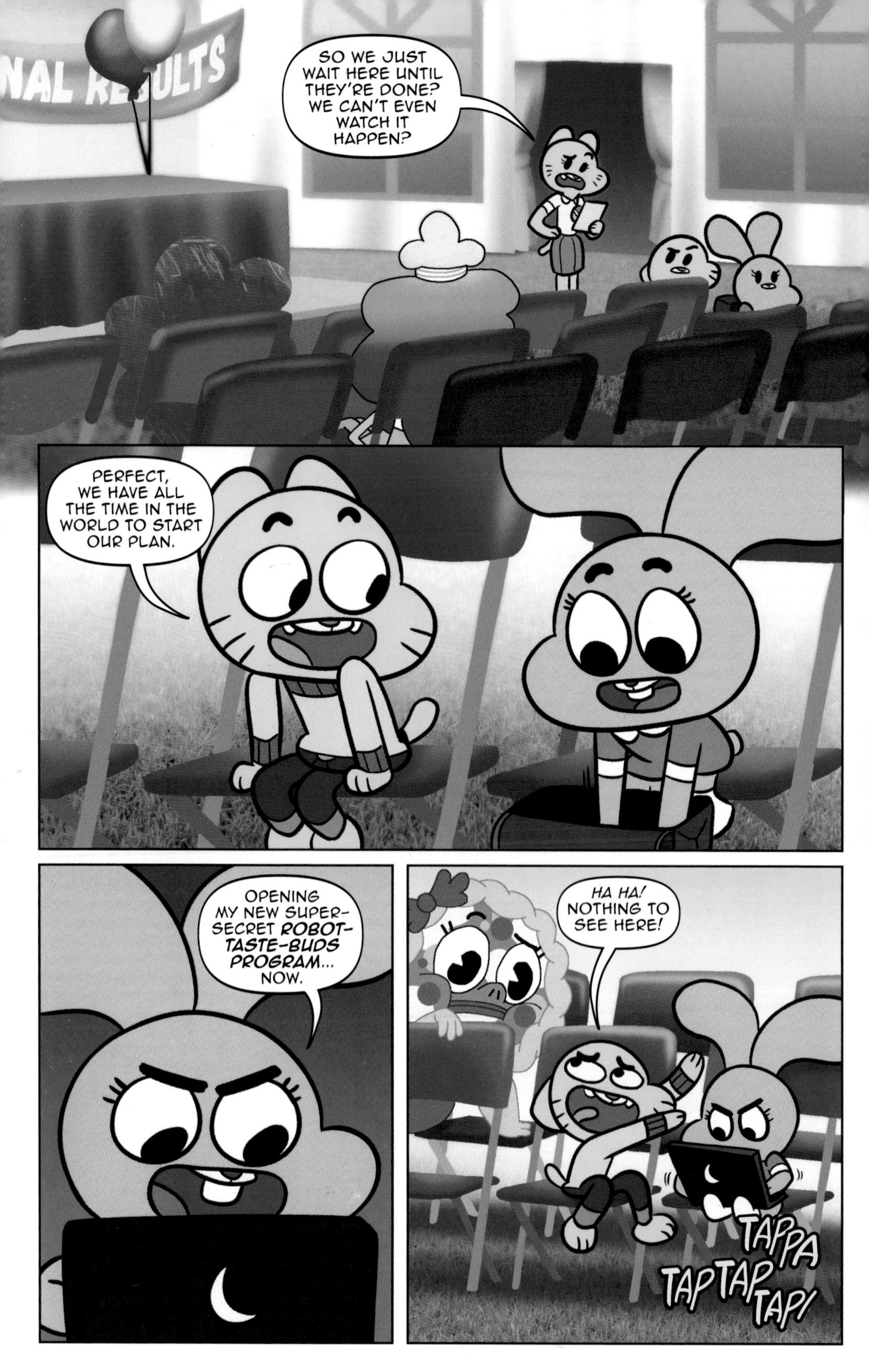
NAL RESULTS
SO WE JUST WAIT HERE UNTIL THEY'RE DONE? WE CAN'T EVEN WATCH IT HAPPEN?
PERFECT, WE HAVE ALL THE TIME IN THE WORLD TO START OUR PLAN.
OPENING MY NEW SUPER-SECRET *ROBOT-TASTE-BUDS PROGRAM*... NOW.
HA HA! NOTHING TO SEE HERE!
TAPPA TAPTAPTAP!

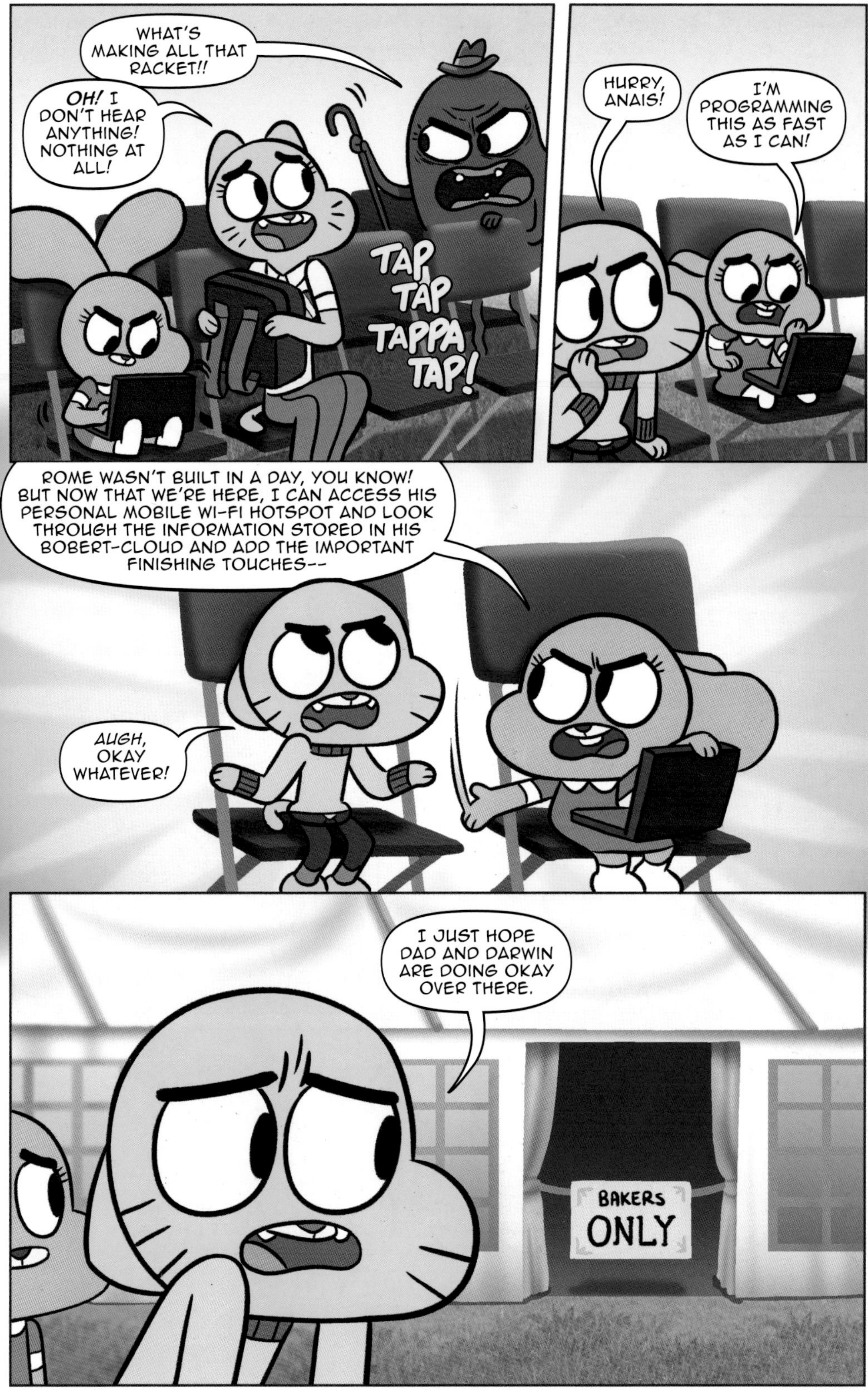
WHAT'S MAKING ALL THAT RACKET!!
OH! I DON'T HEAR ANYTHING! NOTHING AT ALL!
TAP TAP TAPPA TAP!
HURRY, ANAIS!
I'M PROGRAMMING THIS AS FAST AS I CAN!
ROME WASN'T BUILT IN A DAY, YOU KNOW! BUT NOW THAT WE'RE HERE, I CAN ACCESS HIS PERSONAL MOBILE WI-FI HOTSPOT AND LOOK THROUGH THE INFORMATION STORED IN HIS BOBERT-CLOUD AND ADD THE IMPORTANT FINISHING TOUCHES--
AUGH, OKAY WHATEVER!
I JUST HOPE DAD AND DARWIN ARE DOING OKAY OVER THERE.
BAKERS ONLY

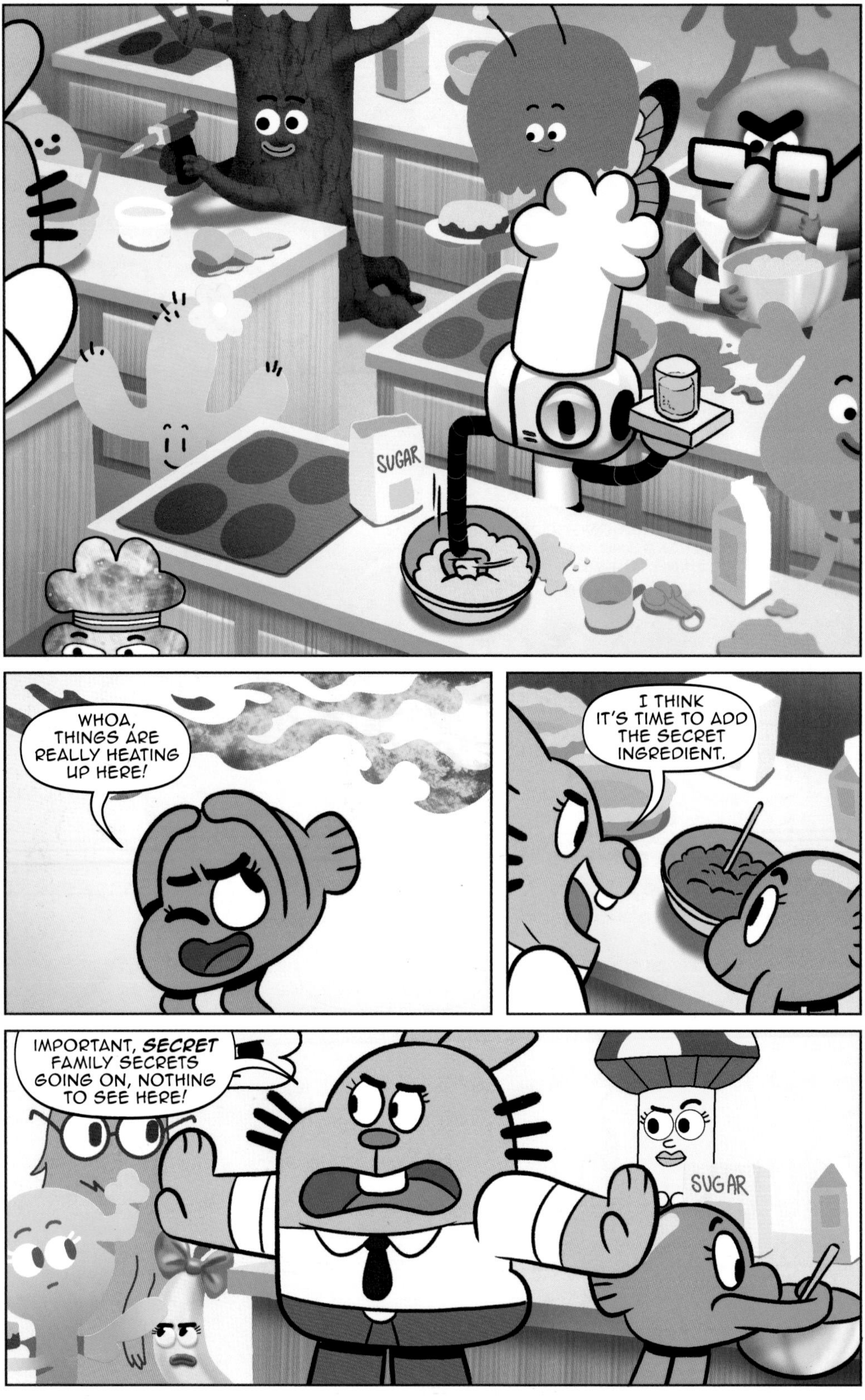
SUGAR
WHOA, THINGS ARE REALLY HEATING UP HERE!
I THINK IT'S TIME TO ADD THE SECRET INGREDIENT.
IMPORTANT, SECRET FAMILY SECRETS GOING ON, NOTHING TO SEE HERE!
SUGAR

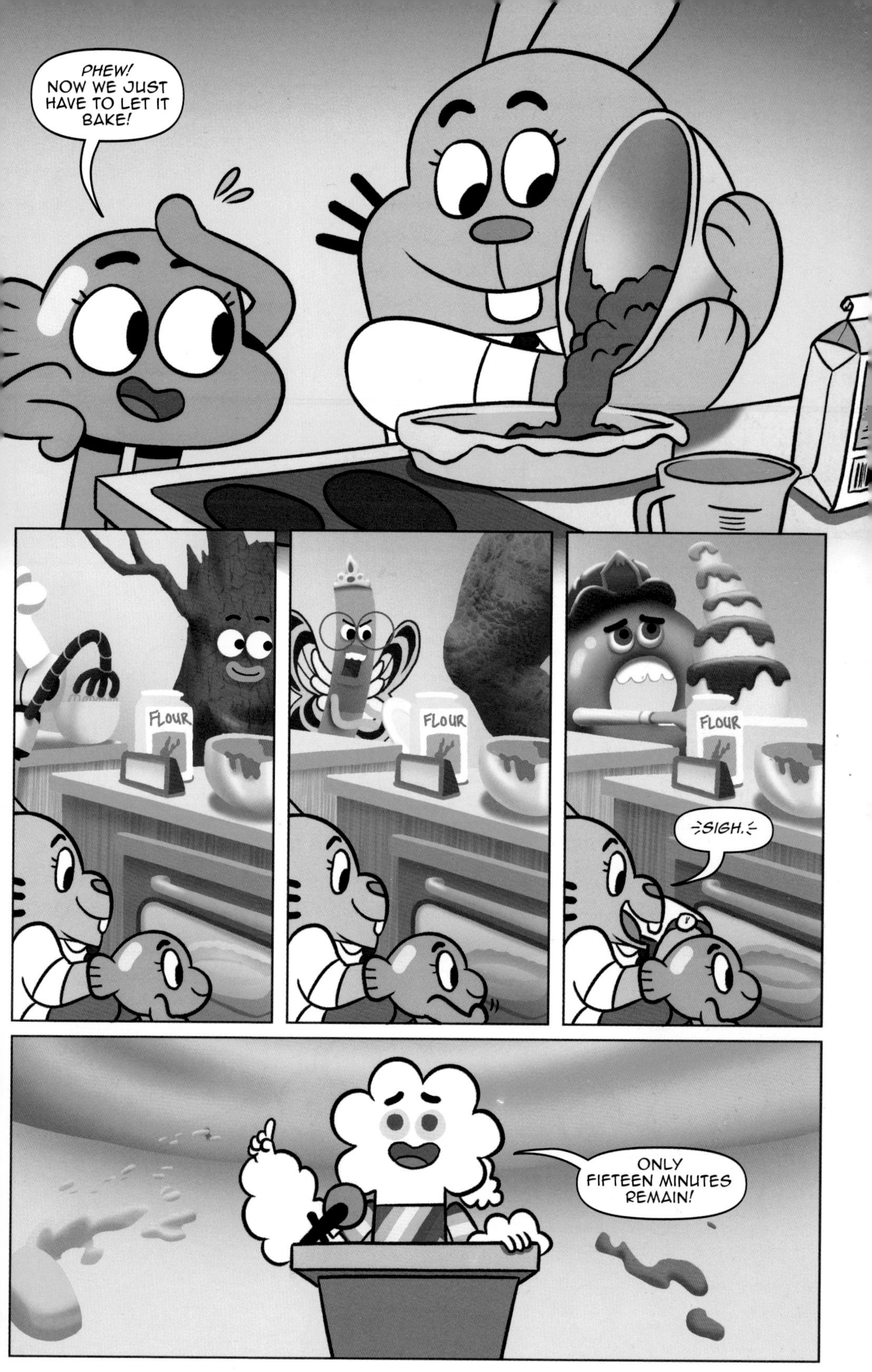
PHEW!
NOW WE JUST HAVE TO LET IT BAKE!
FLOUR
FLOUR
FLOUR
SIGH.
ONLY FIFTEEN MINUTES REMAIN!

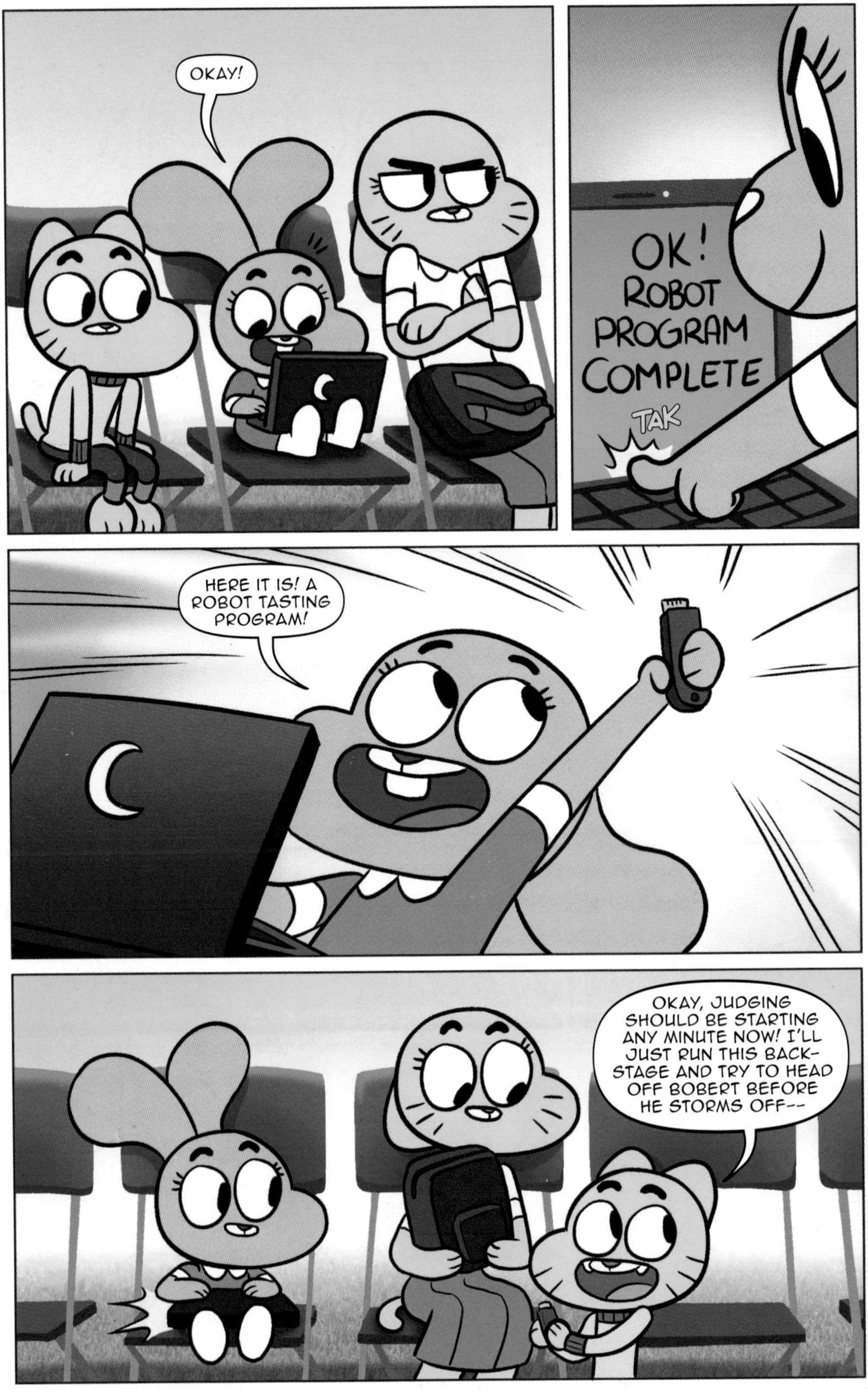
OKAY!
OK! ROBOT PROGRAM COMPLETE
TAK
HERE IT IS! A ROBOT TASTING PROGRAM!
OKAY, JUDGING SHOULD BE STARTING ANY MINUTE NOW! I'LL JUST RUN THIS BACK-STAGE AND TRY TO HEAD OFF BOBERT BEFORE HE STORMS OFF--

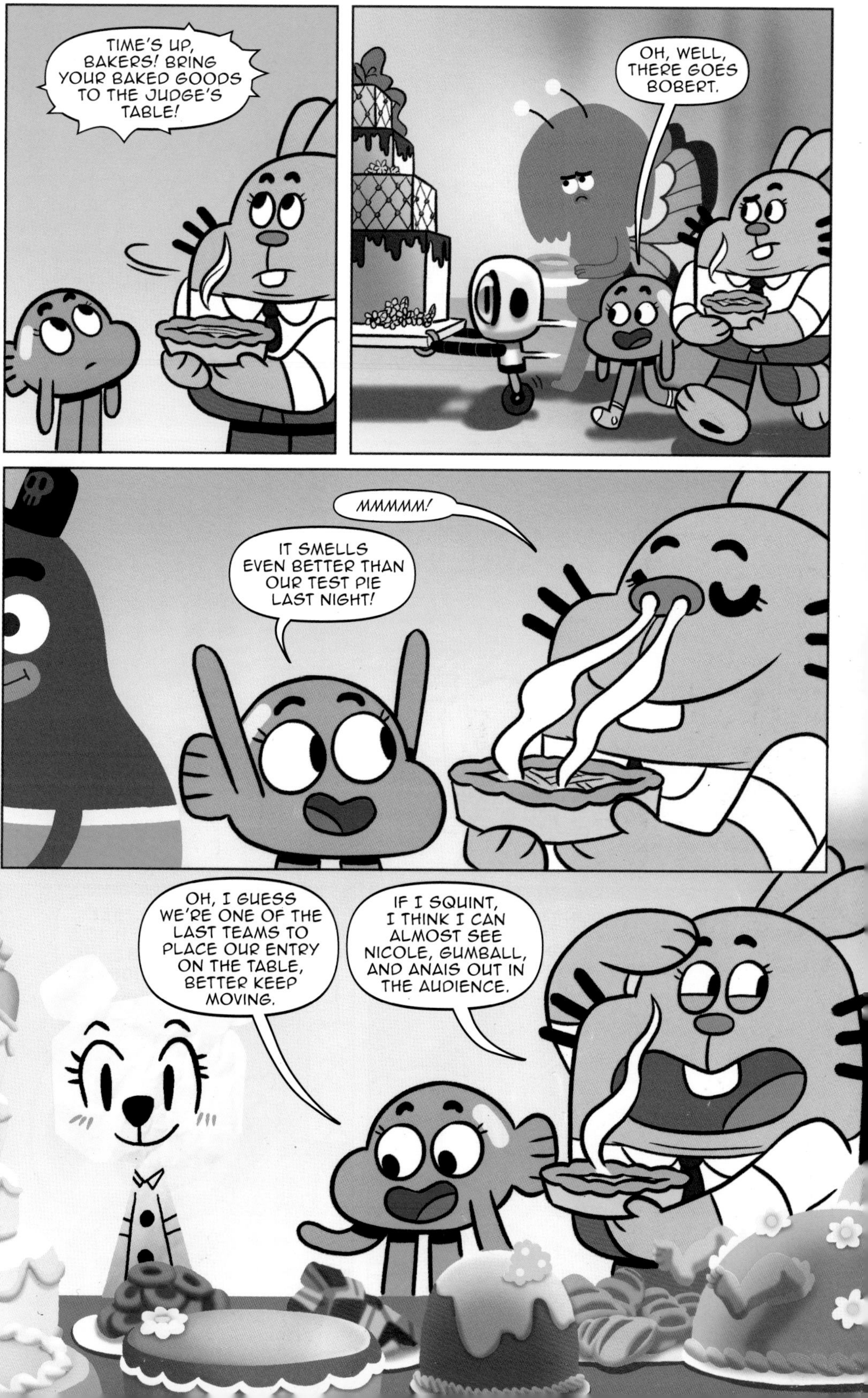
TIME'S UP, BAKERS! BRING YOUR BAKED GOODS TO THE JUDGE'S TABLE!
OH, WELL, THERE GOES BOBERT.
MMMMM!
IT SMELLS EVEN BETTER THAN OUR TEST PIE LAST NIGHT!
OH, I GUESS WE'RE ONE OF THE LAST TEAMS TO PLACE OUR ENTRY ON THE TABLE, BETTER KEEP MOVING.
IF I SQUINT, I THINK I CAN ALMOST SEE NICOLE, GUMBALL, AND ANAIS OUT IN THE AUDIENCE.

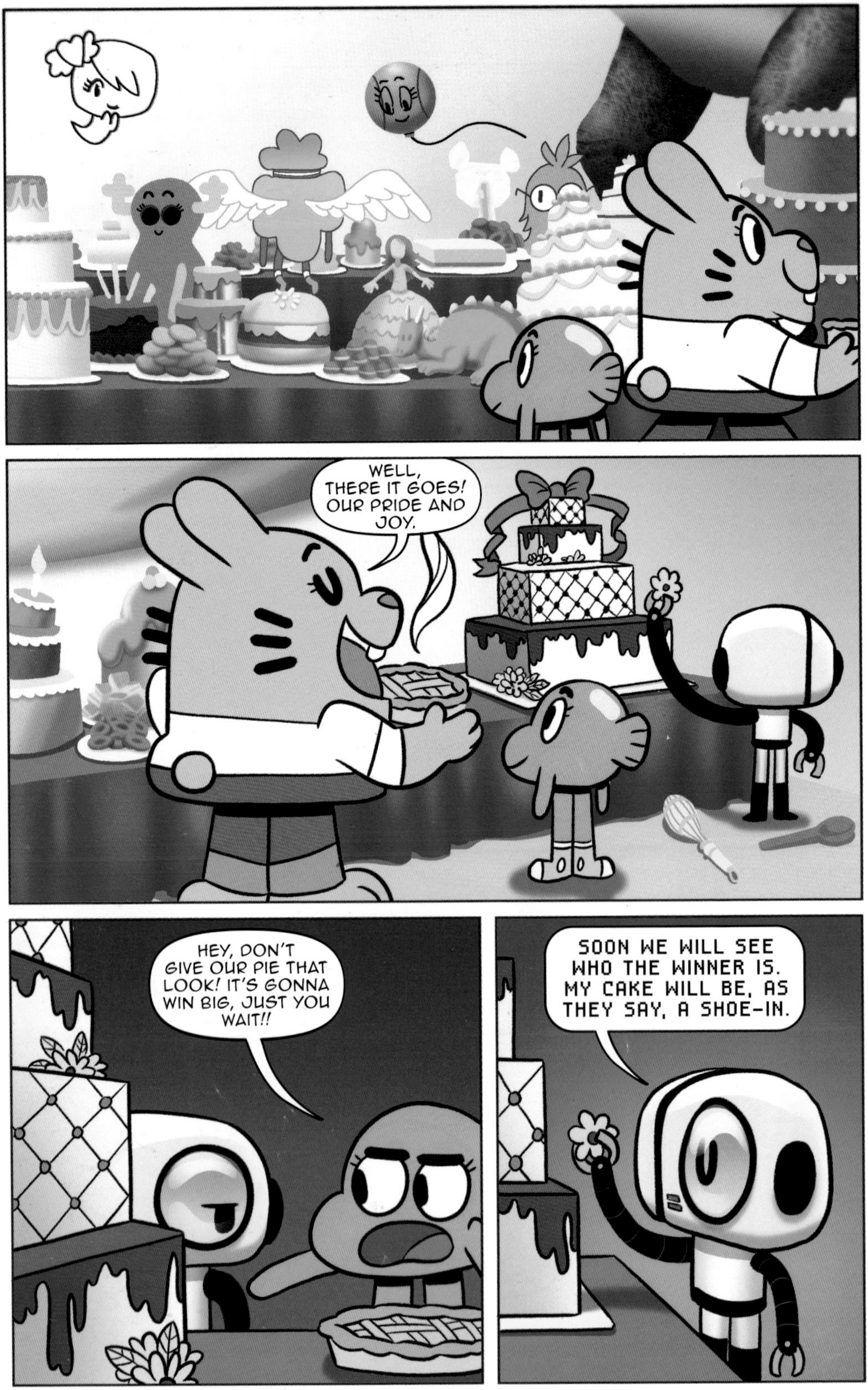
WELL, THERE IT GOES! OUR PRIDE AND JOY.
HEY, DON'T GIVE OUR PIE THAT LOOK! IT'S GONNA WIN BIG, JUST YOU WAIT!!
SOON WE WILL SEE WHO THE WINNER IS. MY CAKE WILL BE, AS THEY SAY, A SHOE-IN.

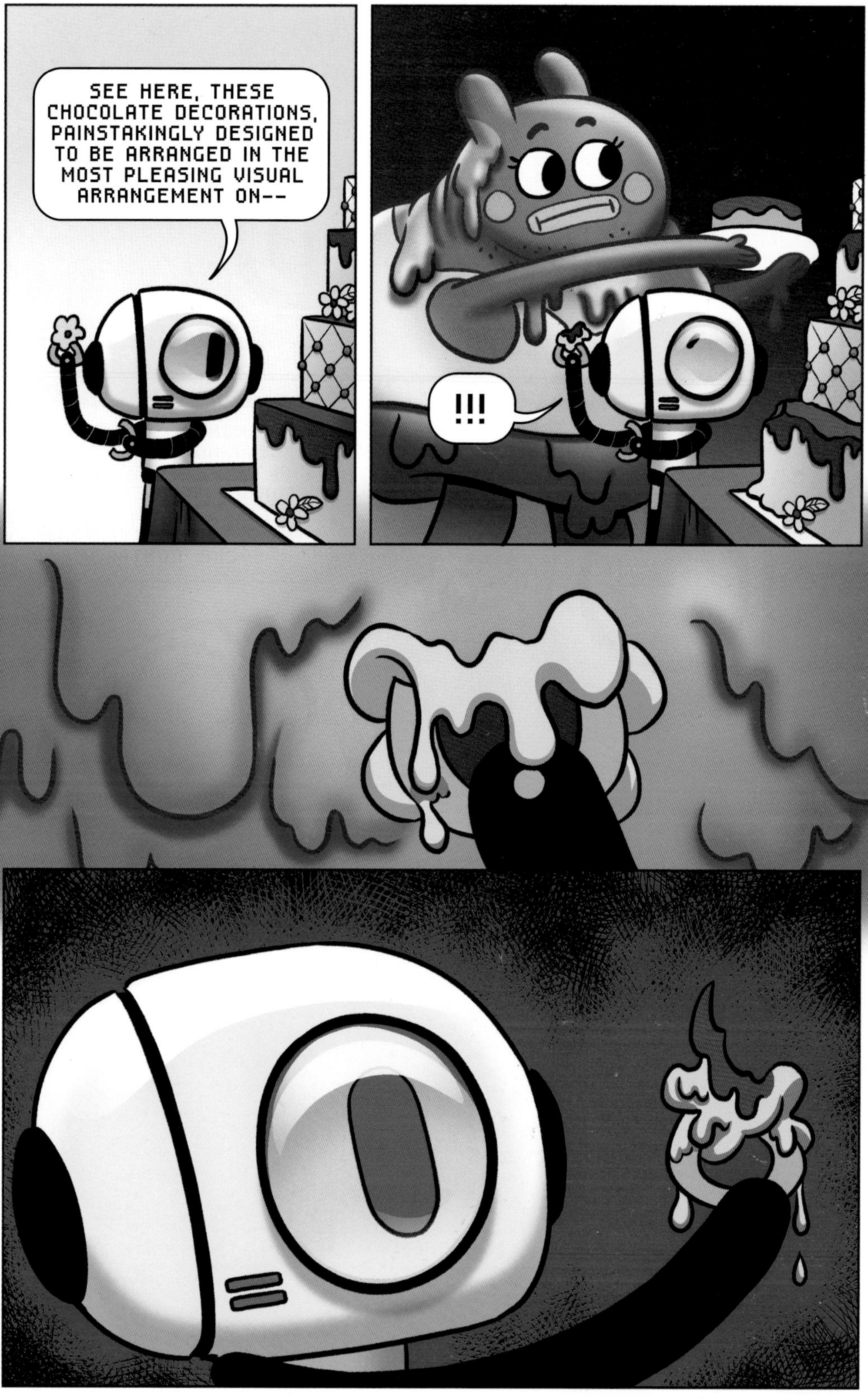
SEE HERE, THESE CHOCOLATE DECORATIONS, PAINSTAKINGLY DESIGNED TO BE ARRANGED IN THE MOST PLEASING VISUAL ARRANGEMENT ON--
!!!

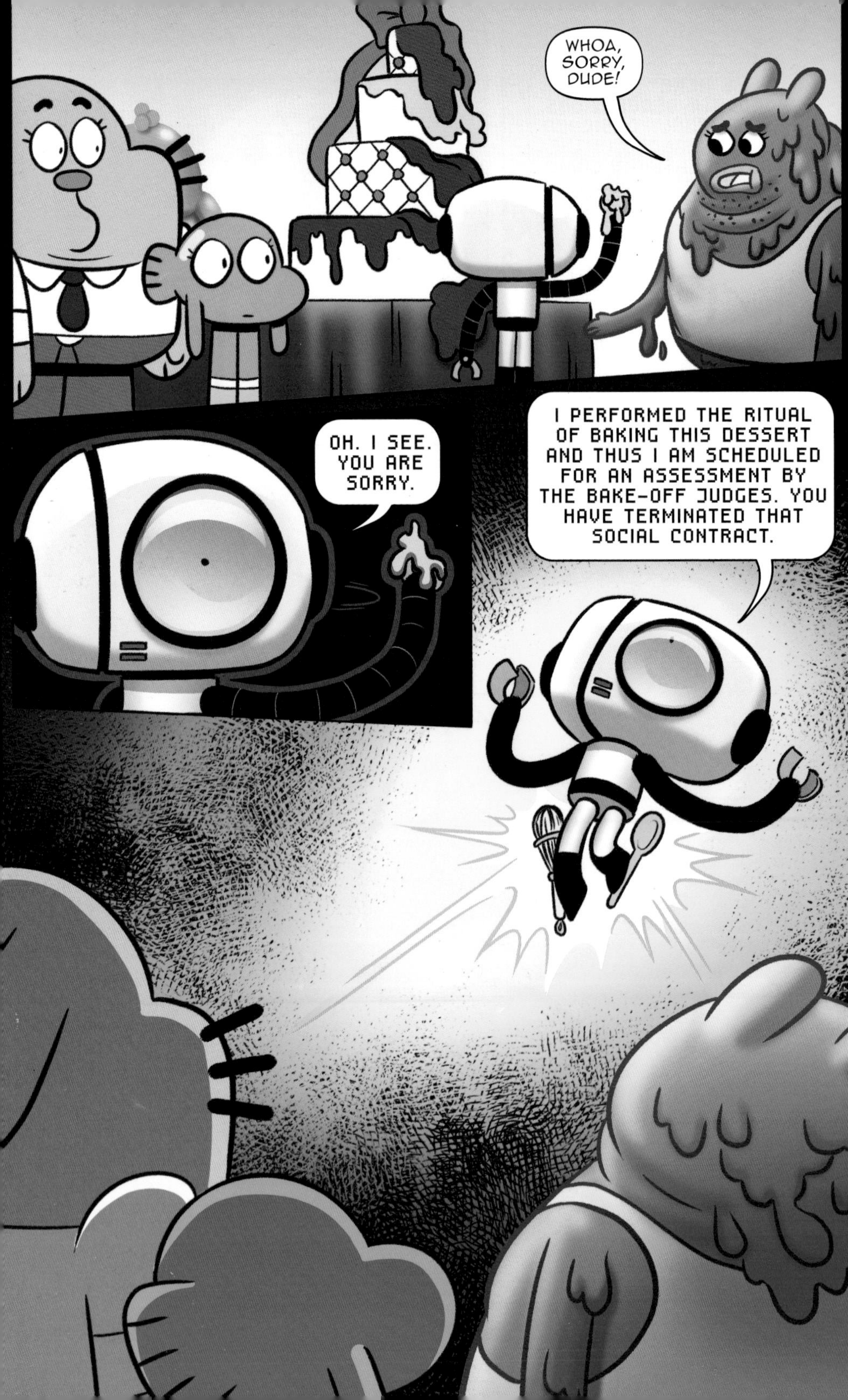
WHOA, SORRY, DUDE!
OH. I SEE. YOU ARE SORRY.
I PERFORMED THE RITUAL OF BAKING THIS DESSERT AND THUS I AM SCHEDULED FOR AN ASSESSMENT BY THE BAKE-OFF JUDGES. YOU HAVE TERMINATED THAT SOCIAL CONTRACT.

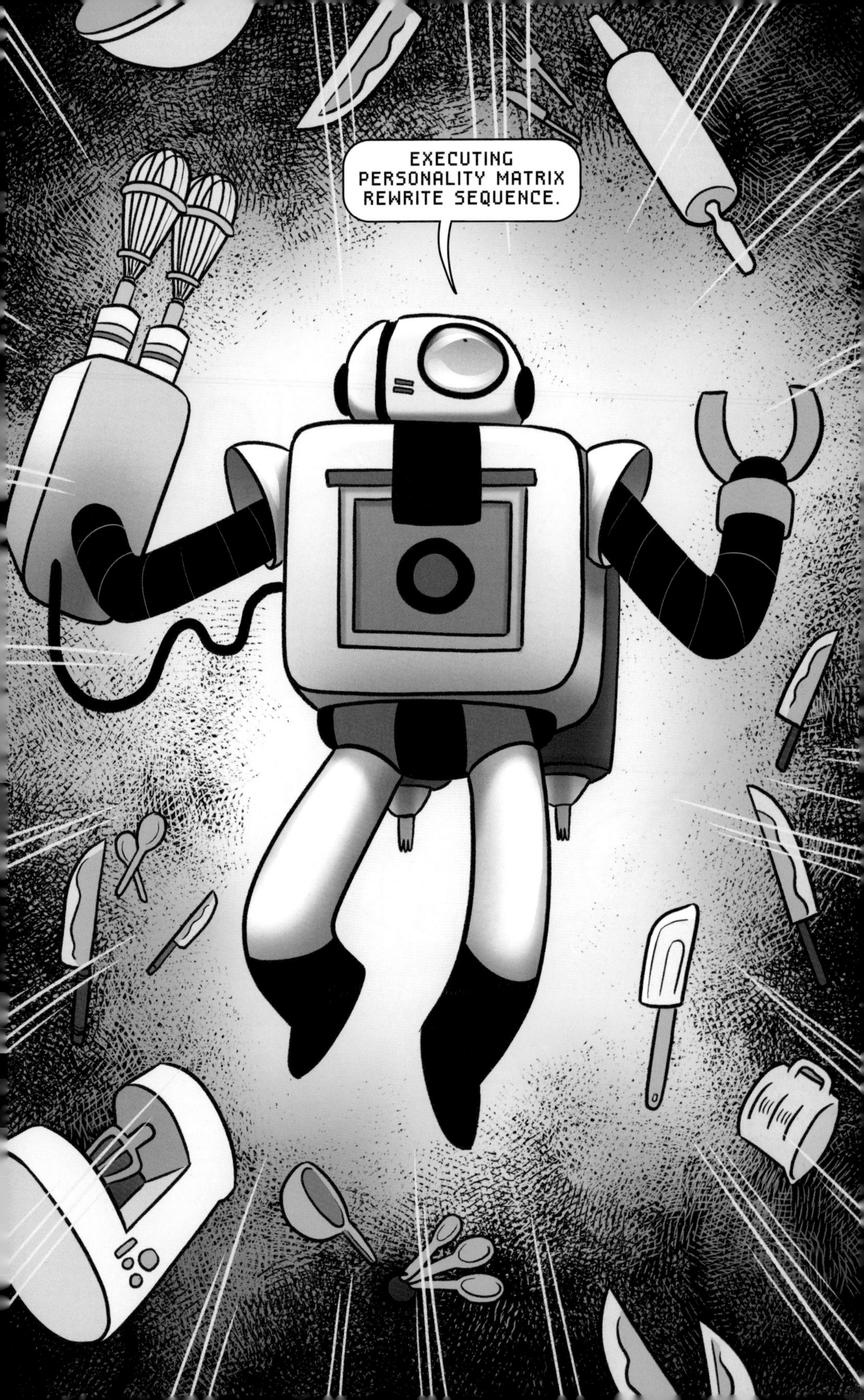
EXECUTING PERSONALITY MATRIX REWRITE SEQUENCE.

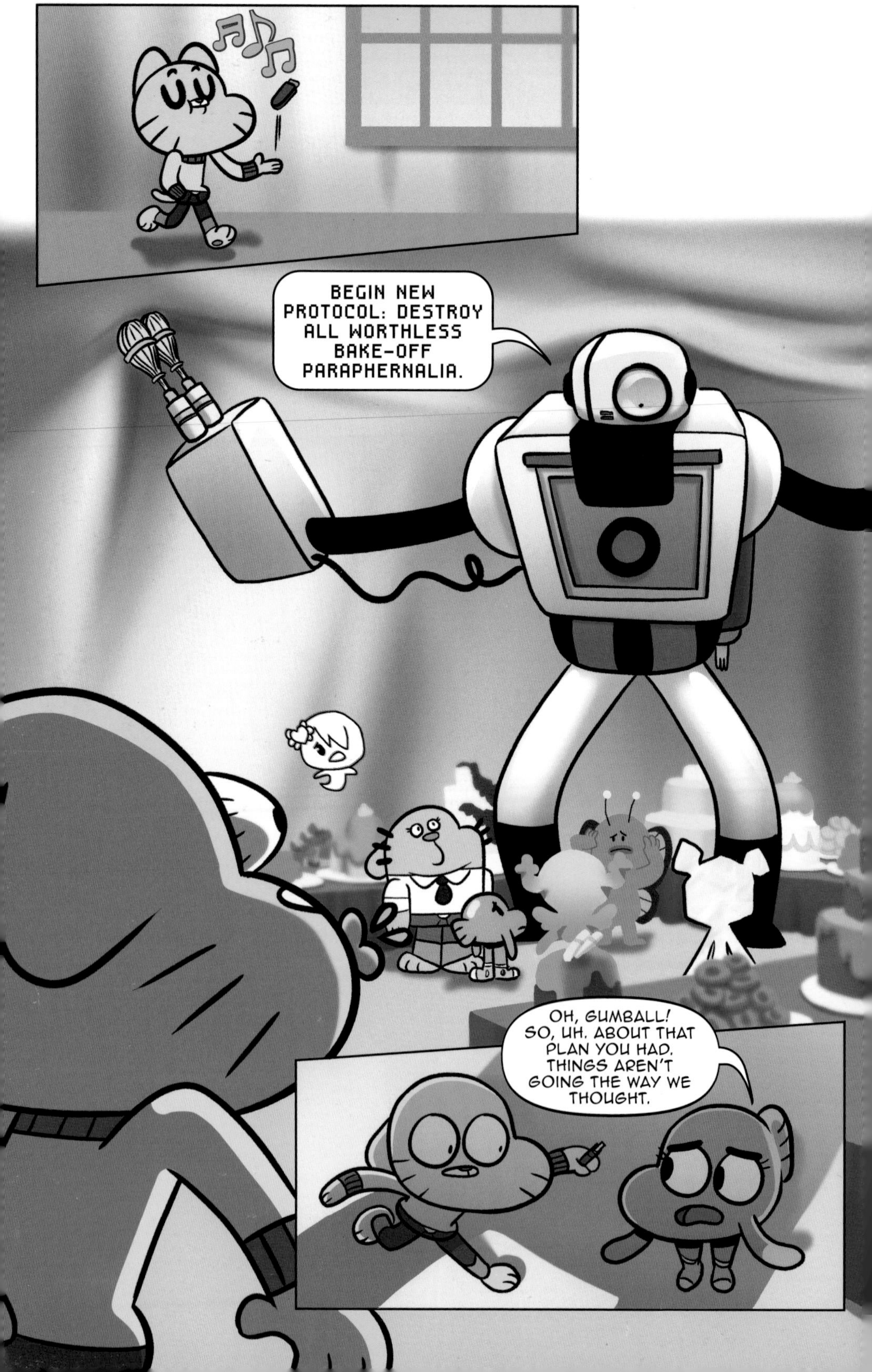
BEGIN NEW PROTOCOL: DESTROY ALL WORTHLESS BAKE-OFF PARAPHERNALIA.
OH, GUMBALL! SO, UH. ABOUT THAT PLAN YOU HAD. THINGS AREN'T GOING THE WAY WE THOUGHT.

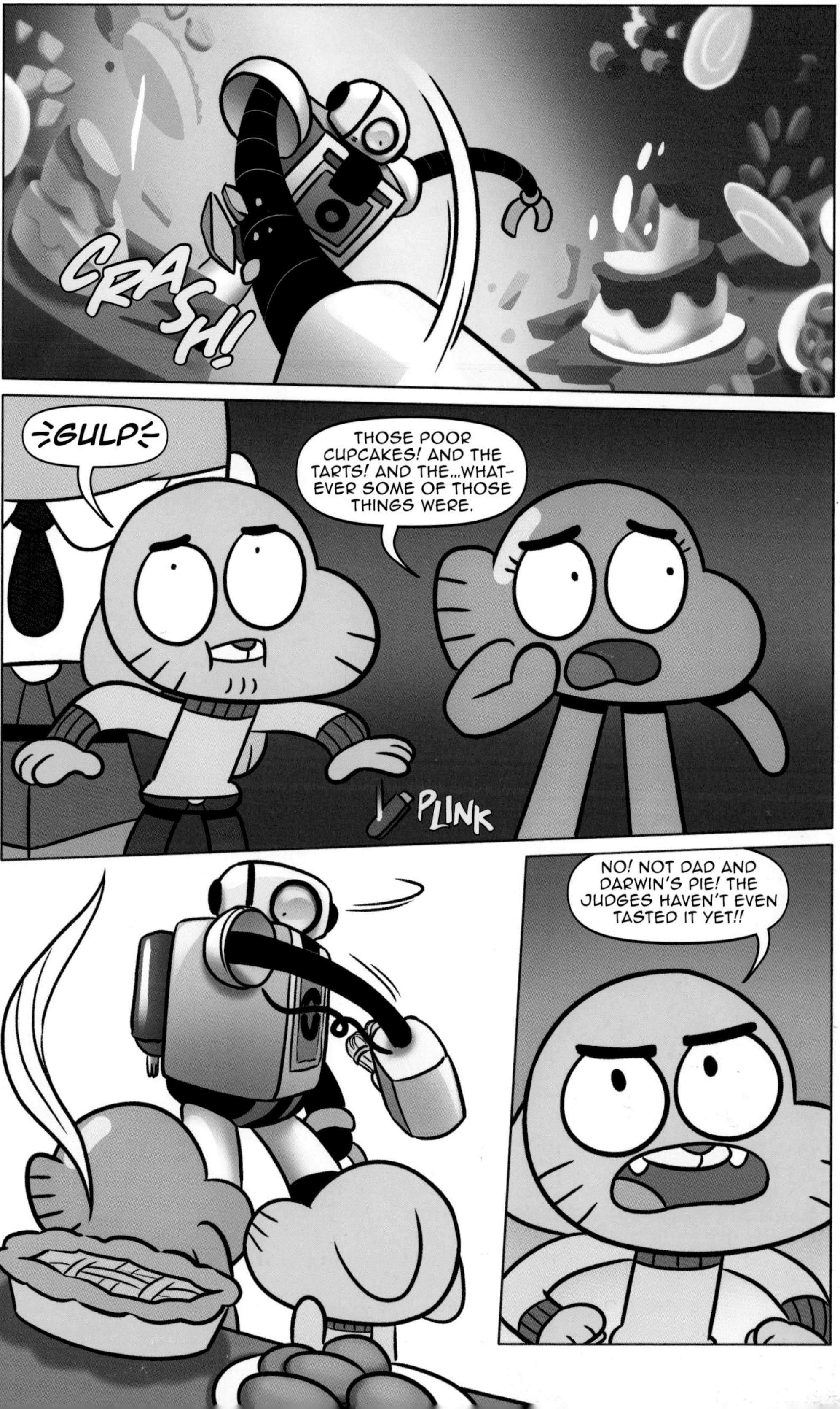
CRASH!
GULP
THOSE POOR CUPCAKES! AND THE TARTS! AND THE...WHAT-EVER SOME OF THOSE THINGS WERE.
PLINK
NO! NOT DAD AND DARWIN'S PIE! THE JUDGES HAVEN'T EVEN TASTED IT YET!!

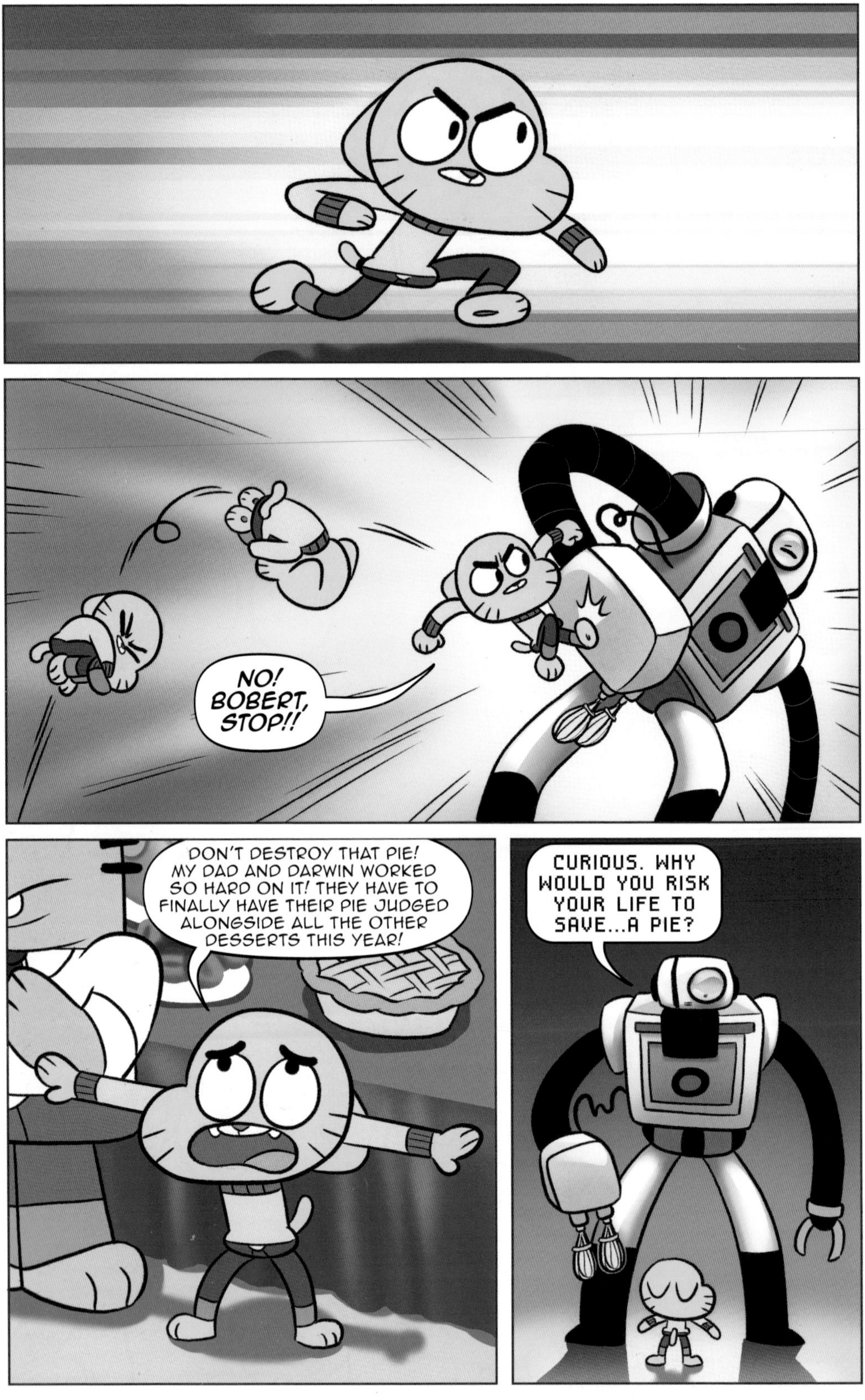
NO! BOBERT, STOP!!
DON'T DESTROY THAT PIE! MY DAD AND DARWIN WORKED SO HARD ON IT! THEY HAVE TO FINALLY HAVE THEIR PIE JUDGED ALONGSIDE ALL THE OTHER DESSERTS THIS YEAR!
CURIOUS. WHY WOULD YOU RISK YOUR LIFE TO SAVE...A PIE?

THIS BAKE-OFF IS POINTLESS! WHY DOES ANYONE COMPETE?!

WHY IS EVERYONE SO OBSESSED WITH COLLECTIONS OF SUGARS AND CARBOHYDRATES?!

DAD AND DARWIN MADE THIS PIE BECAUSE IT'S DELICIOUS, AND BECAUSE IT'S SOMETHING OUR FAMILY HAS MADE FOR GENERATIONS! WHEN THEY MADE THIS PIE TOGETHER, THEY MADE A MEMORY TOGETHER, AND ALSO MADE SOMETHING THEY CAN SHARE WITH OTHER PEOPLE.

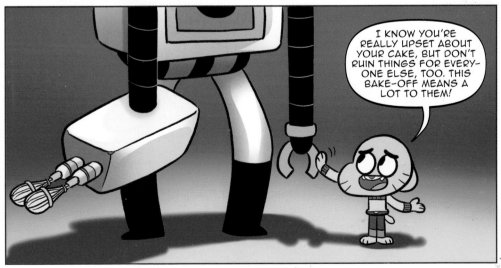

I KNOW YOU'RE REALLY UPSET ABOUT YOUR CAKE, BUT DON'T RUIN THINGS FOR EVERYONE ELSE, TOO. THIS BAKE-OFF MEANS A LOT TO THEM!

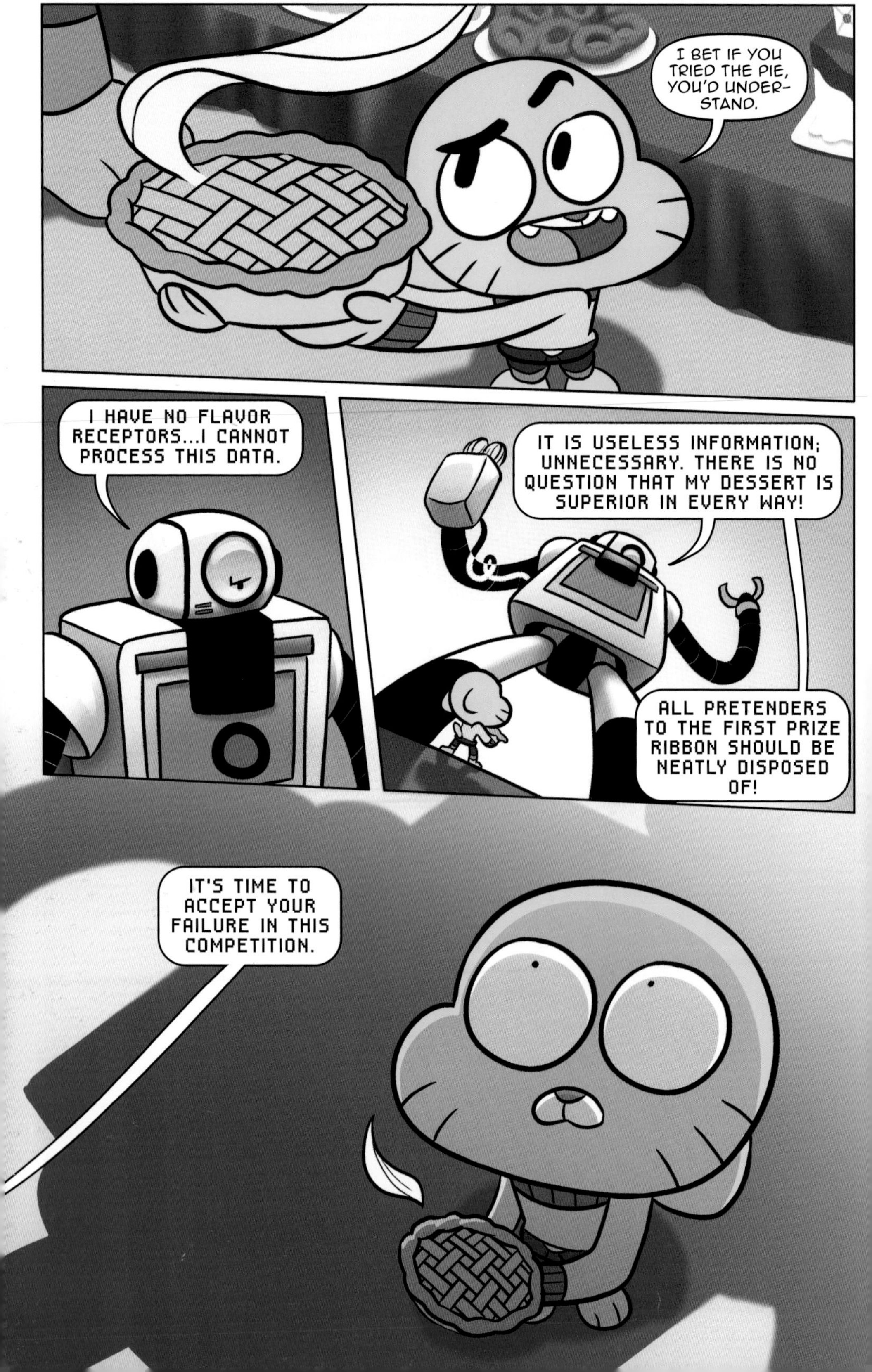
I BET IF YOU TRIED THE PIE, YOU'D UNDER-STAND.
I HAVE NO FLAVOR RECEPTORS...I CANNOT PROCESS THIS DATA.
IT IS USELESS INFORMATION; UNNECESSARY. THERE IS NO QUESTION THAT MY DESSERT IS SUPERIOR IN EVERY WAY!
ALL PRETENDERS TO THE FIRST PRIZE RIBBON SHOULD BE NEATLY DISPOSED OF!
IT'S TIME TO ACCEPT YOUR FAILURE IN THIS COMPETITION.

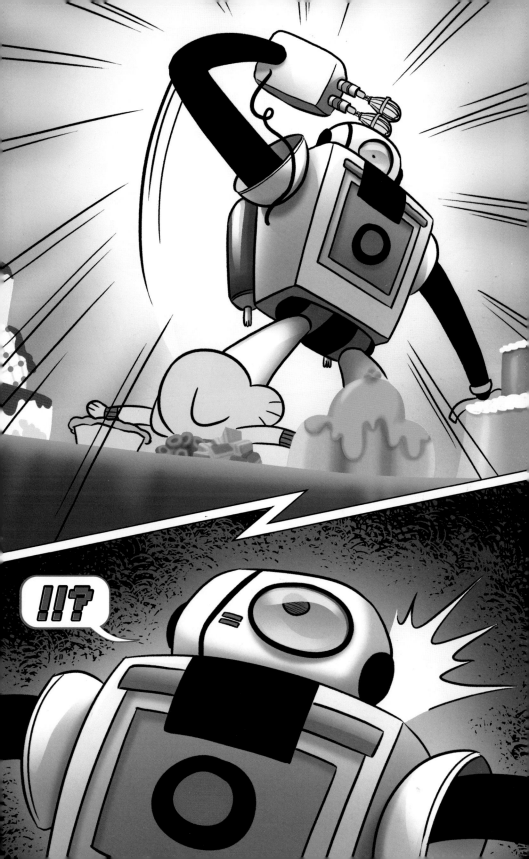

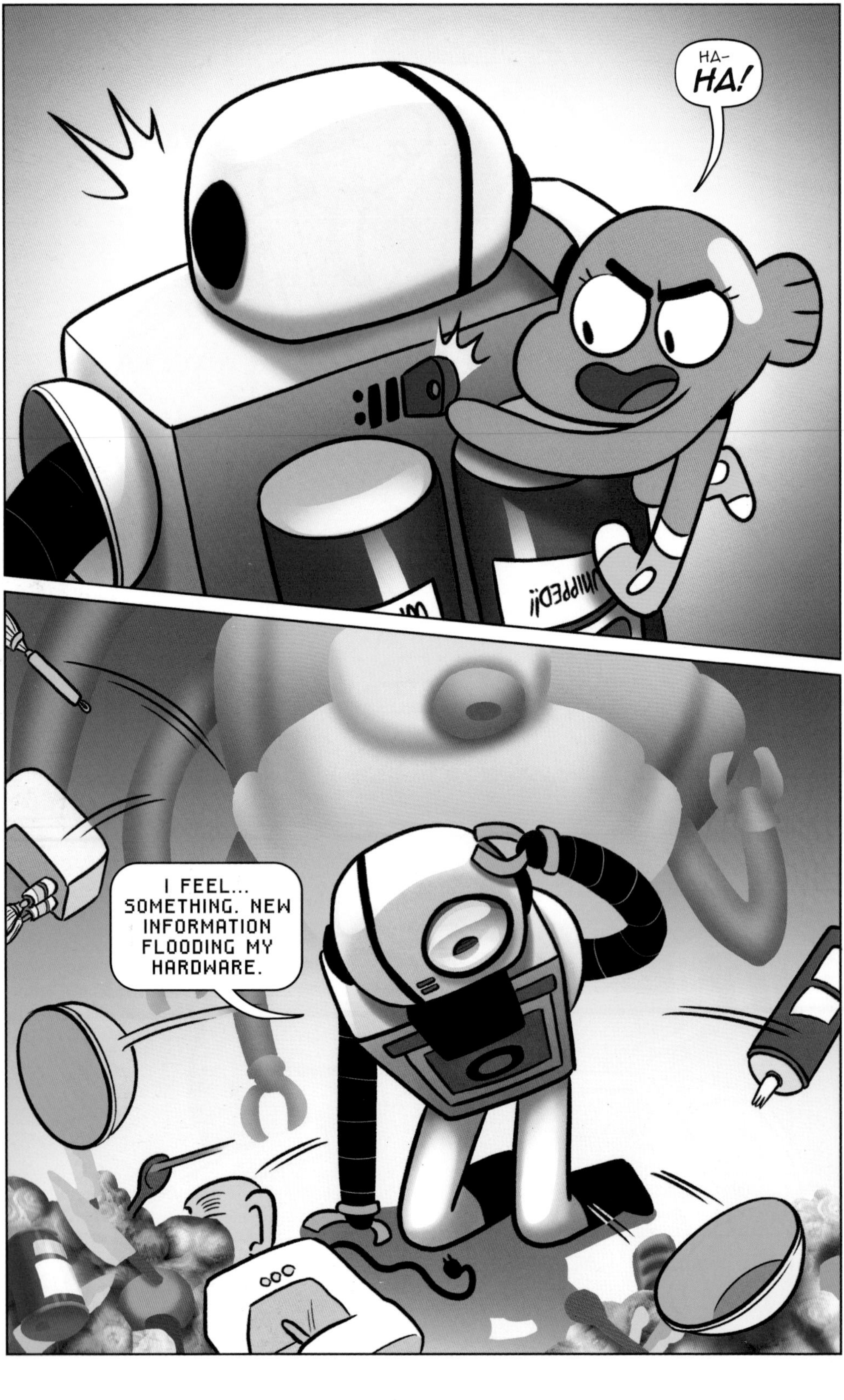
HA-HA!
I FEEL... SOMETHING. NEW INFORMATION FLOODING MY HARDWARE.

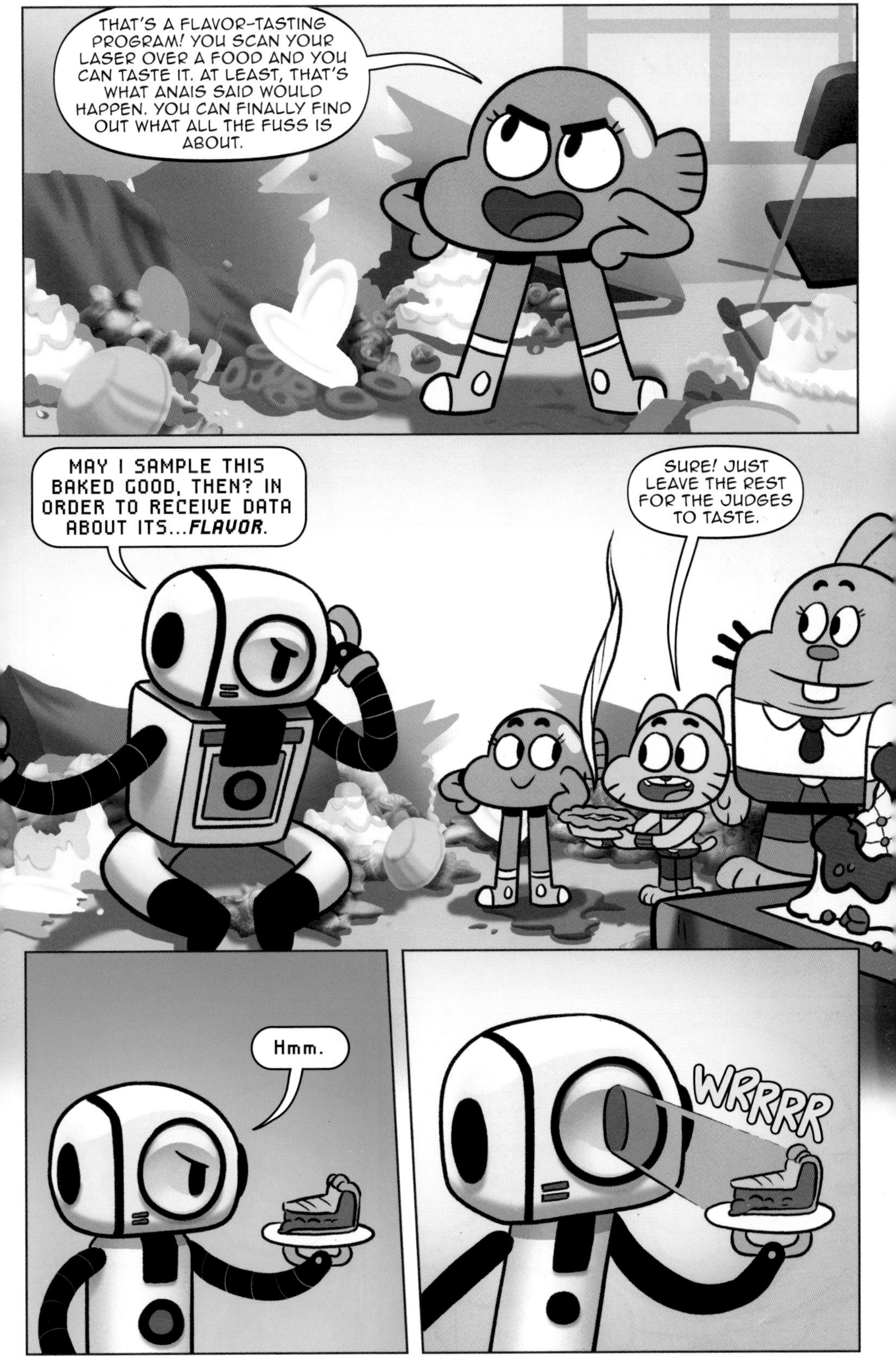
THAT'S A FLAVOR-TASTING PROGRAM! YOU SCAN YOUR LASER OVER A FOOD AND YOU CAN TASTE IT. AT LEAST, THAT'S WHAT ANAIS SAID WOULD HAPPEN. YOU CAN FINALLY FIND OUT WHAT ALL THE FUSS IS ABOUT.
MAY I SAMPLE THIS BAKED GOOD, THEN? IN ORDER TO RECEIVE DATA ABOUT ITS...FLAVOR.
SURE! JUST LEAVE THE REST FOR THE JUDGES TO TASTE.
Hmm.
WRRRR

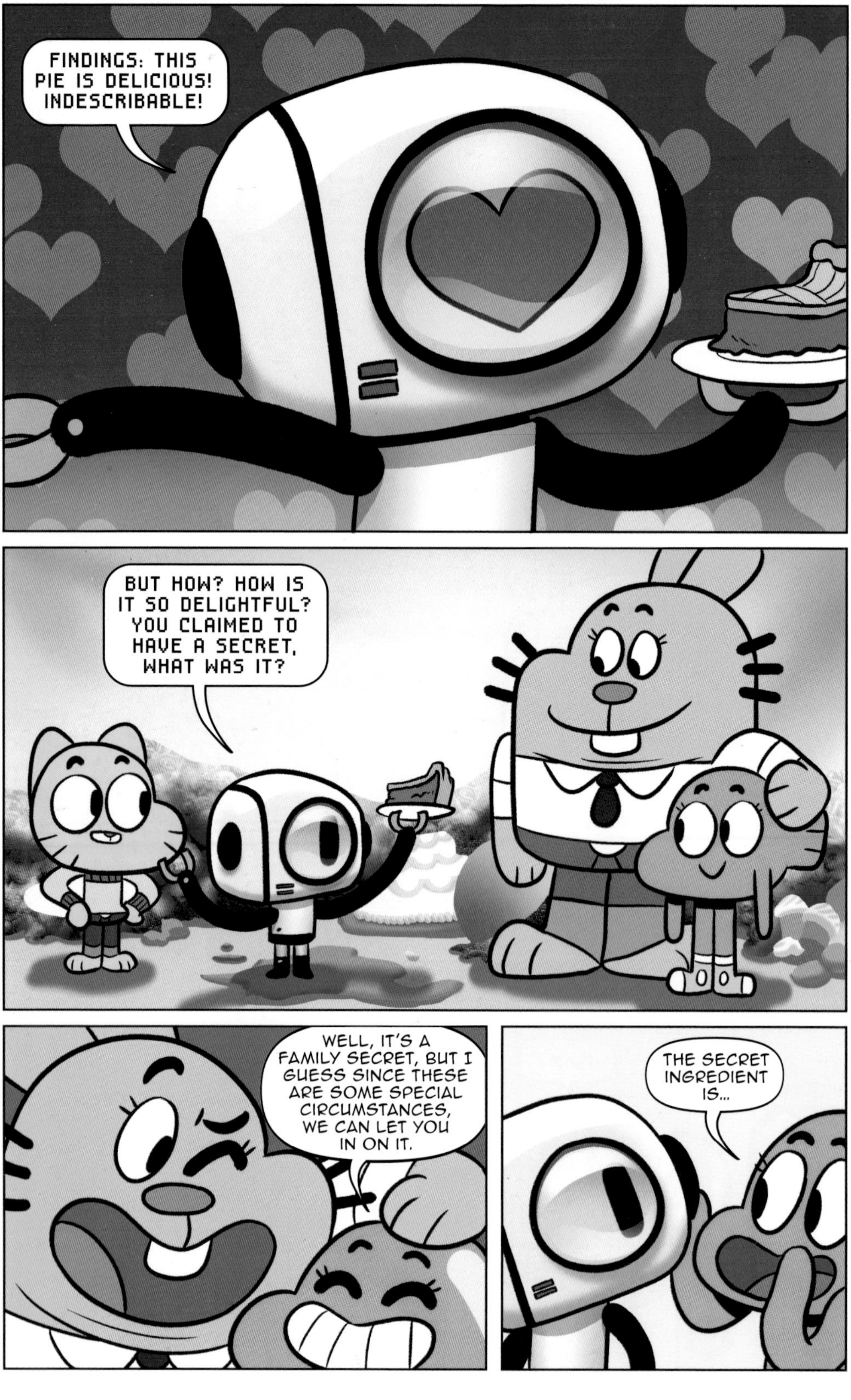
FINDINGS: THIS PIE IS DELICIOUS! INDESCRIBABLE!
BUT HOW? HOW IS IT SO DELIGHTFUL? YOU CLAIMED TO HAVE A SECRET, WHAT WAS IT?
WELL, IT'S A FAMILY SECRET, BUT I GUESS SINCE THESE ARE SOME SPECIAL CIRCUMSTANCES, WE CAN LET YOU IN ON IT.
THE SECRET INGREDIENT IS...

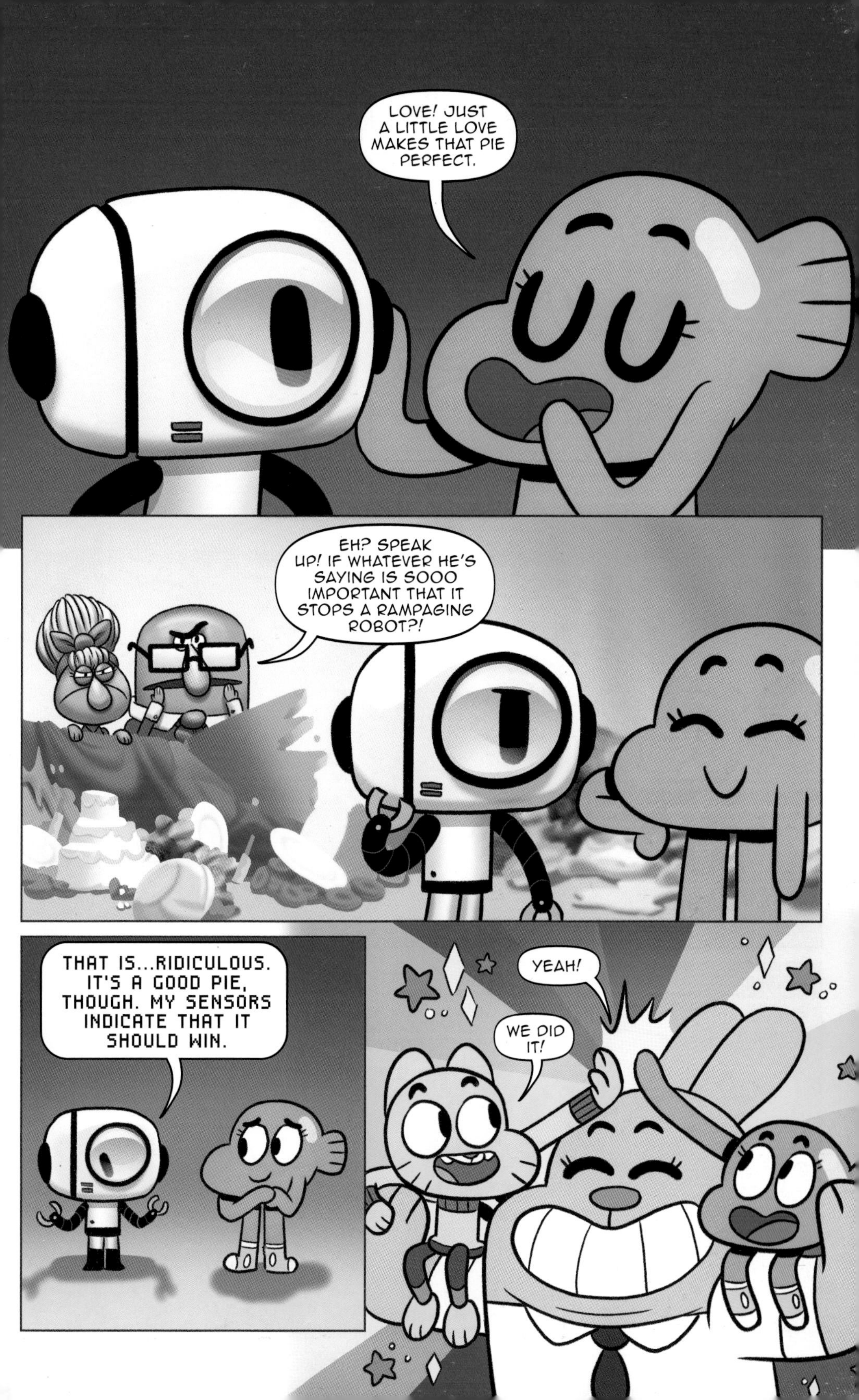
LOVE! JUST A LITTLE LOVE MAKES THAT PIE PERFECT.
EH? SPEAK UP! IF WHATEVER HE'S SAYING IS SOOO IMPORTANT THAT IT STOPS A RAMPAGING ROBOT?!
THAT IS...RIDICULOUS. IT'S A GOOD PIE, THOUGH. MY SENSORS INDICATE THAT IT SHOULD WIN.
YEAH!
WE DID IT!

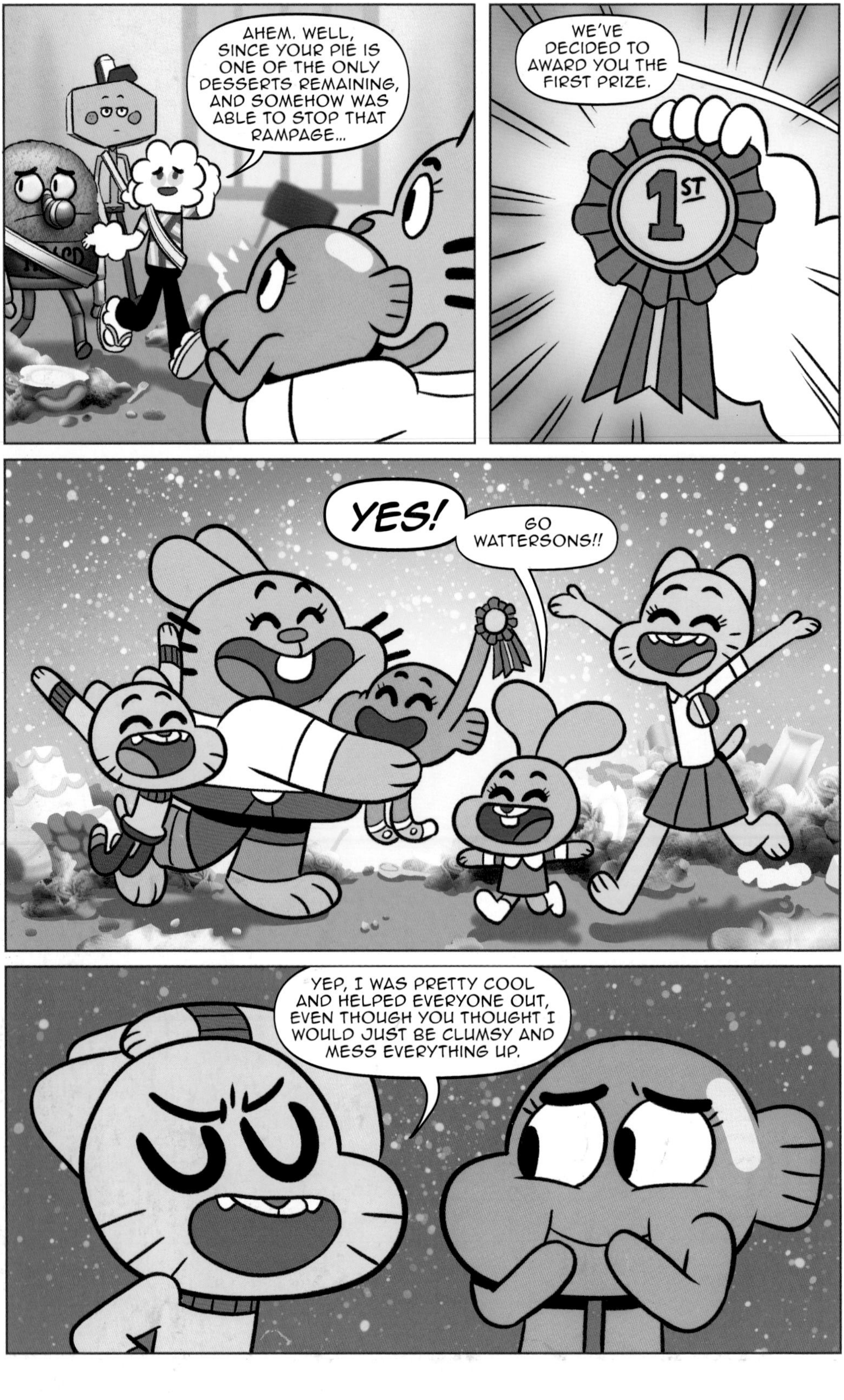
AHEM. WELL, SINCE YOUR PIE IS ONE OF THE ONLY DESSERTS REMAINING, AND SOMEHOW WAS ABLE TO STOP THAT RAMPAGE...
WE'VE DECIDED TO AWARD YOU THE FIRST PRIZE.
1ST
YES!
GO WATTERSONS!!
YEP, I WAS PRETTY COOL AND HELPED EVERYONE OUT, EVEN THOUGH YOU THOUGHT I WOULD JUST BE CLUMSY AND MESS EVERYTHING UP.

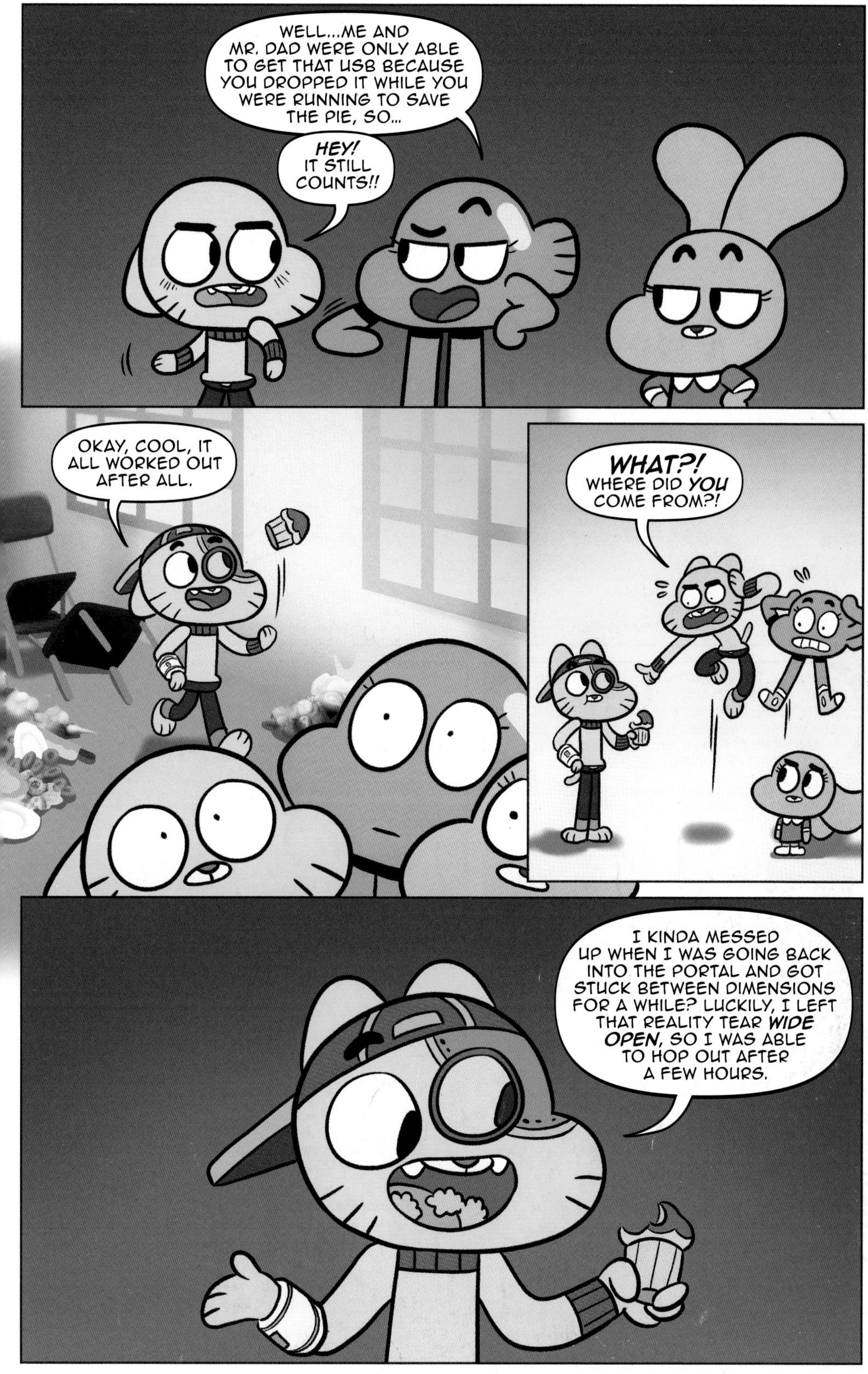
WELL...ME AND MR. DAD WERE ONLY ABLE TO GET THAT USB BECAUSE YOU DROPPED IT WHILE YOU WERE RUNNING TO SAVE THE PIE, SO...
HEY! IT STILL COUNTS!!
OKAY, COOL, IT ALL WORKED OUT AFTER ALL.
WHAT?! WHERE DID YOU COME FROM?!
I KINDA MESSED UP WHEN I WAS GOING BACK INTO THE PORTAL AND GOT STUCK BETWEEN DIMENSIONS FOR A WHILE? LUCKILY, I LEFT THAT REALITY TEAR WIDE OPEN, SO I WAS ABLE TO HOP OUT AFTER A FEW HOURS.

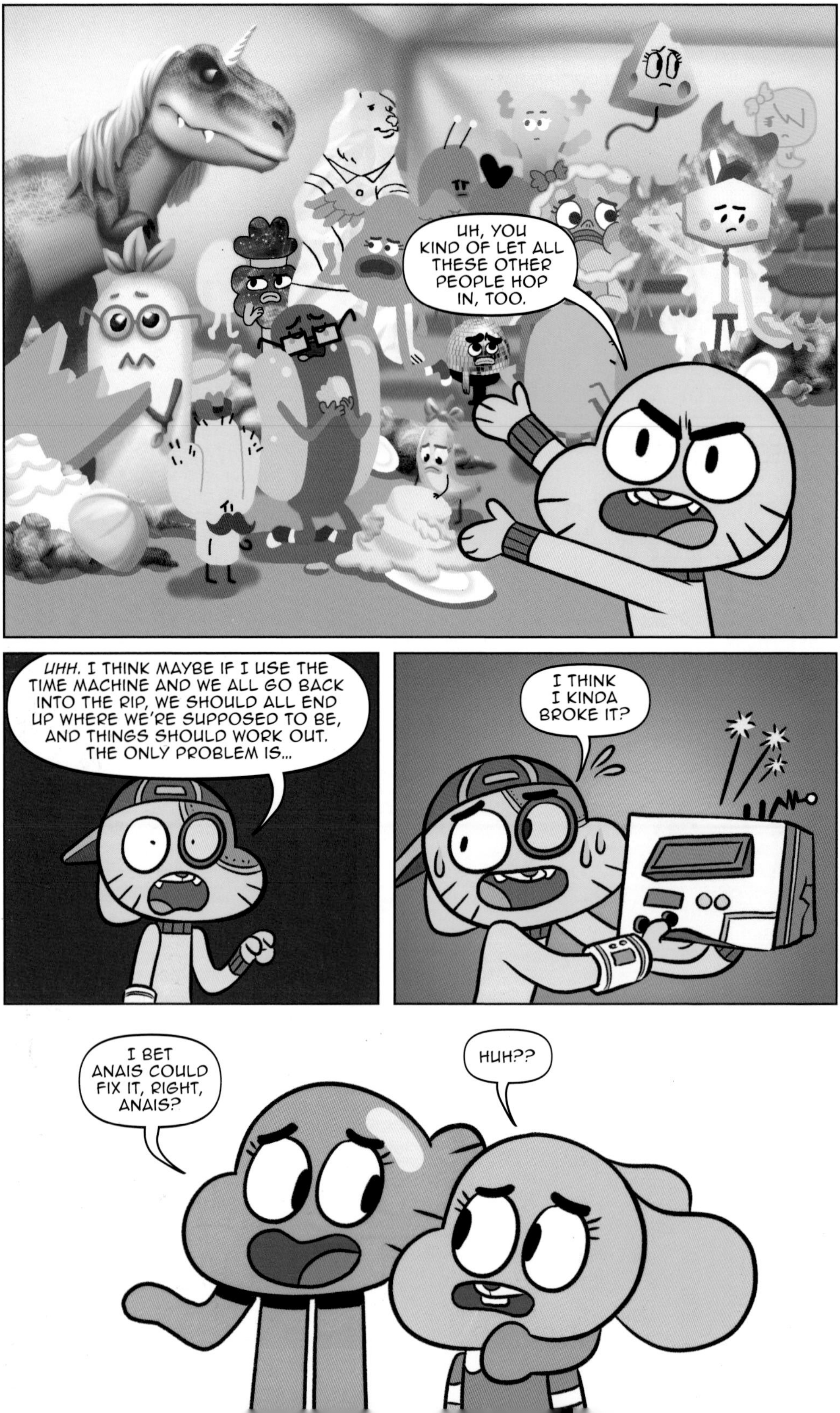
UH, YOU KIND OF LET ALL THESE OTHER PEOPLE HOP IN, TOO.
UHH. I THINK MAYBE IF I USE THE TIME MACHINE AND WE ALL GO BACK INTO THE RIP, WE SHOULD ALL END UP WHERE WE'RE SUPPOSED TO BE, AND THINGS SHOULD WORK OUT. THE ONLY PROBLEM IS...
I THINK I KINDA BROKE IT?
I BET ANAIS COULD FIX IT, RIGHT, ANAIS?
HUH??

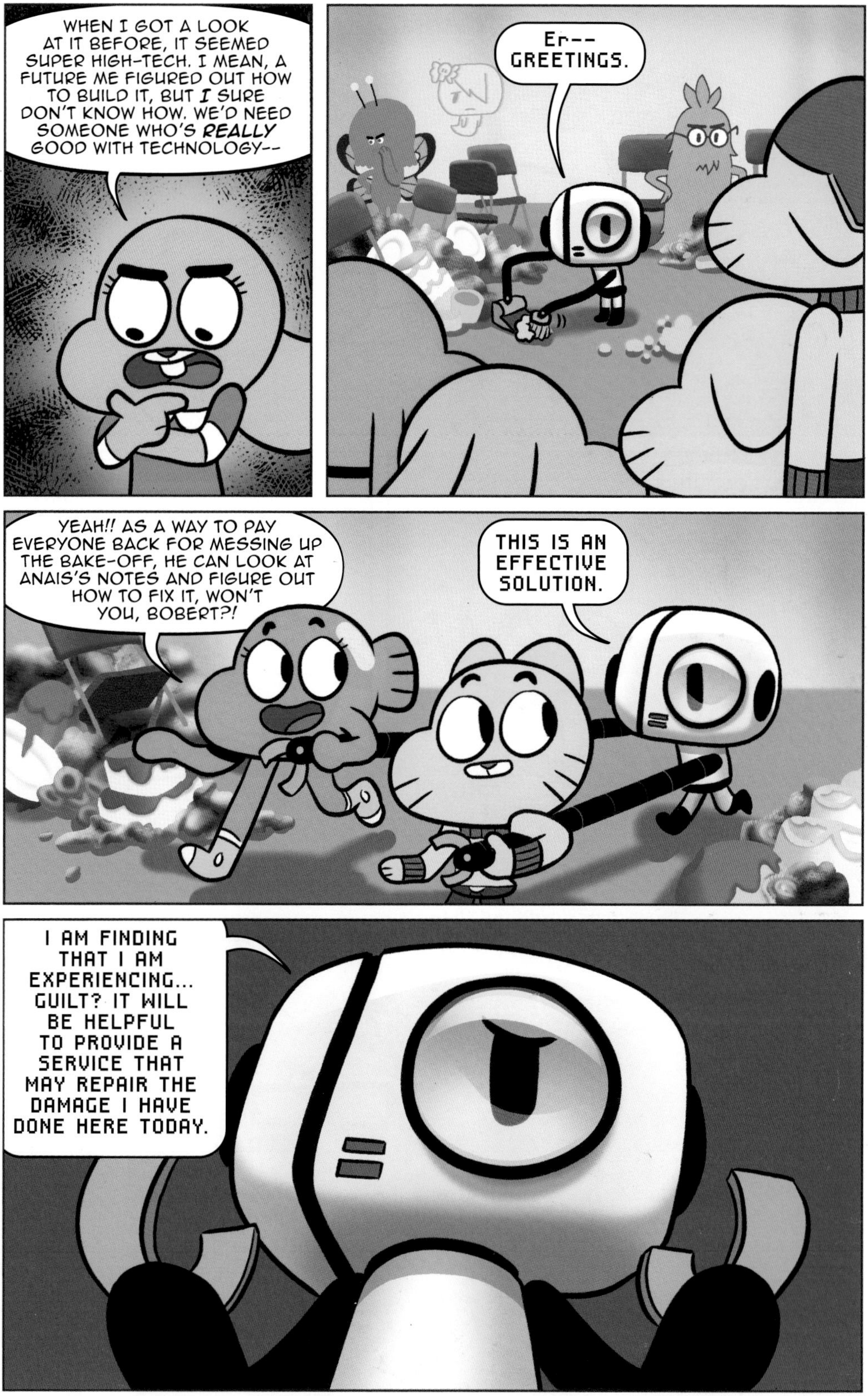
WHEN I GOT A LOOK AT IT BEFORE, IT SEEMED SUPER HIGH-TECH. I MEAN, A FUTURE ME FIGURED OUT HOW TO BUILD IT, BUT *I* SURE DON'T KNOW HOW. WE'D NEED SOMEONE WHO'S *REALLY* GOOD WITH TECHNOLOGY--
Er-- GREETINGS.
YEAH!! AS A WAY TO PAY EVERYONE BACK FOR MESSING UP THE BAKE-OFF, HE CAN LOOK AT ANAIS'S NOTES AND FIGURE OUT HOW TO FIX IT, WON'T YOU, BOBERT?!
THIS IS AN EFFECTIVE SOLUTION.
I AM FINDING THAT I AM EXPERIENCING... GUILT? IT WILL BE HELPFUL TO PROVIDE A SERVICE THAT MAY REPAIR THE DAMAGE I HAVE DONE HERE TODAY.

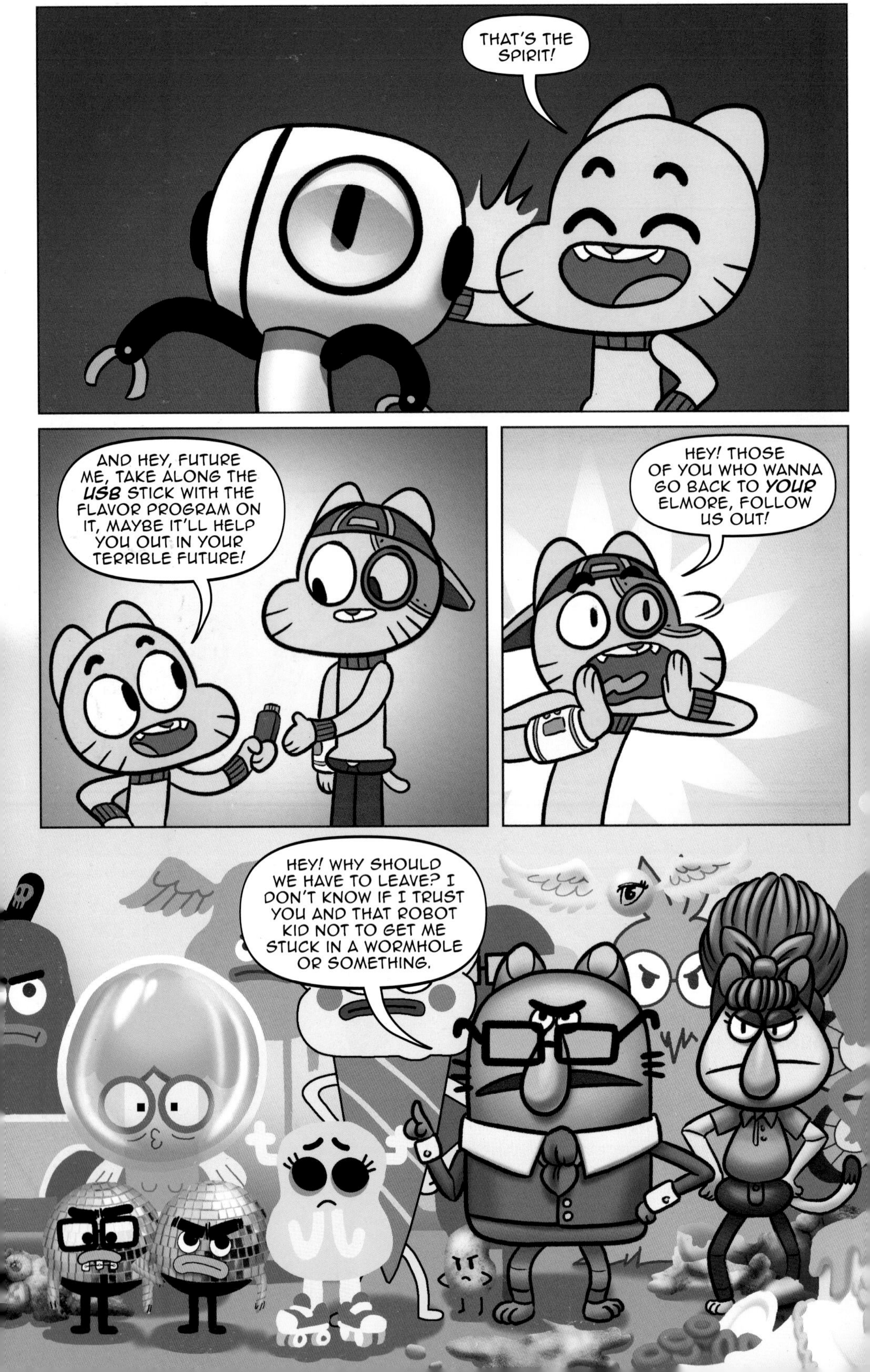
THAT'S THE SPIRIT!
AND HEY, FUTURE ME, TAKE ALONG THE USB STICK WITH THE FLAVOR PROGRAM ON IT, MAYBE IT'LL HELP YOU OUT IN YOUR TERRIBLE FUTURE!
HEY! THOSE OF YOU WHO WANNA GO BACK TO YOUR ELMORE, FOLLOW US OUT!
HEY! WHY SHOULD WE HAVE TO LEAVE? I DON'T KNOW IF I TRUST YOU AND THAT ROBOT KID NOT TO GET ME STUCK IN A WORMHOLE OR SOMETHING.

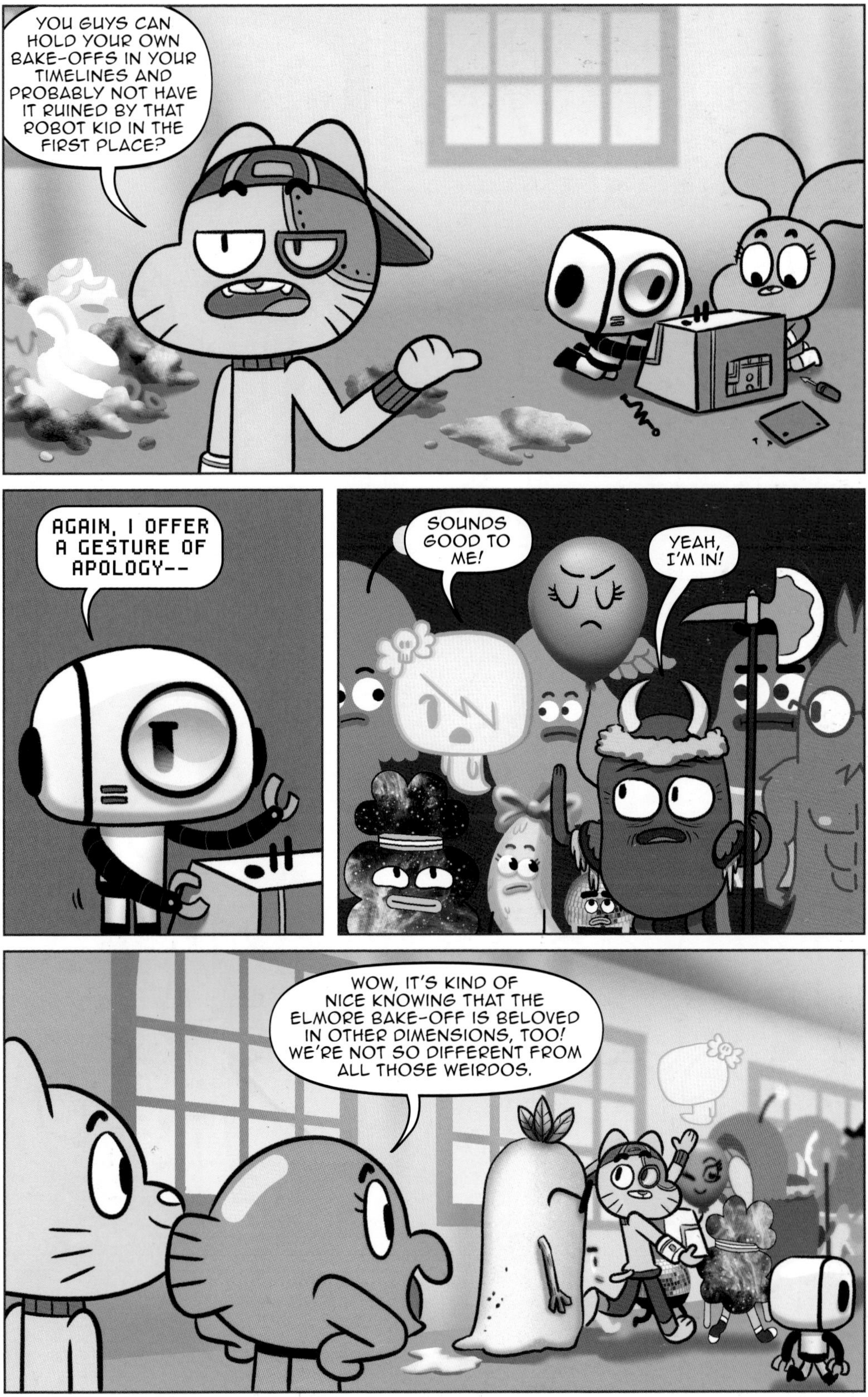
YOU GUYS CAN HOLD YOUR OWN BAKE-OFFS IN YOUR TIMELINES AND PROBABLY NOT HAVE IT RUINED BY THAT ROBOT KID IN THE FIRST PLACE?
AGAIN, I OFFER A GESTURE OF APOLOGY--
SOUNDS GOOD TO ME!
YEAH, I'M IN!
WOW, IT'S KIND OF NICE KNOWING THAT THE ELMORE BAKE-OFF IS BELOVED IN OTHER DIMENSIONS, TOO! WE'RE NOT SO DIFFERENT FROM ALL THOSE WEIRDOS.

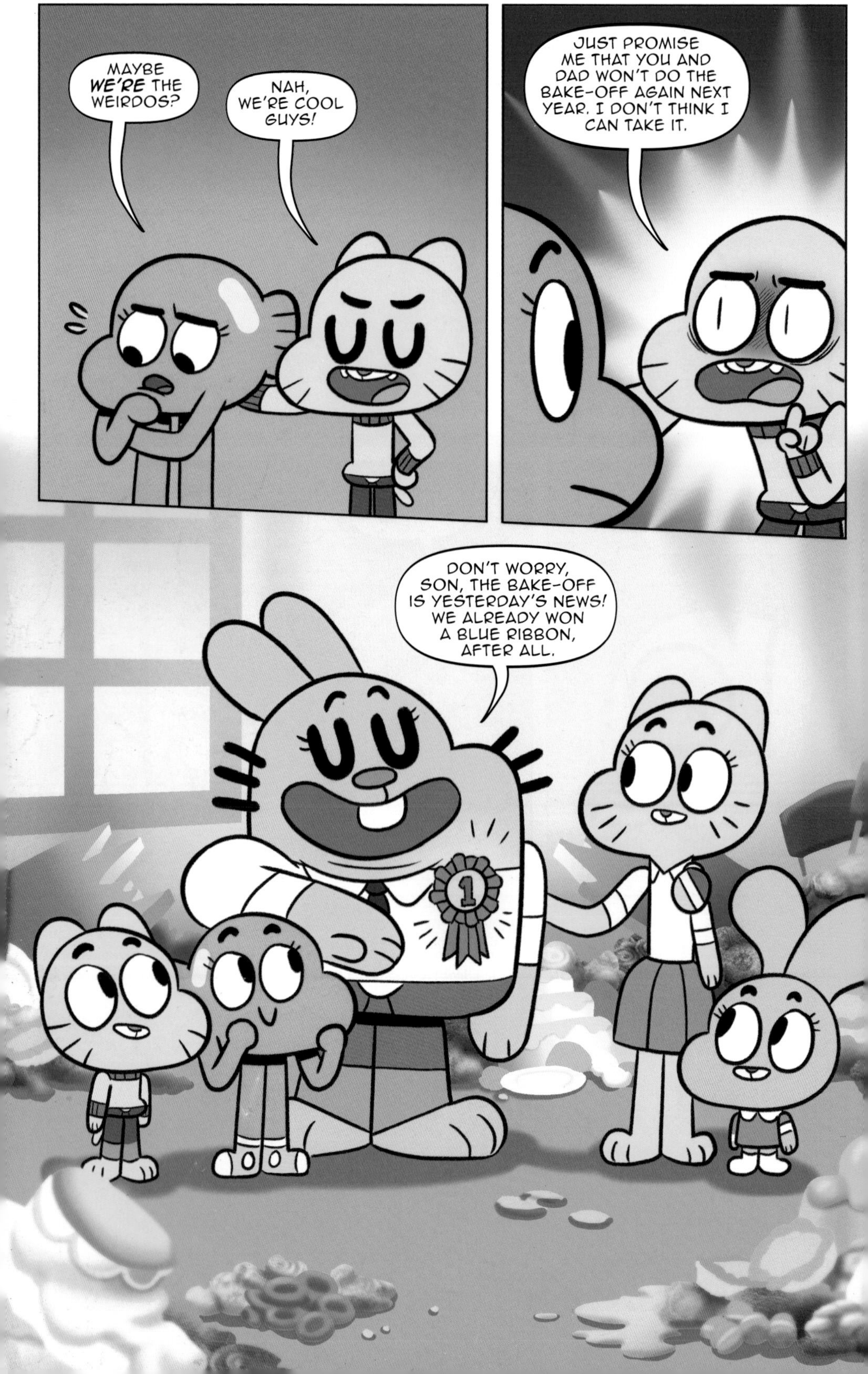
MAYBE **WE'RE** THE WEIRDOS?
NAH, WE'RE COOL GUYS!
JUST PROMISE ME THAT YOU AND DAD WON'T DO THE BAKE-OFF AGAIN NEXT YEAR. I DON'T THINK I CAN TAKE IT.
DON'T WORRY, SON, THE BAKE-OFF IS YESTERDAY'S NEWS! WE ALREADY WON A BLUE RIBBON, AFTER ALL.

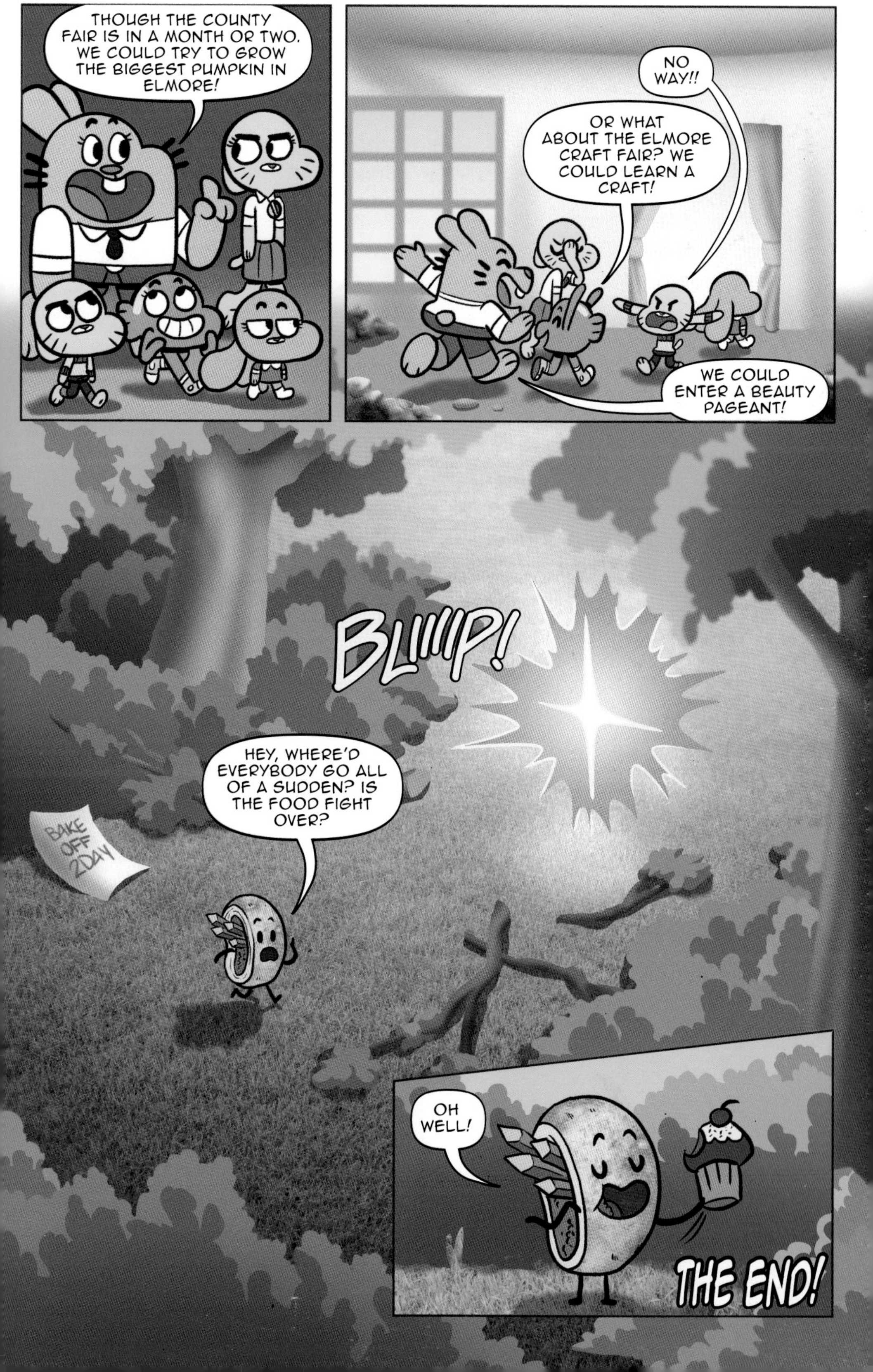
THOUGH THE COUNTY FAIR IS IN A MONTH OR TWO. WE COULD TRY TO GROW THE BIGGEST PUMPKIN IN ELMORE!
OR WHAT ABOUT THE ELMORE CRAFT FAIR? WE COULD LEARN A CRAFT!
NO WAY!!
WE COULD ENTER A BEAUTY PAGEANT!
BLIIIP!
HEY, WHERE'D EVERYBODY GO ALL OF A SUDDEN? IS THE FOOD FIGHT OVER?
BAKE OFF 2DAY
OH WELL!
THE END!

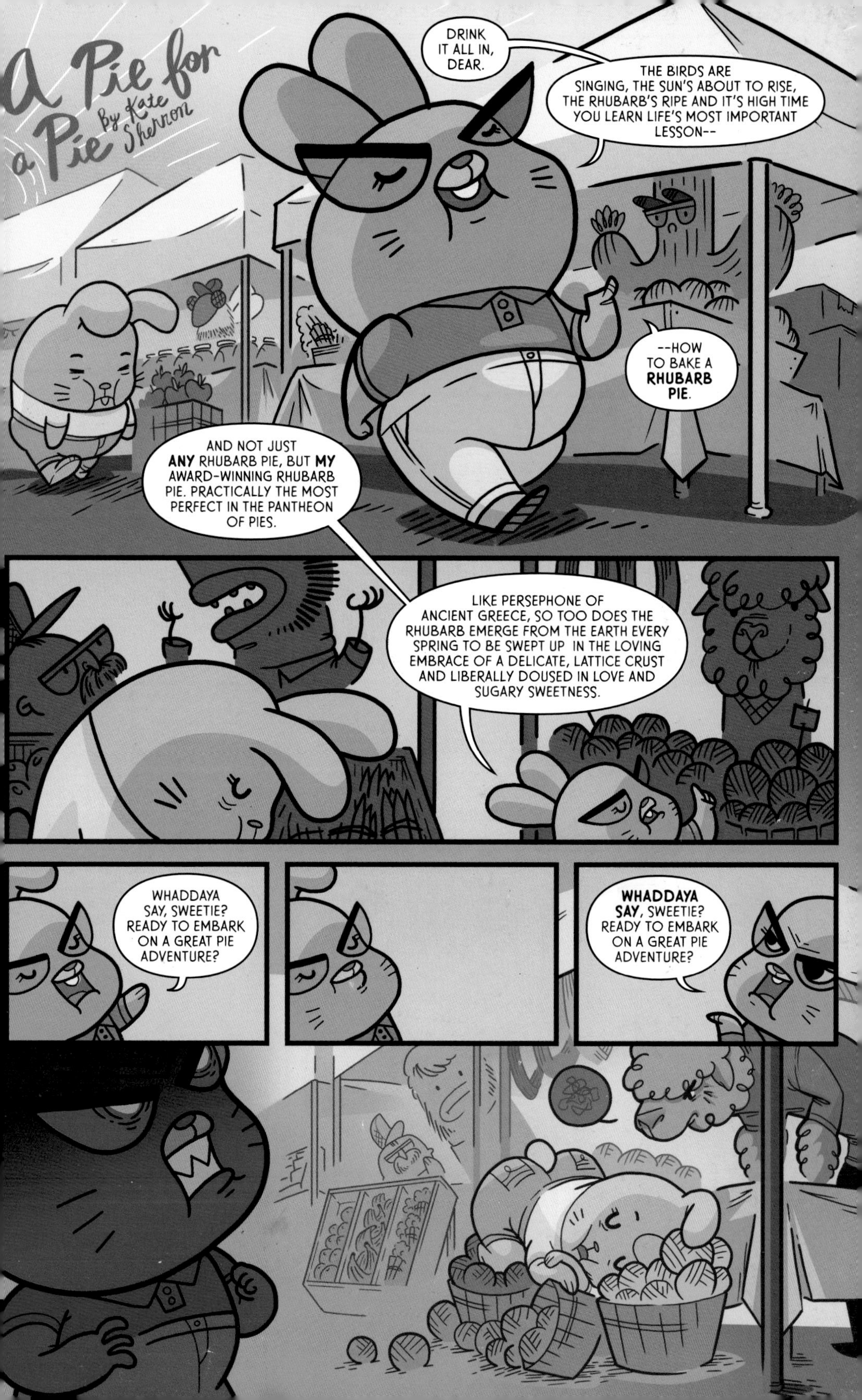
A Pie for a Pie
By Kate Sherron
DRINK IT ALL IN, DEAR.
THE BIRDS ARE SINGING, THE SUN'S ABOUT TO RISE, THE RHUBARB'S RIPE AND IT'S HIGH TIME YOU LEARN LIFE'S MOST IMPORTANT LESSON--
--HOW TO BAKE A **RHUBARB PIE**.
AND NOT JUST **ANY** RHUBARB PIE, BUT **MY** AWARD-WINNING RHUBARB PIE. PRACTICALLY THE MOST PERFECT IN THE PANTHEON OF PIES.
LIKE PERSEPHONE OF ANCIENT GREECE, SO TOO DOES THE RHUBARB EMERGE FROM THE EARTH EVERY SPRING TO BE SWEPT UP IN THE LOVING EMBRACE OF A DELICATE, LATTICE CRUST AND LIBERALLY DOUSED IN LOVE AND SUGARY SWEETNESS.
WHADDAYA SAY, SWEETIE? READY TO EMBARK ON A GREAT PIE ADVENTURE?
WHADDAYA SAY, SWEETIE? READY TO EMBARK ON A GREAT PIE ADVENTURE?

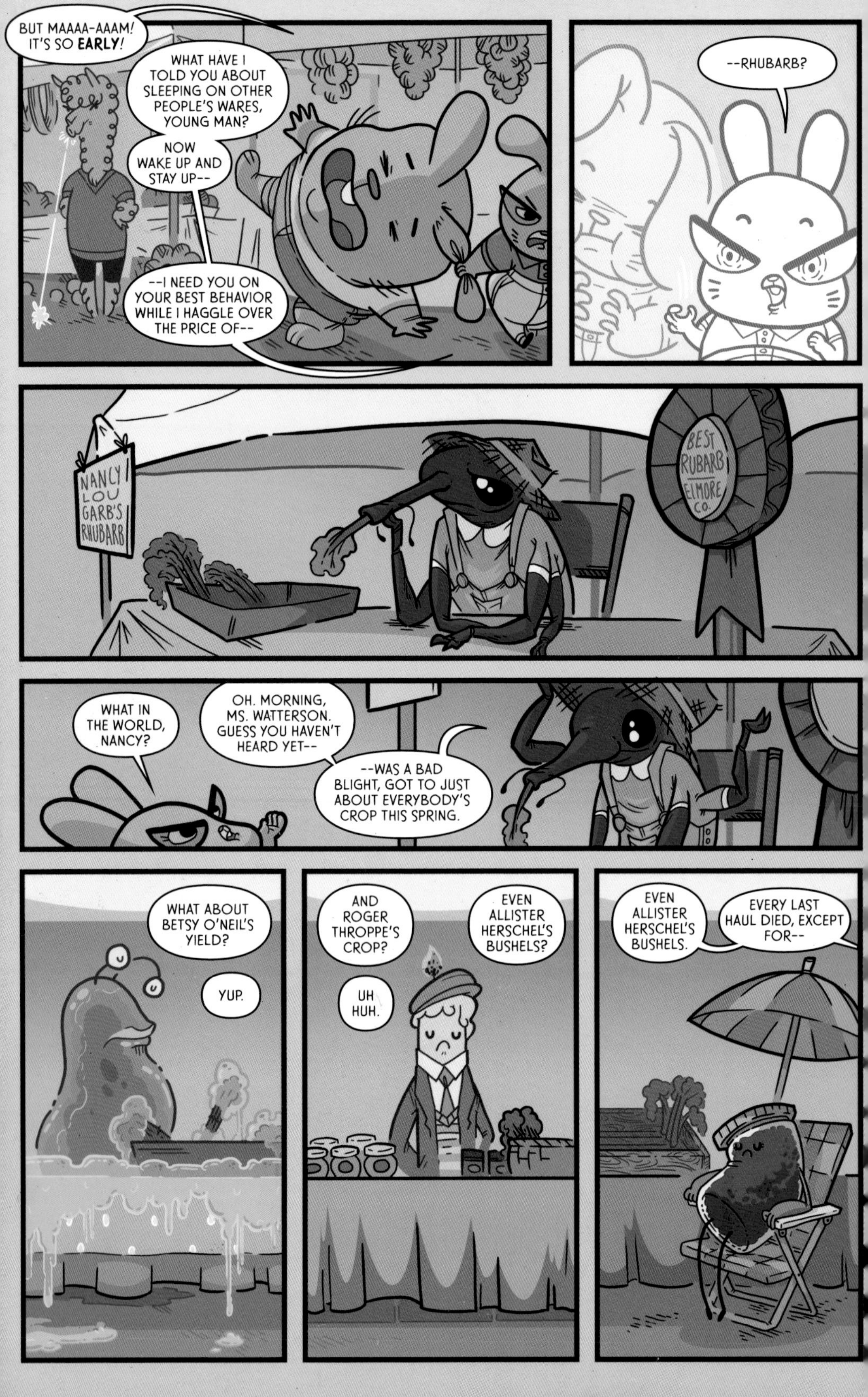
BUT MAAAA-AAAM! IT'S SO EARLY!
WHAT HAVE I TOLD YOU ABOUT SLEEPING ON OTHER PEOPLE'S WARES, YOUNG MAN?
NOW WAKE UP AND STAY UP--
--I NEED YOU ON YOUR BEST BEHAVIOR WHILE I HAGGLE OVER THE PRICE OF--
--RHUBARB?
NANCY LOU GARB'S RHUBARB
BEST RUBARB ELMORE CO.
WHAT IN THE WORLD, NANCY?
OH. MORNING, MS. WATTERSON. GUESS YOU HAVEN'T HEARD YET--
--WAS A BAD BLIGHT, GOT TO JUST ABOUT EVERYBODY'S CROP THIS SPRING.
WHAT ABOUT BETSY O'NEIL'S YIELD?
YUP.
AND ROGER THROPPE'S CROP?
UH HUH.
EVEN ALLISTER HERSCHEL'S BUSHELS?
EVEN ALLISTER HERSCHEL'S BUSHELS.
EVERY LAST HAUL DIED, EXCEPT FOR--

KRIIINGH
KRIIINGH
KRIIINCH

--FRANK FAULK'S STALKS.

WHY ARE YOU MAKING THAT LOUD MOUTH-NOISE, MOM?

FRANK AND I GO **WAY** BACK, DEAR.

I ALMOST FEEL BAD FOR HIM.

POOR GUY **ACTUALLY** THINKS FOLKS LIKE HIS PIE.

ALMOST.

AND THE BAKE-OFF JUDGES LETTING FRANK WIN EVERY OTHER YEAR ONLY ENABLES HIS DELUSION.

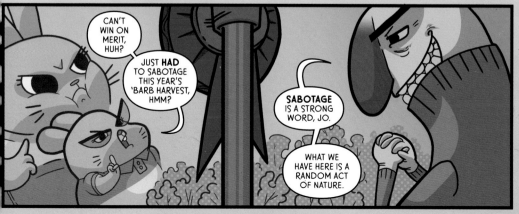

CAN'T WIN ON MERIT, HUH?

JUST **HAD** TO SABOTAGE THIS YEAR'S 'BARB HARVEST, HMM?

SABOTAGE IS A STRONG WORD, JO.

WHAT WE HAVE HERE IS A RANDOM ACT OF NATURE.

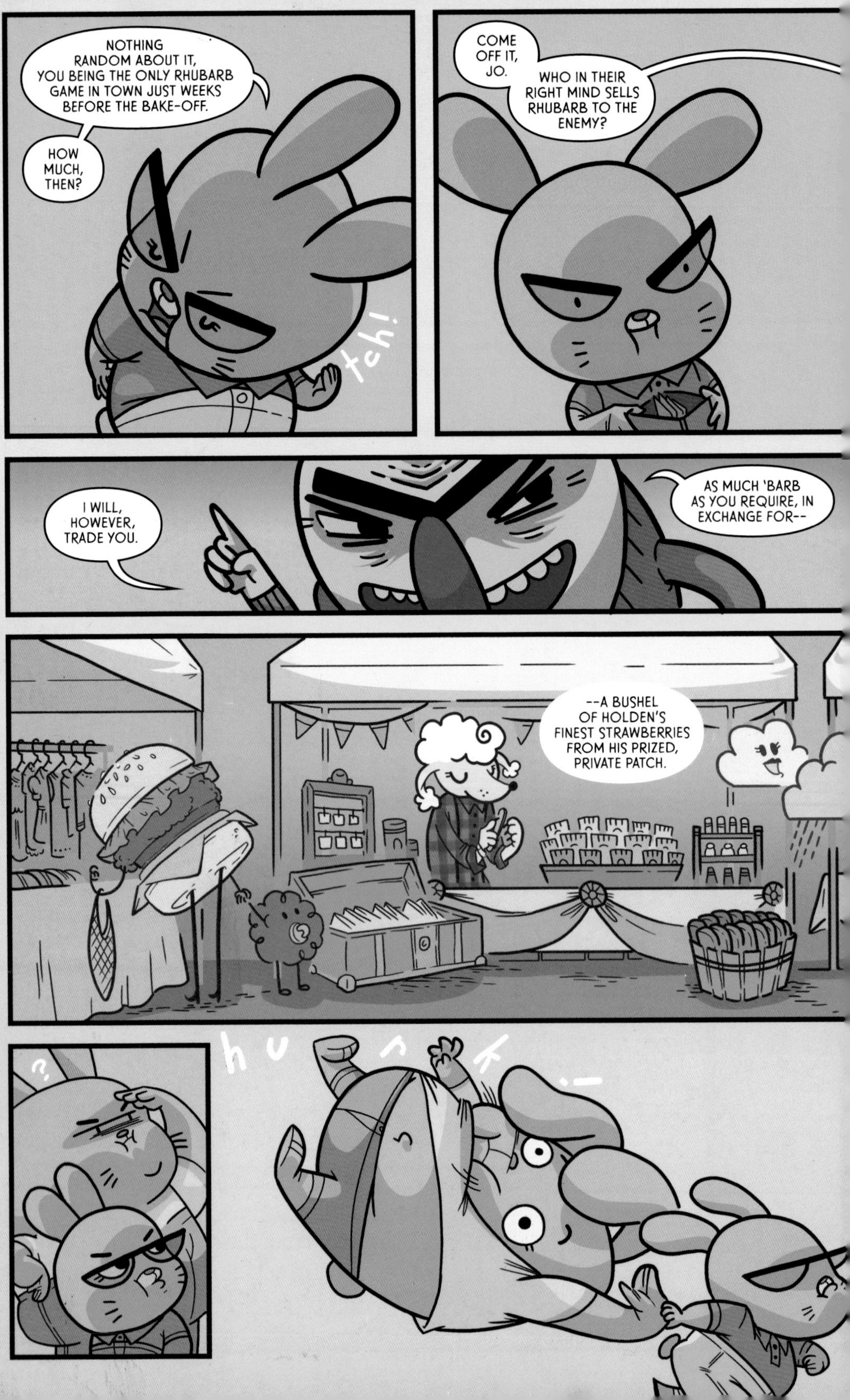
NOTHING RANDOM ABOUT IT, YOU BEING THE ONLY RHUBARB GAME IN TOWN JUST WEEKS BEFORE THE BAKE-OFF.
HOW MUCH, THEN?
tch!
COME OFF IT, JO.
WHO IN THEIR RIGHT MIND SELLS RHUBARB TO THE ENEMY?
I WILL, HOWEVER, TRADE YOU.
AS MUCH 'BARB AS YOU REQUIRE, IN EXCHANGE FOR--
--A BUSHEL OF HOLDEN'S FINEST STRAWBERRIES FROM HIS PRIZED, PRIVATE PATCH.
?.
hunk

MORNING, HOLDEN. HOW'RE THE CROWDS TODAY?

GOOD MORNING JOANNA. IT'S PRETTY SLOW...

TELL YOU WHAT, JOANNA. IT'S BEEN A SUPER ROUGH SPRING THUS FAR. CROWDS'RE DOWN, NO ONE WAN... THE BEESWAX SO... THOUGH THEY COULDN'T G... NOUGH... AST SEASON AND TO TOP IT ALL O... ME **RAB**... TING ALL M... **STRAWBERRIES**... T... TH... S ENOU... TO DRIVE A MAN T... ...OU WHA... AND DID YOU HE... ...E UNILA... DECIDED THA...

RABBITS GOT INTO YOUR BERRIES, EH? THAT'S ROUGH.

YOU WOULDN'T BELIEVE ALL THE FINAGLING REQUIRED TO GET RID OF THE RELATIONS POST HOLIDAYS.

YOU CAN MAKE THEM LEAVE?

JUST BY TALKING TO THEM?!

WELL, SOMETIMES A LITTLE HORSE-TRADING'S REQUIRED, BUT--

OH, MR. HOLDEN... THE **THINGS** MOM CAN TALK YOU INTO!

BRUSHING YOUR TEETH, USING YOUR INSIDE VOICE--

--EATING BOTH FRUITS **AND** VEGETABLES--

--LOOKING BOTH WAYS BEFORE CROSSING THE STREET, PUTTING "I" BEFORE "E," EXCEPT AFTER "C"--

HEY, NOW... YOU MIGHT BE ON TO **SOMETHING** THERE, JOANNA.

WOULD YOU BE WILLING TO TALK SOME SENSE INTO THESE PESTS FOR ME?

MY PLEASURE--

--WEARING CLEAN UNDERWEAR, WEARING CLEAN UNDERWEAR UNDER YOUR PANTS INSTEAD OF OVER THEM, EVEN THOUGH IT'S MORE SLIMMING THAT WAY...

--IN EXCHANGE FOR A BUSHEL OF YOUR BEST BERRIES.

YOU GET RID OF THOSE PESTS FOR ME AND I'LL GIVE YOU **TWO** BUSHELS.

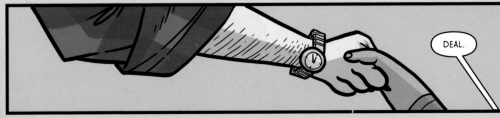

DEAL.

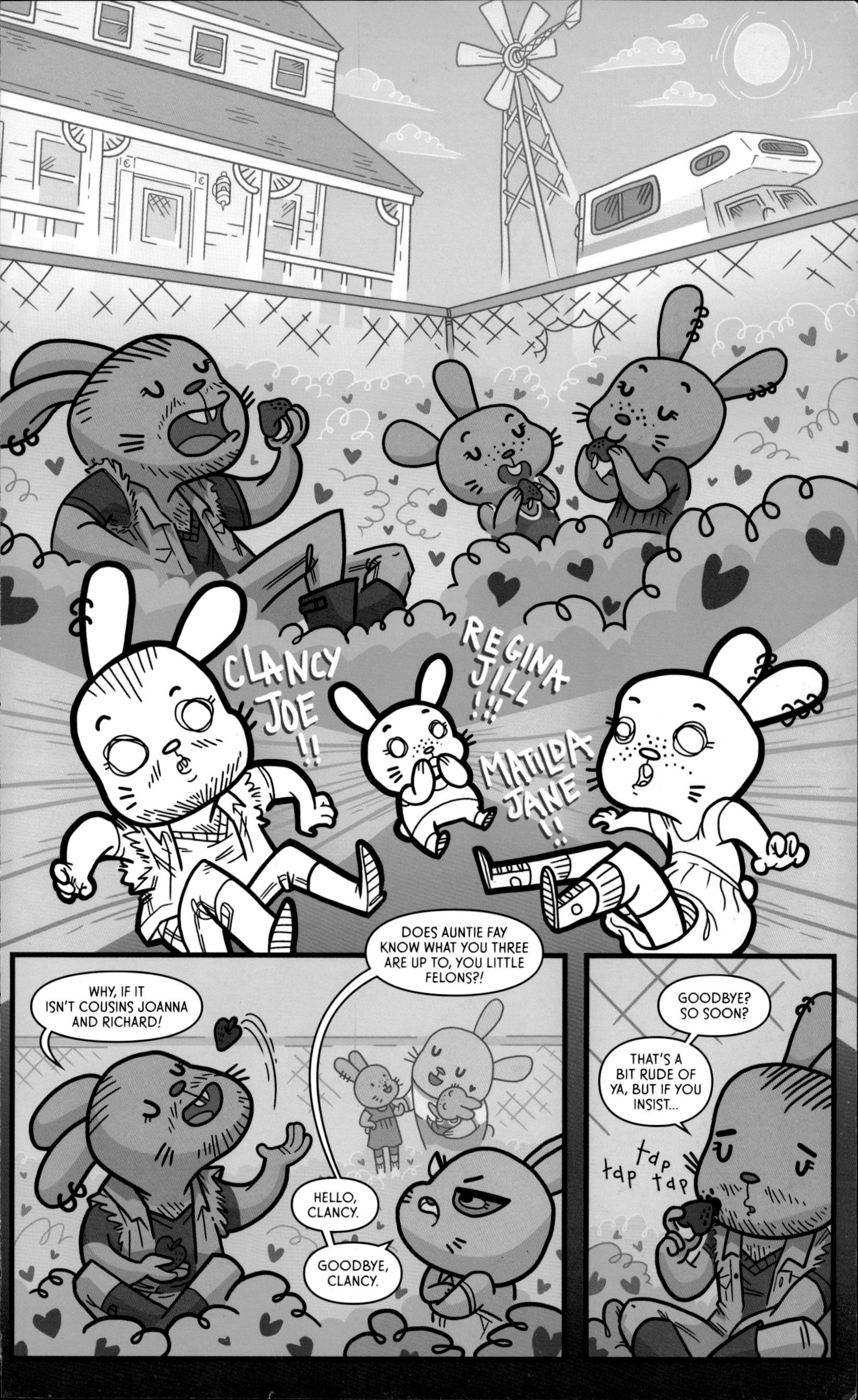
CLANCY JOE !!
REGINA JILL !!!
MATILDA JANE !!
WHY, IF IT ISN'T COUSINS JOANNA AND RICHARD!
DOES AUNTIE FAY KNOW WHAT YOU THREE ARE UP TO, YOU LITTLE FELONS?!
HELLO, CLANCY.
GOODBYE, CLANCY.
GOODBYE? SO SOON?
THAT'S A BIT RUDE OF YA, BUT IF YOU INSIST...
tap tap tap

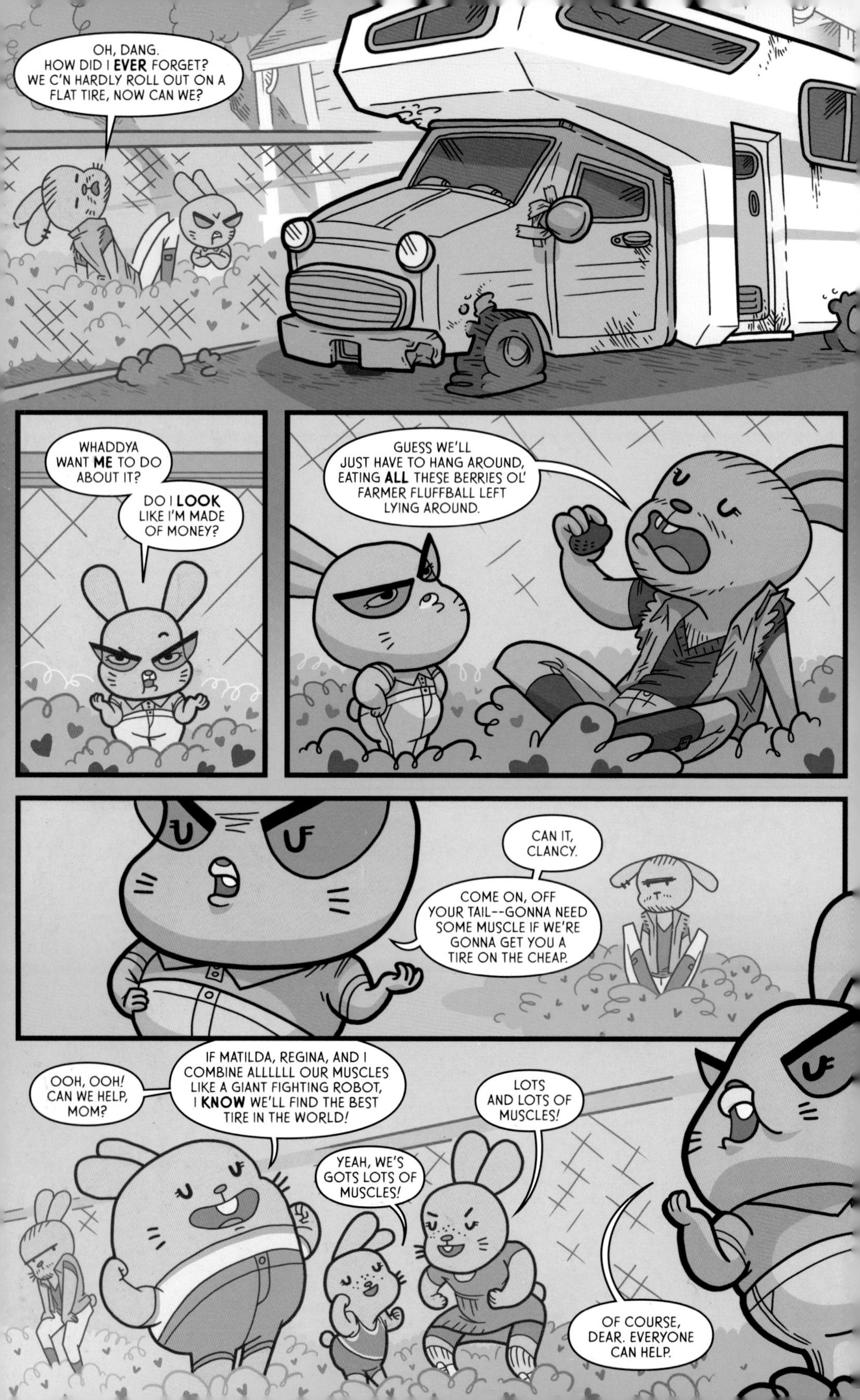
OH, DANG. HOW DID I **EVER** FORGET? WE C'N HARDLY ROLL OUT ON A FLAT TIRE, NOW CAN WE?
WHADDYA WANT **ME** TO DO ABOUT IT?
DO I **LOOK** LIKE I'M MADE OF MONEY?
GUESS WE'LL JUST HAVE TO HANG AROUND, EATING **ALL** THESE BERRIES OL' FARMER FLUFFBALL LEFT LYING AROUND.
CAN IT, CLANCY.
COME ON, OFF YOUR TAIL--GONNA NEED SOME MUSCLE IF WE'RE GONNA GET YOU A TIRE ON THE CHEAP.
OOH, OOH! CAN WE HELP, MOM?
IF MATILDA, REGINA, AND I COMBINE ALLLLLL OUR MUSCLES LIKE A GIANT FIGHTING ROBOT, I **KNOW** WE'LL FIND THE BEST TIRE IN THE WORLD!
YEAH, WE'S GOTS LOTS OF MUSCLES!
LOTS AND LOTS OF MUSCLES!
OF COURSE, DEAR. EVERYONE CAN HELP.

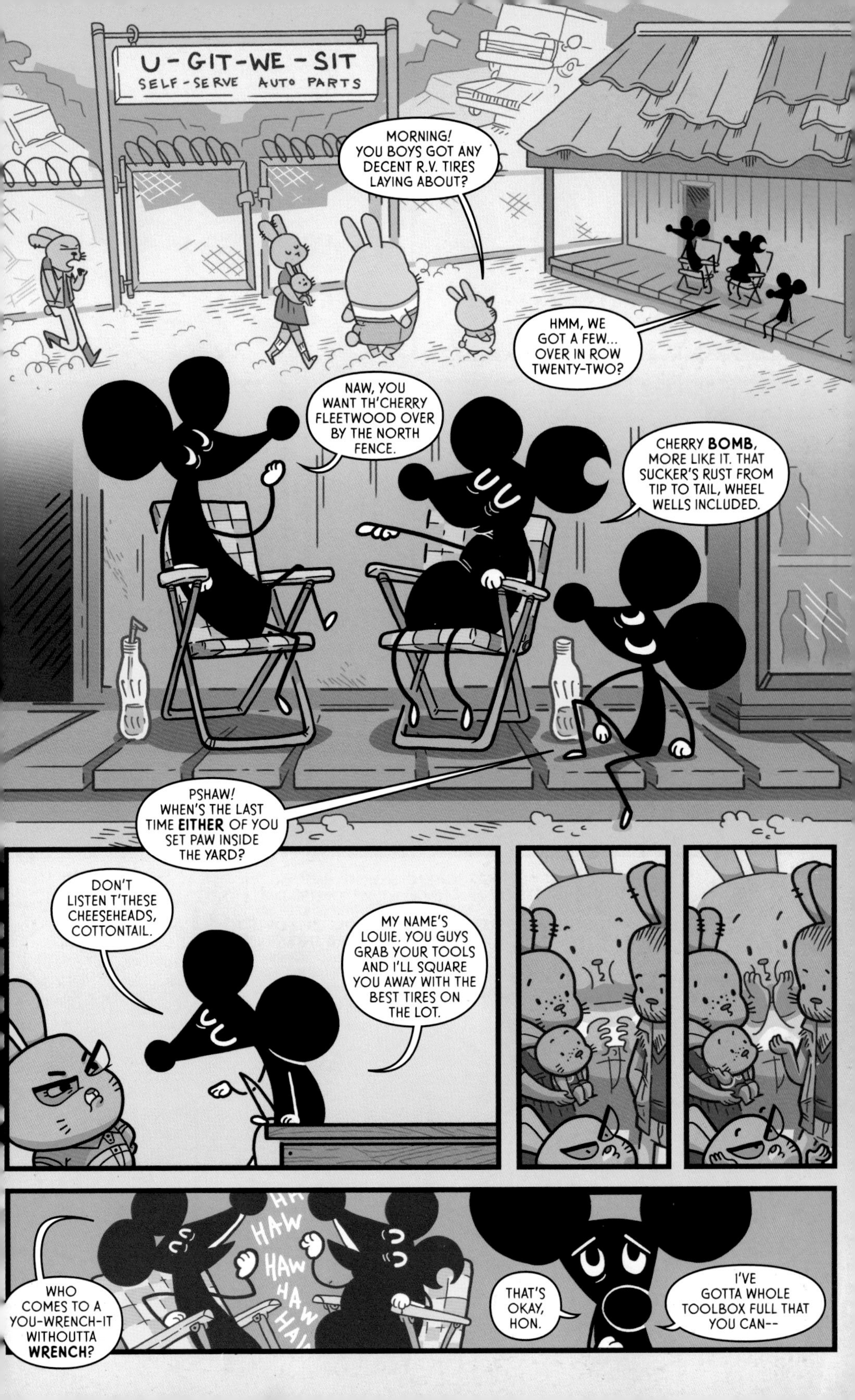
U-GIT-WE-SIT
SELF-SERVE AUTO PARTS
MORNING! YOU BOYS GOT ANY DECENT R.V. TIRES LAYING ABOUT?
HMM, WE GOT A FEW... OVER IN ROW TWENTY-TWO?
NAW, YOU WANT TH'CHERRY FLEETWOOD OVER BY THE NORTH FENCE.
CHERRY **BOMB**, MORE LIKE IT. THAT SUCKER'S RUST FROM TIP TO TAIL, WHEEL WELLS INCLUDED.
PSHAW! WHEN'S THE LAST TIME **EITHER** OF YOU SET PAW INSIDE THE YARD?
DON'T LISTEN T'THESE CHEESEHEADS, COTTONTAIL.
MY NAME'S LOUIE. YOU GUYS GRAB YOUR TOOLS AND I'LL SQUARE YOU AWAY WITH THE BEST TIRES ON THE LOT.
WHO COMES TO A YOU-WRENCH-IT WITHOUTTA **WRENCH**?
HAW HAW HAW HAW
THAT'S OKAY, HON.
I'VE GOTTA WHOLE TOOLBOX FULL THAT YOU CAN--

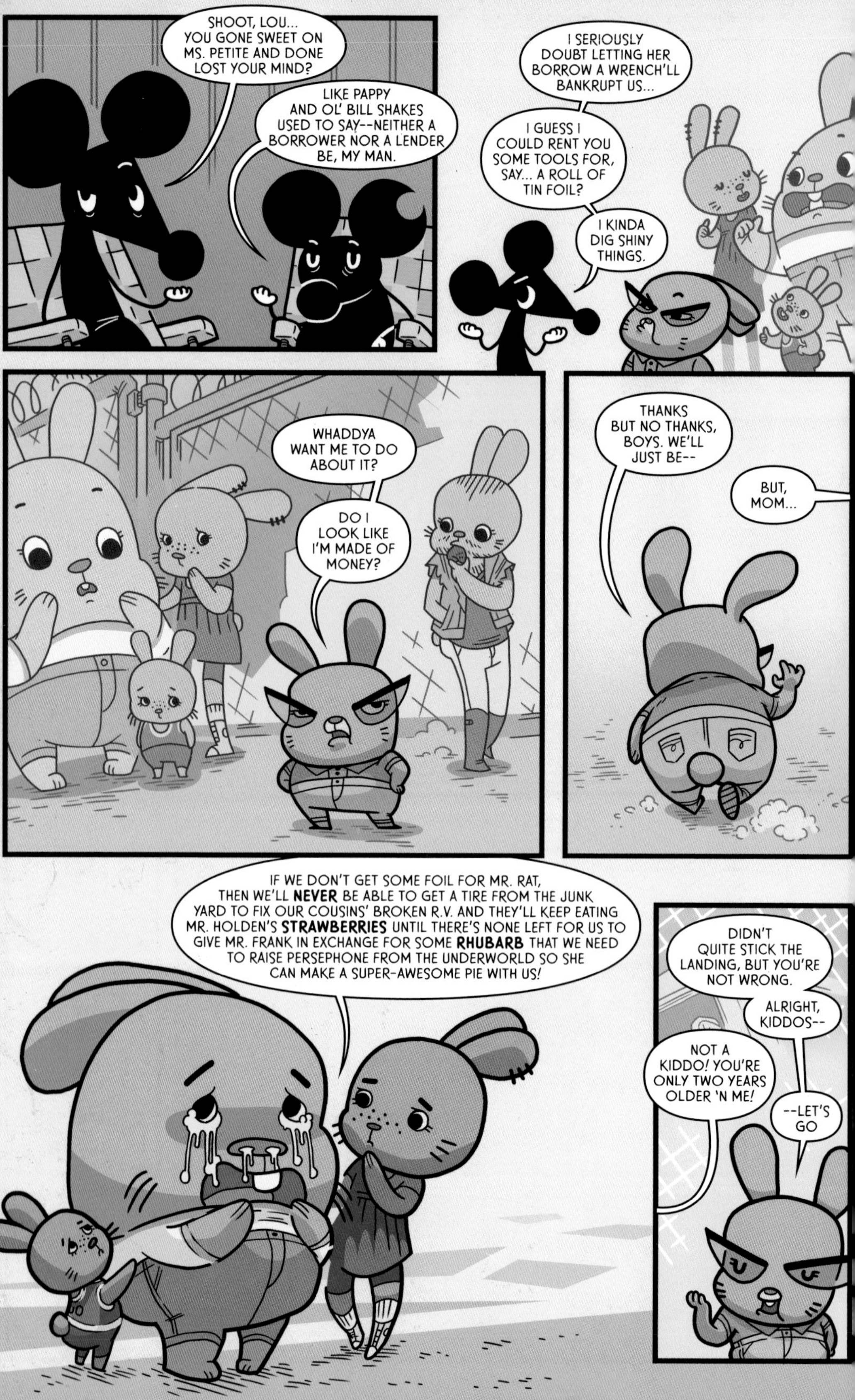
SHOOT, LOU... YOU GONE SWEET ON MS. PETITE AND DONE LOST YOUR MIND?
LIKE PAPPY AND OL' BILL SHAKES USED TO SAY--NEITHER A BORROWER NOR A LENDER BE, MY MAN.
I SERIOUSLY DOUBT LETTING HER BORROW A WRENCH'LL BANKRUPT US...
I GUESS I COULD RENT YOU SOME TOOLS FOR, SAY... A ROLL OF TIN FOIL?
I KINDA DIG SHINY THINGS.
WHADDYA WANT ME TO DO ABOUT IT?
DO I LOOK LIKE I'M MADE OF MONEY?
THANKS BUT NO THANKS, BOYS. WE'LL JUST BE--
BUT, MOM...
IF WE DON'T GET SOME FOIL FOR MR. RAT, THEN WE'LL **NEVER** BE ABLE TO GET A TIRE FROM THE JUNK YARD TO FIX OUR COUSINS' BROKEN R.V. AND THEY'LL KEEP EATING MR. HOLDEN'S **STRAWBERRIES** UNTIL THERE'S NONE LEFT FOR US TO GIVE MR. FRANK IN EXCHANGE FOR SOME **RHUBARB** THAT WE NEED TO RAISE PERSEPHONE FROM THE UNDERWORLD SO SHE CAN MAKE A SUPER-AWESOME PIE WITH US!
DIDN'T QUITE STICK THE LANDING, BUT YOU'RE NOT WRONG.
ALRIGHT, KIDDOS--
NOT A KIDDO! YOU'RE ONLY TWO YEARS OLDER 'N ME!
--LET'S GO

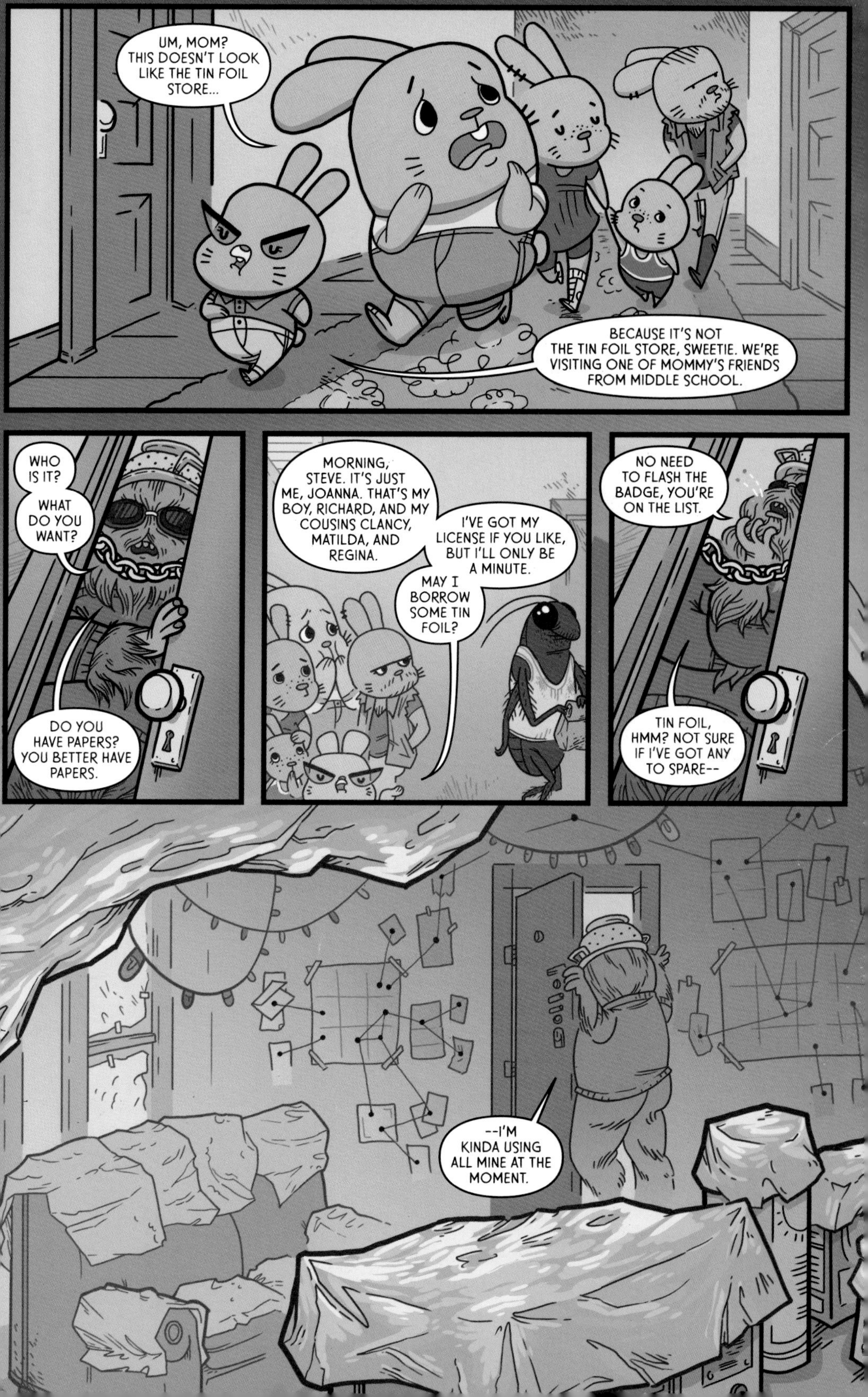
UM, MOM? THIS DOESN'T LOOK LIKE THE TIN FOIL STORE...
BECAUSE IT'S NOT THE TIN FOIL STORE, SWEETIE. WE'RE VISITING ONE OF MOMMY'S FRIENDS FROM MIDDLE SCHOOL.
WHO IS IT?
WHAT DO YOU WANT?
DO YOU HAVE PAPERS? YOU BETTER HAVE PAPERS.
MORNING, STEVE. IT'S JUST ME, JOANNA. THAT'S MY BOY, RICHARD, AND MY COUSINS CLANCY, MATILDA, AND REGINA.
I'VE GOT MY LICENSE IF YOU LIKE, BUT I'LL ONLY BE A MINUTE.
MAY I BORROW SOME TIN FOIL?
NO NEED TO FLASH THE BADGE, YOU'RE ON THE LIST.
TIN FOIL, HMM? NOT SURE IF I'VE GOT ANY TO SPARE--
--I'M KINDA USING ALL MINE AT THE MOMENT.

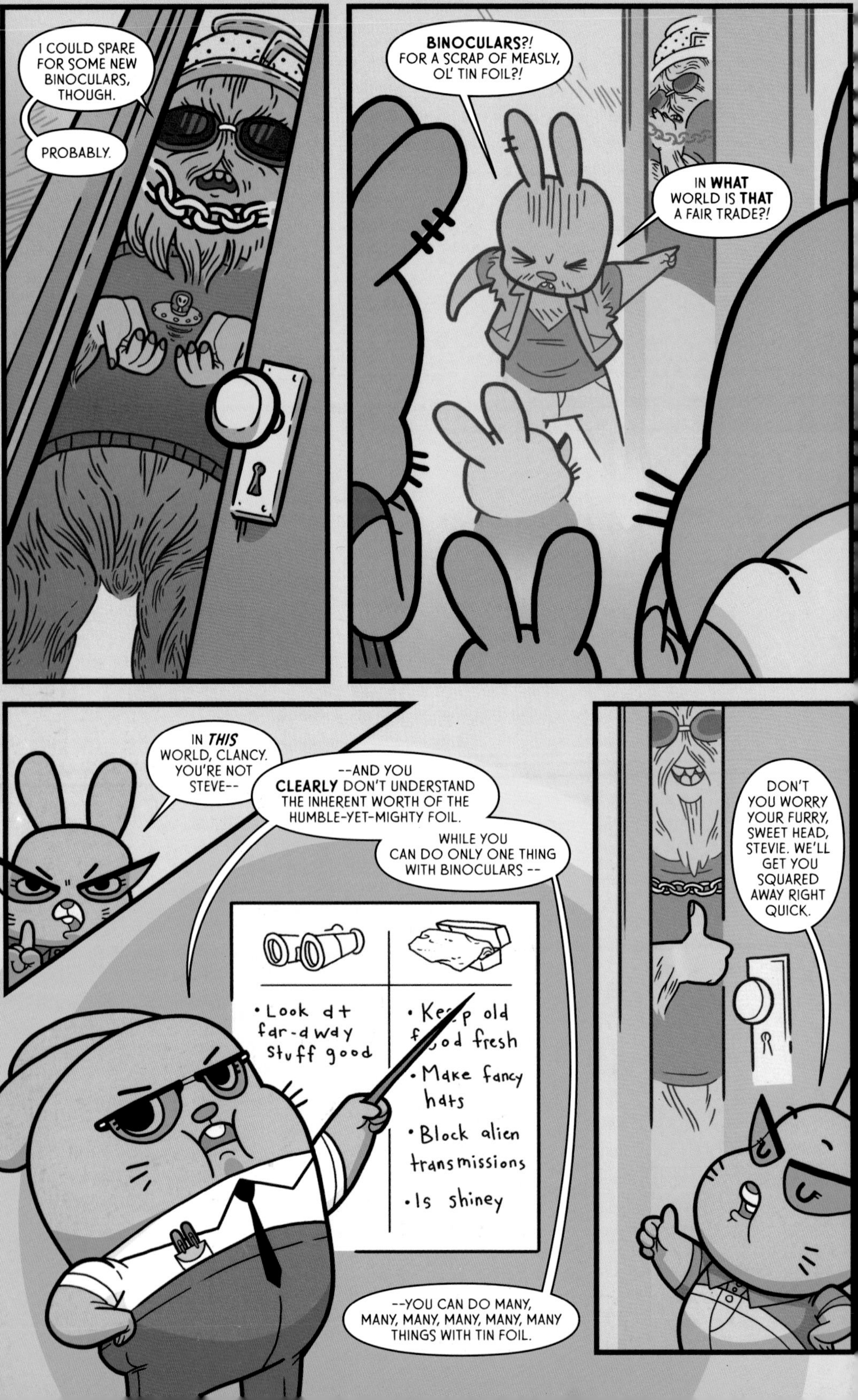
I COULD SPARE FOR SOME NEW BINOCULARS, THOUGH.
PROBABLY.
BINOCULARS?! FOR A SCRAP OF MEASLY, OL' TIN FOIL?!
IN **WHAT** WORLD IS **THAT** A FAIR TRADE?!
IN ***THIS*** WORLD, CLANCY. YOU'RE NOT STEVE--
--AND YOU **CLEARLY** DON'T UNDERSTAND THE INHERENT WORTH OF THE HUMBLE-YET-MIGHTY FOIL.
WHILE YOU CAN DO ONLY ONE THING WITH BINOCULARS --
• Look at far-away stuff good
• Keep old food fresh
• Make fancy hats
• Block alien transmissions
• Is shiney
--YOU CAN DO MANY, MANY, MANY, MANY, MANY, MANY THINGS WITH TIN FOIL.
DON'T YOU WORRY YOUR FURRY, SWEET HEAD, STEVIE. WE'LL GET YOU SQUARED AWAY RIGHT QUICK.

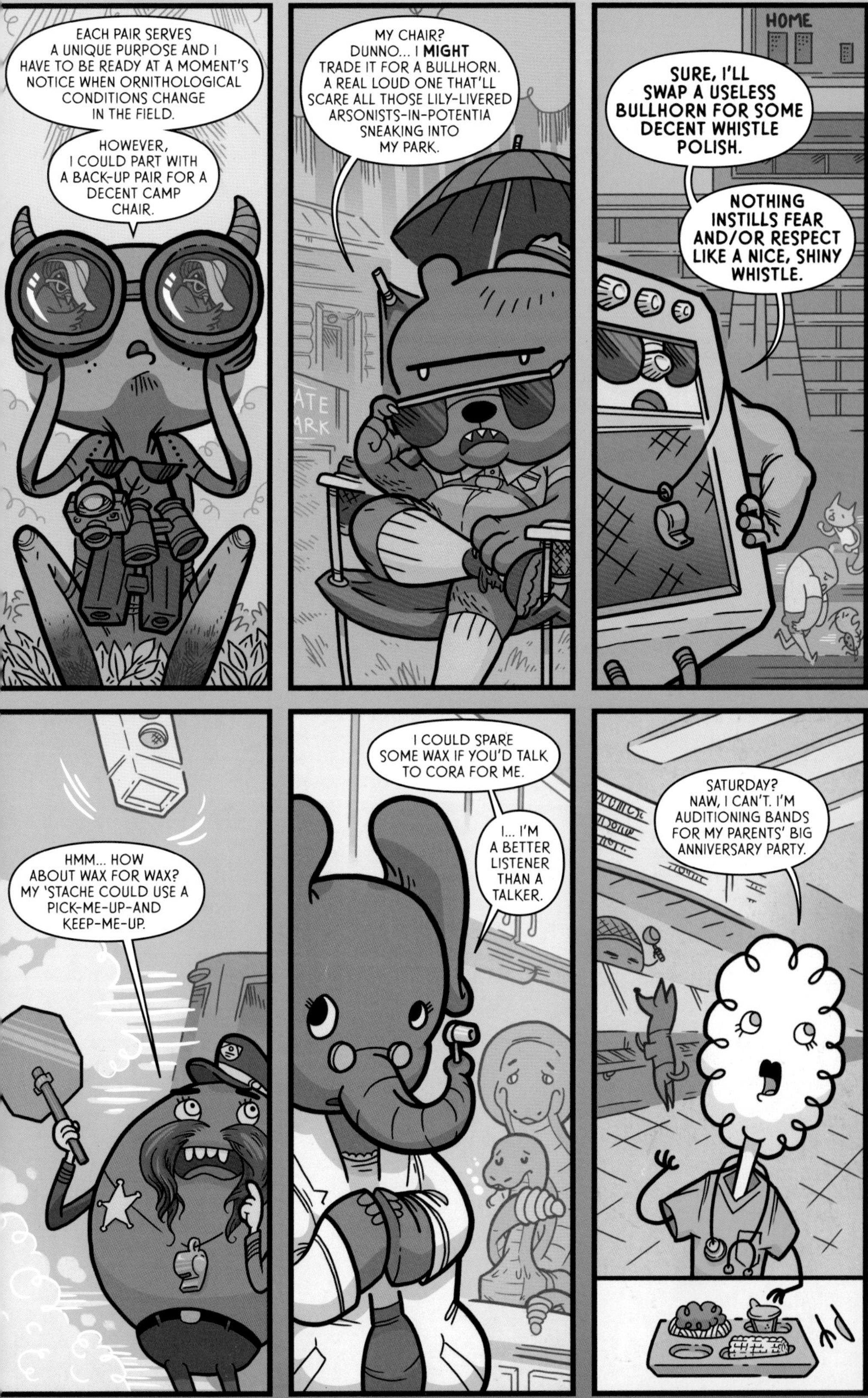
EACH PAIR SERVES A UNIQUE PURPOSE AND I HAVE TO BE READY AT A MOMENT'S NOTICE WHEN ORNITHOLOGICAL CONDITIONS CHANGE IN THE FIELD.
HOWEVER, I COULD PART WITH A BACK-UP PAIR FOR A DECENT CAMP CHAIR.
MY CHAIR? DUNNO... I **MIGHT** TRADE IT FOR A BULLHORN. A REAL LOUD ONE THAT'LL SCARE ALL THOSE LILY-LIVERED ARSONISTS-IN-POTENTIA SNEAKING INTO MY PARK.
HOME
SURE, I'LL SWAP A USELESS BULLHORN FOR SOME DECENT WHISTLE POLISH.
NOTHING INSTILLS FEAR AND/OR RESPECT LIKE A NICE, SHINY WHISTLE.
HMM... HOW ABOUT WAX FOR WAX? MY 'STACHE COULD USE A PICK-ME-UP-AND KEEP-ME-UP.
I COULD SPARE SOME WAX IF YOU'D TALK TO CORA FOR ME.
I... I'M A BETTER LISTENER THAN A TALKER.
SATURDAY? NAW, I CAN'T. I'M AUDITIONING BANDS FOR MY PARENTS' BIG ANNIVERSARY PARTY.

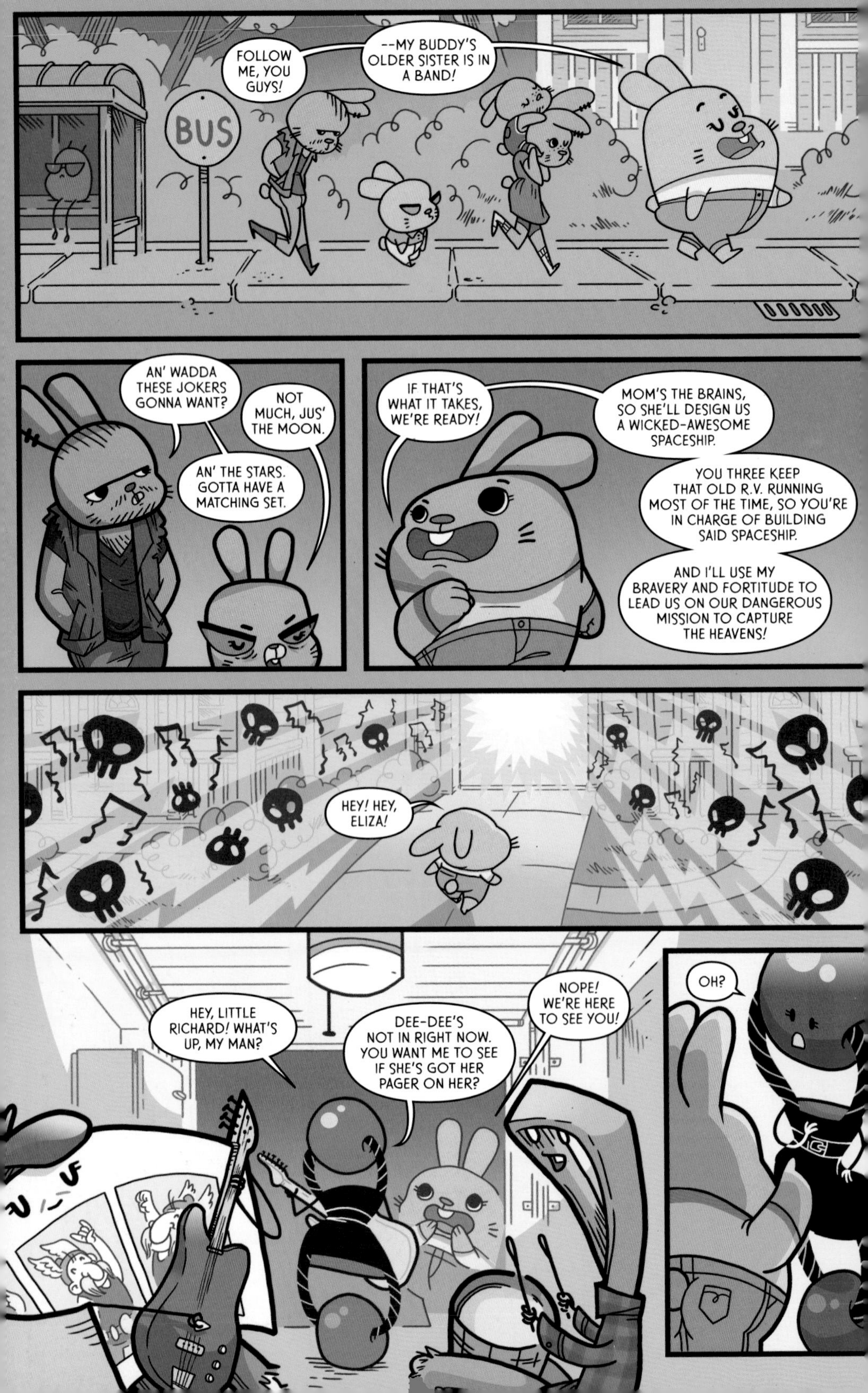
FOLLOW ME, YOU GUYS!
--MY BUDDY'S OLDER SISTER IS IN A BAND!
BUS
AN' WADDA THESE JOKERS GONNA WANT?
NOT MUCH, JUS' THE MOON.
AN' THE STARS. GOTTA HAVE A MATCHING SET.
IF THAT'S WHAT IT TAKES, WE'RE READY!
MOM'S THE BRAINS, SO SHE'LL DESIGN US A WICKED-AWESOME SPACESHIP.
YOU THREE KEEP THAT OLD R.V. RUNNING MOST OF THE TIME, SO YOU'RE IN CHARGE OF BUILDING SAID SPACESHIP.
AND I'LL USE MY BRAVERY AND FORTITUDE TO LEAD US ON OUR DANGEROUS MISSION TO CAPTURE THE HEAVENS!
HEY! HEY, ELIZA!
HEY, LITTLE RICHARD! WHAT'S UP, MY MAN?
DEE-DEE'S NOT IN RIGHT NOW. YOU WANT ME TO SEE IF SHE'S GOT HER PAGER ON HER?
NOPE! WE'RE HERE TO SEE YOU!
OH?

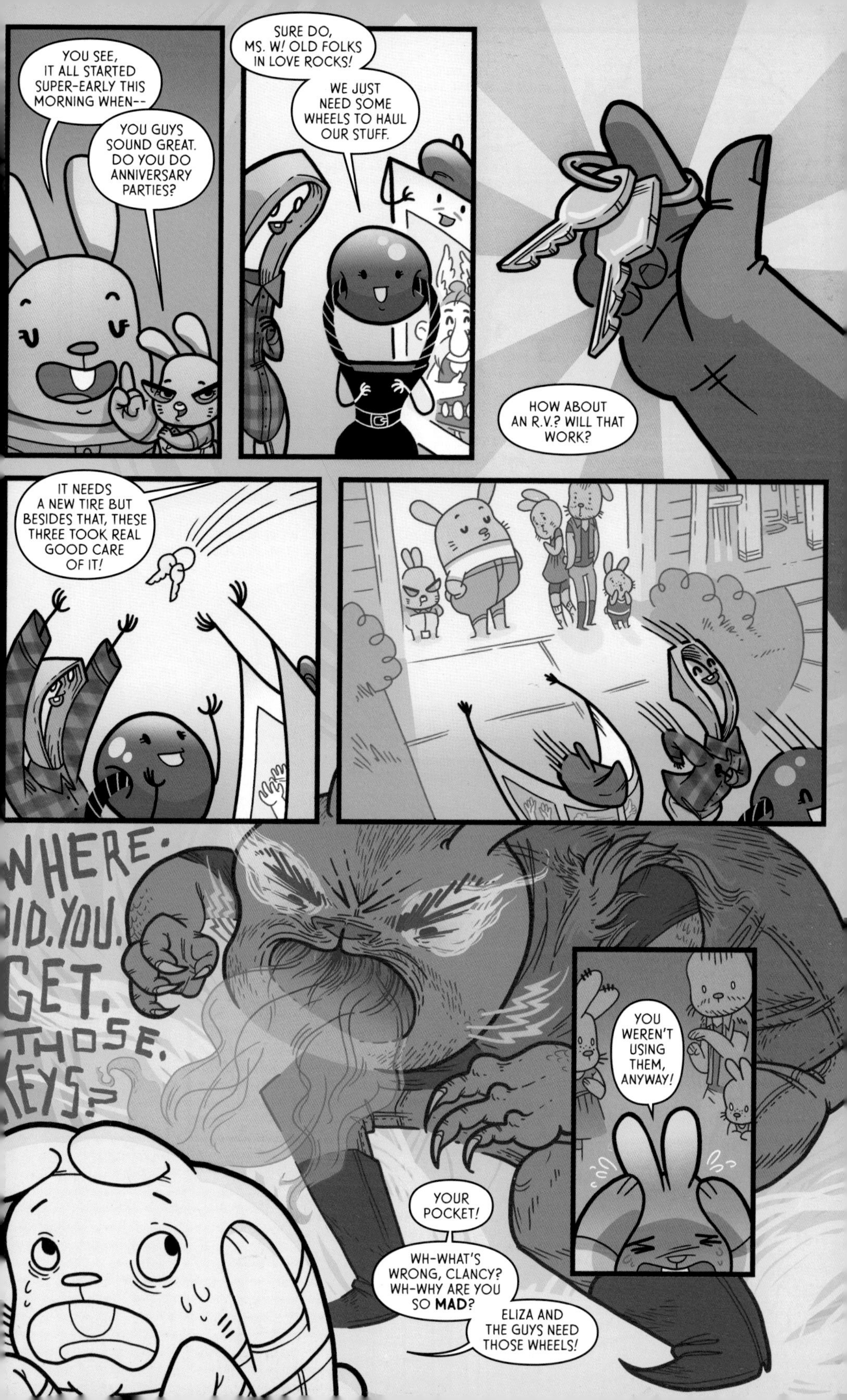
YOU SEE, IT ALL STARTED SUPER-EARLY THIS MORNING WHEN--
YOU GUYS SOUND GREAT. DO YOU DO ANNIVERSARY PARTIES?
SURE DO, MS. W! OLD FOLKS IN LOVE ROCKS!
WE JUST NEED SOME WHEELS TO HAUL OUR STUFF.
HOW ABOUT AN R.V.? WILL THAT WORK?
IT NEEDS A NEW TIRE BUT BESIDES THAT, THESE THREE TOOK REAL GOOD CARE OF IT!
WHERE. DID. YOU. GET. THOSE. KEYS?
YOU WEREN'T USING THEM, ANYWAY!
YOUR POCKET!
WH-WHAT'S WRONG, CLANCY? WH-WHY ARE YOU SO **MAD**?
ELIZA AND THE GUYS NEED THOSE WHEELS!

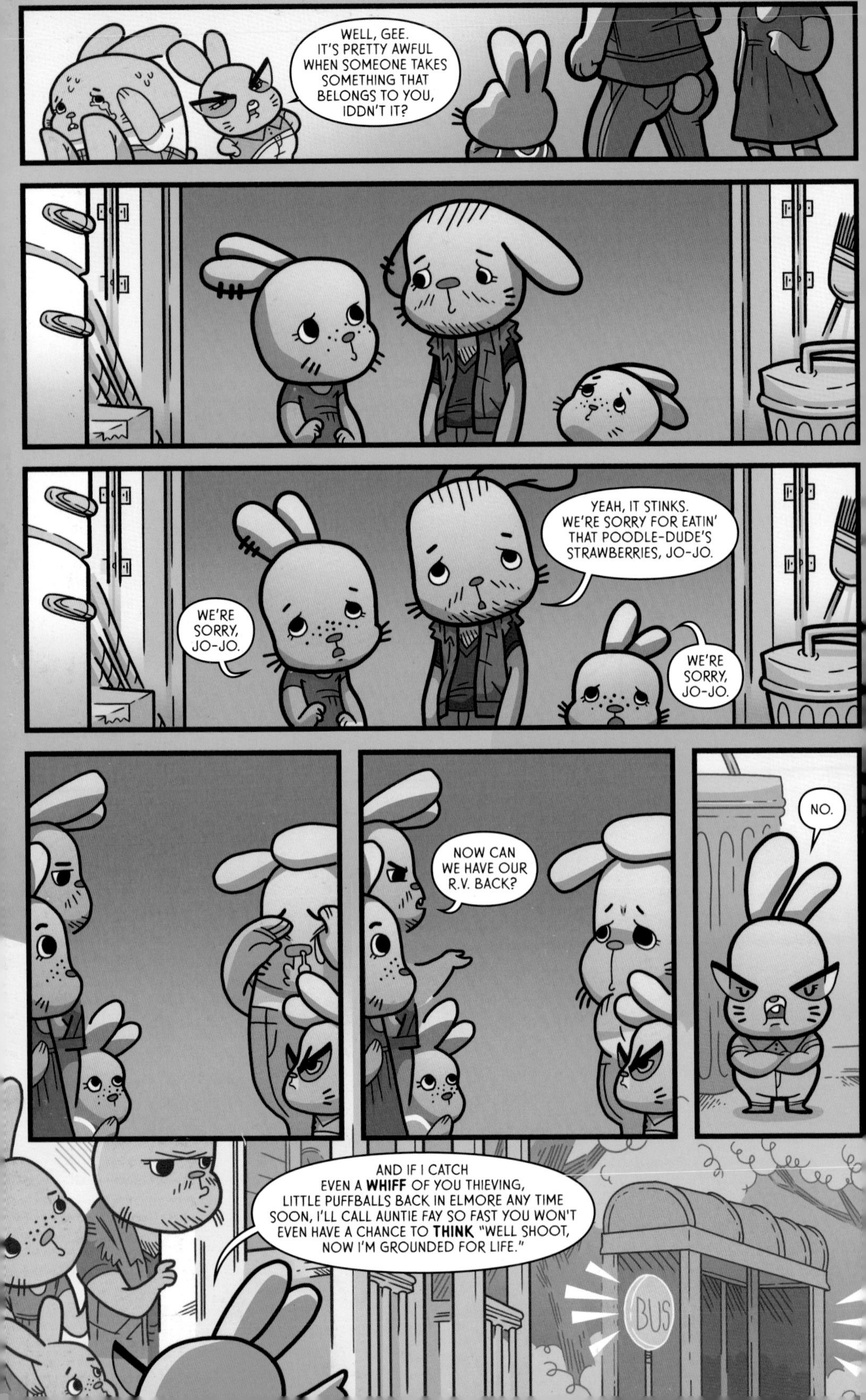
WELL, GEE. IT'S PRETTY AWFUL WHEN SOMEONE TAKES SOMETHING THAT BELONGS TO YOU, IDDN'T IT?
YEAH, IT STINKS. WE'RE SORRY FOR EATIN' THAT POODLE-DUDE'S STRAWBERRIES, JO-JO.
WE'RE SORRY, JO-JO.
WE'RE SORRY, JO-JO.
NOW CAN WE HAVE OUR R.V. BACK?
NO.
AND IF I CATCH EVEN A **WHIFF** OF YOU THIEVING, LITTLE PUFFBALLS BACK IN ELMORE ANY TIME SOON, I'LL CALL AUNTIE FAY SO FAST YOU WON'T EVEN HAVE A CHANCE TO **THINK** "WELL SHOOT, NOW I'M GROUNDED FOR LIFE."
BUS

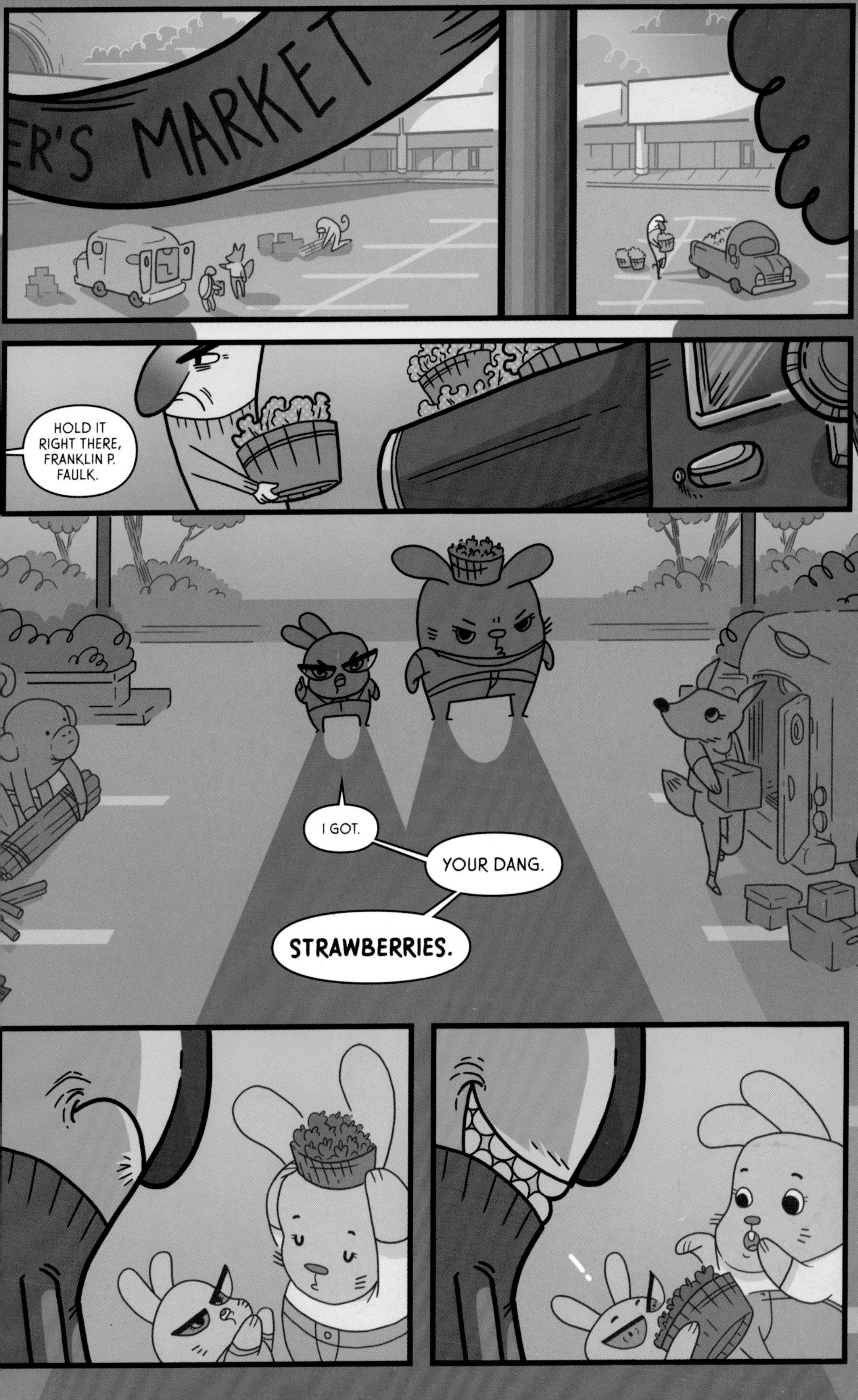
ER'S MARKET
HOLD IT RIGHT THERE, FRANKLIN P. FAULK.
I GOT.
YOUR DANG.
STRAWBERRIES.
!

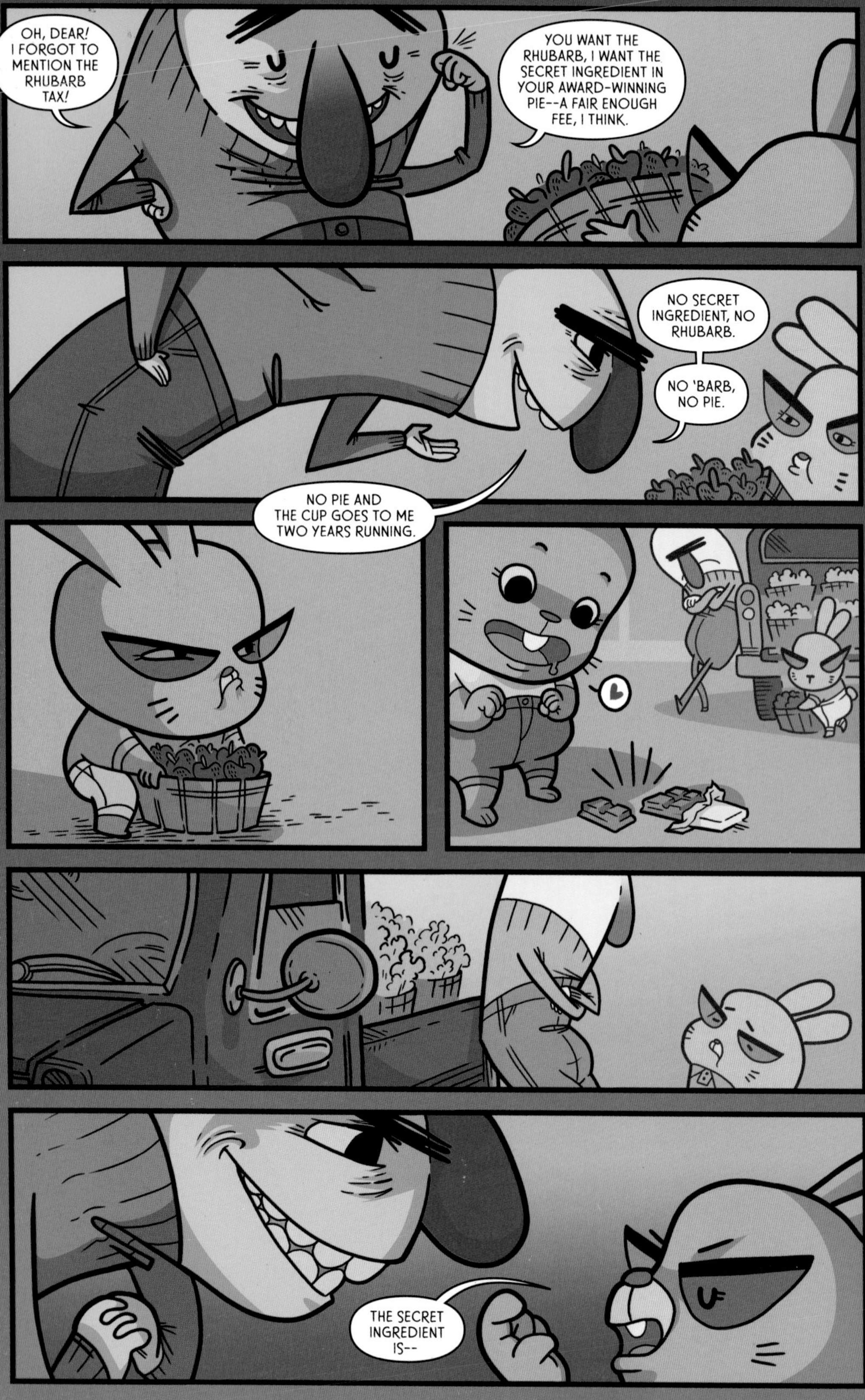
OH, DEAR! I FORGOT TO MENTION THE RHUBARB TAX!
YOU WANT THE RHUBARB, I WANT THE SECRET INGREDIENT IN YOUR AWARD-WINNING PIE--A FAIR ENOUGH FEE, I THINK.
NO SECRET INGREDIENT, NO RHUBARB.
NO 'BARB, NO PIE.
NO PIE AND THE CUP GOES TO ME TWO YEARS RUNNING.
THE SECRET INGREDIENT IS--

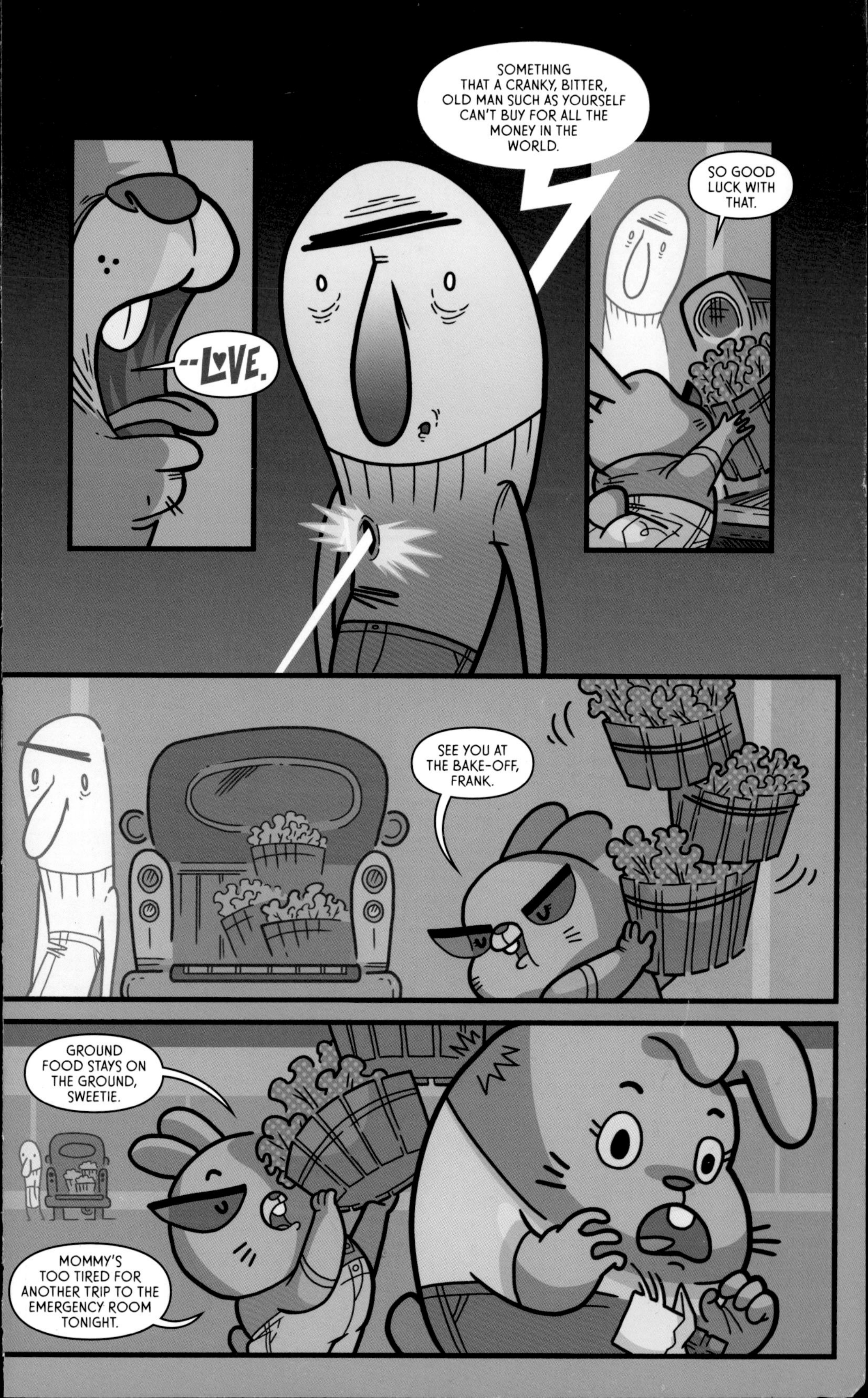
--LOVE.
SOMETHING THAT A CRANKY, BITTER, OLD MAN SUCH AS YOURSELF CAN'T BUY FOR ALL THE MONEY IN THE WORLD.
SO GOOD LUCK WITH THAT.
SEE YOU AT THE BAKE-OFF, FRANK.
GROUND FOOD STAYS ON THE GROUND, SWEETIE.
MOMMY'S TOO TIRED FOR ANOTHER TRIP TO THE EMERGENCY ROOM TONIGHT.

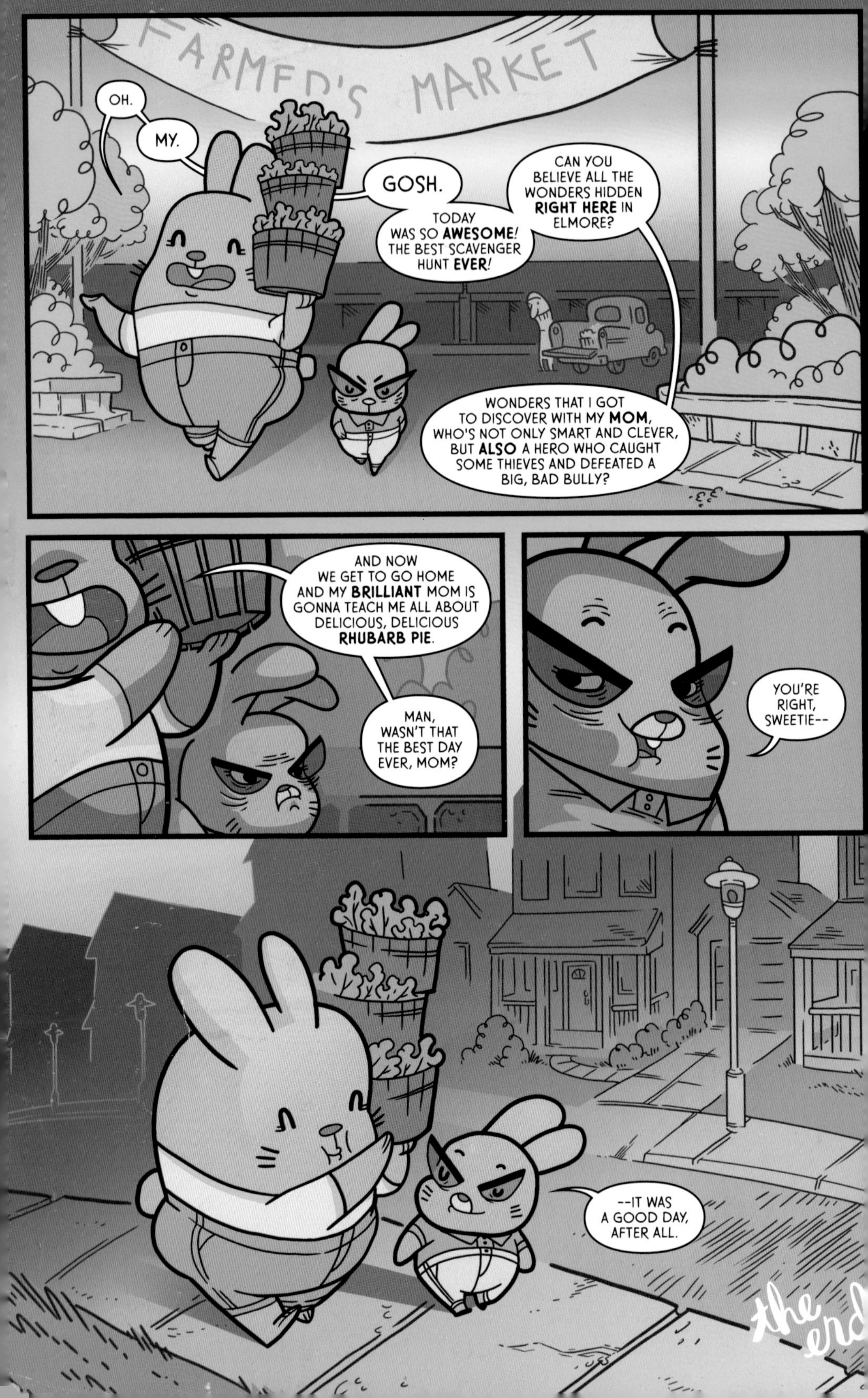
FARMER'S MARKET
OH.
MY.
GOSH.
TODAY WAS SO AWESOME! THE BEST SCAVENGER HUNT EVER!
CAN YOU BELIEVE ALL THE WONDERS HIDDEN RIGHT HERE IN ELMORE?
WONDERS THAT I GOT TO DISCOVER WITH MY MOM, WHO'S NOT ONLY SMART AND CLEVER, BUT ALSO A HERO WHO CAUGHT SOME THIEVES AND DEFEATED A BIG, BAD BULLY?
AND NOW WE GET TO GO HOME AND MY BRILLIANT MOM IS GONNA TEACH ME ALL ABOUT DELICIOUS, DELICIOUS RHUBARB PIE.
MAN, WASN'T THAT THE BEST DAY EVER, MOM?
YOU'RE RIGHT, SWEETIE--
--IT WAS A GOOD DAY, AFTER ALL.
the end

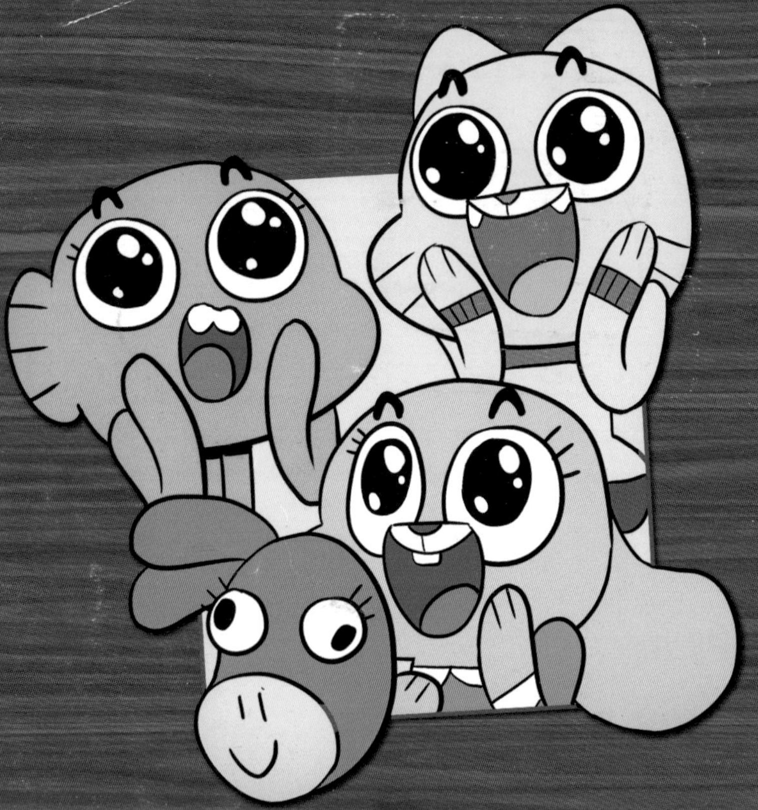

The AMAZING WORLD OF GUMBALL™

CONTINUES IN 2018